# DEATH OF
# A SELKIE

## D.P. Hart-Davis

Merlin Unwin Books

First published by Merlin Unwin Books 2021
Text © D.P. Hart-Davis 2021

Merlin Unwin Books Limited
Palmers' House, 7 Corve Street,
Ludlow, Shropshire, SY8 1DB
www.merlinunwin.co.uk

The right of D.P. Hart-Davis to be identified as the author
of this work has been asserted by her in accordance with
the Copyright, Designs and Patents Act 1988.

A CIP record of this book is available from the British
Library.

Designed and typeset by Merlin Unwin
Printed and bound by CPI Antony Rowe, Chippenham
England

ISBN 978-1-913159-29-0

# Contents

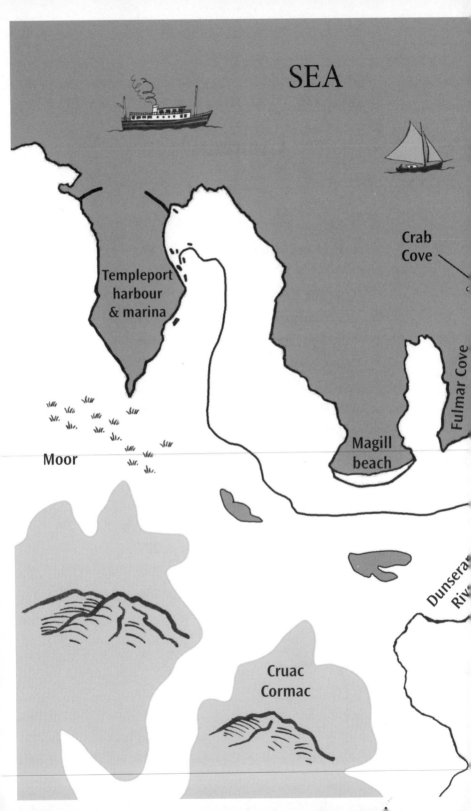

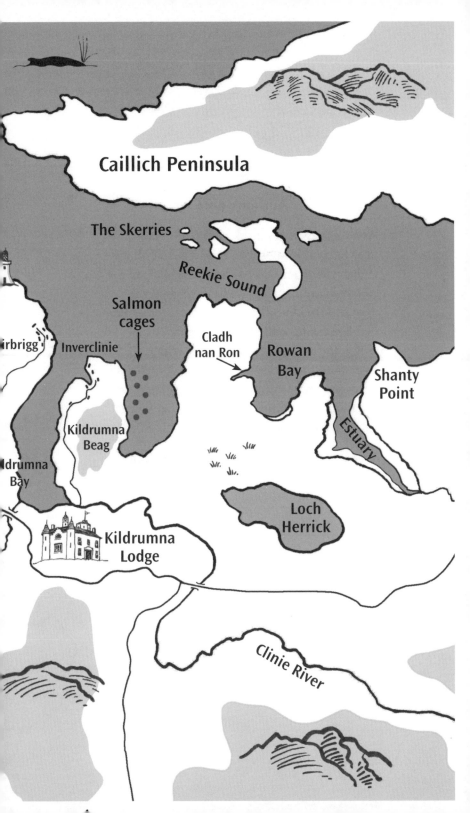

## Author's note

As a lifelong water-funk with an ineradicable
fear of total immersion, I must thank all the
scuba-diving enthusiasts who have helped me
with advice, and vividly described the
joy and freedom they themselves feel when
exploring underwater. In particular
I am grateful to Andrew Powell, who not only
explained the basics of buoyancy control and
corrected my terminology, but suggested ways
to scupper enemies underwater that would
not have occurred to me.

Any errors that may have slipped through the
net are entirely my own.

## Half human, half seal, a selkie is...

Myth or fantasy? Fairy tale or product of one
dram too many on a foggy night?
Or could it be a long-buried folk memory of
far northern kayakers drifting south on summer
currents, to shed their sodden sealskin craft and
resume human form? Whatever its origin, the
legend of the mysterious selkie still haunts the
western fringes of the Celtic world.
They may live ashore for a while, but in the end
the sea always calls them home...

# PRINCIPAL CHARACTERS

Luke Balfour, 39, owner of Kildrumna Fishing Lodge

Jessamine Balfour, 39, his ex-journalist wife

Gunnar Larsen, 55, marine conservationist / cruise ship owner

Ravenna Larsen, 31, his wife

Danna Murison, 72, fishing ghillie

Mhairi Brydon, 46, crofter and jeweller

Elspeth McTavish, 48, her sister

Davie McTavish, 52, Dive Shop owner

Alick McTavish, 19, his younger son

Logan Brydon, 17, Mhairi's son

Dougal 'Big Dougie' McInnes, 44, businessman and ex-MSP

Lady Jean Allan, 60, owner of Eilean Breck Aquaculture

DCI Martin Robb, 45, widowed father of three

Marina Clare Robb, 14, his youngest daughter

Detective Sergeant Jim Winter, 29

# CHAPTER ONE

# The Escapers

A SWIRLING RIPPLE broke the glassy black surface of Stockpot, the best holding pool on the lower beat of the Clinie river, and Luke Balfour – beanpole-tall, angular, and beaky as a heron – who had been staring half-hypnotised at the smooth flow of current sweeping his Stoat's Tail in a semicircle round the shelf of rocky bank on which he stood, stiffened to full alertness and cast again just above it.

Nothing... and then a quick, irritated pluck before the white line straightened out where the tail of the pool broadened into a swift, shallow, gravel-bottomed run. Snagged on that big underwater rock – yet again – he thought, relaxing and taking a couple of steps along the bank before casting once more.

This time the quivering tug that signalled interest was unmistakable. Luke counted two before he struck, and a moment later the satisfying screech of the reel told him the fish was firmly hooked.

Jess will be pleased, he thought. With fishing guests about to arrive and the weekly grocery order held up by last night's storm, he had been obliged to put aside both his Catch-and-Release principles and the barbless lures that had caused such hilarity among locals when he first bought Kildrumna Lodge, and concentrate on filling his creel in the old-fashioned way.

Back and forth across the pool darted the salmon while Luke played it patiently, guiding it clear of the submerged group of rocks, and checking its run towards the shallows, now letting it take line out, now reeling in quickly as it launched

1

itself towards him, only to dive to the bottom when he raised his rod point and bent to bring it up to the net. Six or seven minutes passed before he felt confident that he had it under control, moving smoothly towards the net, with only the occasional fluttering attempt to break back into midstream.

Not a big fish, he thought, catching a glimpse as it broke the surface, and wondered for an instant why it felt odd. Could it be foul-hooked? But as he brought the net in behind to scoop it from the water and bent to see what he had caught, the question was answered in the way he most dreaded.

'Hellfire!' Luke exclaimed, staring in disgust.

Tattered fins, blunted nose, and bloody lesions behind the gills identified his catch as no native wild fish but an escapee from the Moontide fish farm whose feed barge and cages floated in the sheltered neck of the Reekie Sound between Stairbrigg and the peninsula of Inverclinie, close – far too close – to the unprotected mouth of the Clinie river.

Fat, flabby, grey of flesh and loaded with prophylactic antibiotics, it was probably carrying umpteen diseases as well: definitely not one to return to the water. Luke killed it quickly and lobbed it into the deep heather well clear of the path. Bonanza for the otter, he thought, frowning, as he stowed his priest in an inner pocket and picked up his rod to cast again towards the underwater rocks.

Bingo! Another salmon impaled itself on the Stoat's Tail: same lie, same size, same tattered appearance, same meek acceptance of its fate. By the time an identical third and fourth had joined them on the riverbank, Luke – the laid-back, the unflappable – was simmering with anger. They must be packed in behind those rocks like sardines in a tin, he reflected. Made a break for freedom, poor creatures, and now they don't know what to do with it. I won't have them polluting my river, though. Dougal McInnes can damn well beef up the wiring on his cages, or I'll be on the hotline to Scottish Natural Heritage before he can say knife. Classic angler's nightmare: a fish hooked at every cast and none of them fit to put on the table, certainly not in front of three French gourmets who have already made their gastronomic preferences very clear, and they do not include diseased, antibiotic-loaded, mutilated farmed salmon.

Detective Chief Inspector Robb and his problem teenager were due to arrive tonight, and would probably eat whatever Jess put on their plates, but his wife had her pride. Hell would freeze over before she served farmed fish to guests who were paying through the nose for the best local Scottish produce, and with supper scheduled for half past seven there was precious little time for her to revamp tonight's menu.

Despite the expense, lobster it would have to be, together with a fervent prayer that the finicky Frogs did not suffer from shellfish allergy. Surely, they would have mentioned it in one of their exhaustive food-related pre-arrival missives that had so irritated his darling wife?

Gathering up rod, net, and fishing bag, Luke concealed the four farmed fish where the otter would be the first to find them, and set off with long strides for the little harbour to see what luck young Logan Brydon had had today with his creels.

As his size twelves traced the familiar river path, he considered the composition of this week's fishing party, and wondered how DCI Martin Robb would fit into it.

'You'll like him,' Amyas, his Anglesey-based cousin and lawyer, had said in his breezy way when he rang out of the blue to ask if Luke could fit in two extra guests. 'I've known him most of my life, though I haven't seen a lot of him lately. In fact, it now occurs to me that you have met him already, way back, because he used to come and stay with his parents at Ti-Bach, that cottage at the end of our drive, during the Easter hols and we all used to climb the cliffs for gulls' eggs. Remember?'

Luke delved in his memory and came up with a stocky, solid, red-cheeked boy with curly black hair and a ready smile. 'He had a fantastic head for heights,' he recalled. 'And didn't he play for the Bangor Colts?'

'That's the one.' Amyas hesitated, then said, 'He's had a rough time lately, and I'd like to give him a bit of a hand.'

'What kind of rough?' Luke had asked cautiously.

'He was badly smashed up in a crash that killed his wife, and was in and out of hospital for weeks. Off work for over a year, and now when he's almost fit again, he's worried about his youngest daughter, who's gone off her grub and can't face school. She's a competitive little devil, and from what I can gather she had a meltdown after a bunch of her – ahem – friends began trolling her and claiming she cheated in some swimming race, though don't ask me how you can do that. Anyway there was a great hoo-hah, tears, recriminations, parents called in, threats of expulsion all round, and the upshot was that the kid was sent home at half-term with her future uncertain, and now with the summer stretching ahead of them both, poor old Robbo wants something to keep her occupied. A complete change of scene. A much-needed break from social media... The doctor's threatening to put her on antidepressants, which is worrying the hell out of him. If you ask me, it all stems from missing her mum, but what do I know?'

'Tricky,' Luke agreed. 'How old is she?'

'Around fifteen, I think. Robb's got three girls: one married, one at uni, and this Marina is the youngest.'

'Would she enjoy fishing?' asked Luke doubtfully. 'You know what it's like here: choice between river or loch and precious little else to do. Plus no company of her own age. I'd have thought she'd be bored stiff.'

'Far from it, apparently.' Amyas gave the deep, confidential chuckle that always made his cousin smile. 'Swims like an eel and loves anything connected to the water. The family used to spend most of the summer hols at Ti-Bach when her grandparents were alive, and they called Marina their water baby. Robbo would have liked to take her back there to cheer her up, but now the cottage has been sold, so that's why he got in touch and asked if I could suggest something. I just wondered if you'd be able to fit them in.'

'Um-hmm,' Luke thought it over and said, 'Well, I'll do my best, but I'll have to have a word with Jess. She's the boss when it comes to numbers.'

'Good man! I knew I could rely on you,' said Amyas heartily, though Luke was less sure. He was well aware that his wife wasn't keen on having extra guests shoehorned into the party at short notice, particularly since they were expecting the arrival of Luke's godfather Gunnar Larsen any time this week, and with him his new wife, Ravenna. As their major benefactor who had been instrumental in helping them buy and equip Kildrumna, Gunnar's rare visits always put Jess on her mettle, sending her into a frenzy of cooking and cleaning, and the prospect of entertaining Ravenna – reportedly beautiful, clever, and twenty years younger than her husband – had added to her stress.

'She sounds quite a girl,' said Luke as Jess squeezed past him on her way to the ironing room, though whether he spoke in admiration or trepidation was hard to judge.

'Why? What's she done?' Jess was instantly alert.

'Keen rower at Cambridge, apparently, and although she didn't quite make the Eight she got a 2:1 in NatSci Bio and was sports nutritionist to the squad which won the European rowing championships.'

'Sports Nutrition – oh, God!' murmured Jess, hurriedly reviewing her menus for the week. 'OK, got that. What else? Tell me the worst. How did Gunnar come across her?'

'Well, she was working on the cruise ship line that Gunnar bought after selling his trawlers, and she just happened to mention her interest in Viking culture and artefacts –'

Jess breathed deeply through her nose. 'Serendipity, I believe it's called.'

'You could be right. And lo and behold, a couple of years later...'

'Well, I hope she makes him happy.'

'So do I. But you see, darling, you're wearing yourself

out and it's all quite unnecessary.' Luke took the heavy laundry basket she was carrying. 'This isn't a royal visit, far from it. Ravenna's a working girl and Gunnar's quite used to roughing it, so long as everyone does exactly what he tells them to.'

'There speaks his adoring godson,' said Jess, and he laughed.

'Well, you know what I mean!'

'I do indeed.'

'Anyway he's only dropping in to see how we're getting on, and spend a few days on the river. Ravenna stayed here once or twice in her teens as the guest of Isla, old Major Philpott's niece. Apparently they were at school together.'

Far from reassuring Jess, this raised her stress level. 'Oh, God!' she exclaimed. 'Women always notice if things are in a mess. And if she knew the house in its glory days, what's she going to think of it now?'

'Don't worry so much, darling. She must know things have changed. She won't expect to find seven maids with seven mops and a bamboo butler at the door. OK, old Philpott lived here en prince, but what happened? It ruined him; and as for her, she's a career woman. She was keeping the books on these cruise boats when Gunnar met her, not exactly a life of luxury, and she still works on archaeological digs now and then. I don't suppose she'll be running a finger along the bookcases looking for dust.'

'I don't want him thinking we're letting things slide,' Jess insisted edgily. 'We owe him so much already. What if he decided to withdraw his support? We'd be in the soup, that's what. We're in enough trouble already with this damned application for more fish cages in the bay. If we can't rely on the rivers to produce wild salmon for our guests and on Gunnar to fight our corner against Moontide, we might as well give up and be done with it. Honestly, darling, it worries me how dependent we are on him. I lie awake at night, thinking about it.'

Luke had looked seriously at his wife's narrow, fine-drawn face framed in its cloud of wiry dark curls, and the persistent groove between her hazel eyes that seemed to grow a little deeper every day. 'Then you must stop thinking about it because it's not going to happen,' he said firmly. 'Gunnar's not like that. He's always backed us to the hilt and it's not in his nature to let his friends down.'

'You don't think he's been cooling off towards us lately? Wasn't it a bit odd that he didn't tell you he was getting married until after the ceremony?'

'Well...' Luke considered the question. Seeing the bald announcement in the *Telegraph* had come as a shock, certainly; but then Gunnar's unpredictability had always been part of his personality. Besides, when a long-term bachelor marries, he doesn't always welcome the teasing and astonishment of old friends. Particularly when, as in this case, there is a large disparity in age. How old was his godfather? Luke himself was pushing forty, which would make Gunnar around fifty-five.

'Not really,' he said slowly. 'I suppose he thought it easier to present us with a fait accompli in case we tried to change his mind. Not that we would have, of course, but he might have felt a bit awkward.'

Gunnar feeling awkward? That would be a first, thought Jess, but she knew exactly what her husband meant. Gunnar was a rich man and it had always been plain to her that he looked on Luke as a substitute son, a situation that might change upon his marriage.

'Gunnar won't let us down,' said Luke firmly. 'Trust me.'

For a moment she held his gaze in silence, then nodded. 'OK. I'll try. But all the same, I wish...'

'What do you wish?'

'That we didn't have so many of our eggs in one basket,' she said in a rush. She picked up the laundry and whisked away before he could answer.

'Everything's going to be fine,' he muttered to her retreating back, but even as he watched her hurry to her self-imposed thousand and one tasks he wondered, not for the first time, what his wife really felt about the charismatic, larger-than-life, heroically bearded godfather who had dominated most of Luke's adult life. Sure, she paid lip service to his generosity, and never failed to welcome him as a very special honoured guest, but was it possible that deep down she resented – even distrusted – him?

Jess is artistic, imaginative and super-sensitive, prey to wild fancies and unexpected forebodings, whereas I'm just a slow, patient plodder, he thought. Mr Cautious, that's me. Gunnar used to joke that I had an old head on young shoulders, always following him at a safe distance, ready to pick up the pieces. Not that he wasn't glad of it on the odd occasion when he ran out of road.

Jess and I could hardly be more different. I stick with what I know, while she darts from one thought to another and sometimes comes up with brilliant ideas, and with crazy ones almost as often. I know she's cleverer than me, and she's tough: she wouldn't have been deputy editor of *What's Good for You?* magazine for ten years unless she could stand up to the bullyboys of the food and drink lobby.

I make up my mind about people over a period of time, but Jess relies on flashes of intuition based on nothing you could call rational – gut feeling just about sums it up. Yet when it comes to people and their motives, she has an uncomfortable knack of hitting the nail on the head while I'm still hunting around for the hammer.

Could she be right about Gunnar? Would the man who had always been Luke's hero, his lodestar, be capable of ditching them without warning? Of withdrawing his financial support and leaving them in the lurch? Feeling as he did, it was easy for Luke to lose sight of the fact that his godfather was a hard-headed businessman, and no one could pretend that Kildrumna was a profitable investment.

Gunnar had dominated not only his adult life, but his childhood too. From his earliest years, Luke's favourite story had been his mother's account of how Gunnar – at that time just a tall, skinny teenager on a fishing holiday with his father on the Kola Peninsula in the far north-west of Russia – had saved her husband's life. It had been while waiting for a transit flight to Murmansk from the base camp on the Varzuga river that Gunnar had watched the ancient helicopter bringing in another fishing party overshoot the rudimentary helipad. The main rotor stalled, the chopper lurched from side to side like a drunken insect, and seconds later dropped vertically, smashing its skids, and ploughing nose down into the mossy, squashy ooze of the riverbank.

As the hatch sprang open and the structure broke up in a column of mud and flames, Gunnar had sprinted towards it, reaching the tangle of wreckage before anyone else on the ground reacted.

Pulling aside the smashed canopy, he had reached into the cabin and dragged out Luke's father Johnny, then plunged back into the flames a second time to grapple with the unconscious pilot. Every time Luke saw the raised diagonal scar across Gunnar's forehead, he thought of that heroic rescue; and the rest of their relationship had followed as if pre-ordained.

Gunnar had agreed to stand godfather to Johnny's month-old son, interpreting this role less as a moral mentor than as a guide to field sports. Throughout Luke's teens, Gunnar had introduced him to shooting and stalking, fly and deep-sea fishing, scuba-diving and heli-skiing. As every school holiday began, he could expect his phone to ring and hear the deep, amused voice with the faint Norwegian lilt say, 'Well, little godson, what would you say to some fishing in Chile?' Or it might be boar hunting in Poland, or canoeing on the Zambezi, or paragliding in Nepal. Always exciting, always unexpected.

Years passed, and Gunnar took over his father's company, and when, as so often happens, his love of hunting morphed into a passion for conservation, the invitations continued though the focus was rather different. With deep reluctance Luke had to refuse the chance of joining an anti-poaching patrol in the South Pacific, and a whale-counting survey off the coast of Brazil, for as a married father of two struggling to turn around a family business while predatory rivals encircled it like sharks, he had neither the time nor the money to take advantage of them.

Had Gunnar been offended? Was that when their relationship faltered? Surely not: for the very day when Luke finally abandoned the struggle and a small paragraph in the Business pages announced that Huskinson Hosiery had been taken over by Sox 'R Us, once again the well-remembered Norwegian lilt, amused and mischievous, promising fun and adventure, crackled over a bad signal from Vladivostok.

'So you are free at last, little godson. My congratulations! Now you need a holiday to clear your head and forget all about balance sheets and redundancy payments while you look to the future. Now listen: in the month of May I have taken three rods on a little river on the West Coast that I love. It is called the Clinie – you won't have heard of it because it is very remote, very private – and the lodge is owned by an old friend of mine. He doesn't usually let his fishing, but for me he makes this exception. I would be so happy if you and your wife would be my guests – ja?'

What could he say? Three years later, Luke remembered vividly the rush of delight with which he recognised that Gunnar was right. He was free! No need to think up excuses why he must turn down this invitation. No need to wheedle Jess into agreeing they could afford a real holiday. The boys were at boarding school; the money from Sox 'R Us had thudded into his bank account; even the senior staff had greeted the takeover with relief once their pension arrangements had been satisfactorily negotiated.

'Free,' he repeated wonderingly. 'I suppose I am. After so many years it's – it's quite difficult to take in.'

'So you are a lucky fellow,' said Gunnar, the laughter gone from his voice. Lecture alert, Luke had thought. Now he's going to tell me I must invest all the money in something solid. Government bonds, perhaps. But the message was so different it took him by surprise.

'A very lucky fellow,' his godfather repeated. 'How old are you now? Mid-thirties? Less? Not everyone of your age gets a perfect chance to make a new career better suited to his personality. To his talents. Do you understand me? This is your chance: don't throw it away.'

'What do you mean?'

'I mean, little godson, that to be happy – truly happy – you need to work at something you love. Something that occupies you body and soul. You see, I know you very well. You are a man for outdoors – not one to wear a dark suit and stare at a screen all day.'

He was right, Luke thought. Family pressure had kept him working his way up through the family business. Starting at the bottom, ending at the top; chained to a desk and a screen for eight years of servitude, but now at last he was free. The thought had been intoxicating. This was his chance to change course completely.

'I'll – I'll think about it,' he stammered, wondering what Jess was likely to say to the hare-brained schemes that had started to flood his mind.

'No, no, no! This moment is for action, not for thinking. Come with me to Scotland and we will see what we can find.'

What they found, of course, was Kildrumna Lodge at Inverclinie, and by the end of that week both Jess and Luke were head over heels in love with it. For any keen fisherman, the narrow peninsula with its two spate rivers – the rocky tumbling Dunseran punctuated with many foaming waterfalls, and the dark, sinuous Clinie – its network of trout-filled hill lochs, and the deep, sheltered estuary thronged with seatrout might seem a slice of paradise, but it was the lodge itself that was the icing on the cake.

Solidly situated on a shelf of rock above the dark mouth of the river, Kildrumna was a mini Neuschwanstein absurdity – a Gothic folly, with turrets and crenellations – typical product of the Victorian fascination with Scotland. A little Big House that needed a dozen servants, awkward to run, difficult to heat, and slowly crumbling, Jess had thought, but Oh! It's adorable. A sidelong glance at Luke's star-struck expression confirmed that he felt the same.

Squelching along the river path three years later, his feet so familiar with every tussock and puddle that he could have found his way blindfold, Luke knew in his very bones that Jess's fears were groundless. Gunnar would never let them down. After all, who had encouraged them to put in a sealed bid when ramrod-backed old Major Philpott decided to call it a day, and who had topped up their money from his own bottomless coffers when it looked as if they would be outgunned?

His godfather had attended the sale in the bar of The Clinie Arms, and sat beside him, overflowing the hard little plastic chair. Jess chose a seat against the wall on the other side of the room, next to mahogany-faced Danna Murison, ex-ghillie to Major Philpott, a wizened sprite and source of much local gossip, delivered in a hoarse sepulchral whisper that made even good news sound ominous.

'Who's that?' she asked him through the hubbub as the sale concluded, watching the dark, burly, curly-headed underbidder shoulder his way with tanklike momentum across the crowded bar towards the door, slapping a back here, shaking a hand there, jovially greeted by one and all of the fishermen and crofters.

'Yon's Dougal MacInnes – Big Dougie, as he's known. A braw gallus and an ill yin tae cross,' muttered Danna.

'Gallus?'

'Born tae be hanged,' said Danna unequivocally. 'Ye've bested him the noo and he'll not forget and forgive, mark my words. He married the Major's niece, Isla Mackay, for all his dad was no more'n the Major's boatman and never drew a sober breath between one Hogmanay and the next, but the marriage lasted no more'n five years before she'd had enough

of his temper and his politics, and was awa' tae the States wi'
a new man.'

Dougal MacInnes. Jess recognised the name and nodded
slowly. Top of Major Philpott's list of the 'damned Nats' to
whom he had refused to sell Kildrumna. Yes, he looked
the type to enjoy the political gravy train, she had thought,
observing him closely. He had slipped into the room late,
when the sale was already in progress: a good-looking bull of
a man, dark-haired and heavy eyebrowed, with a politician's
easy camaraderie and perpetual smile. Unlike most of those
present, he wore a city suit and tie, as if he hadn't had time to
change. Big Dougie: an ill man to cross.

'Is he your local MSP, then?' she whispered, and a
shadow of a smile crossed Danna's weather-creased features.

'Lost the seat tae an incoming Liberal twa year syne –
only by a whisker, mind – and withdrew frae the political
arena tae "concentrate on his business affairs".' His gnarled
fingers sketched inverted commas and his grin widened into
a wicked leer.

'What are they?' she asked as he obviously wanted
her to.

'Everything and nothing, ma'am, but where there's
skulduggery tae be found, ye can be sure Big Dougie has a
hand in it. Och, he's a big man round here, and canny folk
steer clear of him.'

'Thanks for the warning, Danna.' She filed away the
information and watched McInnes leave the bar.

Big Dougie. An ill man to cross.

It wasn't until she and Luke were well ensconced at
Kildrumna and had two successful seasons' hosting fishing
parties under their belts that the shadow of Big Dougie
loomed again, with the arrival of an official notification to
the Stairbrigg council of a planning application from the
Moontide Salmon Farming Organisation, to site six fish cages
in Kildrumna Bay at the neck of the Reekie Sound.

Much alarmed, Luke banged back an objection, asking for an environmental impact assessment by the local authority, citing well-known cases of damage to the seabed in a sensitive area, and studies of increased mortality among wild salmon populations, and his stance was staunchly backed by every man and woman living on the Inverclinie peninsula.

'A dirty, dangerous business and no way to treat God's creatures,' said plain-speaking Mhairi Brydon, the faded blonde beauty who lived with her son in a croft facing the harbour, and made delicate silver jewellery set with semi-precious stones to sell in Stairbrigg's gift shops. Her late husband Seamus had worked on fish farms before he took to the oil rigs, so her opinion counted.

'Well, at least it's a good way for us to get to know our neighbours,' said Jess, energetically distributing leaflets and knocking on doors, heartened by the degree of resistance to the Moontide proposal; but in Stairbrigg, the nearest town, the reaction was very different. Numbers count and money talks; even with Gunnar's strong opposition and conservationist credentials, the result of the planning board hearing was never in doubt.

One after the other, members of the Council rose to point out the benefits of a well-resourced fish-farming enterprise in the Sound, far enough from the town to be out of sight and smelling distance, yet handy for the associated processing plant and access to the big markets. Along with the existing smokery, it would put Stairbrigg on the export map, key to unlocking government grants as well as generating much-needed revenue and even-more-needed jobs.

With local youth unemployment hovering around 80%, the lure of jobs and investment effortlessly trumped ecological concerns, and when the Moontide application was put to a vote, it was unanimously approved.

'Half of them in McInnes's pocket and the other half licking his arse,' growled Gunnar, loud enough for his words to reach the Chairman and, as the Council members shuffled out,

14

closing their files and chatting, Big Dougie had caught Luke's eye and gave a small, satisfied nod that said unambiguously, 'Quits.'

If only it had stopped there, thought Luke. As usual, he tried to put himself in the other chap's shoes. McInnes belonged here, and he did not. Why should incomers like him and Jess prevent those born and bred on this coast from making money from one of its few commercial possibilities?

At first he had been hopeful. The six cages had not caused a significant drop in Kildrumna's catches of wild salmon for the first two years; nor had there been any major escapes as the captives were transferred between cages until they had grown to the optimum size for marketing, and were then killed and taken to the processing plant. It was true that more seals now congregated on the offshore skerry and also at the mouth of the Clinie river, and at times of flat calm an ominous turquoise bloom would spread from the sheltered water where the cages were anchored; but as far as he could tell the operation was well-run and largely staffed by locals.

Any form of factory farming, whether above ground or under water was anathema to freedom-loving Jess, who said she couldn't look at the cages without feeling sick.

'Thank God we can't see them from the house!' she said with a shudder as she watched them being towed into position.

Luke himself preferred not to dwell on the horrors of lifelong imprisonment with thousands of captives jumping continuously as they tried to exist in too small a space, fouling the seabed with their faeces, frequently vaccinated or doused with pesticides to rid them of sea lice, and fed with fishmeal derived from sand eel, anchovies, or herring, so depriving both seabirds and other predators of their natural food.

A horrible life followed by stressful premature death: hardly surprising that Jess found it difficult even to greet

McInnes civilly when they met – as they could hardly avoid doing – on shopping trips to Stairbrigg's supermarket or car park and she thought he took a perverse pleasure in engaging her in conversation, asking how many fish their guests had caught, and volunteering quite unnecessary information about his progress with renovating the smokery and processing plant.

'Typical politician,' Luke said soothingly. 'Hide like a rhino. Feels he's got to engage with all sides even if they'd rather he didn't. For goodness sake don't start a row with him, darling.'

'As if I would!'

But her resolve was tested on the March morning when he came swaggering out of the harbour cafe to intercept her as she waited for the ferry across the bay to Inverclinie. In place of suit and tie he wore a thick dark-blue guernsey and faded jeans, his rubber boots turned over at the top as the lobstermen wore them. With his broad shoulders, mop of dark curly hair and three-day stubble he looked less politician and more West Coast boatman, but there was no denying he was a handsome devil, admitted Jess grudgingly to herself. A braw gallus, as Danna had said, but a bonny one too – and boy, does he know it!

Tucked under his arm was a copy of the *Stairbrigg Gazette*. She had the distinct impression that he had been waiting to waylay her.

'Hot off the press. Thought you'd be interested,' he said, and without waiting for a response spread the news-sheet on top of the wall, pinning it down with both big hands as the wind plucked and rustled the pages. The headline leapt out at her.

### Local Firm Wins Top Award

Only two years after harvesting its first crop of salmon, Moontide Aquaculture, owned by local businessman and former MSP Dougal McInnes, has been honoured with the Scottish Salmon Producers top award for Marine Enterprise. 'Our team has worked very hard to achieve this recognition of excellence,'

Mr McInnes told our reporter. 'We hope that by being seen to raise standards in aquaculture we can counter the myths put about by our opponents and secure the future of Stairbrigg as a beacon of best practice in salmon farming and associated industries.'

'Astonishing,' said Jess stiffly, and tried to move on, but he detained her.

'Aren't you going to congratulate us?'

She bit back the furious responses that sprang to her lips. *I don't believe you. Who did you bribe to get that endorsement? Why does every escaped fish that we see suffer from lesions and discoloration? Why did so many die when you raised the water temperature to kill the lice?*

All this and more she had heard from their neighbours' gossip, but she dared not voice them for fear of Big Dougie's cosy relationship with the Press. It was too easy to imagine how the reporter would frame his next paragraphs.

*Opposition to the success of Moontide was voiced by Mrs Jessamine Balfour, 39, whose husband recently bought the exclusive Kildrumna fishing lodge on the Inverclinie peninsula...* and there would follow everything she had said, twisted to emphasise the Balfours' Englishness, the supposed wealth of their fishing guests, their selfish preoccupation with keeping Scottish rivers private instead of opening them for 'hard-working families' to share in their bounty... and so on and so forth.

She dared not risk it.

'Well?' Though his mouth smiled, his eyes were watchful. He wanted to trap her into an unguarded remark, and she was damned if she would give him that satisfaction.

'Yes, of course. You must have worked very hard,' she said as casually as she could. 'Now, if you'll excuse me...'

He wasn't ready to let her go. 'Oh, we did, we did! And it was well worth it.' He paused, and when she said nothing he went on, 'This means we can put a premium on our product, and market it as top of the range. Success breeds success, you know, and we must strike while the iron is hot.'

This sounded ominous. 'What do you mean?'

'We've put in an application to the DSFB – that's the District Salmon Fishery Board – for ten more cages in the Sound. That ought to help with our advertising and put the business on a firm footing.'

'But you can't! Not here. It would be environmental vandalism! Didn't SEPA's report warn that the Sound can't take any more pollution without risk of depleting all the rivers on Inverclinie and the coast?' She had read and re-read the report by the Scottish Environment Protection Agency on the environmental impact of salmon farming until she almost knew it by heart. 'If the District Board permits your application it'll drive a coach and horses through SEPA's advice, and I promise you we'll fight it every inch of the way.'

'Best of luck with that, Mrs Balfour,' he said with a grin, 'but I think you'll find local opinion on our side. People are queuing up to work for us, and the economy of Stairbrigg is booming thanks to the Smokery. I'll be surprised if the Board turns down our proposal.'

Ten more cages! Jess felt sick and turned away, unable to endure his taunts any longer. She was hardly aware of how she got home, but when she blurted out the news, Luke simply nodded.

'Gunnar said this was bound to happen sooner or later. I'd better ring him tonight and say it's time to bring up the big battalions. He told me to avoid getting into a fight with MacInnes because he's still so well in with the Scottish Government, but Gunnar's promised he'll step in and calm things down when he visits us in June on his tour of inspection before writing his report for SEPA.'

Thunderstruck, she stared at him. 'You mean you've been talking to Gunnar about this?'

'Well, emailing.'

'That's just as bad. Why did you never mention it to me?'

'He asked me not to because he thought it might upset

you,' said Luke, avoiding her eye. 'Well, actually I was pretty sure it would, so –'

'I'll tell you what upsets me, and that's you going behind my back and making plans with Gunnar without a word to me!' said Jess fiercely. Her smouldering resentment of his godfather's influence burst into sudden flame. 'Come on, Luke! We're supposed to be a team! You've no right to keep me in the dark about something that affects our whole future. We should deal with this together, not go bleating to Gunnar.'

Luke shook his head with his usual maddening calm. 'Steady on, darling. You're getting ahead of yourself. Don't you see – this is exactly why I didn't tell you about the application for more cages – I was afraid you'd lose your rag and do or say something –' He broke off.

'Something what?' she asked with dangerous calm.

'Something... undiplomatic. Something that would make things worse. Look, my love: it's no use going ape about this. MacInnes is a pretty big cheese around these parts, and he's got a lot of local support. We'll have to handle it carefully, and Gunnar's the obvious one to sway opinion our way.'

'But he's a foreigner! He's got nothing to do with Scotland. *We're* the people this application is going to affect – whose business it's likely to ruin. Why should anything Gunnar says make a difference?'

'Don't forget he's a well-known conservationist and belongs to any number of regulatory bodies around the world. He loves Scotland, and has written umpteen papers opposing the degradation of the sea bed in coastal waters. He was instrumental in proposing strict limits on the number of cages fish farms are allowed and where they are sited. And he's an ex officio member of the Advisory Committee on Fisheries and Aquaculture, even though he's Norwegian.'

He looked at her closed, stubborn face and went on, 'Believe me, he's a serious figure in the world of conservation and when he talks, people pay attention. People who matter. He was instrumental in drumming up support for the right of the Press to publish photographs of sick salmon – over 300 of them – taken by fish health inspectors. Some of them are absolutely revolting. Of course the fish farmers fought tooth and nail to have them suppressed, but now the government has decided that those images will be published regularly. I tell you, darling, when Gunnar launches a campaign, he's an unstoppable force.'

It's useless; he won't listen, thought Jess. The habit of deferring to his godfather is too strong. He'll never shrug off his advice, or choose to deal with problems in his own way. Or even in my way. Gunnar's been very kind to us, I don't discount that, but he's old-fashioned and personally I don't trust his judgment. Look at the loss he made when he sold off his trawlers and went into cruise boats; it's not beyond the bounds of possibility that he'd welcome the chance to get rid of Kildrumna, which even I can see is a black hole of expense and never likely to do more than wash its face.

But spelling out these thoughts to Luke was not an option. For one thing it would shock him that they should even occur to her, and risk appearing disloyal; for another that to shake his faith in Gunnar might undermine his own belief in their future here.

I know we can make it work, she told herself; and as she thought again of the newspaper article he had taunted her with the outline, an idea floated into her mind. Two could play at that game, and if Luke was prepared to share their troubles with an outsider, so could she.

When she returned to her laptop that evening she clicked on Contacts and sent a message to her former editor.

As Luke squelched along the river path three months later, his thoughts were also dominated by the Larsens' visit. Estimated Time of Arrival uncertain, as usual. Gunnar's plans were never cut and dried: he took a mischievous delight in surprising his friends by his sudden appearances, though this was seldom appreciated by his hosts and certainly not by Jess, who liked to know times and numbers for meals.

Commissariat apart, he must plan for his guests' entertainment. Fishermen and women would happily spend all day on the rivers and lochs, but partners who did not enjoy sketching or watching from the bank were a problem. Wi-fi was erratic and slow, and mobiles could not get a signal: so once they had taken a few walks and finished telling him he was lucky to live in such a beautiful place, such surplus visitors were apt to settle down by the drawing-room fire, from time to time invading the kitchen for unscheduled coffee and biscuits, or chatting up the team of cleaners as they tried to restore order to bedrooms, all of which drove Jess up the wall.

Old Danna had turned out to be a skilled and resourceful carpenter with a talent for design, and each of the little fishing huts he had constructed alongside the holding pools had a charming balcony with benches and a pull-out table, besides a two-ring gas-fired stove and tiny kitchen. These made an attractive refuge for non-combatants when the fish wouldn't bite or rain came down in stair-rods, but even in the height of summer you could be chilled to the bone after sitting still for more than an hour.

A lot depended on the weather, of course, but after the last downpour the water for the next few days would be high enough to put fishermen onto the top beats until Wednesday, at least; and when the de la Caves and Marianne Labouchere left on Thursday morning to continue their gastronomic tour on Skye, Robb and his daughter would probably enjoy fishing from the boat on any of the lochs – note to self, he thought, send Logan to check there was fuel for each of the outboards and that the oars were in good nick. Earlier in the season, a loch-fishing party of German ladies had been outraged to find only the charred remains of oars which had been used as firewood by some benighted hiker, and ever since then, Luke had insisted they were locked in the bothy.

Even without the added complication of Gunnar and his bride, it was going to be a busy week, thought Luke, but first things first, and that meant securing six lobsters for dinner tonight.

From the north-facing window of the studio she had constructed from a redundant calf-shed set at a right angle to her long low croft, its roof weighted down with heavy turf as insurance against westerly gales, Mhairi Brydon recognised the ancient tweed fishing hat perched on Luke's black hair, and as the rest of his tall, loose-limbed figure came first into sight and then within shouting distance, she pushed aside the baskets and bowls that held her jeweller's tools – tweezers and delicate hooks, tiny silver links and a minuscule hammer – and leaned out of the double-glazed casement to call: 'If you're looking for Logan, Mr Balfour, he's down the jetty, helping with the nets.'

Instead of deviating from his course, he continued towards her and as she hurriedly shut the window to stop the wind scattering all the materials on her work bench, she caught just fragments of his reply: 'Sorry... emergency... raid your larder...'

Moments later he pushed open the door of her spartan kitchen. 'Those damned farmed fish!' he said without preamble, and she raised her eyes to heaven.

'I heard from Logan there's been another escape – a big one, too. The bottom ripped out of the middle cage, and they say there's seals feasting all round about the feed barge. Like as not it was them caused the damage, and the good Lord knows how many salmon have gone up the rivers by now.'

'I caught four of them this afternoon,' said Luke grimly. 'Hauled them out and donated them to the otter, but now we've nothing for supper. I wondered if you'd enough lobsters in your chiller to feed our visitors tonight?'

'Och, aye. You can have them and welcome. Logan brought in nigh on a dozen and I boiled them last night, so they're good and fresh. How many do you need?'

'You're a star,' said Luke gratefully, and Mhairi shook her sandy head so that wisps from the loose bun at her nape escaped to flutter round her cheeks.

'Wait now: I'll put them in a cold-bag right away.'

As she hurried out to the larder, he gazed round the neat warm kitchen with its bright rag rugs and haunting whiff of turf smoke. Even though the ash in the basket grate was dull grey, just a few puffs of the bellows would rouse it to glowing embers again, he knew, to be economically 'smoored' once more when Logan finished his homework. He was heading for university next September – or so his mother hoped – and she was ruthless at ensuring that his re-takes in Maths and Biology, which he was due to sit in the spring, came up with better results than first time round.

Poor devil, thought Luke with feeling. He had never shone in exams either, and thought Logan's practical skills would be wasted by four years of academic work, but Mhairi was adamant. She was a traditionalist to her fingertips and believed in hard work. Something for nothing was anathema to her, and learning meant the kind of knowledge that came from books. Her son might be a born fisherman and very useful mechanic but in her view that counted for nothing beside a degree which would liberate him from island life and send him fully fledged into the world of business.

'I've done all that,' Luke had assured her, 'and I can tell you it's one big headache. I wouldn't wish it on a dog. Every CEO I ever met was longing to throw it up and retire to Scotland where he could spend his time fishing. Lord, how they envied me!' and she had laughed.

'Get away with you, Mr Balfour!' Mhairi's high cheekbones flushed and her grey eyes, which could look so dreamy, fastened on Luke with sudden intensity. 'Say what you like, you'll not change my mind. Logan's going to have the chance to get a top job, and that means he'll need a degree. Look at Big Dougie now. Who'd have thought the poor wean that he was would wind up an MSP with a finger in every pie you can name. I've heard he has only to drop a hint in the First Minister's ear for her to change a law that would hurt his business.'

None of which had made comfortable hearing for Luke, and Mhairi's mind must have been running on the same lines because now she said as she returned with the cold-bag, 'It's a disgrace for him to destroy our rivers for the sake of a grudge, for that's what I believe it is. We'd have had none of this fish farm trouble if the old Major had agreed to sell him Kildrumna, but once Big Dougie's offer was turned down he took a scunner to the place, for all that he was born and bred here.'

She paused, then added delicately, 'Ye'll have spoken to him yourself, of course? I've heard that now and then Mrs Balfour shares a table with him in the harbour café when the ferryboat's late.'

'Better than freezing to death on the quayside,' said Luke, laughing; and she looked at him narrowly. Couldn't he see what was all too plain to her – that along with half the female population of Stairbrigg, Mrs Balfour fancied Big Dougie and was doing her best to deny it?

'As for speaking to him – I've done my best. Written, spoken, asked him for a drink to discuss it... and all the response I get is that salmon is Scotland's biggest food export, and it's not right that the interests of a few rich landowners should be put before those of ordinary people trying to earn a living.' Luke sighed. 'All of which is perfectly true. Unanswerable, really.'

'What about environmental costs?'

'Waste of breath.' Luke picked up the cold-bag and hefted it, then looked inside. 'Thanks for these, Mhairi. They're beauties – absolute crackers. Where did Logan catch them?'

'Wheesht, Mr Balfour. I'm surprised at you. Don't you

know better than to ask where a lobsterman sets his traps? If he tells, he'll likely find them empty tomorrow,' she said severely. 'That's the tradition.'

'Oh, lord! Sorry, I didn't know. Thanks, anyway: you've certainly saved our bacon tonight. Let me know what I owe you and I'll drop it over tomorrow.'

He moved towards the door, but Mhairi put out a hand to detain him. 'Wait, now, Mr Balfour. D'ye ken what's the word down the harbour about Moontide joining forces with the other independent fishfarms here on the West Coast?'

Luke stiffened and a chill seemed to grip his stomach. This was the last thing he wanted to hear. Fending off McInnes alone was bad enough, but if he amalgamated his business with others it could be a death blow for Kildrumna. 'I've heard nothing about that. Tell me more.'

'Well, it's hush-hush just now, but Danna's niece Jamie-Lee, who's a bright lassie and has a boyfriend works as a packer at the Smokery, told Danna they mean to form a consortium strong enough to take on the big boys like Mowi and Scottish Sea Farms, and they've asked Dougal McInnes to chair it.' She paused, then added the clincher. 'The Council's all for it, but they're after dragging their feet until Mr Larsen makes his report.'

'Ah.'

'Danna says Yanis and his boys have been ordered to weed out all sick or dopey fish – white heads, amoebic gills, anything with sores and fungal growths – and test each cage for signs of pancreatic virus. He saw a tipper truck of dead fish driven away from the quay yesterday at 4am, just as it was getting light.'

'Where were they taken?'

Mhairi shrugged. 'Och, there's many a bog hole between here and Templeport will tell no tales. But if Mr Larsen puts in a bad report, says Jamie-Lee, other West Coast fish farms would take fright and then as regards the consortium all bets are off.'

'Hmm.' Luke thought it over. Could be good news or

bad… He said, 'Thanks for putting me in the picture, Mhairi, grim as it is. Forewarned is forearmed. And thanks for these.' He hesitated, then added, 'Please ask Danna to keep his ear to the ground, and let me know if he hears anything more about this amalgamation. We may not be able to stop it, but at least we won't be taken by surprise.'

'Where's the fighting spirit, Mr Balfour?' Mhairi scolded. 'Whiles ye have to fight fire with fire. I'll get a petition started among the ladies, and we'll lobby local councillors until they beg us to hold our tongues. With an election coming up, they'll be clamouring for our votes against vested interests ruining our coast and stealing our children's heritage, for that's what this will be. Man, we'll make those fish farmers wish they'd never set foot on Inverclinie.'

# CHAPTER TWO

# Marina

MARINA CLARE ROBB lifted the mane of crinkly ginger hair off her sweating neck, twisting it like a rope and skewering it with a slide through the scrunchie into a rough topknot, and instantly a swarm of midges descended on the pale exposed skin to torment her.

'Don't forget your Jungle Juice,' her father had said before she set off up the twisting path behind Kildrumna Lodge, leaving him to make slow conversation with the French guests; but after the long hot drive to the ferry, followed by navigating on bumpy tracks across the peninsula, and then standing awkwardly, by turns scrutinised and ignored, while Mrs Balfour introduced them to her other visitors and showed them their bedrooms, she had been longing so much for air and exercise that she had forgotten to transfer the stick of insect repellent from the top pocket of her fishing weskit to her jeans, and was defenceless against aerial attack by thousands of tiny probosces.

Why do they always go for me? she thought, slapping unavailingly and only making herself hotter. They never bother Dad, and Hels and Sal can be bitten a thousand times without showing a mark, but Mum and I... With sudden shocking clarity came the memory of her mother laughing as she slathered calamine on the hundreds of red pinprick bites on her youngest daughter's arms and legs after a singsong round the campfire in Wales.

'Thank goodness at least one of you knows what I go through,' she had said, hugging her; and now Marina felt her throat tighten. Oh, Mum... If only you were here too! She and her mother had shared so much: jokes, interests, and phobias, as well as the same complexion, typical small, skinny strawberry blondes with heart-shaped faces and pointed chins, barely visible eyebrows, and a tendency to freckles. They had the same trouble with stings and allergies; but Mum was dead, killed in the crash that put her father on eighteen months' sick leave, and now Marina had to deal with such problems alone.

The steep winding path meandered upward, making a wide loop round the Kildrumna policies and giving spectacular views of the sea far below. In the distance it was possible to glimpse the blue blur of the mainland, with the little port of Stairbrigg shrouded in turf smoke that had no wind to disperse it. She halted, wondering if it was worth going any farther, then as the midges redoubled their attack, her eye caught the distant gleam of water. As if drawn by a magnet she turned off the rocky path and let her feet carry her through a gap in the cliffs towards a roughly triangular loch set glimmering in a bowl of heather-covered hills, its peaty water promising a haven for trout too small to tempt any but the most avid fisherman.

Perfect for skinny dipping, though: to a hot, midge-bitten fourteen-year-old there could be few more welcome sights. With renewed energy, she stumbled over the tussocky whinberry sedge and ten minutes later slid down a grassy bank to stand on the pebbly foreshore. In the reeds that fringed the mouth of a little burn she could see fish rising, but beyond them the water was clear and still. An alluring group of small islands halfway across caught her eye, and without pausing to consider how she would dry off afterwards, she stripped off T-shirt and jeans, kicked off her trainers and waded straight in.

The midges vanished as cold peaty water wrapped her like a silken robe, and she struck out strongly for the nearest island, sinking her nose deep at each breaststroke and revelling in this return to her favourite element. As she had expected, the water was alive with tiny fish, and the merest riffle of breeze sent V-shaped ripples skidding across the smooth surface.

It was these that caught the eye of young Logan Brydon, sitting dreamily with his back against a sun-warmed rock with his maths revision book on the ground beside him as if he could absorb knowledge from its cover alone. He had been out with his lobster boat well before dawn, checking his pots and re-baiting them, and after delivering the catch to his mother had spent the rest of the morning patrolling the riverbank on the estate quad bike, making sure that the fishing huts along the Clinie were supplied with butane gas and dry wood for their small stoves.

According to his mother's schedule, Logan's afternoons were meant to be spent revising, but by claiming he found it easier to concentrate outdoors, he had managed to negotiate permission to leave the croft and take his book to this vantage-point above the Lodge where he would be the first to see the arrival of fishing guests and, more importantly, of Gunnar Larsen's yacht.

What would he bring this year? he wondered. It was part of Mr Larsen's mystique that every time he visited Kildrumna Lodge, he sailed in a new and distinctive vessel. One year, while his beautiful Whitbread Maxi 81 was undergoing a full refit before competing in an ARC rally, his appearance in a junk-rigged steel schooner with billowing sails of deepest ochre had excited comment all up and down the coast.

That would take a bit of beating, reflected Logan, who treasured the memory of crewing on it while Mr Larsen visited other islands. The £500 tip he had received had tided them over a bad patch in the crofting calendar before the October cattle sales revitalised their finances, which even his mother – ever sparing of praise – acknowledged. 'You're a good son. What would I do without you?'

That was the opening he unwisely seized to tell her of his ambition to spend the following summer in the boatyard in Marseilles, where Mr Larsen had good as promised him a job; unwisely because before he was halfway through pointing out the merits of this scheme Mhairi was shaking her head, adamant that such plans must take second place to his studies.

'Time enough for that when you've your place in college, laddie.'

Her tone had brooked no argument and he cursed himself for blurting out his private dream. Despite her sweet voice and ethereal looks, Mhairi was an activist, an environmental warrior, and she took a keen interest in politics. She read the financial pages of *The Scotsman* and disagreed in almost every respect with her uncle Danna's feudalist views. Many a night Logan had drifted to sleep with half-heard, half-understood phrases in his ears. "The bottom line..." and "He'll have to listen to the bean counters now," had begun to appear in their discussions recently, and this made him unaccountably uneasy. Were they talking about Mr Balfour? Surely not. Or Mr Larsen?

Mhairi made no secret of her opinion that Mr Larsen was too rich for his own good, and now she would very likely forbid her son to spend any time aboard whatever new and beautiful craft came gliding round the headland to moor at the jetty.

For a moment he allowed himself to dream: he stood tall and proud in the cockpit of a sleek, Bermuda-rigged schooner, bearing down on the final marker buoy as the wind rose, whipping up white horses, and the angle of the deck steepened until the rails were lost in a flurry of foam.

'Ready about!' he would shout.

'Ready!'

'Helm's alee!'

And like the thoroughbred she was, the schooner would tack, nearly scraping the marker buoy as she made the turn...

A nick in the horizon – a distant sail. There she was! Abruptly he returned to the here and now and reached behind him for the telescope his father had been given after ghillying for Jerome Kleinweld, overweight chairman of an American pharmaceutical company and one of Major Philpott's oldest friends.

'I guess I won't be doing this again,' Mr Kleinweld had gasped, lying flat on his back in the heather as Jock Brydon set about gralloching the handsome ten-pointer that had taken them four hours to stalk. 'My heart won't stand it. If you care to take it, this will be more use to you than me.' And he had handed to his bloody-handed ghillie the top-of-the-range Swarovski CTS 85 which Jock had been eyeing covertly all day, a thousand-plus pound's worth of sleek, streamlined technology that would be the envy of every stalker and ghillie on the peninsula.

Even that magnificent gesture had not gained Mhairi's full approval. She disliked any hint of accepting charity, and a hard time Logan had had to persuade her not to sell it after his father's death. Even now he kept it very firmly under his own eye in case she should be tempted to turn it into cash. After ten years' hillwork it was not quite the sleek masterpiece of optical engineering it had once been. Scratches and dents marred its shining surface and the carrying-strap was in dire need of attention from the cobbler but, like his father, Logan treasured it and never went to the hill without it.

Extending it to its full length, he focused carefully on the strange sail and felt a twinge of disappointment. Not a racing yacht at all, but a fat little ketch, sloop rigged and sturdy with olive-green paintwork, more suitable for family cruising than taking on the cream of international yachtsmen in ARC rallies. What could have impelled Mr Larsen to choose such a utilitarian vessel?

Then he remembered the new bride. As the little boat came closer, tacking across the bay in a series of short boards, Logan could see that the woman at the helm was being instructed – one might almost think hectored – by the big, blond-bearded, unmistakable figure of Gunnar Larsen himself, hand possessively on her shoulder as he bent to speak in her ear, gesturing emphatically, striding forrad to trim the sails, or aft to peer down at the wake, from time to time seizing the helm himself in a way that left no room for doubt that the pilot was under instruction and might at any moment be told to move aside and let him take over.

Logan was hungry. A glance at his watch told him he would have to hurry home if he wanted tea before his mother went off to her evening's work in the bar. As he closed the Swarovski with two decisive clicks, movement on the surface of the little Dubh Lochan, enclosed by its hills, suddenly caught his eye and he extended it once more, hoping to see an otter and possibly her kits swimming to one of the islands.

No otters; but what he did see with 25 x magnification clarity was the pale body and contorted face of a near-naked girl in the water halfway between island and shore, splashing and thrashing in a way that instantly suggested to him that she was in trouble.

Cramp, he thought.

She turned on her back, bringing first one leg and then the other out of the water, apparently trying to massage her calf muscles, but it was clear to him that this manoeuvre was making things worse.

Silly little cow: what a place to choose to swim alone! he thought. Serve her right if she drowned.

For a moment more he sat staring, wondering what to do, hoping the cramp would go off and he wouldn't have to do anything. Ten to one, he reasoned, if he ran over to the loch that when he got there he would find her back on the bank, wondering what the fuss was about; she must be a pretty good swimmer to have got as far as the island, and if she could get there she could perfectly well get back. On the other hand, how would he feel if she did drown? How would he explain just sitting here watching her struggles and thinking about missing his tea?

That settled it. Clicking shut the Swarovski once more, he shoved the maths book into his pocket, and started to run, praying that the boat would be in its proper place and no benighted camper had chopped up the oars for kindling.

'Just look at her! Isn't she beautiful?' Gunnar flung an expansive arm around his godson's shoulders and pulled him close in a bear hug as they strolled along the jetty above the slipway where the Kildrumna boats moored. 'The first moment I saw her I knew I must have her.'

Luke stared obediently at *Shield Maiden*'s dull olive paintwork and clumsily furled sails, and her pointed Newfoundland dory towing behind, searching for words that were both truthful and could – with a bit of a stretch – be interpreted as praise. *Workhorse? Looks as if she's done a bit in her time? Handsome is as handsome does?* None of them quite fitted the bill. He was about to compromise with, 'Looks thoroughly seaworthy,' when he glanced sideways and saw that his godfather was not gazing at the fat little ketch, but at his wife Ravenna, sitting on a bollard at the water's edge, smiling up at Jess, who was chattering nineteen to the dozen.

'It seems like a dream to be back here,' he heard her say. 'Just as I remember but also quite different. You've done so much. Those urns on the balustrade, for instance – that's brilliant. Somehow they lighten the whole facade.'

The urns had been Jess's idea. 'I'm so glad you like them,' she said, glowing.

Clearly they were getting on well and that, thought Luke, was a big relief. If this visit followed the same pattern as earlier ones, he would be spending most of the week on hill, riverbank, or office giving Gunnar one-on-one attention and, unless Ravenna proved exceptionally keen on fishing or photography, that would mean leaving her entertainment largely to Jess.

'So it was love at first sight?' he said lightly, half-joking; but Gunnar nodded seriously.

'Immediate. I saw my Raven: I loved her. There was no question.'

Not for you maybe, but what about her? thought Luke. Did the flash of attraction – the *coup de foudre* – strike you both simultaneously? It raised interesting questions in his mind but not ones he could put to the new bride on so short an acquaintance. And wasn't there something a bit strange about Gunnar's choice of words? I had to have her... he might have been talking about an object needed for his collection.

'Isn't she?' Gunnar insisted. 'My dear boy, I wish for your opinion on my own little shield maiden. Don't you think she is beautiful?'

Beautiful, no question; and perhaps from Gunnar's massive six-foot four she might appear little, but like her husband she was built on heroic lines, tall, strong, graceful and slow-moving. A well-proportioned size eighteen, was Luke's guess, beside whom his slim, quicksilver Jess looked like an animated midget.

'Stunning,' said Luke with complete sincerity. 'You're a lucky man.'

And indeed with the sun catching glints of gold in the centre-parted chestnut hair which she wore in two thick plaits framing the broad-browed, rose-apricot face now upturned to smile at whatever tall story Jess was recounting, her full-skirted dress with its embroidered hem and figure-hugging bodice, Ravenna looked like an illustration from a child's book of Norse myths, calm, capable and serene. Was there fire and passion beneath that quiet surface? Could she be roused to axe-wielding fury in defence of hearth and home? Hurriedly he pushed away such unsuitable thoughts.

'Sorry! I thought at first you meant your boat,' he said quickly. 'Not quite your usual style, is she?'

Gunnar waved a dismissive hand. 'Oh, that. I picked her up in Turkey a couple of months ago and ran her round to Bozburun to have her customised. Just a tub, of course, nothing special, but I wanted something with a lifting keel so she can run in anywhere, and a diving platform and, of course, extra headroom.'

'Of course.'

'Besides, she's easy to handle; perfect for teaching a beginner. My Raven has never sailed before, but she is quick to learn, you will see.'

'Has she done any flyfishing?'

'Aha!' Gunnar's love-struck expression changed to keen interest. 'So already we come to the big question: are there still wild salmon to fish for? How is the health of the rivers? I hear rumours from my friends in Scottish Salmon Watch that there are very many escapes from the Moontide cages, and the SSFO producers are putting pressure on the government to allow higher concentrations of Slice to combat the sea lice.'

'Too true.' Luke grimaced. He – and almost everyone on the island – blamed *emamectin benzoate*, the powerful insecticide used to kill sea lice and marketed under the trade name *Slice*, for not only degrading the seabed in the hitherto pristine waters of the Reekie Sound, but for its harmful effect on crustaceans. Lobsters, prawns, shrimps and crabs were all susceptible, and lower down the food chain sand eels and shrimps were being indiscriminately wiped out.

'Moontide won't admit it, but given the amount of drift you get in the Sound, there's no way of confining chemical treatments to one area. OK, they have to keep parasite infestations down for the caged fish, I can see that, though I don't like it, but it affects the whole area way beyond the cages.'

'How many treatments do they get?'

'Far too many. Just recently the management sent out a news-sheet, claiming that sea lice are becoming more resistant and they've commissioned a new study that claims that even much higher concentrations of emamectin would benefit salmon without harming other sea life. Personally, I don't believe it. You have only to ask the lobstermen to get a very different answer.'

'Has this study been published?'

'Pending more research, as per,' Luke said with a shrug. 'It's the same old story: almost impossible to pin anyone down to a decision. Compared to most fish farms, this is small, and the owner is keen to get more clout by joining forces with others on the coast.'

'Who's he?'

'The owner? One Dougal McInnes – or Big Dougie, as he's generally known. Local boy made good – I expect you noticed him at the auction.'

Something moved behind Gunnar's eyes, a flicker of recognition. 'MacInnes? Ah, yes. I know him from long ago. Wasn't he the underbidder?'

'That's right. Not a bad chap: he pulled Jess out of a hole when her car went off the road last winter on that nasty corner between Stairbrigg and the White Lady rocks. She was quite shaken. She went through the barrier and in another few yards she'd have been in the drink.'

He didn't add, because Jess hadn't told him, how she had moaned and clung to her rescuer like a terrified kitten as he carried her back up the slope, and felt such a strong surge of desire while wrapped in the comfort of his kammo-jacketed arms that she would have liked him to carry her all the way home and into his bed. Shocking! Not the sort of thing she expected of herself.

'Dinna fash,' he had soothed. 'You're safe now. The car's taken a knock, but no great harm done. Tell me, were you alone?'

'Yes... no!' And with a jolt she had remembered she was on her way back from the vet and poor Pooh-Hi, her Pekinese, was still in her basket on the back seat.

All of which Jess had edited from her account of the incident, reducing it simply to skidding on ice, over-correcting, and slipping sideways towards the cliff. Dougal's role was similarly tailored to spotting the skidmarks, climbing down to investigate, and pulling first Jess herself and then the dog from the stranded car.

Naturally enough it had altered their relationship; Mhairi's were not the only pair of sharp eyes to have noted how Mrs Balfour's colour rose when Big Dougie asked if she would join him for a coffee while waiting for the ferry, or her look of disappointment when he was not on the quay.

Now on the jetty in the evening sunshine, Gunnar asked, 'This question of escapes from the cages: why are they not secure?'

'What can you expect when they were cobbled together from a job lot of cheapo equipment being sold off by a failed fish farm in Chile, and shipped here courtesy of the taxpayer in the wake of an MSP's freebie, aka fact-finding tour? If you ask me, it's a wonder they keep the fish in at all.'

Gunnar nodded heavily. 'In Norway there are big fines for those that allow farmed fish to mix with wild ones. Three strikes and you're out, you know? Then the licence can be withdrawn – in theory, at least. But –'

'Don't tell me: I'll tell you,' said Luke grimly. 'Producers lobby the government until they agree to make an exception... is that what you were going to say? Because that's what happens here. So important for trade, Scotland's biggest food export, blah-blah. Forget the suffering of the fish, close your eyes to the environmental damage, focus your thoughts on the bottom line.'

'As you, my dear godson, must focus your thoughts on how to outwit these villains,' said Gunnar, his slitted, mischievous eyes hinting at barely legal plans about to be proposed. 'Why do you think I have come here at great inconvenience to myself if not to show you how to fight for your precious river by foul means as well as fair?'

Luke smiled reluctantly but his spirits began to rise. This didn't sound like the talk of a man who was contemplating cutting his losses at Kildrumna. 'I thought it was for the pleasure of my company. My mistake! Never mind why you've come, I'm damned glad to see you, Gunnar, and whatever you have in mind, you can count on my full support.'

'He treats her like a child,' hissed Jess, whipping shot-glasses and brandy balloons off tables and chair-arms onto a tray as soon as the drawing-room's heavy door closed on the last of their guests to opt for bed.

Luke would have liked to follow them without delay, but long experience had taught him to recognise storm cones when he saw them hoisted. Better to lower them now than let Jess fret and fume all night over some perceived injustice.

'She doesn't seem to mind,' he said quietly, 'and remember, she is so much younger than him. Not all relationships are even-stevens like ours, darling. Gunnar's probably the father-figure – sugar-daddy – whatever you like to call it that Ravenna never had, and she's quite happy to settle for child-substitute status.'

'You mean being bossed around?'

'That's one way of putting it.'

'But it was so blatant! Correcting every single thing she said, and giving orders on what she could and couldn't wear. She's a clever, well-educated woman! She practically ran those cruise ships he bought. How dare he undermine her like that?'

'Oh, darling, it's not that bad.'

'You can't have been listening. Didn't you hear him tell her to stop talking and finish her food because the Frogs would miss the sword dancing?'

'Don't call them that. What if the girls heard you? What is this sword dancing, anyway?'

'Oh, they're putting on traditional dancing at the pub tonight to entertain some wedding party, and Jerome wanted to watch. Local colour, you know. Anyway, Gunnar ordered Ravenna to hurry up because she was keeping everyone waiting. I tell you my blood was boiling! I kept hoping she'd answer back and put him in his place, but she never did.'

'That's why I say we can't interfere. If that's the dynamic they've settled on, it's no one else's business. As my dad used to say, "*Ne messez pas.*" Leave well alone. Honestly, honey, I mean it.'

If he adds, "Trust me," I'll hit him, thought Jess mutinously, but he didn't. Instead he raised a hand to massage his eyes, looking suddenly grey with fatigue, and she felt a rush of pity. Poor Luke! He tried so hard to keep everyone happy, and she was making things worse by challenging him about his godfather's attitude to women. What did it matter, anyway?

'Sorry,' she said with an effort. 'You're right. It's none of our business. It's just that what with the serving and trying to keep tabs on that poor kid who looked as if she was going into meltdown, and listening to Gunnar banging on about his damned Vikings, I got a bit frazzled.' She took a deep calming breath. 'Forget it. Now, what's the plan for tomorrow? At some point I'll have to go over to Stairbrigg for a major shop, so if you and Gunnar want some quality time together, I'll see if Ravenna would like to come with me – it might appeal to her more than tramping along the riverbank.'

This was a handsome offer from someone who preferred to whizz alone round the little town, provisioning the lodge at top speed with maximum economy and efficiency in half the time it would take anyone else.

'Would you really?' he said gratefully. 'That would fit in perfectly. I'll send the Robbs to the Dunseran's top pools with Logan to ghillie for them and just keep my fingers crossed that they don't haul in any more of Big Dougie's damned escapers. We can do without that.'

'What's kept you? Your dinner's burnt to a cinder and I've no time to make anything else,' snapped Mhairi Brydon, already shawled and booted for her evening shift at the Clachan Inn when Logan appeared, breathless and scarlet-faced, having run the last two miles home. 'There's a wedding party come in on the six o'clock ferry, wanting to hear me sing the old ballads while they eat their meal, and Fergus will skin me if I keep them waiting.'

'Go on, then. Dinna fash, I'll be fine with bread and cheese,' Logan muttered, unwilling for the moment to explain how he had come to lose his most treasured possession. Unwilling, indeed, even to admit that he had lost it until he could go back tomorrow and search more thoroughly. He tried to remember exactly the sequence of events. He had spotted the strange girl swimming in the lochan, decided she was in difficulty and run to fetch the boat. At what point had he put down the Swarovski? He had no memory of laying it on the grass, or even of unslinging the case.

By the time he had turned the boat the right way up and launched it, the girl had disappeared again, and thereafter he had wasted perhaps half an hour rowing over to the islands looking for her, dreading all the time to find her floating face down in the black water.

Not a sign of her. She had apparently vanished into thin air and now he began to question if he had really seen her at all.

Giving up at last, he had rowed back, heaved the boat above the high-water mark, and gone back to where he had been revising. There was the rock he had been sitting against, the book was in his pocket, but of the telescope there was no sign. Cursing freely, back he went again to the lochside, but it wasn't there either although he could trace exactly where the boat had been and see the prints of his own trainers on the gravel beach.

Daylight had been fading when at last he turned for home, still mystified.

No prizes for guessing what his mother would say when she heard. Either, 'What have I been telling you all these years? Easy come, easy go.' Or perhaps, 'A stitch in time saves nine,' which would be fair enough in this case. That damned strap! He knew the buckle was coming loose, but had put off taking it to the saddler in Stairbrigg because it would mean doing without it for a few days. Now he might have to do without it for ever.

Moodily munching a hunk of stale soda bread slathered with butter, Logan decided to leave his lobster pots to look after themselves next morning, and go back to search every foot of heather between path and lochan before his mother was awake.

Detective Chief Inspector Martin Robb hovered outside his daughter's bedroom and wondered if he had been a fool to bring her here. On the journey north she had seemed in much better spirits, munching crisps, listening to the continuous tinny thumping leaking from her headphones, and teasing him about his refusal to follow Sat-Lady's advice on parts of the route he used to know.

'Bossy cow,' he would mutter, diving down a side street and provoking a flurry of disembodied corrections as well as Marina's giggles. 'Doesn't know what she's talking about. She never pounded the beat here like I did.' But times change and so do road signs: more than once his shortcuts ended in a cul-de-sac or one-way street, to Marina's unconcealed delight.

'I told you, Dad. She really does know the best route. Now let's try her in German.' And until she tired of the game Robb was forced to listen to directions he couldn't understand at all while his daughter, who was taking German for GCSE, supplemented Sat-Lady's orders with wild guesses of her own.

So the journey had passed without any worrying incident, and when Marina asked if she could skip tea and walk up the hill behind the lodge for a breath of air, he hesitated only a second before agreeing. Friendly as the French visitors appeared, it might test Marina's mental balance to sit with them too long.

Supper that night had been less propitious as far as

Marina was concerned. They had eaten in the long stone-flagged room that had once been the servants' hall, with guests and hosts alike in good spirits. On their final day at Kildrumna both Ginette de la Cave, plump and twinkly-eyed, and her tall, thin serious sister Laure had caught salmon in the upper reaches of the Clinie, and returned them to the water; and to his delight Jerome had managed to photograph three golden eagles. '*Voyez, tous les trois*, parents and ze juvenile, *j'en suis certain*,' he said, scrolling rapidly.

Marina had returned to the lodge later than Robb had expected, so he had not had a chance to speak to her until, pink-faced and rather damp about the hair, she slid into her place opposite him at the supper-table; to his dismay he recognised at once that she was on the verge of a panic attack, head down, breathing shallowly, and gripping her arms around her as if to hold her body together.

'I've given you a bit of everything, is that right?' Jess Balfour had said, putting down a plate, but Marina barely responded. Just the slightest nod from her bowed head, but no attempt to pick up knife and fork as the rest of the company began to talk and eat.

'You are not 'ongry, mon petit?' asked kindly Madame de la Cave, herself a notable trencherwoman, eyeing the untouched lobster. 'You wish I should 'elp you take 'im from ze shell?'

No answer.

Oh lord, thought Robb, hoping against hope that Marina would shake off her demons. He was sitting between his hostess and Ravenna, and didn't want to draw more attention to her than he absolutely had to.

Minutes passed. Jess finished serving and sat down to allow Gunnar to continue the long monologue about Vikings which he had launched into with his first gin and tonic. Wonderful sailors. Astonishing shipbuilders. Amazingly cultured, too; not at all the violent horn-wearing raiders and rapists of popular imagination.

Robb listened with half an ear, keeping an anxious eye on his daughter. Would she master the attack, or would it master her?

The omens were not good. Marina ducked her head still lower and began to shake. Robb put his napkin on the table and half rose, but before he could take a step Ravenna was on her feet, gliding swiftly round behind the chairs to put a gentle hand on the girl's shoulder.

'Come,' she said softly; and as if in a trance Marina got up and followed her out of the room.

'Half a sec,' said Jess, scooping up Ravenna's plate and returning it to the sideboard. Gunnar's monologue faltered momentarily, and the quick glance he directed at Robb showed the incident had not escaped his attention.

'Leave them, my friend,' he advised. Cheerfully he resumed his masterclass on the Vikings, and Robb sank back into his chair.

Twenty minutes later, Ravenna slipped into her place with a word of apology to Jess.

'Don't worry,' she said to Robb. 'Marina's just tired. I tucked her into bed and gave her something to help her sleep. Oh, nothing strong,' she added, smiling to deflect disapproval. 'She was already dozing when I left. I doubt if she'll remember anything tomorrow.'

Hardly reassuring for Robb, but what could he say? Any damage was already done, and he was certainly grateful for her prompt action. 'Well... thank you.'

Her long green eyes crinkled sympathetically. 'No need to thank me, none at all. I asked what was making her unhappy and –' for a moment she hesitated, then went on – 'she told me she can't stop remembering how her mother was killed. Just one year ago. I am so sorry.'

So the cat was well and truly out of the bag, he thought resignedly, but at least he wouldn't have to go through it all again with her. Yet to his surprise, because he usually preferred to operate on a need-to-know basis and believed family problems should be kept in the family, he found himself telling Ravenna how he blamed the accident for the way Marina had changed from a chatty, cheeky child full of jokes and confidence to this pale, worried shadow of her former self, prone to panic attacks and sudden bouts of weeping.

'Then for days at a time she will be perfectly happy and normal again,' he ended. 'I can't work out just what triggers the trouble. She has always loved the water – fishing, and swimming and boats and so on, and I hoped that coming here would cheer her up. You know, take her out of herself, but so far it doesn't seem to be working.'

'Give it time. She's got so many other worries it's hardly surprising that she feels the world is going too fast and she can't cope with it.'

Robb frowned. This was alien territory. He said stiffly, 'What kind of worries?'

'Oh, big ones – really big ones.' She ticked them off on her fingers. 'There's air pollution. Plastic in the oceans. Climate changes. Destruction of the rain forest. Too much rubbish in the world. Too many people. It's all far too much for a teenager to tackle on her own.' She sighed. 'Children are taught about these problems at school long before they are capable of seeing them in proportion. From hearing that the world is over-populated, it is only a short step to thinking perhaps it would be better if they themselves didn't exist. And then, I gather, she's had trouble on Twitter. Other girls objecting to something she said – is that right? Calling her names?'

Robb nodded. 'They call it trolling. I got her to shut down her account, but of course it was too late.'

'Girls can be so cruel – worse than boys, I sometimes think. Like a flock of hens spotting a wound and pecking at it,' she said sympathetically.

Extraordinary that the most guarded and reticent of his daughters should reveal so much to a complete stranger. Robb said, 'I'll talk to her – see if I can persuade her it's all overblown.'

'Go easy, then,' Ravenna warned, and as if reading his mind, she added, 'Sometimes children find it a relief to unburden themselves to someone they don't know. Someone outside the family. Somehow it feels more private.'

Was she right? All Robb's instincts screamed at him to tell her to stay out of it and let him deal with Marina's hang-ups himself.

For a couple of minutes Ravenna ate her interrupted meal in silence, then she said tentatively, 'I don't know what you'll think of this, but I did suggest she might like to come to Stairbrigg tomorrow with me and Jess. We're going to do a big shop and have lunch in the pub. Girls together, you know.'

Robb thought it over. 'What did she say?'

'Well, I may be wrong, but I thought she liked the idea. You better check with her in the morning. We won't be leaving early; Jess is aiming for the 10.30 ferry. You might both be glad of the break.'

Does she think I'm trying to escape my daughter's company? he thought with a touch of indignation, or she's bored with mine? On the other hand, he found the prospect of a day on his own very alluring, and when he managed to rouse the sleepy, tousled Marina next morning, she mumbled that was fine by her. Trying not to feel rejected, Robb scooped up discarded clothes from the floor and dumped them on the suitcase rack.

'Watch out you don't miss the ferry,' he warned, but before the door clicked behind him, Marina had drifted back to sleep.

# CHAPTER THREE

# The Dunseran

LUKE UNCLIPPED THE ten-foot carbon fibre rod from holders on the Volvo's roof, inspected the reel and joints and gave it a couple of experimental swishes before handing it to Robb. 'That should do the trick. Now, let's see what else you need.'

Stepping back a pace he gave his guest a quick once-over. Form-fitting neoprene waders, nailed and felt-soled wading boots, net, life jacket, many-pocketed weskit, fishing bag with waterproof lining and inside it hat, midge veil, fly-box, Leatherman multitool, spare casts already made up with droppers, sandwiches, fruitcake, matches – what a lot of gear he had to carry compared to his childhood expeditions equipped with Grandpa Tom's ropey old split-cane rod, whose reel was inclined to stick at crucial moments, and three sizes of tattered March Browns. In those days he used to drag out by force any fish he chanced to hook, and beach it on the bank, but that wouldn't do here, where the rule was to take one fish only and return to the river any others you were lucky enough to catch.

'Got a stick? No? Take one of mine,' said Luke, rootling in the cluttered back of the car, and handing over a spiked wading-stick with a sling, which Robb could see was going to be a pest to carry. 'I like my guests to have a third leg, because you have to wade in some pools where the rocks are slippery.' For the third time he glanced at his watch and then back down the second fork of the track. 'Now, where's young Logan? I told him to meet us here at ten and he's usually pretty punctual. Maybe his stirks broke into the oats again and he's trying to get them out before his mother gives him an earful.'

He blinked rapidly and Robb noticed the tight skin round his eyes and dark shadows hinting at a sleepless night. Under strain, poor chap, he thought. I wonder what's bugging him? Money? Wife trouble? It was usually one or the other. Ever since they arrived, Robb had been aware that underlying Luke's friendliness there was a feeling of barely contained anxiety, as if he was walking on the edge of a precipice.

With an embarrassed duck of the head, Luke added, 'I'm sorry to leave you without a ghillie, but don't waste your morning waiting for him. No doubt he'll turn up in his own good time, and give you a lift back to the Lodge when you decide to pack it in. I'd stay myself, except that Gunnar's waiting for me to give him a hand with his engine – and between you and me he's not the most patient of men. And then after lunch he wants to go through the books. He's our major shareholder, you know; but now he's gone into cruise ships instead of trawlers he only manages to come here and check things out once in a blue moon, so he likes to make the most of it.'

Running you ragged in the process, diagnosed Robb. He said hastily, 'Don't worry about me, for heaven's sake! There's nothing I like more than exploring a river on my own – and frankly,' he added disloyally, 'it's a treat to be on my own for once. Doesn't happen often enough.'

'Right, then, I'll be off.' Plainly relieved, Luke slammed the car door, shouted, 'Tight lines!' through the window, and bumped away down the track in a spatter of mud, while Robb began to pick his way down the thread of path that led to the river.

It was a damp, misty morning with occasional breaks in the cloud that gave alluring views of rolling, heathery hills intersected by trickling burns. In a narrow cleft between steep cliffs, the Dunseran was a chatty, bubbling thread of silver as it splashed from one rocky basin to the next in a series of shallow waterfalls, a far cry from the smooth treacly sweeps and curves of the majestic Clinie. There were tight rock gorges where an active fisherman could leap from one side to another, and bigger pools dotted with huge free-standing rocks like primitive croys.

Michie's Run read Robb, consulting the outline map that Luke had pressed on him; Round Pool, dotted with boulders which looked like stepping stones from this height; and Slithers which was probably self-explanatory.

Lower downstream the Dunseran broadened out through a band of woodland, and though the upper reaches did eventually straighten between the grassy flats and finely-gravelled redds of spawning pools, at the point where Luke had deposited him there was no obvious advantage in casting from one bank or the other.

My kind of river, Robb thought with satisfaction. Deep, narrow, full of incident: highly promising because his kind of fishing depended less on accurate casting than on opportunism and enterprise. Even the most awkward lies might be holding a salmon if you could get to them.

Rule One: don't let the fish see you.

Standing well back from the edge of Michie's Run, concealed by a twisted thorn bush, he stared into the water through polaroid glasses, astonished — as always — how the lenses revealed an underwater world of rocks and eddying weed invisible from the surface. As his eyes adapted to the stream-scape they began to pick up movement: just on the edge of the current, under the opposite bank, two long shapes lay parallel, inches apart. As he watched, a larger dark torpedo glided up to join them, dislodging the first two, which vanished into deeper, darker recesses under the rocks.

No shortage of customers, he thought. The question was, how to tempt them? Casting in such a narrow gorge was impossible, but unless he could get closer to the water he would not be able to trickle his fly past that somnolent nose. Was that better done from this side or the other?

Hampered as usual by his newly mended leg, he

clambered awkwardly over loose slabs at the top of the pool until he stood on a ledge about four feet above the water and could inch along it with his back to the rock face. As he had anticipated, the wading-stick tangled with his folding net, and after a few yards he dumped it on the ledge.

When he reached the spot he had marked, he again resorted to the polaroids, and saw with a leap of satisfaction that the larger salmon still lay, with fluke gently waving, in the same position, and three more had joined it. Very careful not to make a splash, he dipped his rod-tip close to the surface and let a short line take the fly downstream, passing so close to the torpid fish that it might have scraped their sides, had not a sudden swirl destroyed their close formation.

Blast! he thought, reeling in. Perhaps something bigger to catch their attention? A little old Jock Scot that had belonged to Grandpa Tom?

Patiently he waited until the fish again lay parallel, but once more they let the fly pass unmolested. At his fourth attempt he detected what could have been a bump on the short line; his heart began to thud with the age-old message: Fish interested. Action stations! and he unslung the folding net for easy access before sinking the fly again.

Another bump on the line, a definite drag and then, as he struck, the pool erupted in a boil of foam as the salmon fled downstream for the shelter of the undercut rock face, pulling out line as it went. For a moment all movement ceased though the steady drag continued, and Robb wondered if his cast was wrapped round some underwater obstacle; then this worry was banished by a bout of furious tugging and another dash across the pool. So fast did the line come in that Robb had to raise his rod vertically to maintain tension.

He seemed to hear Grandpa Tom's slow voice. 'Don't hurry him, lad. Give him time,' but this fish seemed determined to ignore the advice, thrashing and wriggling so eccentrically that he began to suspect it could be foul-hooked.

Time dragged past while they struggled – by his watch

no more than seven minutes though it seemed an eternity – before Robb managed to bring the failing, flailing fish within reach of the net. Not big, five or six pounds at a guess, and sure enough the hook was not lodged in the angle of the jaw but firmly through the dorsal fin. Furthermore, the cast had become tightly wound about its fluke in a complicated cat's cradle that would take both hands and scissors to untangle; he was glad there was no scornful ghillie to watch him snipping away while the fish flapped and gasped in the net.

With relief he lowered his catch back into the dark pool, waited a moment for it to recover, then tipped the net free. Not a good start, he thought. Time to try somewhere else.

Following the faint trace of path left by other anglers, he made his way downstream. Michie's Run ended in a smooth sweep down to a double waterfall, at the foot of which the current swirled round a pothole leaving plenty of promising places for fish to rest before leaping upward through the glittering spray. After the claustrophobic gorge, it was liberating to have space around him, and Robb prowled round the pool, surveying the bank attentively to see where others had stood to cast. The most trampled and therefore favoured spot seemed to be close to the waterfall, and here again his polaroids revealed a fine selection of fish moving languidly on the edge of the current.

The June sun had burned off the morning mist and struck comfortably through his denim weskit. Revelling in silence broken only by natural sounds, he settled with his back against a warmed rock to eat a Mars bar and listen to the faint mewing of golden eagles interspersed with croaking from ravens larking about the heights and a far-off bleating from crofts clustered along the shore line. Not an engine to be heard; only the gentle chuckle and splash of water ironing out his soul, as Grandpa Tom used to say. At the time this had surprised Robb, for it was hard to imagine anyone less interested in the workings of the soul, but here in the empty landscape dominated by the little river, he knew exactly what his grandfather had meant.

*Peace, perfect peace*, with loved ones far away... he mused, and at once his mind returned to Marina. Was she bored stiff with the company of older women she hardly knew? Was she being a nuisance for them? Unlike her sisters Helen and Sally, both of whom let you know exactly what they were feeling the moment they felt it, Marina had always been a bit of a mystery to him; she played her cards close to her chest and let others do the talking. It was strange that she had chosen to confide in Ravenna Larsen last night, and when she returned to the dining room he would have liked to continue their conversation and discover something of her background, but Gunnar's loud voice put paid to that.

'Less talk and more eating, my little one,' he commanded. 'If you chatter so much I must call you Magpie, not Raven.'

What a boor the man was! And yet he was highly regarded both in business circles and as a conservationist. Could he be jealous to see his wife talking to another man? Surely not. The super-civilised French guests had looked shocked, but Ravenna seemed undisturbed. Quickly she cleared her plate and Gunnar beamed approval.

'Good girl! Now we shall be in time for the dancing. Also I wish very much to hear Mhairi sing ballads and laments of olden days, about lost battles and betrayed maidens to bring tears to my eyes.'

The sun had vanished behind a bank of cloud. Robb got up stiffly, licking his fingers. 'You can't catch a fish unless your fly is in the water,' Grandpa Tom used to say when he found him idling on the bank. Wading into the shallows of the Round Pool, he made three casts before remembering that he had left his stick – Luke's stick – on the ledge above Michie's Run.

Oh well, I can pick it up on the way back, he thought, or if this Logan chap turns up, I'll ask him to fetch it.

Marina was enjoying the shopping trip and the way both the older women went out of their way to include her in their conversation. After whisking in double-quick time round the enormous Morrisons which dominated Stairbrigg's main street, they wheeled the resulting three trolley-loads of food and drink down the street to the harbour and left them at the ferry terminal, then turned to the more interesting business of beefing up Marina's armoury of salmon flies at the Sports shop and discussing the relative merits of spray and cream-based midge deterrents.

'The ghillies swear by Avon cosmetics, even if it makes them smell a bit girly,' said Jess, buying two tubes and giving one to Marina. 'Try it and see if it works better than Jungle Formula. Now, what next? Shall we pop into the Museum and see the Bonny Prince Charlie exhibition before we get some lunch?'

'Oh, yes, please!' Marina was a fan of the bonny prince, but Ravenna said she wanted another look at the knitwear boutique where an Icelandic sweater had caught her eye.

'I'll meet you at the Harbour café in – what? An hour? Forty-five minutes? How long will the museum take?'

They agreed on an hour and went their separate ways, though Marina noticed that instead of heading back to the knitwear shop in the main street, Ravenna vanished down a small alley in the network of lanes leading to the fish market and Smokery.

The museum was a disappointment. Jess had never been there herself, saving it as a possible way of amusing non-fishing guests with no taste for shopping, and she was startled to find the dour little stone building at the top of Bridge Street consisted of two rooms only, with a few showcases containing trivia such as buckles and sporrans along with well-known portraits of the Bonnie Prince. Far from detaining them for an hour, their inspection was done and dusted in twenty minutes, and guessing correctly that Marina would have no spare money to spend, Jess decided to head straight for the café and secure a table before the lunchtime rush.

Vain hope. As always, the Harbour café was full-to-bursting, with an untidy queue stretching beyond the ramshackle little wooden building, and every table occupied.

As Jess hesitated on the threshold, Marina exclaimed, 'Look! There she is.'

'Where?'

'In the far corner, talking to a man in green.'

'I can't see her.'

'Follow me.' Marina darted off, weaving like an eel through the wall of shoppers with carrier bags, while Jess followed more slowly, greeting friends on the way. When at last she reached the table, Ravenna was alone and Marina was already prospecting for another chair.

'Well, that didn't take you long,' said Ravenna, rearranging the chairs and removing an empty coffee cup. 'How was the museum?'

'Not great.' Jess pulled a face and beckoned to the waitress. 'What did you think, Marina?'

'Well...I don't want to be rude, but it was pretty small and there wasn't much to see.'

'Spot on,' said Jess, laughing. 'Just two rooms filled with the usual BPC tat.'

'It'll look different when the extension is built,' said Ravenna and Jess's eyebrows rose.

'Extension? At the museum?'

'It's so they'll be able to display their Viking Hoard properly instead of keeping it in a storeroom under lock and key. I've done a bit of work on the catalogue; Gunnar was keen that I should lend a hand, and I must say it's rather fascinating. It gives one quite a different perspective on the Viking incursions – wasn't he talking about it at dinner last night?'

Reluctant to admit that she had zoned out most of Gunnar's masterclass, Jess made an indeterminate noise, and

Ravenna went on, 'I gather that someone dropped a word in the right ear, and the Minister of Culture decided to showcase local enterprise by extending the scope of the museum. Moontide proposed an architect, the plans were approved, and hey, presto! Stairbrigg's museum gets a complete facelift.'

Any mention of Moontide raised Balfour hackles. Jess frowned. 'I hadn't heard anything about this.'

'Well, it shouldn't affect you, should it? You told me you hadn't seen the museum until today, and the whole plan is really Moontide's baby. My guess is they'll end up paying for most of it, too, because however keen the Minister is, the Scottish Government is chronically short of cash.'

Jess filed the information to tell Luke, and beckoned the waitress. 'Come on, let's order and then perhaps you can tell us a bit about the Hoard. What's it to be, Marina? Orange or Coke, and then the choice is between haggis or cheeseburger. Brilliant of you to get a table,' she said to Ravenna as the food and drink arrived. 'Sometimes one waits for hours.'

'I thought I'd better get one while I could. A chap was just leaving, so I took it before anyone else did.'

Marina looked up in surprise: this didn't quite tally with what she had seen from the door, but rather than contradict her new friend, she buried her nose in her Coke and wondered how her father was getting on.

Poor Dad! Illness – particularly mental illness – was certainly not his scene. Despite his attempts to be sympathetic, instinct told her that part of him longed to tell her to get a grip. Snap out of it. As if she could! She had glimpsed his worried face across the table as the Black Wave swamped her last night. All afternoon she had been aware of it closing in and tried to evade it by walking and swimming in the little loch, practising aquabatics in the hope of distracting her thoughts from the looming threat. But when she saw a rowing boat being dragged down to the water she had a sudden panic that perhaps she was breaking some rule that forbade swimming in a fishing loch, so she had swum back to shore as fast as she could, dragged herself into her clothes, and run away from the water.

There had been a nasty moment when she wasn't sure she was heading in the right direction, and that was when she had spotted the cylindrical leather case with a broken strap lying in the heather. She stopped to pick it up, and recognised the tall stand of Caledonian pines that sheltered the lodge from the prevailing wind, with the path just above them at the point where the midges had first attacked her.

But however fast she ran, the Black Wave followed; when she slid into her place at table she knew it was about to overwhelm her and she had no way to escape it except by holding herself tight while the shudders ran through her body, making herself as small as possible in a dark fog in which any step she took threatened to tip her into an abyss.

The touch of Ravenna's hand on her shoulder and her gentle murmur of 'Come!' had broken the Wave's grip last night. Before she knew what had happened Marina found herself tucked up in bed in her pyjamas, with Ravenna sitting beside her offering two pills and a glass of water.

'Swallow those and they'll help you sleep,' she had said matter-of-factly. 'My brother used to get panic attacks when he was just about your age, and he told me the best cure was to sleep them off.'

'Did he grow out of them?' whispered Marina, and Ravenna smiled.

'Oh, lord, yes. Long ago. He's a professor of mathematics at an American university now. I don't suppose he's thought about panic attacks for years. According to him, they affect only the most intelligent people, usually in their teens.' She made the Black Wave sound perfectly normal, even a mark of distinction. For a few minutes longer she sat in silence, with her hand on Marina's shoulder, then she gave it a pat and rose briskly. 'Now I'd better go and finish my supper or the others will wonder where I've got to; and you must close your eyes. Sleep well!'

'OK.' She snuggled into her pillows, but at the door, Ravenna turned. 'By the way, Jess and I are going over to Stairbrigg tomorrow. She's got to shop, and I want to see the town. Would you like to come?'

When Marina said nothing, she added, 'Think it over and tell me in the morning,' and quietly left the room.

As Luke had said, the Round Pond was trickier to fish than it looked. A freshening wind made it hard for Robb to cast into the swirl of foaming water below the waterfall, and the sinuous tail of the pool which had looked so promising was full of concealed shelves of rock on which his fly snagged so often that it was hardly worth fishing there. After losing three in a row, he reeled in and sat on the bank to eat his sandwiches – cheese and pickle, his favourite, and a chunk of dark fruitcake – washed down with a can of lager; as he munched, a couple of salmon jumped at the tail of the pool, but the showy splashes did not suggest a taking mood, and he ignored them, too comfortable with his back against sun-warmed rock to start the frustrating business of casting against the wind again.

He must have dozed off, because when he opened his eyes again he felt stiff and chilled, and it was an effort to lever himself up and collect his gear. He stumped back to the river path and set off for the wooded gorge marked Slithers on his map, along with a little symbol indicating a fishing hut. Here and there on his way downstream a seductive stretch of water tempted him to take a few random casts, but nothing came of them, and presently he found himself climbing cautiously down a cleft in the rocks above a strongly flowing, dark and clearly very deep L-shaped pool, with a high cliff undercut by the current at the angle, opposite which was a wide fringe of shingle. It was very quiet. The current made hardly a gurgle as it swept along without bubbles or foam to break its sinuous smoothness.

After considering the possibilities for a while, Robb clumped across the plank bridge supported at each end by telegraph poles guyed with thick cables, and stood in its shadow to cast almost squarely across the current, which whipped his fly downstream and out of sight round the L.

Two steps on, two casts, and he was suddenly into a fish in midstream, before the line had even straightened... and without a shadow of doubt this was a whopper. Fresh-run, gleaming silver, fifteen pounds if it was an ounce. He saw it jump clear of the water, a shining flash followed by a scream from his reel as it took off downstream, making his rod bend in a hoop as he struggled to keep the tip up.

This was more like it! The age-old excitement gripped him. This was one he wanted to take home in triumph. *Catch your fish before planning what to do with him* warned the echo of Grandpa Tom's voice. There's many a slip... But despite all his efforts to behave calmly and rationally, his thundering heart and shaking hands urged him not to hang about – to get leviathan out of the water and onto the bank before it found a means of escape.

A glance at his reel showed that the line was already down to the backing, and the salmon showed no sign of stopping its run downstream. What was round the bend of the pool? Rocks? Maybe a waterfall that could break the cast? There was nothing for it but to follow the fish, stumbling along the bank at first, reeling in carefully whenever he could, but finally, inevitably, forced to take to the water himself, splashing clumsily in the shallows and wishing he had not discarded the wading stick.

Suddenly the line went dead. Out of breath and glad of the check, Robb kept up the strain, testing it gently, fairly sure that the fish was still there, sulking in some deep refuge before another dash for freedom.

Five minutes passed. Six, seven, eight... Surely it must soon move? Robb knew his grandfather would have told him to get below it, so that the fish had the current to contend with when it started to run again. Moving very carefully, for the weed-covered rocks were slippery, he worked down the pool until he was waistdeep and level with the point where his line disappeared in the water.

Nothing doing. The fish stubbornly refused to move. For the first time since the salmon had taken, Robb looked around him to assess where it might be possible to beach it, and got a shock. Lying on the very edge of the bank not fifty yards farther downstream was what appeared to be the body of a child, with its head overhanging the water, and one arm immersed to the shoulder.

As Robb stared, blinking, and wondering what the hell to do, the hooked fish came suddenly to fighting, furious life, dragging out the line again and jerking him forward in a stumbling run. Before he could adjust his balance, one foot slipped on a flat slab while the other sought and failed to find the river-bed; seconds later he was floating, buoyed by his waders and inflated vest, being swept along by the strong current, still grimly clutching his rod.

Broken water ahead, with rocks scattered halfway across the pool. He touched bottom, floundered towards the bank, and sank again in the still water beyond the mainstream. As he stood wondering how to cross those treacherous underwater slabs while still maintaining tension on the line, something jabbed his shoulder and a voice spoke in a hoarse whisper.

'Get a holt o' this, sorr, and let's hae ye oot o' there.'

Spluttering and gasping, Robb brushed water from his eyes and saw that what he had mistaken for a dead child was a short, wizened, weather-beaten gnome of a man clad from hat to heels in green-brown tweed, now upright on the riverbank and holding out a long shepherd's crook for him to grasp. Far from being child-like, the gnome had powerful shoulders and a vice-like grip in the hand with which he hauled Robb onto dry land, and firmly took the rod from him.

'Gie me that till ye're sorted out, sorr. I'll bring him into the bank forbye. But losh, mon, whaur's yer stick?' he chided.

'Yon rocks are a sight ower slyke for wading.'

'Thanks. Thanks very much.'

Water gushed from waders and pockets as Robb lay down to drain them as best he could. The gnome clearly knew his business and under his careful guidance the long silver torpedo was gradually approaching the bank as the hoarse compelling commentary continued.

'Bring the net ahint the fluke and dinna spook him. Nae rushing, tak yer time. Yon's a bonny fush... Canny, now, sorr... sink the net deep.'

Foot by foot, slowly the line came in until nearly all of the cast was visible and the silver shape only a few inches below the surface. Net clutched in both hands, its handle fully extended, Robb crouched on the bank where a small runnel made a break in the undercut turf.

Limping heavily, the gnome stepped backwards, carefully guiding the tired fish's head right into the runnel.

He said sharply, 'Now, sorr! Quick.'

Robb scooped. There was a flurry of movement and for an instant he wondered if the fish would overflow the net. Then it was safely in the deep pocket, twisting and thrashing, with the net bending under the weight as he, too, withdrew from the river and laid his burden on the heather.

'Brawly fecht, sorr.' The wizened face cracked in a smile. He removed the salmon from the net and dispatched it with a couple of smart taps from a lead-loaded 'priest.' 'Ye'll be Mr Robb, nae doot,' he went on, extending a brown and sinewy hand. 'Allow me to name masel': Danna Murison, here in place of young Logan who's awa' tae the hill a–hunting the spyglass he lost yestreen.'

They shook hands. 'Good of you to come instead,' said Robb. 'For a moment back there I thought I'd the choice of losing the fish or losing my life.'

'Nae, nae. Ye'd have gotten yersel' oot the stream, though I doot ye'd hae lost yon bonny fush,' said Danna, surveying him solicitously. 'Ye'll be fair clemmed wi' the dousing. Come awa' tae the hut. I've a braw fire in the stove tae dry those duds afore ye catch yer death.'

Beside the roaring stove in the next hour, Robb learnt more. Danna had to be well into his seventies, 'runt o'the litter,' as he cheerfully described himself, and had served as 'The Major's' soldier servant in the Scots Guards, then worked for him for another quarter century as ghillie, butler, and general factotum here on Inverclinie. His eldest brother had married Seamus Brydon's sister, so he was kin to Mhairi, who had sung at The Clachan last night, while he accompanied her on the fiddle and her cousin Neil played the pipes.

'Some of the guests from the Lodge went to listen to her. They said she was well worth hearing,' said Robb.

'Oh, aye. I taught her the old songs when she was a wee bit lassie. She had aye a douce voice,' Danna agreed with a gusty sigh. 'That was before she went stravaiging off tae Glasgie, the daft quean, wi' a bunch of gaberlunzies and ended up –'

He broke off abruptly as if conscious of saying too much but Robb was convinced he would have ended his sentence "in gaol."

'Ye'll forgive an auld mon his blether,' he muttered. 'Whiles it gets lonesome on ma ain, but since I lost ma voice I canna sing wi' Mhairi for the towerists, nor tell the auld stories: damn you, John Player!'

Following with an effort Danna's cracked whispers and trying to work out relationships, Robb steamed cosily by the stove and munched his fruitcake while Danna gutted a pair of brown trout and fried them in a blackened skillet. He decided he had done enough fishing for the day, but the loss of the wading stick bothered him. He could hardly ask little lame Danna to slog back up the river to fetch it, but presently the problem was solved when the door burst open and the laughing face of a tall, fresh-complexioned young man with high cheekbones and wild, wind-blown hair peered into the smoky fug.

'I'd a notion I'd find you here, Uncle Danna,' he said, grinning cheekily. 'I smelt fish frying from half a mile. Fine sort of ghillie you are, sitting here on your backside eating guddled trout while your client – Oh!' He broke off as Robb rose stiffly from the bench behind the door. 'Beg pardon, sir. I never saw you there. Logan Brydon's my name, and Uncle Danna took over ghillying for you today so's I could search the hill for my glass.'

'Good to meet you, Logan.' Robb shook hands and nodded at the big fish on the window-ledge. 'Your uncle's done a grand job – take a look at that. I'd never have landed it alone. What about the telescope? Did you find it?'

The smile faded. 'No luck at all. I've searched every hag and clump of heather between the wee lochan and the rocks where I was reading, and it's just not there.'

'How did you come to lose it? Could someone have taken it?'

Logan considered the question and shook his head. 'There's not many use that path behind the Lodge.' He hesitated, unwilling to risk his uncle's mockery with a tale of a damsel in distress, and decided not to mention it. Instead he said, 'Have you a mind to fish the next pool, sir? The rain will have freshened it up and it'll be worth putting a fly over it before the water goes down.'

In the face of such keenness, Robb hadn't the heart to say he was wet, tired, and had had a bellyful of fishing already, and he guessed that Logan wanted to compensate for his earlier absence. Together they left Danna to finish his meal, and made their way along the winding river path to the pool marked Carol's Catch on the sketch-map.

# CHAPTER FOUR

# Counting the Cost

'NOT A PRETTY picture, you will agree. Not pretty at all,' said Gunnar, saving his work and closing down the laptop. He pushed back his chair and looked at Luke over the top of his spectacles. His expression was uncharacteristically serious, even minatory, and as he shuffled his own papers into order, Luke's heart sank. 'What have you to say?'

'Not exactly pretty, but at least it's an improving one,' he said, trying to sound upbeat. 'Next year's figures will look much better.'

'Ah, but can we wait for them? You must believe me when I tell you it gives me no pleasure to throw you to the wolves, but as my accountants keep reminding me, these days I have a duty to my shareholders. They are not impressed to hear of such losses year upon year, and would like to see action to reduce them, perhaps even turn a profit – modest, no doubt, but a profit nonetheless. Then my Board would feel more... indulgent, shall we say? More prepared to back you for another five years?'

By which time, thought Luke, both the Clinie and the Dunseran may well have no native salmon in them, and Big Dougie will be able to pick up Kildrumna for a song. Jess and I will be out on our ears and all our work gone to waste, along with our dreams. He felt a sudden surge of rage, not all of it directed at Big Dougie and his caged fish. Blindly relying on his ever-generous godfather to bail him out had begun to seem a highway to catastrophe, just as Jess had warned it might.

'What kind of action do you suggest?' he asked. 'We could extend the season, perhaps offer other kinds of holiday – bird-watching, for instance, or sailing. Jess is a pretty good cook, as you know. She could run courses...'

'No, no, no,' broke in Gunnar, his usual expression of benign amusement now tinged with exasperation. Could his dear godson truly not see that this was only a preliminary skirmish, since the battle between wild and farmed fish was already lost here? Restocking both rivers was the best, possibly the only answer, though the costs were prohibitive unless the source of trouble – the reason for diminishing native stocks – was removed. That meant getting rid of the fish cages, and in Gunnar's view there was only one way to do that. It was a pity that ultra-correct Luke could not see it and, without compromising his own neutral status he, Gunnar, could not suggest it.

'She could,' insisted Luke. 'There are all sorts of courses we could run here during the close season: wildlife photography, for instance, or craft workshops...'

'No, no! You and your clever Jess have done wonders here but even you cannot extend yourself any further. No, it is about one of your wife's other activities that I am concerned.'

'What do you mean?' Luke felt his colour rising. Gunnar might be the very bedrock of their support, but he was damned if even he would be allowed to slag off Jess's efforts to make this place pay. 'Do you mean the jewellery business? Selling the stuff Mhairi makes for her?'

'My dear boy, what a talent you have for taking hold of the wrong end of the stick!' said Gunnar. 'No, no. I admire Mhairi's work and your wife's entrepreneurial spirit in finding a market for it. My concern is to find out if you know *What's Good for You?*'

Luke blinked at him: was he mad, or was Gunnar?

'Of course I know what's good for me! Why shouldn't I?'

'I am speaking of the consumer affairs magazine. Do you know of that? Do you read it?'

'Well, yes and no. I know it exists – or used to – because Jess worked there before we married; but no, I don't read it. I think she told me it was more of a trade magazine than aimed at the general public. As I say, it was all a long time ago.'

'Would it surprise you to hear that she is working for it now? And that the articles she writes are undermining confidence in the safety of eating farmed salmon?'

Luke opened his mouth, shut it again, and counted slowly to ten. 'I would find that very hard to believe.'

'But you do not deny it.'

'Jess works extremely hard. You know that,' said Luke deliberately. 'Without her, our business would come to a grinding halt. She barely has time to write a shopping list, let alone articles for the press.'

'My dear boy, I wouldn't challenge that for a moment. Please don't take this personally. You and I share one mind. We cannot fall out, ja?' Gunnar waved a placating hand. 'Let me explain. My friends in the SSPO – the Scottish Salmon Producers Organisation –'

'I know what the SSPO is, 'said Luke tightly, 'and as far as I'm concerned they're a –'

'Please allow me to finish! As I was saying, my friends are concerned that the attacks this magazine has been making on their industry is undermining consumer confidence in their products. These risk creating – and I quote, "unnecessary confusion or fear about consuming healthy Scottish seafood." They have asked me, as an impartial referee and member of the Advisory Committee on Fisheries and Aquaculture, to look into the allegations made in these articles, and in particular to their accusations against the cages in the Reekie Sound belonging to Moontide. There! Is that clear enough for you, little godson?'

'Nothing new in that. Anyone you speak to in Inverclinie would say exactly the same: that salmon farming is a dirty, dangerous business,' said Luke heatedly. For the first time ever Gunnar's habitual "little godson" jarred, infantilising him, suggesting contempt rather than affection. 'I told you yesterday that the Moontide operation is notorious for cutting corners. Their cages are overcrowded and filthy. They rely on antibiotics and slick publicity to conceal the fact that they are degrading the seabed and plundering the marine food chain, as well as destroying crustaceans with toxic chemicals; and to add insult to injury, they have started using ADDs to keep seals away. You know about those?'

'Acoustic Deterrent Devices? I have heard of those, ja; and also I know that noise underwater can disorientate marine mammals and disrupt their navigation systems. Have you proof that this happens here?'

'Not exactly,' Luke admitted, 'but a pod of whales stranded on a beach not far from here last summer and there was a lot of muttering about ADDs being the cause. It's common knowledge that Moontide sails as close to the wind as it dares, and relies on government support for business even when its activities run directly counter to advice from Scottish Natural Heritage.'

'That toothless watchdog! Poor beast, he has a hard task keeping the peace between so many opposing interests. Commerce, conservation, employment.'

'I know. By the standards of the big multinationals, McInnes's operation is tiny and it's difficult to get them worked up about polluting somewhere they regard as marginal, barely worth worrying about when they've got so many more urgent problems demanding attention.' Luke shook his head, frowning. 'I'm not being entirely selfish. I can quite see why McInnes wants to play with the big boys by increasing his output, but if they allow him to ruin the wild fishing here it sets a precedent. Where will they draw the line and say enough is enough?'

'Your forbearance does you credit, dear boy.' Gunnar regarded him quizzically. 'Instead of thinking how you can defeat your opponent, you try to see his point of view. All I am asking is, does your wife share your distaste for fighting dirty, or has she secretly launched her own campaign to discredit him, using a weapon with which she happens to be familiar?'

Luke said stiffly, 'I don't believe it. There are dozens of activists opposed to salmon farming's effect on the environment who could have written those articles! What I can't understand is why you should accuse Jess.'

'You don't think her past association with the magazine is – let us say – suggestive?'

'I certainly don't. Look here, Gunnar. What is all this? I thought you were planning how to get their licence withdrawn. That you were – well – were on our side.'

How childish it sounded, put like that! He almost expected his godfather to pat his head and tell him it would all be all right in the end.

Instead Gunnar said with a definite hint of pulling rank, 'How can I take sides? I have been asked to investigate this matter as an impartial referee, whose only interest is in the truth.'

'Then perhaps instead of making unfounded accusations against my wife you should ask the editor where he got his information.'

'But naturally! And naturally I received the standard reply that he – no, actually she – was bound to protect her sources. That is why I have arranged an urgent meeting with Dougal McInnes before I send in the first draft of my report to the SSPO. He has agreed to show me his firm's records and production process, and take me out to his feed-lot and cages so I can see for myself that everything is above board.'

So the enemy would get the chance to put his case first, no doubt having ordered his workforce to clean up any irregularities beforehand. Luke's stomach seemed to have tied in a hard knot. This was worse than he had expected.

He said, 'You're not likely to see much if you've got McInnes breathing down your neck. He's a plausible bastard, and I can guarantee you'll only see what he wants to show you. His foreman Yanis Kyriakis is a tough nut with a hotline to the police, and they come speeding out to see off any boat that comes too near.'

'Is that allowed? Surely the Sound is a public waterway?'

'Of course it is. Moontide has no right to call the police to act as private security for them. I tell you, they're obsessed with secrecy, and that's because a lot they do doesn't bear scrutiny.'

'Interesting. Very interesting. Of course I would have preferred to make my visit unannounced, but McInnes insisted we meet in his office first so that he could brief me on all the wonderful things he is doing for the local economy.' Gunnar smiled. 'Things that I will not have heard fewer than a hundred times before.'

'Softening you up?'

'Perhaps. But it is also possible that you are under-estimating your old godfather, my dear boy; and he may have sharper wits than you suppose.'

'When will this meeting take place?' asked Luke as calmly as he could, but the tremor in his voice must have given him away, because Gunnar chuckled deep in his beard.

'Do not be afraid, little godson! Our meeting in his office in Stairbrigg is agreed for next Saturday, but before that I have other enquiries to pursue, and many things may happen in seven days. As I say, I have to be impartial, to assemble evidence before I make my report, and first of all I wished to hear what you would say about any involvement of your wife in this matter.'

'I tell you there is no involvement,' said Luke, trying to stifle the sneaking, growing suspicion that Jess might indeed have been pursuing her private feud with the fish farm — perhaps at one remove — without mentioning it to him. It was true she never had time to write articles, but then there would have been no need to. A couple of telephone calls to an old colleague, a few emails, quickly, quietly done. A few stats, a few telling stories of seals shot without a licence and fish suffocated — that was all it would take to put an investigative journalist on the scent of malpractice in a commercially important industry and start a crusade. That was the sort of thing consumer magazines thrived on.

'My dear boy, I am very glad to hear it,' said Gunnar. 'Now we will speak of other matters.'

Luke was left hoping to hell that it was true.

'What shall I do with this, Dad?' asked Marina, bouncing into Robb's room bright and early. 'I found it on the hill and forgot to tell you, but it looks worth quite a bit.'

He groaned and opened a bleary eye. Schnapps shots with Gunnar after dinner had not been a good idea. Marina was looking lively and fresh, her thick hair tied back and colour in her cheeks. She was swinging a telescope case by its broken strap, and he knew immediately whom it belonged to.

'Oh, well done, poppet! That must be the one my ghillie was looking for yesterday. Said it had been given to his dad and his mother would raise hell when he told her he'd lost it. Where on earth did you find it?'

She plumped down on the end of his bed and poured out the whole story – the swim, finding the leather case with its broken strap, the race to get back for supper, and how she had knotted the strap and hung it on the bathroom hook and forgotten about it until this morning.

'It's got a name on it,' she pointed out, 'and an address in America.'

'That's right. And it's a Swarovski?'

She nodded. 'Then it's certainly the one Logan lost.. You can give it back to him this morning because he's taking us fishing on the big loch – the one they call Herrich. Off with you now, and get some breakfast, and I'll be down asap.'

Overnight the jetstream had shifted north of the Shetland Isles, and the five blue and gold days that followed had all the perfection of Mediterranean weather without the crowded beaches. Far too hot for salmon to show interest in snapping at flies, but morning and evening rises of trout on the lochs kept the fishing party well occupied. Puttering gently with an outboard along little coastal bays, old Danna showed an uncanny knack for locating shoals of mackerel, which were one morning preceded in spectacular fashion by a silver tide of whitebait, driven ashore to strand themselves gasping and flapping on the sand. Marina scooped them up by the bucketful until Jess begged her not to bring in any more.

'But they're so delicious! It's a waste not to eat them!'

'Honestly, sweetheart, the whole lodge smells of frying fish. Even my hair is full of it. Get Danna to show you where to find chanterelles in the policies,' said Jess firmly. 'Your father tells me they're his favourites.'

As proof that humans are creatures of habit, by Wednesday everyone in the party had established a private routine. Robb spent most of his time with Danna on one or other of the lochs, sometimes accompanied by his daughter, but no longer worried about entertaining her since she, in turn, seemed happy to attach herself to others of the party, either fishing the rivers with Logan to ghillie, or visiting his mother's workshop to watch her designing jewellery and assist with polishing semi-precious stones.

'Yon's a bright wee lassie,' Mhairi told her son. 'Quick to listen and quick to learn. You'd do well to take heed of her ways.'

'She's just a kid,' said Logan with the condescension of seventeen for fourteen.

'Good at her books, too. Learning to speak Mandarin and computer science, as well,' his mother needled. 'She's even after me to teach her the Gaelic, how about that? She'll be running the World Bank or the United Nations before she's forty, I've no doubt.'

'Give over, Mam!'

'It's the attitude, see? She wants to learn about the world and how to make the most of it.'

'I heard she had a fit at dinner and had to be taken to bed,' mumbled Logan defensively, but Mhairi was having none of it.

'Tired to death, poor bairn. Spreading tales? That's a fine way to thank her for finding your father's glass on the hill! As I say, you'd do well to mark her ways instead of mooning over ones you can't have.'

Rather than answering, he carried his plate to the sink and washed it, but her final words disturbed him. Had she been going through the contents of his waste-paper basket again? None of the screwed-up sheets of rejected verse bore the name Ravenna, he was pretty sure, but once his mother got her teeth into a subject she wouldn't let it go until she had discovered every detail. He must be more careful.

Marina also enjoyed the company of Gunnar and his wife, with whom she explored the coastline in *Shield Maiden*, running ashore in tiny bays to picnic and swim in clear water teeming with small fish.

Far from finding Gunnar alarming, she enjoyed his rough teasing and proved quite capable of calling him to order if he overstepped the mark, which reminded Robb piercingly of the way his late wife would discipline a boisterous dog with a single sharp command: there's a lot of her mother in Marina, he reflected. If only she wasn't so damned competitive! There's no shame in coming second, but she can't see that. With her it's winning that counts. He shuddered to remember how her sisters' teasing nickname of 'The Half-Portion' used to be enough to trigger a knockdown, drag-out scrap that ended in tears, slammed doors and, on more than one occasion, a visit to A&E.

Despite his taste for late-night drinking, Gunnar was an early riser and Marina would dive off the jetty to join him before breakfast, challenging him without success to swim the mile to the Skerries, a line of jagged rocks where harbour seals hauled out to slump like grey or spotted sag-bags. These rocks had been the scene of several shipwrecks over the years, and she longed to look into the deep underwater clefts and trenches, where it was said that barnacle-encrusted masts could sometimes be glimpsed through waving forests of seaweed.

She would also have liked to inspect the double line of round fish cages which lay like giant pennies on the shining surface of the bay, but Gunnar refused to allow her to approach them either.

'Their security men do not welcome visitors,' he warned. 'They think you want to steal their fish.'

Marina laughed. 'As if! I only want a look.'

'Then you and I and my Raven will take a picnic on *Shield Maiden* tomorrow and sail over to that island you see in the distance, where dolphins play and there are many kinds of seabirds and seals,' he said decisively. 'You would like that, ja? To get there we must pass by the fish farm cages, and with binoculars you will be able to see everything. Then in the afternoon you and I will dive to thirty metres to look at a big wreck I know of.'

Marina's face lit up. More than fishing, more than swimming, this was what she had been longing to do ever since they arrived. 'Cool! I've brought my diving log-book. Can Dad come too?'

'Certainly he can. And while we dive, Logan will command *Shield Maiden* because it is not possible to anchor close to that island because of underwater rocks.'

So at eleven o'clock on a perfect June day, Robb and his daughter leaned on the rail with the sun on their faces and wind tangling Marina's hair, watching with close attention as

Gunnar ran the fat little ketch parallel to the shore on a course that brought her within hailing distance of the cages. Men in hi-vis jackets were busy with buckets and long-handled nets about the walkways that linked them, and sure enough there was soon a shout from the feed barge.

'*Shield Maiden*, ahoy! Keep your distance, please! I repeat, Keep your distance!' A thick-set figure in oilskins with a loudhailer reinforced the order with emphatic Keep-Off gestures.

'That'll be Yanis, the foreman. It riles him if boats come near his fish,' Logan warned. He knew Yanis well as an eager customer for any under-size lobsters caught in Logan's pots. Selling them was illegal since they should have been returned to the water, but under instruction from his masterful wife Olympia, who ran a fish-bar on the seafront at Stairbrigg, Yanis snapped up anything of questionable size, and Logan added the cash he paid to the stash he was accumulating against the longed-for moment when his mother would allow him to leave home.

Gunnar took no notice, gliding nearer to the protecting ring of barbed wire until all the hi-vis clad workers had turned to stare at the broad-beamed intruder, and its passengers could see right into the round pens where the salmon jumped and splashed ceaselessly.

'*Shield Maiden*, alter course! Alter course immediately,' roared Yanis.

'He'll be calling the police next,' murmured Logan, resisting the temptation to wave to his cousins and former schoolfellows Alick and Hamish, who had taken jobs on the fish farm as soon as they got their Scottish Certificate of Education; and a few minutes later, Marina saw a blue and white chequered launch put off from the Stairbrigg jetty and speed towards them across the smooth water.

'Have you seen enough, kittunge? Then it is time to leave, I think,' said Gunnar coolly, and put the helm over. In silence they watched Yanis tuck the loudhailer under his arm and stump back to his hut on the feed-lot barge as the fish farm dwindled in the distance, and *Shield Maiden* began to bob and lurch on hitting the turbulent currents of the Reekie Sound.

Robb, who was no sailor, endured ten miserable minutes of this on deck before creeping down four steps to the forrad berth to lie prone, hoping he was not going to be sick.

'Are you OK, sir?' called Logan down the hatch.

'Just – go – away,' Robb groaned, and Logan withdrew his head with a complicit grin at Marina.

'Once we're round the headland he'll be fine. There's many can't stand the motion of the Reekie, and the smell of fish doesna help. But if your dad would prefer it, there's a bus back to Stairbrigg every hour and you can meet him down at the harbour,' Logan suggested.

This was indeed the option Robb chose when he surfaced, rather green about the gills, and refused his share of the picnic.

'All the more for us,' grinned Gunnar, wolfing cold mutton pie and haggis washed down with Laphroaig from his flask. 'Mars bar, anyone?'

'Spare me,' said Robb with a shudder.

They put him ashore from the jollyboat with instructions for finding the bus stop. 'You'll miss the seals,' said Marina.

'Then I'll look forward to hearing all about them from you,' he said cheerfully, much relieved to feel his feet on solid earth again. 'Mind you look after her,' he added to Gunnar. 'She only got her Advanced Open Water qualification last October.'

'More likely she will be looking after me,' muttered Gunnar, waving as they headed out to sea again.

Long before they reached the Skerries the high staccato barks, grunting roars and plaintive, bird-like calls of the seal colony drifted across the water, and by the time they were close enough to distinguish between rocks and mammals the noise was so loud and continuous that conversation had to be conducted in shouts. Gunnar cut the engine and let *Shield*

*Maiden* drift on the swell, which carried her along the jagged promontory without disturbing its inhabitants. Some lay placid and inert, others reared up to bite at one another's necks, while the round heads and bulging eyes that popped up close to the boat looked more curious than fearful.

'Like labradors without ears,' said Marina, and Logan grinned.

'They'll bite, too, if you get ower close to their pups. In winter we have to steer well clear of the Skerries.'

They sailed on down the coast to Gunnar's chosen island. By three o'clock, *Shield Maiden* was over the spot where the wreck of a trawler lay in twenty fathoms, and the scuba divers donned their equipment.

This took some time, since Marina's insistence on correct procedure meant rigorous checking and testing of every valve, clip and release. Once they had agreed on how much weight she should carry, she checked the battery on her dive computer and the 0-ring in the tank valve, then turned her attention to the regulators. When she was sure they were both delivering air easily and it had no oiliness or odd smell, she breathed through the main regulator while checking the pressure gauge for wobbles; then used the low-pressure inflator attached to her BCD to inflate it fully and assure herself that no air was escaping. Before she was satisfied that tube, tank and regulators both primary and alternative were in order, gauges tested for air fluctuations, belts secured and releases tried out, Gunnar was growing impatient.

'Buddy-check now,' she said, ignoring his loud groan. 'Shall we use Big White Rabbits Are Fluffy or just ABC?'

Gunnar suppressed a grin: his own favoured mnemonic for BWRAF stood for Before Wanking Ring a Friend, but Marina could not be expected to know that.

'Which one?' she persisted, and he shrugged his massive shoulders.

'You choose. It's all the same to me.'

'Rabbits, then. It's more thorough, my instructor told me.'

What the hell were they talking about, Logan wondered with a mixture of admiration and jealousy as he watched the pair of black-clad figures, so different in size but united in a world they understood and he did not. He tried to catch Ravenna's eye to see if she shared his mystification but she was oblivious, leaning back against the hatch, face raised to the sun, mouth curved in a half-smile.

Once more she began clicking and snapping, pushing him back and forth as she peered at connections and tested tubes, while he fidgeted, keen to get into the water.

'You've done that already,' he grumbled, as she checked his airgauge for the second time, but she would not be deterred.

'It's important to do it properly. No fluctuation, my instructor said –'

With an effort he quelled the desire to damn her bloody instructor to hell and back, and said gently, 'Listen, kittunge, you are right to say these checks are important, but I think you forget that I have been diving since before you were born.'

'My instructor says the most dangerous condition of all is when you become so familiar with your equipment that you are tempted to skip checks,' Marina recited, mantra-style. 'Now answer this question: what is the most common cause of diving accidents?'

'Running out of air, of course.'

'Wrong.'

'How can that be wrong?'

'Well, it is. Try again.'

With masterly self-control, he tried going too deep, damaged equipment, perished hoses, while Ravenna smiled lazily and Logan watched open-mouthed at her cheek. Mam would never let him get away with such impertinence.

'I give up. What is it,' said Gunnar at last.

'You really want to know?'

'I said so.' The edge on his voice showed patience was wearing thin.

'Stupidity!' said Marina with a peal of laughter. 'There!

You didn't expect that, did you? Isn't it true? Most diving accidents are the result of simple stupidity.'

Gunnar growled. 'All right, you win. Now are you satisfied, or must we go on checking valves until it is time for supper? Come, are you ready? Let's dive.'

A double splash that sent a wash over the diving-platform, and they were gone. Logan peered into the water until the black hoods disappeared, feeling curiously empty, resentful and ignored.

When they hauled out to bask on the sun-warmed deck and watch a school of porpoises flashing and curvetting round the bows, Logan looked at Marina with reluctant respect.

'Losh, but you're a braw swimmer! It was never your dad taught you to dive?' he said.

'Oh, no. That was Mum. She took me on a course in Portugal for my birthday treat. It was really cool...' Her voice suddenly trembled as she remembered it had been Mum's very last birthday treat; and Logan, seeing her wrap both arms around her ribs and start to shake, wished he had kept his mouth shut. She ducked her head down to hide her face and much as he instinctively wanted to put an arm round her shoulders he was embarrassed to do so. Gunnar, who had no such inhibitions, heaved up from his seat on the hatch-coaming and rolled forward to envelop her – wet suit and all – in an enormous bearhug.

Holding her close, he announced in a stage whisper, 'Hush! Don't tell anyone! Marina pretends to be a normal English girl, but in secret she is a mermaid.'

Marina sniffed, blinking away tears, and disengaged herself. 'Well, I know who you are in secret,' she retorted.

'Tell me.'

'You're the seal who turns into a man. You know – the one Mhairi sings about.'

Gunnar's big laugh rang out. 'Ha! I am the Great Selkie? And you are a mermaid? Yes, that is good. I like that.'

They smiled at one another, sharing the fantasy. Marina said, 'But where is your lovely fur coat?'

He sighed gustily and made theatrical sorrowful eyes. 'Alas, I cannot tell. Long ago a naughty little mermaid stole it, and now every time I dive I search for it, because without it I can never return to my kingdom under the waves.'

'I'll help you look for it. Together we're bound to spot it.'

'Ah, but then I would put it on and you would never see me again.'

She nodded solemnly. 'At least you would be happy. Perhaps you would come back here from time to time and I could swim out to meet you.'

'Deal,' said Gunnar, and lightly slapped her palm. 'But now you must listen, little mermaid, and remember to stay away from the lights of the big boats.'

'Why?'

Gunnar said solemnly, 'When a fisherman catches a mermaid to live with him on land, he never lets her return to her home under the waves. She has to hide her long tail and work in bars or restaurants all the rest of her life.'

What rubbish they talk, thought Logan. He flicked a glance at Ravenna, but she was staring fixedly at her husband as if she had just understood something, and the look on her face made him shiver.

'I won't forget.'

Marina shook herself, as if waking from a dream, and took the smartphone from her beach-bag. 'Come on, everyone, line up. Selfie-time!' and obediently the others grouped themselves against the mast. Logan hung back diffidently, but Marina insisted, 'All of us,' before draping her arm round Gunnar's neck and putting her face close to his.

'Just a couple more,' she said, examining the result. 'Ravenna had her eyes closed.'

After several more takes she was satisfied. 'Not bad of anyone,' she said, 'though Logan –'

Firmly Ravenna removed the iPhone and began scrolling back through recent images. 'Tell me, who are all these people. Friends? Family? Oh, I know this one, but who is it with him?'

It was Robb in proud grandfather pose, at the christening of his first grandchild. With him stood Helen, holding the baby, and his son-in-law Richard; to their right were Richard's parents, and on the left Marina's middle sister, Sally, and Marina herself.

'Oh, I've got better ones than that,' she said quickly, grabbing back the screen before Ravenna could comment on her missing mother. She scrolled back rapidly and stopped at the picture of a slender, dark-haired girl with an outdoor complexion and a flashing smile. 'This is my sister Sally, just after she passed out of the Agricultural College. She's always been mad about animals and works as a gamekeeper. And that – 'she paused at the next frame – 'is her boyfriend, Jim. He's making that silly face because he didn't want to be photographed.'

'Why not?'

'Some people just don't.' Marina shrugged.

Ravenna stared at the picture. Jim had turned half away from the camera, but his close-cropped head and aquiline profile were clearly delineated. 'Hot,' said Ravenna.

'Yeah, right. That's what Sal thinks. No accounting for tastes,' Marina went on scrolling, giggling from time to time.

Chatter, chatter: typical women! thought Logan. Turning away, he pointed astern and called, 'Look over there! Dolphins! Five – no, six of them. They must be into a shoal of mackerel...'

'Feeding time for dolphins, fishing time for us,' Gunnar decided briskly. 'Start the outboard, boy. Feathers, lines, lifejackets...!' and within minutes the jollyboat was puttering across the choppy, green-blue waves towards the distant pod, leaving Ravenna alone on *Shield Maiden*, wallowing gently in the swell, still scrolling through Marina's iPhone.

Seated in the stern with one hand on the tiller, Logan kept an automatic eye out for underwater rocks and entered his own private world as he searched for a rhyme for "Beauty." He was in love, bewitched by the unattainable, and like a troubadour of old he turned to poetry as the only way to express it. Nothing he had read quite answered: yet somehow this amazing, bewildering emotion must be released in verse even though the perfect rhyme eluded him. Neither "duty" nor "fruity" had quite the romantic ring he sought, and beyond them the alphabet provided little guidance. It was amazing how many words meant nothing at all, he reflected, running through the possibilities: cooty, footy, gooty, hooty... Perhaps he should start again and put "beauty" near the start of the line rather than the end...

There was a roar from Gunnar in the bows: 'Watch your steering, boy!' and Logan hastily changed course.

Shut up, you bloody old gaberlunzie, he thought. No need to shout at me. I won't run you aground. I know these waters like the back of my hand.

But his mother had cautioned him against answering back, even when clients made idiotic remarks, and she would go ballistic if there was any hint that he had been rude to Mr Larsen, so he held his tongue and went back to dreaming of his goddess. Her glowing skin, her long, languorous eyes – were they green or blue? – her copper-gilded hair... Three times he had ghillied for her this week, and because she had no more sense than a five-year-old when a fish was on the line, from time to time their hands had touched, and on each occasion his skin had prickled as if hers held an electric charge. He was sure she had felt it, too. Those lovely eyes had widened, her lips curved in a smile... When he landed her first salmon for her, she had been as excited as a little girl, and for a moment he thought she was going to kiss him on the mouth.

If only he could forget about uni and go to work on one of her husband's cruise ships where he could see her every day...

'Wake up, boy!' shouted Gunnar. 'This is the feeding-ground. Make a circle now and we will find them.'

You'll be lucky, thought Logan, turning his head to hide his scowl, and he was right: the dolphins had long gone, and so had the mackerel. After a fruitless and increasingly chilly half hour even Gunnar had had enough and ordered a return to *Shield Maiden* at full throttle.

Back on deck they sorted out their scuba equipment and heaped it by the mast.

'Logan can wash it all when we return to Kildrumna. Mind you use fresh water, boy,' commanded Gunnar curtly. 'I don't want it sticky with salt when I need it next.' He hefted the used cylinders and told Logan to take them for refilling at the dive shop before he went home for tea.

'Tell them I want Forty/Sixty. They'll understand,' he said brusquely, and a moment later asked: 'What percentages did I ask for?'

'Forty/Sixty,' repeated Logan, flustered and resentful. The extra work would make him late home, where he had all his afternoon chores waiting.

'Correct. Mind you get it right, boy.'

'Yes, sir.'

What's wrong with Logie today? Marina wondered, catching the tail-end of another scowl. Is it because Gunnar keeps bossing him around? But then he bosses everyone around: bossing or teasing, that's just his way, and no one else seems to mind. Or is it because Ravenna stayed on the boat? He seemed pretty keen on her when we were fishing yesterday. Actually, the way he looked at her was quite embarrassing, and when she spoke to him he stammered and went red in the face.

Marina was wise in the ways of burgeoning attraction, having monitored the love affairs of her elder sisters ever since they brought their first boyfriends home, but this unequal pairing puzzled her. Take the age discrepancy: Ravenna must be thirty at least, while Logan had only left school this summer, and the difference in background was even more striking. He was a crofter's son who had never been farther from home than Glasgow, and she travelled the world as the wife of a millionaire. For him to admire her, be dazzled by her – perhaps even imagine himself in love with her – well, that was understandable; but what on earth did she see in him?

Perhaps, thought Marina, calm and serene as she seemed, Ravenna possessed some strange power. Look at the way she had drawn off the Black Wave that so nearly engulfed Marina herself that first evening, even though she had been careful not to swallow the pills Ravenna gave her. Never eat anyone else's medicine had been one of her mother's strictest rules.

Then there was the way Dad looked at her. No one in their senses would call her father a ladies' man, but he seemed to seek out Ravenna's company after supper, and she was able to make even poor Mr Balfour, who always looked so worried, lighten up and laugh. Nor had Marina forgotten the man who had kissed Ravenna in the harbour cafe before melting into the crowd, a proper kiss, not just a bump of the cheekbones... Perhaps she was a genuine femme fatale like Helen of Troy, to whom men were drawn like helpless moths to a flame. Yes, that must be it.

Marina decided to watch Ravenna closely and see if she could pick up some tips.

# Gunnar

AFTER BREAKFAST ON Friday, Gunnar followed Jess out to the kitchen and told her he proposed to skip supper.

'I have seen many seatrout in the Lower Clinie pool just below the Stockpot, and will fish for them off the rocks tonight. It will be cloudy, but the moon is nearly full, so conditions are good.'

'Fine. I'll make you some sandwiches,' Jess offered, secretly glad to have an evening free from his disruptive presence.

'Ja, and put in mutton pies also, two or three.'

'Sure.'

He lumbered out, meeting Luke in the rod room and relaying his plans for the evening.

Luke nodded, his face creasing into its familiar worried lines, 'Yes, I've been noticing a lot of fish in that pool in the last few days. I only hope they're not mixed up with escapers from the cages. Still, it's worth a go. I'll pop down after supper and see how you're getting on,' he promised. 'By the way, is *Shield Maiden*'s engine firing properly now? I think I managed to fix it for the moment, but it's not in its first youth and really what it needs is a complete overhaul by a pro. The boatyard in Templeport is excellent, and I've got their number, if you want it.'

'Always you give me good advice, little godson. Whether I choose to take it – ah, that is another matter.'

Gunnar's laughing eyes mocked Luke's caution, and in a

spurt of annoyance he thought, All right. On your own head be it. If that dodgy old rattletrap lets you down and you get blown halfway to Iceland, don't blame me!

'What time are you meeting McInnes on Saturday?' he asked stiffly.

'We will rendezvous in his office at the Smokery at four o'clock, where he will show me his records and production targets –'

'And give you a few drams of single malt and a taste of his – ahem! – top-grade, sustainably reared and harvested smoked salmon –'

'That is certainly possible,' agreed Gunnar, deadpan. 'After which he will take me to see over the cages, during which inspection he has agreed to answer all my questions. How does that sound to you? Do you have any objections?'

Luke considered the matter, running the schedule through his mind. A four o'clock meeting in Stairbrigg would probably take the best part of an hour, which meant they were unlikely to reach the cages much before half-past five. Yanis and his workforce would not be dousing the fish with pesticide or disposing of dead ones so late in the afternoon. According to Danna, who often went night-fishing and returned at dawn, fish farm clean-up operations took place in the morning, before potentially hostile onlookers were about. Would Yanis even be working at that hour? His domineering wife Olympia would need him to cope with the diners at her thriving restaurant. Most likely no one would be there but Wully, the overnight security man.

'Not exactly,' he said slowly, 'but wouldn't it be better to see the cages earlier in the day? When you could get a better idea of what goes on there and the type of people they employ?'

'I agree, but unfortunately I have no choice in this matter,' said Gunnar, stroking his beard and twisting it into tiny ringlets, a gesture Luke recognised from far back as the prelude to some stretch of the truth. 'This is because McInnes cannot miss an important meeting in Glasgow before he returns to Stairbrigg. He must leave again on Sunday, so this is my best chance to see him.'

So he has nobbled you, just as Jess suspected, thought Luke with dull certainty. You actually want to be able to give Moontide a clean bill of health, so that their application for more cages is approved. He wished he had paid more attention to the details of Gunnar's switch from trawlers to cruise boats, but financial transactions were not his forte and though Jess worried that Gunnar had ceded overall control of his business to the newly-appointed board, Luke had trusted that his godfather's dominant personality would ensure that his wishes remained paramount.

A misplaced trust, it seemed.

'So that's that, then,' he said with assumed cheerfulness. 'But if you're planning some night-fishing off the rocks you'd better take a look at the local forecast. There's a big blow coming. Isobars packed tight, and heavy rain from one to three tomorrow morning. The glass is falling, but you should be all right up till midnight, anyway.'

Gunnar had moved to the window to look down on the tranquil garden with steps leading to the river. The southerly breeze hardly stirred a leaf of the rowans lining the path down to the jetty, where the two Kildrumna outboards and single speedboat moored to their heavy iron rings rocked gently on unruffled water, and beyond them the squat olive bulk of *Shield Maiden* lay peacefully at anchor like a resting toad.

'The calm before the storm,' he said meditatively. 'Well, we must make the most of it. You say you have the boatyard's contact number? I think you are right and I should consult them before taking *Shield Maiden* to sea.'

Robb and Marina had gone to try their luck on the big loch again, crossing the squelchy morass of low-lying bog squeezed uncomfortably into the front of the Argocat, which Logan drove with the ruthless directness of a tank, glorying in its capabilities, heedless of obstacles which would have brought any other vehicle to a juddering halt. Up the precipitous sides of gullies and over peat banks it chuntered, splashing across streams and over plank bridges which Robb would have hesitated to cross on foot.

'This is fun, Dad!' shouted Marina above the ear-numbing high-pitched roar of the transmission.

Robb whose bad leg was being crushed against the door, longed to get out and walk away from the hellish din, but tried to be glad that she was enjoying herself. It seemed a very long journey but when at last the Argocat breasted a slope and looked down on Loch Herrich, dotted with small islands and bustling with wildfowl, he had to admit the view was worth the discomfort.

High enough above the glen to command a great panorama of sea and heather, humps of islands and stark outlines of hills, all silvery-blue, green and purple, Loch Herrich itself was protected by cliffs on the northern side, while several burns trickling down its southern face coalesced in a broad V-shaped bay, thick with reed and weed, perfect for trout.

Through ears still ringing from that monstrous unmuffled roar, he heard the high keening of gulls and teal, oyster catchers and curlews as they rose from the islands and circled the loch in broad sweeps before heading for the sea. Down in the marshy reeds, small ripples and splashes showed that trout were feeding.

'Come on, Dad,' said Marina, gathering up her fishing gear. 'Let's catch our lunch and cook them on a fire, like we used to at Ti-Bach. We can use that driftwood for fuel and for once I've remembered to bring salt.'

There are anglers whose sole motivation is to catch fish, and others who can contentedly stand for unproductive hours in unresponsive water for the sheer pleasure of casting, striving always for a longer line and greater accuracy, and for whom the catching of fish barely matters. Robb belonged to the former tribe, and his daughter, who had won a Junior Angler championship at the age of twelve and was now a keen contestant in the Under-23 category, was definitely part of the latter.

Again and again she sent the fine glistening line snaking across the glassy water in graceful parabolas, letting the fly alight on the surface as softly as thistledown; and time after time she gently recovered it, pivoting or moving a few steps to cover more water.

When Robb attempted to copy her, his line landed in loops and he seemed to feel Logan's censorious eyes on his back. He stumbled off a few hundred yards to the other side of the delta, switched to a spinning rod equipped with a glittering spoon – and be damned to the unsportsmanlike triple hook, he thought. He was here to catch his lunch, not practise fancy casting. As if to confound him, the spoon instantly sank into the weed and, after minutes of fruitless tugging, emerged festooned with dripping tubular stems.

He glanced over his shoulder to see if Marina had noticed, but she was bending forward, intent on carefully lifting her net with what looked like a good-sized trout.

Faintly across the burn her shout reached him. 'Look, Dad!'

He gave her a thumbs-up and splashed back to the bank. Now for the all-important fire. Four stones in a ring; twisted old heather-roots, shards of ancient planks and dry spindrift grass in a neat wigwam, half a packet of firelighters, a long match – instantly extinguished – another, and another, and hey presto! a sudden blaze. He inhaled the evocative scents of paraffin and burning grass with keen enjoyment. This was what fishing was all about.

Logan, who had been brooding and smoking roll-ups from the opposite side of the burn, couldn't resist the atavistic lure and hurried across with an armful of planks from some defunct bridge, and between them they built up a noble blaze.

All it needed was something to cook, but now Marina was taking fish with nearly every cast, ignoring her father's shouts of, 'Lunch!'

More than lunchtime: a quarter to three already and he was starving. 'Run over and fetch her,' he told Logan. 'We don't need a miraculous draught of fishes. Just a trout apiece will do us fine.'

'Very good, sir.'

The boy loped off across the heather, but even from a distance Robb could see that his daughter was resisting the order. He grinned. When she was just a small child it had taken the skills of an ACAS negotiator to persuade her to leave the bath, and anyone who resorted to brute force needed nerves of steel. He imagined the conversation.

'Your dad says you're to come for lunch.'

'Can't you see the fish are taking? I'll come after the rise.'

'He's hungry. He wants to cook the trout. We've a grand fire going.'

'Tell him not to worry. I'll come when I'm ready.'

'He said Now.'

This could take a while, thought Robb, and raised his binoculars to watch mallard and teal clustering at the far end of the loch, then began to look with keener interest at activity in the bay below.

From this eminence, he could survey both Kildrumna Lodge, with its outbuildings, boatshed, and private jetty, and the straggling village of Inverclinie round the point, together with the long tongue of the hill known as Kildrumna Beag that separated them. A winding thread of track linked the two small settlements, too narrow for cars but accessible by walkers or mountain-bikers, and halfway up it Robb recognised Jess Balfour in trainers, shorts and T-shirt, free of domestic cares for the few precious hours between lunch and supper, pounding up the steep bends with a springy, athletic stride.

Barely pausing at the ridge to catch her breath, she started at the same speed down the other side of the hill, emerging in the network of small streets at the back of the village, and then walking at a more sober pace to the last house on the outskirts, which Robb knew from his daughter's description was the Brydons' croft. The porch was built at an angle to deflect westerly gales, and the pitch of the roof hid the doorstep from any watcher on the hill, but a moment later Jess came back into view, accompanied by Mhairi Brydon. The two women walked to an adjoining building set end-on to the main house. Mhairi unlocked its door, and the pair vanished inside.

Interesting, thought Robb, and was wondering if there would be lobster for supper again when a shout from the lochside alerted him to Marina's approach, stumbling over the tussocks with trout in her net and Logan carrying her rod a few steps behind. They were in argumentative mood as they gutted the fish at the water's edge, and he left them alone to work out how best to cook them. Marina's method of rolling each trout in newspaper and soaking the parcel before thrusting it into the heart of the fire won the day, and although it involved another wait, he had to admit the result was worth it.

Yet hardly had the fire died to embers and the last of the trout been divided three ways, than Marina was agitating to get back to the water.

'Come on, Dad. There are thousands of fish just waiting to be caught, and you haven't had a single one yet,' she said impatiently. 'Logan can deal with the fire.'

The boy was sitting a little apart, knee up and stick supporting his telescope in the classic pose as he stared out to sea.

'Yon's Mr Larsen's dory coming into harbour.'

Robb's binoculars picked up the jollyboat's dull olive paintwork, with Gunnar manoeuvring through the moored skiffs and small craft that thronged the jetty. He threw a rope round a bollard and the little boat bounced as he heaved himself ashore.

'Come on,' nagged Marina.

'You go ahead, darling. I'll catch you up.'

He and Logan watched in silence as Gunnar's long strides took him up through the empty streets and along the coast road to Mhairi's isolated croft backing on to Kildrumna Beag.

'That's our house,' said Logan in a strange, breathless voice. Robb saw his fingers whiten as he gripped the Swarovski, staring with painful intensity at the burly bearded figure far below. 'I wonder...'

'Wonder what?' Robb prompted.

But moments later Logan laid the telescope on the heather and bowed his head with a look of utter dejection, turning his head to hide his expression before rising to walk after Marina. Whatever his hopes, they had not materialised, and he was not going to tell Robb about them.

Gunnar had spent a busy morning alone aboard *Shield Maiden*, and twice called the boatyard for advice. The air in the sheltered bay was still and below decks the heat felt stickily oppressive with the threat of the approaching storm, so it was a relief to take the jollyboat into the fresher air round the point in Clinie harbour and after mooring among the fishing boats to amble up the single street, noting what had changed since he last visited it. A few more bungalows crouched along the seafront; a few more small shops had evidently succumbed to lack of trade and were boarded up. Several detached houses sported Rooms to Let signs, and the single hotel was undergoing a much-needed renovation, with ladders and builders' materials stacked in its car park.

Not a thriving economy, he concluded, but not on the brink of collapse, either. Pretty, peaceful, stagnant. All it needed was money – that, and the driving force of someone who would take the little town by the scruff and shake it into activity... and, alas, experience showed all too clearly his dear godson was not the person to do that. He had had his chance –

three years' worth of chance – but now things had to change.

Gunnar sighed, shook his head, and quickened his pace as he passed the last of the cottages and reached the branch lane that led to Mhairi's croft and studio.

Shawl round shoulders, wisps of blonde hair escaping from her loose chignon, eyes guarded and watchful above the enigmatic smile into which he could read anything or nothing, she stood guard at the top of the steps leading to the glass porch watching his approach, vigilant as a hunting cat.

'I wondered when you'd come,' she said.

'So here I am!' he said heartily. 'I hope you are happy to see me. I wish to speak seriously about your son. May I enter?'

Her face hardened as she shook her head. 'You've picked a bad time, Mr Larsen. I'm busy. I've told you before I've nothing to say to you.'

She stepped back, putting her hand on the door, but he caught her arm. Watching from within the studio Jess, who had come for a discussion of additions to the jewellery range, saw with astonishment gentle, soft-spoken Mhairi attempt to shake off the restraining hand. Silently they tussled, but when Gunnar's grip proved too strong, Mhairi stopped struggling, gathered saliva in her mouth and spat directly in his face.

For a moment neither moved, then Gunnar took out a red-spotted handkerchief and carefully wiped his beard. 'That was unwise,' he said with studied calm. 'The truth cannot be hidden for ever. What will you say when it comes out?'

'I'll worry about that when it happens,' she snapped. 'And until then leave me bide. Good day to you, Mr Larsen.' Turning on her heel, she pushed open the kitchen door and, when he moved to follow, slammed it in his face.

I don't believe I saw that, thought Jess, taking a hasty step back from the window. Though she'd been too far away to catch their words, the body language of the confrontation was perfectly clear, and the image of respectful, self-contained Mhairi spitting like an angry cat seemed burnt on her retina. What the hell's going on? she thought. Luke would say it's none of my business, but he'd be wrong. It is our business that's at stake, and if there's a feud we ought to know about it.

'Was that Mr Larsen?' she asked as casually as she could, turning away from the display cases she had been pretending to examine as Mhairi returned to the studio, wisps of hair tucked into place and manner almost surreally calm.

'Aye, so it was.'

Since she seemed disinclined to elaborate, Jess went on. 'I thought so. What did he want?'

To her own ears the question sounded intrusive, almost rude, but Mhairi answered without hesitation, 'Och, just a wee matter of a brooch he wanted me to copy for his wife. I told him all my work is original and I wasn't in the business of copying; but yon's a man won't take no for an answer.' A brittle laugh. 'I told him I was busy and showed him the door, but I don't doubt he'll be back.'

'What sort of brooch was it?'

Mhairi's nose wrinkled in distaste. 'An ugly old thing. Heavy. Not my taste at all, and like to ruin any dress you put it on, but he wouldn't be told.' Briskly she dismissed the subject. 'Now, Mrs Balfour –'

'Jess.'

'If you like. Now let's have a look at your accounts and see what the ladies at the Lodge were buying this season, and if we can come up with something they'll like next year...' It was clear that the subject of Mr Larsen's visit was closed.

Logan arrived home at a run, but remembering his mother's aversion to drama and fuss, he stopped to recover his breath and smooth his hair before pushing open the kitchen door and saying as casually as he could, 'Was Mr Larsen looking for me, Mam?'

Mhairi looked up sharply from the bannock she was shaping. 'Whatever gave you that idea?'

'I was up at Loch Herrich and saw him come to the door, but he didn't stay long, so I thought it must be me he wanted.'

She let a moment of silence develop before saying curtly, 'What would that one be wanting with you?'

*That one* sounded ominous, but Logan ploughed on doggedly. If he couldn't make Mam understand what a chance this was for him to get on in life, he would have to defy her, follow his own path and hope she grew to accept it. 'Did he leave a message for me?'

'Be done wi' ye now!' she said in exasperation. 'There's no call to keep blethering about Mr Larsen. He and his wife will be gone by noon on Sunday, and perhaps then ye'll get back to your books and stop ettling after a life that's not for you.'

Strangely he found it encouraging that she knew at least part of what he wanted. He said recklessly, 'Mrs Larsen asked if I'd like to work on the cruise boats this winter. She's worked there herself and she'd put in a good word for me. I could learn how they operate, and where they go, and maybe do a bit of teaching myself if the passengers wanted instruction in sailing. Mam, they employ hundreds of people! They send boats all over the world! It's a fantastic opportunity, and she said I was ideal for it –'

'So instead of going to university you want to skivvy for fly-by-night strangers in a dead-end job that'll leave you with nothing to fall back on when they kick you out at the end of the cruise season? Foolish bairn! Are those the values I've given you? Is that truly what you're wanting?'

The bitterness in her voice shocked him. Was she right? The proposal sounded less attractive put like that, but still he hankered to know why Mr Larsen had called on her this afternoon. Ever since Ravenna (as he secretly thought of her) had laid her hand on his arm and offered the job of his dreams, it had been a warm, comforting thought to which he resorted night and day; but now a cold trickle of reality was creeping in to spoil it. Hadn't she said that her husband would have to confirm it? And hadn't old Gunnar treated him with disdain aboard *Shield Maiden* yesterday, making him skivvy as his mother described?

'Well, I tell you now, I'm not having it.' The finality in her tone doused any lingering flicker of hope that she would give in. 'You may not mind ruining your life, but I won't let it go so easy. Away to your chores and homework now, and if you want to please me, never mention working on cruise boats again.'

Furious and defiant, he slouched out to begin his evening chores: bringing in a hod of peat from the stack in the outhouse, mixing meal into the sow's scrap-bucket, and moving the electric fence that kept the stirks out of the little patches of oats and barley that would feed them through the winter. As he worked, he kept raising his eyes to the bay, automatically noting the movement of boats and fishermen around the harbour while his thoughts raged back and forth.

Why was Mam so set against him having any contact with the Larsens? All right, he had always known she didn't approve of rich people who could carelessly dispense charity or withhold it according to a momentary whim; in her view you got what you worked for. Look at the way she had scolded his father for accepting the Swarovski! But he was also aware there were many areas of his mother's life he knew nothing about.

She seldom spoke about her childhood here at Inverclinie, though he guessed from what he had been told of his grandparents that their family life had been grindingly poor; and he had never heard her refer to her career in Glasgow after leaving school. She must have supported herself somehow and learned to design and make jewellery before she returned to her roots, married his father, and became the person she was now: strict, cautious and, with a sense of morality that often, in Logan's view, conflicted with her own interests as well as his. Why did she refuse to sell jewellery in the Stairbrigg gift shops, preferring instead to let Mrs Balfour make her own profit from them? Why did she turn down enticing offers to sing at folk music festivals? Even Angus the publican's suggestion that she should produce an album of ballads had met with a flat refusal. Why?

It was like this ridiculous focus on getting him to uni. Lots of school-leavers took a gap year before sitting their entrance exams. Why shouldn't he work on cruise ships, travelling and learning about the world beyond Inverclinie? Maybe the clientele would be everything she warned: rich, selfish and old. Maybe the job would involve skivvying – horrible word, implying second or even third-class status, obeying orders from bullies one step higher on the career ladder, being given dirty, demeaning work until he hoisted himself up from the bottom of the pile. He wouldn't be there for long. Ravenna would see to that.

Drugs were what Mam dreaded. He cursed himself for ever telling her that his cousins Alick and Hamish at the fish farm had a regular trade with a hard-eyed Maltese dealer off a container ship that docked at Templeport, and had pressed him to try their extra-strong skunk, teasing remorselessly until he gave in. Never again, he had vowed, reeling dizzy and sick from the feed barge, but that cut no ice with Mam.

'Did you not mind a word I said?' she scolded. 'That stuff is dangerous. Two puffs one day, four the next, and before you can say knife you're addicted.'

It was on the tip of his tongue to ask how she knew so much about it, but she forestalled him. 'And if you doubt me, take a look at yon Hamish's friend Morag – Morag Macnamara as she is now – that bright bonny lass who had the world at her feet when she won the talent show three years syne, and now she's an old woman. I've seen her scrounging the Food Bank in Templeport for a can of beans to put on the table, and if that's what your 'two puffs' have done for her, they'll do it to you as well.'

Logan was silent. He had himself been shocked by Morag's haggard yellow face and lined skin, and the look of desperation in her eyes.

'Give over, mam. Dinna fash," he said irritably. 'I tell you it made me sick and I won't be touching it again.' He had slouched away, resenting the fuss over the incident – one that he would have long forgotten if the acid in his vomit had not burned into his boat's polished brasswork as an unwelcome reminder every time he visited his lobster cages. He wouldn't be trying out skunk or any other weed again.

As he fuelled up and headed out towards the line of rocks draped in bladderwrack where the traps were strategically sited in water clear enough to check without hoisting them whether they were occupied or not, the question of Mr Larsen's visit still nagged at him.

This evening he was in luck. Besides the one large hen lobster berried with eggs whom he released, four males well above the minimum size and a couple of crabs made a respectable catch as well as an excuse for calling in at Kildrumna before going back for his tea.

Not that he really needed an excuse. Ravenna had asked him, in the gentle, caressing tones that made his skin tingle, if he would be kind enough to ferry her in his own boat across the narrow neck of water to Stairbrigg before the museum closed at six o'clock. He had assented readily. The extra trip would take no more than ten minutes each way, which with any luck his mother would not notice, and the last thing he wanted was to keep Ravenna waiting.

He spotted her standing quietly at the jetty in the shadow of the boat house, enveloped in a hooded green cloak that reached to her ankles, with a little briefcase at her feet. The moment he cut the engine and tossed her the mooring rope, she stepped neatly aboard without even bothering to hitch it round a bollard.

'Well done, good timing!' she smiled. 'Let's go.'

Watching through the window of the rod room where he was assembling his night-fishing equipment, Gunnar saw the lobster boat's foaming wake describe a tight curve as it sped across the bay towards the distant houses. Where was she off to? He hurried onto the stone terrace with his binoculars.

From there he could clearly see Ravenna seated in the bows, huddled into her cloak as spray dashed over her, with Logan in the stern, gunning the outboard with his hand on the tiller. Raising the binoculars, he focused on the Stairbrigg harbour with its pier and small marina to the right of the ferry company office.

'So!' he murmured, nodding, scanning the figures seated on the harbour wall or benches carefully positioned to catch the last of the sun. Some were obviously shoppers with baskets and carrier bags, waiting for Calmac's final run of the day, while other women gossiped and watched children dangle rods off the pier. The tranquil, timeless pattern of a summer evening in a sleepy fishing port, with grey, white, and pastel-washed cottages stacked against the hill, like so many he had seen in childhood when his father visited his trawlers.

A few fishermen were unhurriedly working on their boats or nets, but the bulk of the day's commerce was over, so the stocky square-shouldered figure striding purposefully down the steep cobbled lane that led to the beach immediately attracted his gaze.

'As I thought!' murmured Gunnar to himself. 'You fly back to him, little Raven. When I took you as my shield maiden you promised me loyalty, but instead you betray me. You have cheated me' – his face hardened – 'so now I must clip your wings.'

Across this narrow channel, body-language was as easy to interpret as words. He watched Logan weave his boat through the throng of moored craft, and the cloaked figure of Ravenna step ashore at the end of the jetty. She exchanged a few words with her boatman – arranging a return trip, perhaps? – before waving or blowing him a kiss; then, picking up her briefcase she sauntered away, round the angle of the ticket office. Gunnar saw her encounter the hurrying stranger and for an instant the two figures merged. Then they walked back up the hill towards the museum, and he returned his attention to the boy still sitting in the boat.

What would he do now? Visit Olympia's Bar to sell his catch and justify to his mother the time spent on this unscheduled trip to Stairbrigg? Mhairi was a martinet who made her son account for every minute of his time. Or would Logan return directly to Kildrumna?

For the best part of five minutes the matter went unresolved, but at last Logan's boat turned in a tight curve, retraced its tortuous route through the marina and headed across the bay. Now he had the choice of making for the Kildrumna inlet or rounding the point to Inverclinie harbour, and presently it was clear that Kildrumna itself was his goal.

Gunnar lowered the binoculars and returned to the rod room, hurriedly snatching up rod, fishing bag, net and wet-weather gear. Awkwardly clutching them and his wading-stick he began to descend the long flight of stone steps that led to the jetty, hoping to encounter the boy on his way up.

It was time – high time – to put young Logan straight about a number of things, one of which was the difference between acceptable and unacceptable behaviour, but first he must lure the fish to the net.

They met at the halfway point. 'Carry your rod, sir?' said the boy, with an engaging smile.

Gunnar, who had been watching his feet on the uneven steps, looked up, feigning surprise. 'So much equipment – I need more hands.'

Leaving the bucket of squirming crustaceans on the middle step, Logan relieved him of some of his burdens and together they walked back to the jetty. Though he could sense that the boy was bursting to say something, Gunnar took back his rod and net in silence, nodded acknowledgment and had turned towards the Rock Pool at the mouth of the Clinie before Logan nerved himself to say, 'Could you spare me a moment, sir? I'd appreciate your advice.'

'I am always prepared to give advice, boy. Whether it is what you want to hear is another matter. So! What is it?'

Logan said in a rush, 'It's my career, sir. Now I've left school, I'm looking for a job. I don't want to stay here all my life. My mother told me you came to our house today looking for me, and I wondered...'

'You are telling me she sent you to find me?' said Gunnar sharply.' What did she wish you to ask of me?'

Logan took his courage in both hands. 'She knows I want to travel and see the world –'

'Like every young man who ever lived,' said Gunnar dampingly. He drew a deep breath and exhaled with a contemptuous snort. 'So you thought I might provide a magic carpet for you, is that right? You are thinking it would be very nice to cruise in the Mediterranean and the Caribbean all winter, and perhaps return to Scotland for a month or two in the summer.' For a long moment he stared speculatively at Logan. 'Well, you have told me what you want, and what you don't want, but now I must know what you can offer in return for this dream. What experience do you have? What qualifications?'

'I'm a hard worker, sir. You said so yourself when I crewed for you three years ago. And I did four months' work experience in the Templeport yard when the yachts were laid up for the winter. My mother said the only way to find out if you would give me a job was to ask you myself.'

There! It was out now. He waited uneasily, watching Gunnar nodding his big head and chuckling as he stroked his beard. What did he find amusing? Did he think it absurd for a teenager to ask the company boss directly for a job?

Should he have applied to some underling, a personnel manager perhaps, who would have given him the brush-off or a bunch of forms to fill out?

'You astonish me, boy,' said Gunnar at last. 'That is not the message I expected from your mother. Well, we shall see.' Again he let an uncomfortable silence develop before saying with a touch of impatience, 'It is not your seamanship that makes me hesitate. It is your character I question. Can you smile when you have to make the same answer to the same fool ten times in one day? Can you work in a team? When you take clients fishing, will you dream of your ladylove and run the boat on the rocks – huh?'

He leaned forward to peer closely at Logan. 'You know what I speak of, ja?'

'Yes, sir.'

'Good. Then think about these things and come back tomorrow at this time, when I will give you my answer. I would not want you to throw over any job I offer when you find it does not suit you. That would destroy my credibility as well as yours. Now tell me where are the tanks which I asked you to get refilled?'

'I put them back in the rack, sir.'

'And the mixture?'

'Forty-sixty, like you said. Initialled by the manager.'

He waited hopefully for praise, but Gunnar merely nodded. 'Good boy,' he said and went on staring at him as if searching for hidden flaws, then gave a slow, thoughtful nod.

'Very well, at the end of the season I will take you on trial for six months, working for me personally until you have learned the basics of the business and may be more of a help than a hindrance to the company.' A pause, then he added the killer question, 'Since you are a minor, you will need your mother's agreement. Do you think she will accept those terms?'

'Yes, sir,' said Logan with a confidence he did not feel.

'Tell her I wish to know if you are like your father.'

'You knew him, sir?' Logan said cautiously.

'Quite well enough.'

As Gunnar turned away with another dismissive grunt, Logan decided instantly that he would tell his mother no such thing. Though generally recognised as a canny fisherman and ghillie, Seamus Brydon had had few admirers and, after he was dismissed by the Major for persistently turning up drunk for work, his career had been one long descent from oil rigs to fish farm and finally poacher.

The less said about him the better, thought Logan, returning to his boat unsure if the interview had been a success or failure. It was disappointing that there had been no mention of payment or thanks for the prompt and efficient way he had carried out extra work, but on the whole things could have gone worse – much worse.

His mood of quiet satisfaction vanished as he unmoored and threw a leg over the gunwale, for there was his lobster bucket neatly stowed in the bows – empty. Bloody hell, he exploded silently, searching under the thwarts and finding nothing.

'The poor things were trying to get out, so I put them back in the sea,' said Marina, appearing silently at the foot of the steps, her expression a mixture of self-righteousness and defiance.

Thrown away his lobsters – deliberately? Logan wanted to shake her. 'What for did you do that, you doaty bampot,' he burst out, quite forgetting the respect due to a client's daughter, but far from looking chastened, she giggled.

'Doaty *bam*pot! Oh, Logan, I've been called a lot of names, but that's a first. Wait till I tell my sisters – they'll love it.'

'Aye, you can laugh, but it's no joke for me,' he growled. 'That was my best catch this week, gone with naught to show for it, and the lobsters like to die from being out of the water too long anyway.'

'Bullshit,' said Marina with a readiness that would not

have pleased her father. She patted her rear pocket. 'I googled it before I tipped them in. You can keep them out of water and they're OK for two days, until their gills collapse.'

No arguing with Google. Logan said bitterly, 'I suppose you don't care about the cash I've lost! You've never had to work your guts out. You don't know what it's like to scrimp and save, with your mother after you all the time to bring in more money.'

'You leave my mother out of this!'

Belatedly he recalled her loss. 'Sorry,' he muttered.

'As it happens, I know exactly what it's like to work hard. You try keeping up with a gang of Romanian strawberry-pickers for a month, day after day, rain or shine, and you'll think sitting in a boat catching lobsters is a rest cure.'

' Why did you do that?'

'Why do you think? Dad bet me £50 I wouldn't stick it for more than a week, so I got that, too.' She paused, then added in a more conciliatory tone, 'Look, I'm sorry you've lost your catch, but you shouldn't have dumped those poor lobsters on the steps. I thought you'd forgotten them and they'd be struggling to get out all night. In any case, you wouldn't have got much for them. Olympia Kyriakis pays rock-bottom prices and that's the only fish-bar that risks buying immature lobsters.'

Logan frowned. He hadn't expected this inquisitive girl to know about his dealings with Yanis's wife. 'They weren't that small, and anyway, what do you know about Olympia?'

'Danna told my Dad she buys anything she can get hold of and when it comes to paying she's as tight as a chicken's – OK, forget it. But why leave your catch on the steps? Anyone could have nicked it.'

'I was helping Mr Larsen carry his gear.' After a pause he couldn't help adding, 'We talked about my career.'

'What career?' said Marina instantly and again he hesitated, wondering whether to trust her with the news he was itching to share. What harm would it do?

He said, 'I asked if he would give me a job on his cruise boats at the end of the season.'

'Cool! What did he say?'

'He's thinking it over. We didn't go into details, but it looks good,' he said carefully, teetering along the line between half-truth and actually lying.

'Does your mother know?'

'Not yet, and don't you go telling her.'

'She won't be pleased.' During their brooch-making sessions, Mhairi had made it very plain to Marina that she wanted her son to go to university rather than taking a job locally.

'When will you start?' she pressed, and Logan shrugged impatiently.

'Don't ask so many questions. I'll know more about it when we've talked it through.'

'And then you'll tell me? And your mum?'

'When I'm ready.'

'When will that be?' Her curiosity irked him: he threw a leg over the gunwale without answering.

'Where are you going now? Can I come too?'

'No, you canna. I'm late for my tea already, and you're not invited.'

'Oh, Logie, don't be horrid!' she pleaded. 'I'm sorry I let your lobsters go. Let me help you catch some more. It'll be such fun – just the two of us. I don't mind getting up early.'

'Five o'clock?'

For a moment Logan hesitated, considering his options. On one hand he was unwilling to disappoint her again. She was a nice kid and his mother was always telling him to be friendly and polite to the Balfours' guests. He admired her fishing and diving skill, not to mention the way she stood up to Mr Larsen's bullying and made him laugh. Secretly he thought she was very pretty, with her long crinkly hair and pale pointed face not unlike the illustration of Ophelia in his tatty school copy of Hamlet. On the other, it would take twice as long to visit his lobster traps with her in tow, and Uncle Danna had warned him never to allow Mr Balfour's visitors to see where he set his creels.

'Please, Logie!'

'OK, then,' and be damned to Uncle Danna, he thought. Even if she saw something she shouldn't, she wouldn't know what it was. 'Not tomorrow, but we'll give it a go the day after. You'll have to clear it with your Dad – OK?'

'Sure.'

'Five o'clock sharp, and I'll pick you up here on my way out. If you're late, I won't wait, mind.'

'Don't worry, I'll be on time. Thanks, Logs, see you then.'

She gave him a radiant smile and waved as he fired up the engine and swung the boat in a tight curve, his mind once again on Mr Larsen's offer of a job.

He wouldn't tell his mother about it, no – but he would go right away and have a chat to his auntie Elspeth, who was less rigid in her views, and more inclined to her favourite nephew's way of thinking.

Davie McTavish, who owned the former Chandlery fronting on Stairbrigg harbour just next door to Olympia's Fish Bar, had long been a worried man. Wiry and skinny to the point of emaciation, he had deep wrinkles round his eyes and grooves between nose and mouth which made him look older than his fifty-two years. The nervous tic that twitched his left cheek signalled the stress of trying to make his business pay.

After a rackety youth in Thailand and the South Pacific, he had returned to his roots in Stairbrigg and transformed his father's well-established Chandlery into a Marine Supply and Dive Shop. Modern sportswear instead of oilskins and sou'westers. Surf boards and scuba equipment to replace ropes, nets and sails. He hoped to capitalise on a new breed of marine sportsmen and promote the wild, remote beauty of the coast as a tourist destination, but after a promising start the business plateau'd and, with the increasing price and sophistication of the stock he needed, cash flow had become an urgent problem by the time Big Dougie's predatory eye noted the signs of a struggle.

'Call it a partnership, if you like, and keep your name over the door. It's well respected hereabouts,' he had said when he made his proposal. He surveyed the disordered racks of clothing and boxes of dive gear as yet unpacked that overflowed the long, scuffed counter. 'There's plenty of scope here for the kind of customer you're needing. It's just that they don't know it yet. Once word gets about, you'll have no difficulty paying me back.'

Sensing resistance, he had added in his easy, confident way, 'I'll not be wanting to take over from you. I've enough on my plate to keep me busy without that. Just call on me to give a hand with the donkey work – I'd enjoy that. It will keep me grounded to see how folk work now that I've escaped the Edinburgh bubble. Maybe I could take a look at your accounts and make some suggestions? I've contacts you might find useful. But as far as the world's concerned, you'll be keeping the business in the family. How does that sound to you?'

With bills piling up in his cluttered office, Davie had been in no position to refuse, however irked he felt at the way money seemed to stick to his former schoolfellow's fingers as fast as it slipped through his own.

How had McInnes become so rich? Everyone knew that his father drank every penny he earned, and Wee Dougie had worn cast-offs from the charity shop, while the McTavish family paid their bills on the nail and were pillars of the kirk. Yet somehow while he, Davie, had been knocking about the world in search of the Perfect Wave, McInnes had broken through the barrier separating the Doing OKs from the Seriously Rich, and become the most powerful businessman in the area.

Swallowing his pride, he had accepted Big Dougie's offer, and tried to convince himself that he had not sold his birthright for a mess of pottage.

As anyone who knew McInnes could have predicted, his involvement with the dive shop did not stop at lending a hand at busy times, nor casting a casual eye over the accounts. On the contrary, Davie was soon uneasily aware that Big Dougie and his accountant were virtually running the business, stocking new lines and cancelling non-performing ones, chasing up slow payments and offering discounts. As a result, McTavish Marine Supplies was making money hand over fist.

Once he was in a position to pay back his loan, Davie would have liked to take the reins again, but Big Dougie was in no hurry to hand them back. The suggestion that he might be surplus to requirement seemed to wound him.

'Man, we're doing great! I tell you, it's no trouble to me. With the marina expanding as it is, trade is bound to increase so unless you want to take on an apprentice there'll be too much for you to handle alone.' He paused, then added casually, 'Unless your own lads want to work with you?'

If only! Davie had sighed and rubbed his eyes. Neither Alick nor Hamish had ever shown the least interest or pride in the Chandlery, and his adored Elspeth was physically incapable of helping in the shop. Though only two years older than her sister Mhairi, Elspeth's crippling arthritis had made her semi-invalid by thirty-six, even struggling with her own cooking. As teenagers, the sisters used to win cups and medals for sword dancing at many a Gathering, and their close harmonising was the highlight of local ceilidhs, but the steroids had blurred her pretty features and swollen her ankles and wrists, though her warm heart and generous nature were unchanged.

Just the luck of the draw, she'd think without rancour, as she limped about supported by two sticks.

'Give me your shopping list and I'll drop the stuff in on my way home,' Mhairi sometimes urged, but Elspeth valued independence too much to burden her sister with extra chores.

'No need, mo achroi, no need at all,' she'd say, laughing. 'I'm doing fine, just fine,' even when every joint ached and the larder was empty. It was no use relying on her sons. They would turn up for supper and eat enormously, but apart from scarred salmon from the cages, they made no contribution to expenses. Her boys were a disappointment and secretly she preferred the company of her nephew, Logan, who shared her taste in romantic fiction.

She was a great home-maker. 'Give Elspeth four walls and a roof, and in two shakes she'll have it fit to house a queen,' her husband would boast, and Logan heartily agreed when he compared her snug, all-electric bungalow smelling of fresh cakes to his mother's spartan croft where whiffs of ancient shellfish filtered under the kitchen door. "Helping Aunty Elspeth" was one of the few excuses for absence which Mhairi accepted without question.

'All she lets me do is work and study,' he complained now to his aunt's sympathetic ear. 'I'm never allowed to have any fun.'

'Wheesht, Logie. Don't say that. It won't be for ever and when you're famous and publishers are fighting over your new book, you'll be thankful she kept your nose to the grindstone,' she said, offering a wedge of shortbread. 'Put the tin back on the high shelf, there's a love, or the boys will empty it when they leave the Clachan tonight.'

Wheezily, she settled back in her chair. 'Now give me the craic from the Lodge. All I've heard is that a passel of lads have come in from the Isles, wanting to add Big Dougie to their salmon syndicate.'

That explained the string of 4x4s which Logan had seen driving down the single-track from Templeport that afternoon. Not for the first time, he was impressed by the way his housebound aunty kept up with the news. She got it, of course, from Uncle Davie, and it also explained the extra activity round the Moontide cages, where Yanis had been chivvying his team.

He asked, 'What about the Smokery?'

'Ah, that's the big draw – and the sticking point, too. McInnes wants to charge the others to use it. Davie says they've asked him to chair the group, even though Moontide's had a bad press lately.' She leaned forward confidentially. 'Some say Mrs Balfour had a hand in that, but don't you go mentioning that at the Lodge.'

Remembering the interest his mother and Danna had shown in the *Templeport Chronicle* recently, and elliptical phrases heard through his bedroom door, he remembered Mrs Balfour's connections with the media. Though he regarded Mr Balfour as a soft touch, his wife was a fighter, no mistake. From time to time he had caught the rough edge of her tongue himself.

So why was Mr Larsen sailing away when things were getting interesting? He said tentatively, 'Mr Larsen's asked me to crew for him when he goes up the Sound to the Viking festival.'

She had been staring at the fire but now her head swung round to face him directly. 'And will you do that?'

Logan nodded. 'If I do well, he's promised me a job this winter. A trial, 'he added hastily, sensing a change in her manner: a sudden coldness.

'What does your mam say to that, laddie?'

'I hoped you'd advise me, aunty. I – I haven't told her yet, but I know she won't let me unless... well, unless you help me persuade her. It's a wonderful chance for me! I've lived here all my life, and now I want to see the world –'

'I – I – I! Don't you think of anyone but yourself? You should be ashamed, Logan Brydon! After all these years when your mam's been working her fingers to the bone to keep you clothed and fed, you want to skip out of her life without a backward glance? How will she manage without you?' said Elspeth angrily. 'Have you given a thought to that? What about her hopes, her dreams for you? Are you going to throw that over for the chance of a dead-end job from a bletherskate

I wouldn't trust as far as I could throw him?'

Such an outburst from easygoing Aunty Elspeth was unprecedented, not only because it was exactly what he feared his mother would say, but also because as far as he knew his aunt never had anything to do with Mr Larsen.

'Why, aunty? Why don't you trust him?'

'Never you mind. The world didn't start when you were born, laddie, and there's things I remember that are best laid to rest. There! That's enough.' She was still angry, and he sensed she had said more than she meant to. 'You've come to the wrong place if you want me to back you against your mam, and if you're hoping I won't mention it to her you'll be disappointed. Now gang yer gait, and dree yer ain weird, as my grandma used to say. Do you understand me?'

Logan was glad to escape.

Gunnar entertained two visitors in *Shield Maiden*'s cabin later that evening, one by invitation and the other unexpected. Both interviews required his full attention, a degree of diplomacy and, in one case, generous tots of whisky.

Idly watching the kaleidoscope of small craft thronging the Stairbrigg harbour, he noticed the dark-green speedboat used by the Dive Shop to tow water-skiers detach itself from the melée and head directly for *Shield Maiden*. Though the years since he had last seen her had not dealt kindly with Mhairi's sister, he had no difficulty in recognising the steroid-puffy face looking up at him from the front seat, but the unannounced visit puzzled him, since she had never hidden her distrust of him and in the old days had done her best to keep him and Mhairi apart.

'Elspeth!' he exclaimed, leaning over the rail. 'To what do I owe this pleasure?'

'I'd be glad of a word with you, Mr Larsen,' she said without a smile. 'May I come aboard?'

Useless to plead another engagement when her hand

was already on the ladder. He watched her heave herself up the rungs, breathing heavily, and put out a hand to steady her as she reached the deck.

'No, no. I can manage fine,' she said, shaking it off and confronting him like an embattled partridge. 'What I have to say will not take long, but nor will it keep. You may say this is none of my business and you could be right at that, but if my sister's too stubborn to ask you herself, I'll do it in her stead.'

'Ask me what, Elspeth?' he asked, though he could guess.

The boatman was revving his engine. 'Ten minutes, Davie,' she called.

Gunnar nodded and gestured to the companionway. 'It is good. Come in the cabin, and let us discuss what is on your mind.'

True to her word, Elspeth stayed no more than ten minutes, steadfastly refusing refreshment but, though wounded by her comments on his character and behaviour, their sparring ended in agreement, after which Gunnar sat thinking for a while before returning to his contemplation of the harbour's evening rituals. There was justice in what she had said, he reflected, and an obligation he had already taken steps to honour, expensive though it was likely to prove. The past was inescapable. However long you managed to duck and weave, in the end it would catch up with you.

Grumbling internally, he set out a brace of bottles while awaiting the arrival of his second, more welcome guest.

An hour later when he, too, had puttered quietly away across the bay, Gunnar washed the glasses, replaced them in an overhead locker and, grimacing, swallowed the pills that would ward off an untimely attack of cramp.

That left him with one more task before embarking on the night's adventures.

Sighing gustily, he settled at the cabin's flap-down table with his laptop, thick fingers pecking carefully at the small keys.

My dear little godson, he wrote and paused, irresolute, tugging at his beard. How much should he tell him? Full disclosure? Half the truth? The upshot of his interview with Jess? That had surprised him. Without Luke's emollient presence as Piggy-in-the-Middle she had shown him quite another side of her character: forceful, marginally antagonistic and quite as unscrupulous as Gunnar himself. Nor had there been any need to insist on secrecy because she had demanded it as a condition of her co-operation. He grinned – how easy it was to be mistaken in people, no matter how long you had known them! But did good ever come of raking over the past? There was no denying that Elspeth's intervention had unsettled him. He took a coin from his pocket and spun it high: Heads, all. Tails, nothing.

The coin missed the table, rolled on to the floor and wedged upright in a crack, refusing a decision. Gunnar grunted in annoyance and returned to his document.

My dear little godson, I believe I owe you an explanation…

Finally, satisfied that he had covered all contingencies, he set about readying *Shield Maiden* for sailing.

After the hot, clear weather, it was plain that the high had drifted west and the weather was about to break; thunderflies danced over the jetty, and anywhere out of the wind inch-long clegs with wicked jaws would alight silently to administer itching bites. As the glass fell, the wind backed into the north and sudden gusts began to whip up white horses outside the sheltered cove. The forecast was right: clearly they were in for a blow.

For such a heavy, cumbersome man, Gunner moved about the small boat with surprising neatness, stowing gear into lockers, coiling down ropes and checking stores: food for a week and drink for six months; only when all below was shipshape to his satisfaction did he go back on deck.

Logan had replaced the re-filled scuba-diving tanks in their correct order.

'All done, sir. Uncle Davie said you should test them yourself,' Logan had added conscientiously, and Gunnar laughed, cuffing him lightly on the shoulder.

'Oh, I doubt if that will be necessary,' he replied absently, his eyes on a cormorant carrying a fish that was labouring heavily towards the cliffs. Yet when he was alone he sampled the tanks through his hand-held analyser, frowned, nodded and, after a moment's thought, dropped the first tank overboard into the weedy depths, where it sank without trace, and put the others back in the rack.

Am I becoming paranoid? he thought, chuckling. An old woman who jumps at shadows? Or as little Marina's thrice-damned dive instructor would tell me, "Better safe than sorry"? How that child makes me laugh with her warnings and mottos, her Big Fluffy Rabbits and silly pranks. If only I had met her when I was young! At odd moments her quirks reminded him of another golden girl he had loved long ago, full of mischief and fantasy, too good for her surly clod of a husband.

His father had stamped on that romance – hard. Olaf had been a ruthless man, even threatening to disinherit his elder son in favour of brother Bjorn, and life itself had crushed that golden girl into dull conformity. But blood would out: already signs of rebellion were apparent. For how long would she be able to restrict the boy's desire to break free? God in heaven, thought Gunnar, has he never looked in a mirror?

Though the milky light of a West Coast summer night bathed the bay in a pearly opalescence far removed from darkness, aboard the feed barge a single light moved sporadically. The day team had left two hours ago, and now the night guard was making his final round before retiring to his bottle in the cabin. Every evening for the past week

Gunnar had studied his routine, but tonight was different – witness the big 4WD vehicles lined up in the car park of the Old Anchor, where no doubt in the Snug their owners were sizing up the prospective chairman of the new consortium, and he was touting the benefit of Big is Beautiful for the salmon-farming industry. The group had already toured the Smokery, tasted its products, and washed them down with a dram or three. Early tomorrow they would be taken to inspect the feed barge and cages in the bay.

He planned to give them a wake-up call. He had laid the train and must be far, far away before the explosion.

He started the engine and puttered quietly beyond sight of Kildrumna Lodge and the long tongue of land that separated it from Stairbrigg, and slid *Shield Maiden* into the narrow appendix known as Clam Bay, skilfully avoiding the line of jagged rocks that guarded its entrance; then on past the dog-leg bend into the sheltered lagoon beyond.

A ruined shieling whose stone-built barn had at some time been used as a hikers' refuge was visible halfway up the bracken-clad slope at the far end, and from it a narrow path snaked down to the shingle in one direction and up to the road in the other. Gunnar surveyed it thoughtfully. An exit? An inconspicuous way of escape?

Massive in his long black 'steamer,' he went down to the cabin and from under the bunk extracted another cylinder marked with a green and yellow band whose re-filling he had overseen personally. Back on the diving platform he strapped it to his BCD with quick, deft movements, checked the pressure gauge and dive computer, and slotted weights into its pockets.

Black hose, yellow hose, regulator and bright yellow octopus: check.

Twist and tighten all valves: check.

He sniffed and tasted the air and nodded: A 1 OK; then clipped on the short snorkel for use near the surface.

On went the BCD and cylinder – heave, click, snap – on went mask and fins, and he was ready.

*Shield Maiden* had begun to rock as the wind freshened, but he left her at single anchor. Once he was clear of Clam Bay the choppy waves would mask his bubbles: no fear now of a patrolling guard spotting a living, breathing intruder.

It was time to go.

Smoothly Gunnar entered the water, seventeen stone suddenly weightless as he hovered a few feet down, waiting to equalise. This is where I belong, he thought. I am a man upon the land; I am a Selkie in the sea... This is where I am truly happy.

Small fish darted away through the milky moonlit water, but larger ones ignored him as he breathed out to descend to just above the weedy rocks, checked his compass, and began an easy flutterkick approach to the cages.

Operation Schmooze is off to a flying start, thought McInnes with satisfaction as he shepherded his guests to their bedrooms. Big Dougie believed in treating his potential colleagues well. Not only had he booked them the best rooms and the best dinner the pub could provide, but had also laid on a film showing Moontide Salmon Products from 'egg to canapé' – as he put it – for after-dinner entertainment.

Lady Jean Allan, the tough little white-haired string-bean who owned Eilean Breck's Salmon Enterprises, was key to a successful deal – and the one he had to watch out for. She was rich, well-connected, and indisputedly the grande dame of the Islands' fish farmers. With her on the board, investors would be scrambling to put money into the new consortium, and he would be able to upgrade his buildings, install electronic surveillance and transportation facilities and, above all, secure his place as one of the big boys of the industry.

His dreams were close to becoming reality, but he warned himself to gang warily. Jeannie was no soft touch – far from it. She had a sharp tongue and such exacting standards that he wondered if he had been over-ambitious in inviting her here. During the Smokery tour, she had barely tasted his smoked salmon and cream cheese wheels, and preferred Highland Spring water to Lagavulin.

She was the only one who had questioned his figures after his presentation, and cast doubt on his marketing projections and the scientists he had quoted on disease control. She had spoken warmly about Gunnar Larsen – "true champion of standards in aquaculture" as she called him – which was hardly surprising since it was his glowing report on Eilean Breck's management that had ensured her products' premium status for the past five years.

It was clear that she had also been following the debate in that damned consumer rag *What's Good for You?* with keen attention, because several of her questions harped on about over-use of antibiotics and the deleterious effects of anthelmintics on shellfish.

OK for her, he thought. Lice were hardly a problem where deep water, strong currents, and the splendid isolation of Eilean Breck meant that chemical-free fish management plus the use of biological cleaners such as wrasse and lumpfish allowed her to produce organic salmon, but her business model was undermined by difficulty in getting her fish to market. Gales, storms, and whole weeks of rough weather could make airlifting to the mainland prohibitively expensive, and then where was her profit? She wanted access to the Stairbrigg Smokery, that was clear enough, but how far would she compromise to get it?

Lady Jean played her cards close to her flat chest, and he had overheard her whispering her doubts about Moontide to that sanctimonious fuzzy-faced old stick-in-the-mud Callum Baillie from Westerewe, who was likely to be voted in as the new company's deputy chair.

'Whosoever toucheth pitch shall be defiled,' whistled Callum through his remaining teeth, though it was well known that his manager shovelled Slice into the cages with careless abandon and the mortality among his fish was well above the average.

String-bean Jeannie and old Fuzzy-Face had been quite ready for bed by ten o'clock, but though James 'Haddock' Findlay and Bruce McEachran, hard drinkers both, would have preferred to stagger down to The Clachran and roar out sea shanties into the small hours, diplomatically but firmly McInnes had wished them a good night and ushered them to their bedrooms.

Relieved of their noisy company, he sauntered along the sea-front as far as Olympia's Fish Bar. Music and multi-coloured lights plus a confused babble of voices spilled out from under its awning, where tables were placed just far enough apart for a harried snake-hipped Yanis to shimmy between bearing trays of heaped plates. The place was heaving with tourists and yachtmen splashing the cash on local produce with a Mediterranean slant.

Behind the glass-fronted bar, two pale girls with tightly-netted hair were working the deep-fat fryers, while the ample form of Olympia herself, flashing-eyed and splendid in a low-cut sequinned top protected by a purple apron, wove back and forth along the counter like a caged bear, taking orders and loading plates. She worked hard and made sure that her staff did too. No wonder they never stayed long, regularly disappearing with their bags and bundles on the early bus to Glasgow.

Plenty more where they came from, he thought, and when Indyref2 finally came to pass every one of them would be needed to build the economy in this sparsely populated country, even if it was a land of oatmeal and whisky, rather than the milk and honey they had been promised. Olympia might be a tough boss to her many 'nephews and nieces,' but she provided them with a start and asked no questions so long as they were not foolish enough to bring up the subject of the minimum wage.

Besides, it was good to know that extended family relationships were still alive and well in southern Europe. He gave her a grin and thumbs-up as he passed the counter.

Where did she get all those lobsters? he wondered fleetingly, working his way through the noisy throng. Some looked remarkably small and certainly wouldn't meet market specifications.

He ducked through a red satin curtain and caught Yanis as he came past with a tray stacked with plates for the dishwasher.

'Any trouble tonight?'

'All quiet, boss, apart from the seals barking their heads off. We checked all the cables. There's a big blow coming down from Iceland in the early hours, but it's not forecast to last. May be a rough night, though.'

Yanis looked exhausted. His tightly-cropped fair hair – legacy of the German stormtrooper who had raped his grandmother in wartime Athens – stood up in spikes, and his pale blue eyes were darkly circled. He tried to wipe his sweating face against his shoulder, and the tray lurched.

'Here, give me that. Come out to the kitchen a moment.' As McInnes took the load of plates and cutlery, he heard Olympia screeching for her husband to hurry up but he paid no attention, and led the way to the brightly-lit scullery, with its row of dishwashers humming and swishing and a team of adolescents loading and unloading the machines.

'Did you have time to stop by the quarry?'

Yanis nodded. 'The boys used the JCB to bury the lot before going home for their tea.'

'Good.' A heap of decomposing fish under a tarpaulin was the last thing he wanted sharp-eyed Jeannie to spot. 'I'll take our visitors out at the top of the morning tide. That'll be – what? Seven? Seven-thirty?'

'But –'

'They won't mind if it's rough. They're well used to it.' And the choppier the sea the less they'd be able to complain about overcrowding, he thought, since the fish would naturally seek shelter near the bottom, giving an impression of more space at the surface.

'Yanis! You idle good-for-nothing! Come here this minute!'

'Sounds like you're needed,' said McInnes, grinning. 'OK, then. I'll take the launch out now and check everything's in order. Where's *Shield Maiden*? I see she's left her mooring.'

'Over to Templeport, I heard. Trouble with the engine.' Yanis gave his drooping trousers a hitch and tightened his belt as Olympia screeched again. 'I must go.'

He darted away. Poor sod, thought McInnes. Imagine being married to a voice like that. Instead of going out through the crush of diners, he exited by the fish-smelling dustbins and strolled casually to unmoor the sleek Gran Turismo launch he had been using on appro for the past two months, switching to voice-mail whenever the seller's number came up on his mobile's display. He'd buy when he was ready: he didn't like being hassled for a decision.

Zooming away from Stairbrigg over the sea's moonlit surface, smooth as polished pewter, he wondered if Yanis was right about the changing wind. It was a question of timing; even with all its charts, the met office could get it wrong. The slap-slap of waves that kicked in as he met the strong current in the Reekie Sound reassured him. By morning it looked like being every bit as rough as he wanted. He might even have to cover the Gran Turismo's leather seats if he didn't want a valeting bill.

Fifty yards short of the feed barge he cut the engine and in the sudden silence allowed the launch to drift broadside on until it kissed against the short wooden pier onto which fishmeal sacks were unloaded.

Scarcely had he set foot on the ladder than the cabin door was flung open and the wild, hirsute figure of Wully Murison was outlined against the light, ancient 12-bore in hand, fully alert and on the lookout for trouble.

'Who goes there?' he demanded, peering into the twilight; and then, 'Och, it's yourself, Mr McInnes. I thocht maybe those bastard seals had come back tae trouble us. There was one heaved out on the board-walk yesterday, cool as you please. Yanis says to scare them off it they get ower bold.'

'You weren't going to shoot them, I hope?'

'Not a bit of it, sorr. Not a bit of it. Just a warning blast ower their heads, like.' Wully opened the door wider and became chattily hospitable. 'Will you come in and take a wee wet?'

'Thanks. Black coffee, no sugar,' McInnes followed him into the fug.

Like his youngest brother Danna, Wully had the knack of making himself comfortable and, in a space no bigger than the cab of a long-distance truck, he had constructed a nest as cosy as that of a harvest mouse. Hot-box and Thermos, cold-box with milk, whisky, Nescafé and smartphone to hand, he could hunker down between patrols while keeping eyes and ears open, and at the first sign of trouble deploy binoculars, shotgun, and a powerful halogen lamp. Under the window-shelf a low, rumbling growl confirmed that Nipper, his cross old wire-haired terrier, was in attendance.

Wully pushed a space clear for the boss and busied himself with kettle and coffee powder. 'Now, sorr. What's the problem?'

McInnes shook his head, frowning. 'I can't explain exactly. Running a bit rough and missing now and then. I hoped you'd be able to put your finger on it. I can't afford it to let me down tomorrow.'

'Verra guid, sorr. I'll give it a go and welcome. Wheesht, Nips.' He shoved the growling dog out of the way with his foot and explained, 'He's aye onaisy when there's seals aboot.'

But tonight seals were not the cause of Nipper's restlessness. Tucked against a massive joist that supported the floor of the barge, Gunnar looked yet again at his dive-monitor and wondered how long McInnes would stay. Lingering near the surface to conserve his air by using the snorkel was risky. Not only might that damned dog betray his presence, but the choppy waves slopped into his mask.

The cages were anchored to the seabed on a shallow shelf some 200 yards offshore. Taking care not to disturb the deep layers of rotting food and faeces beneath them, he had used his battery-driven underwater power-wrench to unscrew vital bolts and then, with an arm round a stanchion for support, worked with heavy shears to slice through all but the last strands of wire and rope that moored the cages farthest from the barge, ignoring the questing, importunate noses of sleek, bulky bodies around him. They were his friends, his kin, but they had a different agenda. Patience, brothers, he thought. Very soon you will have what you want.

Gunnar was a powerful man, and once the coast was clear it would take no more than five minutes to make a breach in the last cage. The approach of McInnes in the launch had forced him to suspend operations, and now he waited with growing impatience for the glow from the opening door to signal his departure.

A rumble of voices, boots on boards. 'A braw nicht,' observed Wully, stamping his feet as he emerged onto the walkway with Nipper bristling at his heels. The dog jumped straight over the rail into the launch and stood on the driver's seat, front paws on the coaming, emitting growls disproportionate to his size.

'Where's that torch of yours?' said McInnes sharply. 'Shine it there – across the corner the dog's telling to.'

As the bright beam swept past him, Gunnar gripped the regulator between his teeth and sank noiselessly off the shelf into deeper water.

'Zero. Naething to see.' Wully thought of his cooling coffee. 'Come on oot o' it, ye mad tyke.'

But the dog held his point, and McInnes said slowly, 'I'm not so sure. I thought I saw something move. Look! There it is again. Fetch me my pop-gun and I'll ginger it up.'

'Bound tae be that thieving bugger of a seal. Wait one...' Wully grinned, ducked back inside and handed McInnes the semi-automatic Beretta 93R machine pistol hidden from official inspections. McInnes checked the magazine, slotted in the shoulder-stock and set it for three round bursts.

'Try this for size,' he muttered, loosing off a tight group into the water.

Too close for comfort, thought Gunnar, going deeper and easing farther away from the shallow shelf. It was unlikely that bullets fired at random would hit him, but the possibility was there, and an unlucky shot might damage his equipment. More dangerous was the expenditure of air, which might force him to surface while the men were watching.

For the first time he wished that the moon was not so bright or the bay so sheltered for beyond the rough waves and strong current sweeping through the Reekie Sound, Kildrumna Bay lay placid as a mill-pool, the big bluff of Cruach Cormac protecting it from the westerly gales as the original builders of the Lodge had intended.

At a safe distance he surfaced and used the snorkel again as he watched McInnes and Wully stand talking for a moment; then the launch zoomed away with a creamy wake streaming behind.

Get inside to your bottle, Gunnar urged silently. I can't wait here all night. But the lone figure seemed in no hurry to return to his cabin, and instead walked slowly round the entire encircling walkway, examining each cage while Gunnar fretted that the few strands now securing the farthest cages would give way prematurely under the press of salmon.

'Sometimes you have to fight dirty,' he had told his godson. Poor Luke! Always so anxious to do the right thing in the right way that he was unable even to consider doing the right thing in the wrong way. A line tugged at his memory: What thou wouldst highly, That wouldst thou holily. Yes, that was Luke to a T. Gunnar scorned such an attitude: in his view the end more than justified the means – any means.

Of course, if he was caught red-handed the consequences would be dire for both of them. The scandal would destroy his reputation and probably Luke's by association, for McInnes could be relied on to plaster the story over every media outlet. Public sympathy – and government opinion – would support him. He would lose no time in re-stocking his cages and applying to set up more.

And so, goodbye Kildrumna Lodge. Goodbye to the little Dunseran and deep smooth Clinie river which held such magic and memories, and eventually, inevitably, goodbye to the wild Atlantic salmon itself. For so many years the dice had been loaded against its breeding pattern which demanded migration to its natal river to spawn. This might be the final straw. What had seemed a fine opportunity to attack McInnes and discredit his business could blow back in his face by having the opposite effect.

Should he abort the operation? Retreat to the safety of *Shield Maiden* and spend the rest of the week, the rest of his life, regretting that he had failed to strike this blow in the wild salmon's defence?

Gunnar glanced once again at his monitor and decided to give it one more shot. Man and dog were quiet in the cabin. All he had to do was cut the final strands and release the caged fish. The state of the seabed alone was enough to excite official disapproval from those who investigated the escape and that, coupled with his own report to Scottish Natural Heritage would scream malpractice to every conservationist body concerned with aquaculture. At the very least McInnes would be forced to move his pollution elsewhere and when the visitors from the Islands saw the extent of the escape they were unlikely to welcome such a ramshackle addition to their new consortium.

It would take only a few minutes. The delicious buzz and whiff of danger which Gunnar craved filled his veins and electrified his nerves as he gripped the regulator between his teeth again and descended to just above the seabed, then glided gently back to the cages.

Surfacing silently by the farthest, he was reassured to see the cabin door closed and only a dim glow around its frame. Ideally Wully would have succumbed to his weed and be slumped stoned in his chair, with Nipper snoring in his lap, but Gunnar was too old a bird to trust in ideal scenarios. In Wully's place he himself would be standing motionless against the cabin wall, armed and alert, watching for movement in the dark water.

Minutes passed, minutes which with air low and a long swim ahead of him, he could ill afford to waste. Nothing stirred except the restless circling and plopping of caged fish, and eventually with infinite caution he eased out the bolt cutters and snipped the two corner cables supporting the mesh, so that one whole side flapped downward and the salmon poured out below the surface in a silver tide. Moontide…

One down, five to go.

Still using the snorkel, with his body tight under the walkway, he moved hand over hand under the boards until he reached the other cages and did the same, but hardly was he beside the last and once again extracting the cutters than the halogen glare swept over the cages, lingered an instant, then returned to pinpoint him.

Before he could grab his regulator and submerge, a burst of shots made the water around him erupt in small explosions.

Close. Altogether too close.

Breathing out hard to deflate his BCD, he was sinking as fast as he could when an enormous blow struck him between the shoulders, jerking out his mouthpiece. Stunned and dizzy, he groped for his octopus, but water was already pouring in through the fractured regulator hose and as other blows struck him he knew his luck had run out at last.

Twenty minutes later, as McInnes moored and drew the cockpit cover over the sleek little launch, he heard the double blast of the old shotgun and grinned. That was the weapon Wully preferred and how he loved blazing away! It must make up for long dull hours with no company but that crotchety old dog.

He looked forward to hearing about it in the morning, but for now – he glanced at his watch – it was a bad strategy as well as bad manners to keep a lady waiting even if, in this particular case, it was far from certain that she was any kind of lady.

# CHAPTER SIX

# Ravenna

'WAKE UP, WOMAN! Time you were on your way!' McInnes removed his square brown hand from Ravenna's right breast and raised himself on one elbow to survey her. The opulence of Olympia's crimson silk bedspread was not entirely to his taste, but he had to admit it made a striking background for the creamy curves of her strong, well-muscled body, hair fanned out against the pillows, arms upflung like a sleeping baby.

'Too early. Leave me alone.'

'It's gone five, and the fish-bar opens at six. The lads will be bringing the boats in and I must take a look at the catch before they start yammering for their breakfast.'

'And pay them off.'

'Paperwork, transport, haulage… A business doesn't run itself, you know.'

'Oh, I know all right. Quite the tycoon these days, aren't you?' she mocked, turning on her side, then yelped as he slapped her naked rump, laughing as her eyes flashed open in outrage.

'You spanked me!'

'Aye, and you'll get the same again if you don't rouse up and get back in your duds.'

'If you dare touch me you'll be looking for another way to shift your clients. I mean it,' she warned as he raised his hand again.

He laughed. 'Come on now, Venny. You wouldn't do that to an old friend?'

'Like to bet?'

'I'm only trying to protect your reputation.'

'A likely tale.'

'It's true enough. Look, you've a good six miles of single-track before you get to the Kildrumna avenue, and that old banger of Hamish's will do well to average twenty on the coast road. If you're not back in your bed by the time your old man comes in from night fishing, he'll want to know the reason why.'

'That's where you're so, so wrong.' She rolled luxuriously on her back, greeny cat's-eyes slitted mockingly. 'Stop hustling and come back to bed. Why are you always in such a goddam hurry?'

But his mood had changed. 'Get up. I've work to do, even if you haven't. Do you want the world and his wife to know where you spent the night?'

'Why should I care?'

Her disdain for what others might think had both maddened and attracted him ever since they met. He slapped her again and caught her wrists when she grabbed his head and tried to yank out a handful of black curls.

'Brute!' she hissed.

'Go on with you. You always liked a bit of rough... I'll kiss it better. There! Now get going. I can't lie here all day.'

Still grumbling, she swung her legs to the floor and he watched critically as she dressed. 'You're putting on weight, Venny,' he said as she struggled with the waist button of her jeans. 'Are you pregnant?'

Her nose wrinkled. 'Not bloody likely.'

'Why's that?'

'Young girls are Gunnar's thing, didn't you know?' Her mouth turned down. 'The way he looks at that daughter of Martin Robb's – ugh! It makes me sick. He's besotted. He's always patting and hugging her, pretending to frighten her by jumping out of dark corners, making out it's a big joke.'

'How does she like that?'

'What do you expect? It's gone to her head completely. She twists him round her little finger. They make up fairytales, and play silly tricks on one another. Once she put a branch of bladderwrack in our bed and I put my foot on it.'

He laughed.

'You may think it funny, but I didn't. Typical schoolgirl. You should have heard her bossing him around when he took her diving, scolding him for not doing his safety checks the way she'd been taught. That would have made you laugh. He told her he'd been diving long before she was born, but she did that stop her? Not a bit of it. Nag, nag. Check this, test that. The look on his face!'

'He's done a fair bit of diving this week,' he said thoughtfully.' Davie McTavish told me he sent two cylinders in for re-filling a few days ago, and another four yesterday. That adds up to a good few hours underwater.'

She said offhandedly, 'That's what he's doing when he goes out night-fishing the sea-pools. Isn't it odd how he never seems to catch anything? You'll have to beef up your security if you want to keep him away from your fish.'

'Someone must be helping him. It's dangerous to dive alone at night.' He steepled his fingers, running through possibilities, testing and discarding them. 'I wonder who?'

'Does it matter? You've got a nightwatchman, haven't you?'

'Och, aye. Larsen would get more than he bargained for if he tried anything at night. Yanis said he was sniffing around the cages again in broad daylight yesterday. Brought the boat right up close and wouldn't back off until the police launch came out.'

He lit a cigarette and moved to the window, considering how best to undermine Gunnar's credibility. A paedophile scandal would suit him fine. 'Tell me about the girl. Shouldn't you have a word with her father?'

'Warn a copper his daughter's being groomed? That's a little above my pay-grade, mate. If he can't see what's under his nose, he's hardly likely to listen to me.'

'Copper?' he said, frowning. 'Robb?'

'DCI – didn't you know? Has your all-seeing, all-hearing grapevine missed a trick?'

'I thought he was just a bloke who'd lost his wife in a car crash. No one said he was a cop.'

'They don't always shout it from the rooftops, you know, especially when they're on holiday.'

She took a brush from her bag and began to force it through her long thick hair, cursing the tangles as she separated it into three hanks and pulled it over one shoulder to braid.

'That plait makes you look like a schoolgirl,' he needled.

'Excuse me! This is genuine Shield Maiden style circa 850 AD, according to my husband.' She secured the end with a twist and pulled it forward to lodge under her chin.

'You mean you let that old bully dictate your hairstyle? I thought you had more – more...'

'More what?'

'Self-respect. Sense.'

She stuffed the brush back in her bag and turned to confront him, hands on hips. 'Money and sense don't always go together. When you've seen how A-listers live – when you've been waiting on them, pandering to their whims and putting up with their insults for four long years – you start to want some of the action yourself. And, believe me, at that point a millionaire who says you're the girl he's looked for all his life has an undeniable appeal. If indulging his fantasies is part of the deal, it doesn't seem too high a price.'

'You've been lucky.'

'Took more than luck, I can tell you,' she snapped.

'Lucky to bring it off, I mean. Most rich old men can spot a gold-digger at fifty paces.'

'Don't call me that!'

'Isn't it the truth?

She smiled and wrinkled her nose. 'He's not that old. And I can tell you it took some doing.'

An uphill slog of scheming, tantalising, approaching, retreating before she had him hooked. Two whole years between deciding he ticked all the boxes and wedding bells.

He wouldn't leave it alone. 'So you showed him round and introduced him to the crew –'

'I happened to be assistant purser and my boss – er, happened – to be ashore.'

'– and you looked into each other's eyes, he was smitten, popped the question…'

'It wasn't quite like that.' Time and again she had thought he would escape her as she played him like a salmon, letting him run and then carefully, delicately, reeling him in again. Two years of agreeing, adapting, humouring his whims. She wasn't going to tell Dougie about that anxious hiatus; let him think she had secured her big fish with ease.

'What about the Happy Ever After, eh?'

She shrugged and waggled her fingers. 'Comme ci, comme ça. Nobody's perfect, you know. Men who marry late tend to be a bit – well, let's call it set in their ways.'

'Be honest.'

'He's a complete nightmare. Sometimes I think if he says, "my little Raven" just once more I'll explode.'

'You should have married me.'

She gave him a sideways look. 'You weren't much of a catch in those days. Besides, Isla got there first, didn't she? She made you what you are now – deny it if you dare. Taught you to speak proper, put you in touch with people who would give you a leg up? Without her you'd still be nothing but the Major's under-gardener. Gardener's boy, never on time, always in trouble. Too busy chasing skirts to attend to his work. Remember?'

That must have come from Danna, he thought. Who else still referred to old Philpott as 'the Major'?

'We didn't all have your educational advantages,' he said coolly. 'All right, Isla put me on the road, I'd be the last to deny that, but don't forget I've made my own way since we parted, and not done so ill, forbye.'

It amused her how his speech switched between English RP and Scots vernacular. Hallmark of a politico, she thought, a colour-changing chameleon. She said at random, 'I've heard you own half the businesses in Stairbrigg.'

Danna blabbing again, he thought, nodding. 'Aye, and I'd have the other half if yon busybodies in Scottish Bloody Heritage and your old man would take their fingers out of my affairs.'

'Don't worry, he won't be bothering you much longer. He's sailing up the Sound to Kinvarnoch. There's a Viking festival where they burn a replica longship. Just the kind of rubbish he loves.'

'You're not going with him?'

She shook her head. 'Not my scene. He's taking young Logan to crew for him – if he can get him away from his mamma. She thinks he has designs on her precious son, and she could be right.'

'That wouldn't surprise me.'

Ravenna smiled reminiscently. 'Logie's a big lad now, and it's time he cut the apron strings. I kissed him once when he landed a fish for me, so he thinks he's in love.'

'Ah, the classic triangle. Rich old git, sexpot wife, randy trainee – remind you of anything? Potiphar and his missus? Oedipus?'

'Wrong story, dumbo,' said Ravenna icily, swinging round from the mirror. 'Oedipus killed his father, not his boss.'

'So?'

'Don't be ridiculous.'

'But you'd admit your old man's looking for a successor, if only to keep Brother Bjorn and his brats at bay. Have you ever met Bjorn?'

'He came to our wedding. I thought he was charming and so was his wife.'

'Was she the third or fourth? I'd advise you to stay clear of Bjorn if you want to enjoy your golden meal-ticket, and while we're on the subject, try thinking ahead when you next feel the urge to canoodle with a minor. What a honeypot you are, to be sure. Who else at Kildrumna have you enslaved? Has the cop fallen victim to your charms?'

She gave him a sideways glance. 'Work in progress.'

'What about the Balfours?' He was always keen to hear how matters stood in the enemy camp.

'Oh, I get on OK with Jess, poor pet. Toils away from morning to night, is twice as clever as her husband, and is – how shall I put this? – not wholly indifferent to your own rough charms, according to various accounts.'

He grinned. 'What about that smug bastard Luke?'

'Oh, he's not so bad.'

'Privileged, entitled, born with a silver spoon in his mouth. Everything he's ever wanted handed to him on a plate. Harrow, Cambridge, family firm – and then a takeover that let him buy Kildrumna.'

'You have been doing your research!'

He ignored her mockery. 'I tell you, it makes me sick to see him there when he's never done an honest day's work in his life. Old Philpott would have sold to me –'

'To a damned Nat? I don't think so.'

'You know nothing about it. Along comes Luke Balfour with his godfather to bankroll him, and snaps up the whole place under my nose, then tries to turn it into something it was never meant to be. He should have stayed down south and practised his fancy fishing with barbless hooks in chalk streams with a bailiff to check licences instead of ruining a good Scottish river.'

She went on, 'Well, you'll be glad to hear that as regards Luke, I'm not exactly flavour of the month. He can't hide the fact that he doesn't like me. Doesn't trust me. Can't think why.'

'Don't be disingenuous. It doesn't suit you.'

'Because I have displaced him in Gunnar's affections?'

'Because you or your offspring must have displaced him in Gunnar's will. New wife, new will, eh? You'd better be careful he doesn't go tearing that up. I hope you've got a watertight pre-nup all signed and sealed?'

Ravenna was silent: too close to the bone. She had indeed angled for one but Gunnar insisted all that mattered was loyalty and trust.

Dougie's face darkened as he stubbed out his cigarette. He said with controlled anger, 'I've had about enough of him. His damned niggling and meddling is doing us real damage. He was behind the government's decision to publish all those photos of sick salmon taken by health inspectors. Over three hundred of them, and never mind the knock that'll give consumer confidence. We did our best to block their release, and a pretty penny it cost in lawyers' fees. I tell you I'll be glad to see that little green boat sail over the horizon and far, far away. Now I'm on the edge of the big time I don't want him snooping while the lads from the islands give Moontide the once-over.'

'And make you Chair of their consortium?'

'Maybe.'

'Have they signed on the dotted line?'

'None of your business, Venny. Until the deal's in the bag the less anyone knows the better. And that includes you.'

'Don't you trust me?'

'In a word, no. The temptation to mention it to your friends the Balfours might get the better of your famous discretion, my sweet.'

'Won't you be sorry to see me sail away on that little green boat?' she said, hamming up maiden-all-forlorn, but he was impatient for her to leave.

'You? Oh, you'll always fall on your feet,' he said indifferently, adding with sudden venom, 'But your man's an interfering old sod who should have been put out to grass years ago, and he's thick as thieves with those damned marine conservationists, for all he claims to be impartial. He wants to see over my fish farm before he reports to SNH, and that'll be another day's work wasted. In the office first, where no doubt I'll get a lecture about sustainability and pollution of the seabed; and after that I'll have to take him out to the feed barge and show him everything he wants to see. Correction: everything I want him to see.'

'Which might be rather different?'

His teeth flashed. 'What do you think?'

'You'd better be ready to turn on the rough charm.'

He yawned and stretched. 'And you'd best scoot before every tattletale in Stairbrigg tells him you're sleeping with me.'

'All right, all right, give me a chance. I'm going.'

'Off wi' ye, then. Same time, same place tomorrow?'

'You'll be lucky.'

She waited for him to kiss her or at least tell her he'd enjoyed their love-making, but he had turned away and was pulling on his shirt and jeans as she left the room. Isla might have taught him how to succeed in politics, but she'd done little to civilise him, she reflected. Perhaps she had preferred him as he was – a ruthless self-centred bastard, who cared little for her or any of his other women. So why, wondered Ravenna, did her heart speed up and her mouth go dry whenever she saw him? Why did she allow him to treat her as he did?

Pure animal attraction, she told herself crossly as she clattered down the uncarpeted stairs and out into the misty morning. Though he had not been much of a catch when she first knew him, things were different now. Very different. Besides, he'd always been a handsome hunk and his hard, muscular body did make a welcome change from sleeping with a blubbery old walrus who snorted and snuffled through the night and tickled her with his whiskers, but she wasn't going to risk her hard-earned golden meal ticket. If Big Dougie wanted her help to continue, his manners would need a significant upgrade.

Fierce though it was in the early hours, overnight the gale blew itself out, and the still, pellucid water of Kildrumna Bay glimmered like gold as McInnes set off from Stairbrigg on his PR campaign, with Jeannie Allan in the launch's cockpit and the other fish farmers settled in the stern.

A good sound sleep on The Old Anchor's memory-foam mattress and early morning tea had softened Jeannie's attitude towards her host. You can't judge a book by its cover or damn a man because his father was a rogue, she thought, glancing with approval at his long-nosed, square-jawed profile and competent hands. Beside the alert, freshly-shaved McInnes the other men looked half-asleep and frowsty, with rough hair and low-mow beards. Old Callum was nursing a hangover after hitting the grain on top of the grape, and Bruce McEachran's eyes were bleary and bloodshot.

'The sort of morning that makes you glad to be alive!' she declared with a brightness that the others found offensive and made no effort to answer. 'I see you've plenty of seals here in the bay,' she remarked, turning to McInnes, and he flashed her a rueful grin.

'Too many – but what can you do? The tourists like watching them and the conservationists won't hear of culling. There's a big nursery on that skerry – over there to the right – and SNH has put it off limits. No one's allowed to land there to avoid disturbing them, and I can tell you in autumn when the pups are born the noise does your head in.'

'Target practice!' shouted Bruce McEachran, his weatherbeaten face looming over from the stern. 'Great sport. Ye've got to be quick, mind. Every time a little round head pops up, give it a blast. I've shot dozens of the thieving buggers this year alone. Have ye tried it, Lady Jean? I hear ye're a grand shot.'

Jeannie pursed disapproving lips, but Dougie said easily, 'Och, man, they're no' so bad. I like to see them, myself. Balance of nature, you know.'

'Sod the balance of nature,' muttered McEachran, and Jeannie gave him a look of dislike. Did she really want to join forces with such a barbarian?

In silence they crossed the turbulent waters of the Reekie and rounded the point into the mouth of Kildrumna Bay, smooth as glass under the shelter of Cruach Cormac, but even from a distance it was plain to the visitors that all was not as it should be. McInnes's shoulders tensed as he gripped the wheel: in the few hours since he left the feed barge something had gone very wrong.

An eerie moaning and splashing was coming from the nearest cage, and though the McTavish boys would not be clocking on for another hour and Wully should still be on duty, the cabin door was ajar and Nipper, who usually announced visitors with a volley of barks, was uncharacteristically silent.

As he cut the engine and brought the launch gliding up against the boardwalk, McInnes caught sight of a bulky body thrashing against a loose section of net in which it was entangled, the mesh wound tightly from flippers to tail. A dark bloom of blood stained the water within and without the breached cage, and the high keening, grunting sounds came from the remains of a seal's sleek head with most of the lower jaw missing.

'God in heaven!' Jeannie leaned over the gunwale, looking sick. She turned to McInnes and grabbed the wheel. 'Quick, man!' she ordered. 'Finish it off. Hurry!'

Scrambling up in a daze, trying to take in the scale of the calamity, he jumped the gap from the launch, stumbled on the boardwalk and shoved the cabin door fully open. Sprawled in his chair, snoring and dead to the world, was Wully, an empty bottle at his feet and the air thick with the reek of skunk. There was no sign of Nipper.

Seizing the Beretta from its hiding place and checking the magazine, McInnes ducked out of the cabin again and shot the injured seal at point blank range, sending a fountain of bloody water over the launch and its occupants. The flailing body subsided into spasmodic twitches and when it was still, he turned away, unwilling to face the expressions of his would-be colleagues. Grim-faced, he inspected the other cages: empty, all of them, their netting sagging loosely and the cables that anchored them to the walkway cleanly severed. Rage swept over him, choking up his throat.

'There's nae a seal on airth could dae that,' muttered McEachran, joining him. He picked up a metal end and examined it. 'Yon's the work o' someone wha doesna care for ye, laddie.'

McInnes nodded. 'Sabotage,' he growled, adding silently, 'I know exactly who did it, and that bastard's going to pay in blood.'

# CHAPTER SEVEN

# The Big Fish

'WHAT TIME DID Gunnar get in?' Luke asked his wife as she stirred the bubbling vat of oatmeal that had soaked in the bottom oven all night.

'What time did you?' She gave him a quick, anxious glance before returning her attention to the pot. Luke's face was grey under its usual tan, and dark circles under his eyes were evidence of sleeplessness.

She knew he had failed to find Gunnar down at the Lower Clinie Pool after supper, and had gone out again when she was in bed. As usual she had slept heavily, but at some level she'd been conscious of him moving about in the bedroom, pulling the curtain across to stop moonlight shining into her eyes; then later – much later – she had put out a hand in the darkness and found his side of the bed empty and cold. When was that: late night or early morning? He was a poor sleeper and when worried about their finances he would often wake at dawn and go down to the river to watch the sunrise and remind himself why this place was worth everything they put into it.

And it was, it was! She never needed reminding, however demanding the guests or rough the weather.

'That brute Yanis has been shooting seals again,' she said, and he turned sharply.

'Shooting at? Or shooting to kill? He says he only tries to scare them off.'

'Then how come the two seals washed up at Cladh nan Ron on Monday had bullet holes in their skulls?'

Luke said angrily, 'That's illegal! They're a protected species and this is a conservation area. You need a licence to shoot them, and Yanis hasn't got one. The Tourist Board was getting too many complaints so Marine Scotland refused Moontide's renewal application.' He began dropping cutlery on the table helicopter-style, muttering, 'I'll bloody well ring McInnes and have it out with him. He can't simply ignore his employees breaking the law.'

'Remember when they tried those Acoustic Deterrent Devices which sent whales and dolphins doolally? Marine Scotland didn't approve of them, either.'

Luke shook his head despairingly. 'It reminds me of playing noughts and crosses as a child. Whatever you did would get blocked and this is the same. The fish farms aren't wholly to blame, because once seals know where they can get an easy meal it's difficult to keep them off, and there are an awful lot of them on the Skerries. I've seen them crowd up against the wire and literally suck salmon through the netting. They soon get used to any kind of deterrent except a bullet.'

'Hardly surprising when the oceans are being stripped of the wretched creatures' natural food so that it can be ground into meal and fed to their natural prey huddled together just out of their reach,' said Jess, on auto-pilot. This was ground they had been over so many times that they had almost stopped being angry about it.

They stared at each other, and she said with sudden energy, 'Whatever one thinks of Gunnar – and as you know I'm not his greatest fan – you have to admire him for fighting it all the way. He could have stood back when he lost so much money on the trawlers, and said he'd done his bit and now someone else could hold the ring between fish farmers and conservationists, but here he is, still committed to protecting the underdog and speaking truth to power, just as we were taught to at school, but most people soon decide it's not worth the hassle.'

'I haven't.'

'Thank God. And nor have I. But it's uphill work keeping the faith.'

It was on the tip of his tongue to ask if she had been helping *What's Good for You?* with their articles, but as usual he shied away from confrontation and decided it was better not to know for sure.

Jess said, 'I've asked Olympia to come across and cut my hair before it drives me mad. Do you want her to do yours, too?'

He ran a hand across his head. 'Um, well – maybe. I've got a lot to do today.'

'Yes or no?' she said impatiently.

'What time?'

'She said she could pop across when she's finished the fishermen's breakfast... say 11.30. I'll see what she has to say about those seals.'

'OK, but go easy on her,' warned Luke. 'It may not be Yanis at all. I know he sometimes leaves those boys in charge when he's helping out in the Fish Bar.'

'Alick and Hamish McTavish?'

'That's right. Davie the Dive Shop lets them both run wild. Typical teenagers. I can quite imagine one of them picking up a gun and having a go at a tempting target.' He turned as the side door crashed open to admit Ravenna with a flushed and triumphant Marina, carrying a wicker basket overflowing with a golden mass of chanterelles.

Jess looked at it with dismay. 'Oh, poppet!' she said weakly. 'We can't possibly eat that many. Put them on the draining board and I'll deal with them later.'

'We went out early so we could have them for breakfast. Dad loves them,' said Marina, her smile fading, and Jess capitulated with an inward sigh. Beautiful as they looked when raw, the little fungi would disintegrate into a watery greyish mush in the frying pan – mush generally leavened with a quantity of grit.

'OK, I'll cook them right away, before he comes down.'

Back came the smile at full wattage. 'Cool! I'll clean them up, no worries. There's hardly any earth and no maggots at all; Venny made me throw out anything with nibbled bits. But, you know, there are thousands and thousands more. Danna showed me a really good place.'

'This is plenty to be going on with,' said Jess firmly. 'Coffee, Ravenna? You look as if you could do with it after your exertions.'

She certainly did, thought Luke, curious as to the nature of those exertions. Blooming, glowing, she radiated health and... what? Satisfaction, he decided. Like a sleek, beautiful panther digesting a fawn. Now why? Or rather, why now? Where had she been and what had she been doing?

Sleepless as the skies began to lighten towards dawn, and uneasy that he had not heard Gunnar's heavy step on the stairs, he had slid out of bed and wandered along the wooded path towards the Rock Pool. Looking back towards Stairbrigg to watch the rising sun, he saw the twin glow of sidelights turn off the single-track road at the ivy-covered gateposts which marked the limit of the Kildrumna demesne. There they were doused completely.

In and out of the trees bumped the shadowy vehicle, creeping along the rutted track, the only moving object in the still landscape, and he watched until it vanished at the junction where one branch led to the Lodge and the other to Inverclinie village.

Minutes later, he saw a tall figure shrouded in a hooded cloak come swinging back along the track and take the fork towards the Lodge, running lightly up the two flights of steps to the gunroom door where it was again lost to view. Ravenna's cloak, he thought with certainty.

Where had she been? The early hour, doused lights, and the way she had hurried along in shadow suggested haste and secrecy. Though it was no part of his job as host to monitor the movements of his guests, Luke could not help wondering why she had so clearly chosen a night when Gunnar would be out on the river. None of my business, he thought, but a flicker of doubt about his godfather's marriage would not be dispelled.

"He treats her like a child," Jess had whispered that first evening; and even Luke had sensed something artificial, even stagey, about the submissive way Ravenna accepted her husband's advice, orders and frequent criticism. Beyond his orbit, alone with Jess or even Robb, she was very different, a person in her own right with ideas and opinions far removed from that childish persona.

This morning was a case in point. The early exercise had given her an extra glow of health and vitality, beside which his dear Jess looked faded and worn. She works too hard, he thought. At the end of the season I will – I really must – take her on a real holiday, somewhere sunny where she can forget all about household chores for a week or two. We could close up Kildrumna and fly out to visit her sister in the Cape; walk in the Drakensberg, perhaps...

He became aware that people were looking at him. Someone had asked a question and was waiting for his answer. 'Sorry. I was dreaming. Say again?'

'What was the biggest salmon ever caught here?' said Marina, blushing as faces turned towards her.

Luke saw her grip her elbows in the telltale sign of a panic attack, and said quickly, 'Danna caught a whopper back in 1998. A real whopper. Forty-two pounds, I think it was. I'll show you the photograph old Philpott took – it's on my desk. I keep it there to show our tenants what they might catch if they're very very lucky.'

He returned with the commemorative photograph in its big red leather frame and put it in front of Marina. Everyone crowded round to look.

'Tell us about it,' said Ravenna, peering at the caption neatly written with a mapping pen in black ink:

*Danna Murison. 42LBS. August 20, 1998. Slithers*

'Well, Danna was ghillying for Olaf Larsen – Gunnar's father – and while he was snoozing in the sun after eating his piece, Danna says he just flicked a little black Zulu into the water under the bank at the top end of Slithers on the Dunseran, where your dad was fishing the other day, and this enormous fish took the fly. You must get him to tell you about it himself.'

Marina had released her elbows and leaned forward, eagerly scanning the photograph of Danna and his record catch. In the foreground was the diminutive ghillie, grinning from ear to ear, years younger but instantly recognisable, holding upright a thick-bodied salmon that reached as high as his shoulders. Carefully posed against the backdrop of the lodge, leaning on sticks or sitting on the low walls flanking the front step, a motley collection of servants and guests gazed admiringly at his great catch.

'Who are they all?' asked Marina.

'Danna told me that old Philpott wanted everyone who worked here to be in the picture. Made Mrs Lloyd, the cook, leave the joint to look after itself, and roped in all the gardeners and ghillies. That's the Major, in the middle, with the moustache, and beside him is his niece, Isla. Such a lovely girl – I'm told her hair was so long she could sit on it. You were at school with her, weren't you, Ravenna?'

'She was a year ahead of me, so I didn't know her well, but yes: it's true about her hair – and it was an amazing colour, too. Real spun gold. One summer when my parents were abroad, she kindly asked me to stay here during the holidays.' She sighed. 'Looking back, it seems like a dream – the sea, the sun, the freedom... Oh, it was wonderful. They were all so kind. The Major – and Isla, too. I had a real crush on her.'

Jess left the stove and came round the table to join them. 'Beautiful, yes; but quite strange, according to Mhairi. Contrary. Impulsive.' She smiled, 'Mhairi wouldn't say so, but frankly I thought Isla sounded a right little madam.'

'And that couple over there, on the right, are Gunnar's parents, Olaf and Christina,' said Luke.

Marina stared at them. Gunnar's mother was a tall, statuesque blonde, her hair piled high with combs, while Olaf's thick eyebrows and jutting jaw reminded her of someone.

'There's Mhairi,' she said, pointing.

'That's right, and the girl next to her is her sister Elspeth. They both worked in the house. Of course they all look older now. And that –' his finger pointed at a thickset, dark-haired young man whose rebellious expression made it clear that he, at least, had no intention of smiling to order – 'that, if you can believe it, is none other than our local bigwig, Dougal McInnes, in what you might call his chrysalis phase.'

Marina caught the note of sarcasm and looked up quickly. 'The fish-farm man? Why is he in the photograph?'

'Because at the time his father was the Major's gardener, though I must admit I find that hard to remember when I hear him spouting his political rubbish nowadays. Scotland for the Scots, and all that. He ran off with Isla, which scuppered his chances of getting a job with Major Philpott, but I suppose in a way that was the making of him...' Luke broke off and turned, as the kitchen door was flung open. 'Ah, here comes your dad,' he told Marina, 'Just in time for the last of the chanterelles. But what have we here?'

Robb entered, beaming. 'Special delivery!' he announced, lifting both hands to display a shining silver grilse wrapped in dock leaves, which he deposited ceremoniously on the table in front of his daughter.

'Dad!'

'I hope you don't mind but after such a struggle I couldn't bear to put it back,' he said to Luke.

'Good lord, no. What a beauty – well done!' Luke schooled his features to display nothing but approval although he could see at a glance that Robb's prize was a gravid hen who would have been better returned to the water. Too late for that, so what else could he say in the face of Robb's delight?

'Up and down the pool we went. Time and again I thought I'd lost it. In fact I doubt if I'd ever have landed it if young Logan hadn't come by on his 4x4. You see, I'd left my net on the other side when I crossed the bridge, basic error, but I thought I could pick it up on my way back, and as it was I had just about decided to head for home when this fellow took the fly. That's why I'm so late. Actually, I don't suppose he was on for more than ten minutes, but it felt like eternity.'

Questions came thick and fast: which pool? What fly? From the bank or in the water? Marina had never seen her father so talkative, so lit up, and wished she had been with him at the scene of his triumph. Mushroom-hunting had been less fun than she expected. Ravenna had been dreamy and abstracted, hardly paying attention to Marina's chatter except to insist on throwing out any fungi that looked discoloured or dirty, and kept urging Marina to hurry in case they were late for breakfast.

She said, 'Where's Gunnar? We must keep some chanterelles for him,' but Ravenna shook her head.

'He's won't be here for breakfast. He told me he meant to take *Shield Maiden* over to the boatyard at Templeport, to get the engine checked before he takes her up to that Viking festival at Kinvarnock. And when he gets back from Templeport he's got a date to see Dougal McInnes at the Smokery before inspecting the fish farm.'

'Then I won't see him at all today,' said Marina, disappointed. 'He said if it was fine he'd take me to explore the wreck properly. It's amazing what you see down at the bottom, and the fish almost bump into you. They're not at all scared. The colours are fantastic, too. When will he be back?'

'What's this Viking festival all about?' cut in Robb, correctly interpreting Ravenna's glance as a plea for help. Marina could be very persistent: it was difficult to deal with her whims without sending her into what she called the 'black wave' of gloom or a full-blown panic attack, and just lately he had begun to wonder if she was deliberately exploiting this mental fragility. Surely not? Would his youngest daughter be so devious?

He couldn't help noticing that these meltdowns appeared to be triggered by any setback to her personal plans, and had been privately horrified by how quickly she had picked up the jargon of the child psychiatrists he had consulted. Part of him longed to tell her to snap out of it and do as she was told, because she couldn't expect to have everything her own way; and part of him was – well, frightened – of what such directness might provoke. Rage? Depression? Self-harm? Even the ultimate possibility he shrank from thinking about.

So he said as unemphatically as possible, 'Time and space, sweetheart. Gunnar's got a busy day. He's going to have difficulty cramming all that in without taking you diving as well.'

'He promised,' said Marina mutinously, tearing her toast into tiny pieces and arranging them round the edge of her plate. 'He's going to show me a secret cave. Tomorrow the sea will be too rough. Didn't you hear the forecast?'

There was an awkward silence, and then both Luke and Jess began describing the Viking festival which had sprung into being only ten years ago and now attracted visitors from all over the world.

'Completely phoney, of course,' said Luke. 'Horned helmets, hairy men marching about wearing swords and shields and lots of trumpet-blowing, though they don't call them trumpets.'

'Trombones?' suggested Robb. 'Pipes? Slughorns? Yards of tin?'

'No, no. Some Gaelic word – or perhaps it's Norse. They parade up and down the harbour and make speeches, and when it's nearly dark they drag this longship onto the beach and set fire to it, while all the tourists snap away, and the whole thing ends in a tremendous booze-up.'

'Followed by a tremendous hangover,' said Jess. 'I told you, it's completely phoney, but it raises a lot of money which a place like that can certainly do with. Perhaps we should start one here.'

Everyone laughed, but Marina leaned forward again, her face alight with interest. Drama was far and away her greatest enthusiasm at school.

'Oh yes! That would be great. Something different from Vikings, though – 'she thought for a moment – 'you could make it about sea-stories and legends, and call it, um... Monsters, Mermaids and Myths. Or... wait... I've got it. Call it 'Kingdom of the Sea,' and get Gunnar to organise it: he'd do it brilliantly. He loves all the old stories and songs and he's got a terrific imagination. He could be Neptune, calling the shots and ruling his kingdom under the waves.'

I wonder if she's got something there, thought Luke. After all, it was Gunnar's streak of romanticism that had brought him here in the first place, and fuelled his determination to stop McInnes and his cronies from wrecking it. Why else would he have bankrolled Kildrumna so lavishly when anyone could see it was a bottomless pit of expense? But wouldn't a festival of the kind Marina envisaged be just another kind of exploitation? Attracting hordes of tourists to trample and pollute the land just as the fish farm polluted the sea?

'If you held it next summer, I could help, couldn't I, Dad?' said Marina eagerly. 'Remember that pageant our village did about flying, From Icarus to Stealth? This could be a sea version, with Danna telling spooky stories about Krakenwakes and monster snakes, and Mhairi singing ballads and sea shanties, and – and – fifteen men on a dead man's chest, and fishwives gutting caller herring on the strand... I could be Grace Darling...'

'Steady on,' said Robb, laughing.

'Don't forget Red Donald's Skillet,' called Jess over her shoulder from the stove. 'That's our local spine-chiller.'

'Who was Red Donald?'

Luke took up the tale. 'A particularly nasty red-bearded chief whose clan ruled this part of the coast. He had a beautiful daughter – don't they all? – but no son, and when he was getting old he announced that any man who wanted to succeed him would have to row across the very dangerous whirlpool just around the headland from here and fetch back his daughter's gloves from a rock on the other side. So one after another his rivals attempted it and were drowned. Then a bright spark named Callum persuaded Donald's beautiful daughter (who was in love with him) to give him an identical pair of gloves, waited for a foggy day, when the sea-fret lay like a blanket, and launched his boat as if to cross the whirlpool, but actually stayed in the safe water on its rim.'

'The dirty cheat,' said Robb. 'Then I suppose he produced the gloves and claimed the prize.'

'Exactly.'

'And they all lived happily ever after,' finished Marina, who liked a satisfactory end to stories.

'Not sure about that bit,' said Luke. 'Anyway, that whirlpool has been known thereafter as Red Donald's Skillet, because it's rather the shape of a frying pan, with the handle stretching back to Craig Head.'

Now Marina had the bit between her teeth. 'Oh, why isn't Gunnar here? I know he'd love it. I'm going to write down all my ideas and show them to him the minute he gets back.'

'After you've given Jess a hand with the washing-up,' said Robb, but too late. His daughter had darted out of the room and the door crashed behind her.

'Seems like you've started something,' murmured Luke to his wife.

Withdrawing his attention from the conversation, he began to worry: where was Gunnar? He had known this week was liable to be tricky because his godfather not only liked to have him and Jess dancing attendance during his visits but took a keen pleasure in keeping them guessing about his movements. It was no use expecting him to make a plan and stick to it: Plan A might without warning be replaced with Plan B or even C. Take this sudden proposal to sail up the Firth to Kinvarnoch's Viking beano. He had never even mentioned it to Luke, but now it sounded as if they would be unlikely to see him again until Wednesday at the earliest, and that was when the new fishing guests would arrive.

Luke had cleared his diary and kept these vital weeks free – apart from agreeing to Amyas's plea to host Robb and his difficult daughter – but on Monday Kildrumna Fishing must be back in business or the year's accounts would look even worse than they did already, and Gunnar would have every excuse to cut up rough about them.

Oh, lord! he thought helplessly. Why were other people so awkward? The Robbs had been no problem, so far; and the difficult daughter had actually been quite useful in the matter of keeping Gunnar amused – he took a childish pleasure in arguing with her and in their silly practical jokes – but as soon as next week's serious fishermen arrived, schoolgirl pranks would have to stop.

By noon, news of the mass break-out from the salmon cages had reached everyone in Stairbrigg. With a thunderous face, McInnes watched the four SUVs wheel out of the Old Anchor car park and bump away up the single-track to Templeport. And that's the last I'll be seeing of them, he thought grimly.

Each of his potential colleagues had reacted differently to the debacle: 'Haddock' Finlay vowed revenge on all saboteurs while old Callum shook his fuzzy head sadly. 'This is the thanks you get for putting this wee toun on the map,' he mourned. 'Ingratitude more sharp than serpent's tooth.'

Red-faced Bruce McEachran slapped him on the shoulder and urged him to take it on the chin.

'Brace up, man. Don't let it get to you. Install CCTV and beef up your security. Show them you're in it for the long haul.'

Yet none of the men mentioned the consortium, waiting for a lead from Lady Jean, who said nothing, waxed cotton hat-brim pulled low and rat-trap mouth tight shut. She had followed McInnes into the cabin and listened silently to Wully's tale of woe. Nipper had gone into the water after a seal and been swept away – Nipper, reared from a pup and the canniest tyke on the whole West Coast, had leaned too far and slipped off the walkway; borne away by the current before his master could grab the long-handled net to scoop him to safety.

'So you sat here and drank yourself stupid,' raged McInnes, keeping his voice low. 'You've your mobile. Why didn't you call me? You knew I'd be here early. You knew I'd be bringing visitors. Why...' He stopped abruptly, noticing Jeannie's presence behind him as Wully subsided, mumbling excuses, a heap of misery. 'Come on, let's get back ashore. I'll deal with this lot later.'

In strained silence they returned to the jetty, then made their excuses and left, the men muttering awkwardly that they'd be in touch very soon. This he doubted. More likely they would order stiff drinks at the Templeport ferry terminal and resolve that, Smokery or no Smokery, they wanted nothing more to do with Moontide. In salmon farming as in any food-production business, consumer confidence is key, and this morning's fiasco had given his reputation such a nasty knock that no one was likely to risk associating themselves with him. The prize he had manoeuvred towards with such care had been snatched from his grasp and McInnes had no need of outside advice about revenge.

He was aware that though widely respected in Stairbrigg, he was not universally loved and, as he returned to his office in the Smokery, even the commiserations of neighbours and colleagues like Davie McTavish seemed to hold hints of schadenfreude: there is, after all, an undeniable pleasure in watching a friend fall off a roof, and those whose toes he had trodden on in his ascent found it hard to conceal their secret satisfaction at seeing him cut down to size.

Don't get mad, get even, he thought, rehearsing the coming interview with Gunnar Larsen as he ate a sandwich lunch at his desk. Be cool, unconcerned; dismiss today as a minor setback. These things happen when you deal with wildlife, he imagined himself saying. You can't blame the seals. Yes, talks with the Islands producers were still ongoing, and he'd already rung the hatcheries about re-stocking.

'When Mr Larsen comes, show him straight to my office,' he told young Donny Pearson, his assistant. 'Coffee first, and we'll give him a taste of smoked salmon before going round the Smokery.'

'Verra guid, sir.' Donny had the sense not to ask if they would be visiting the cages later.

'And tell Ishbel to bring our inspection reports for the past three years,' McInnes added, seating himself in the big swivel chair that faced the sea so that his visitor would have his back to the light. No sense in drawing his attention to the intense activity around the cages as Yanis and the boys cleared and replaced the damaged netting.

Posed and poised, with temper under control and stats at his fingertips, he waited for Gunnar to keep the rendezvous.

And waited. An hour passed. Ninety minutes. McInnes was not a patient man, and when the clock's hands crept towards five, he picked up his mobile.

'This is Ravenna's voicemail,' she purred after six rings. 'Sorry I can't take your call right now, but leave a message and I'll come back to you as soon as I can.'

Just when would that be? He needed an answer at once. Drumming his fingers on the windowsill, itching to get out to the cages and restore order, he imagined her glancing at her little screen, recognising his number and deciding she'd give him a few hours to simmer down before telling him what he wanted. Or perhaps she was working on an alibi? She must know what her husband had done and where he was now.

He thought back. When had he noticed that *Shield Maiden* had left her mooring? Someone had told him she had been taken for an engine check at Templeport – but who?

The intercom beeped. Ishbel said nervously, 'Mr Balfour's on the line, sir. Shall I put him through?'

'Of course.'

'Sorry to bother you at a busy time, McInnes.' Luke's hesitant, apologetic manner strongly suggested he had been forced against his will to make this call. 'Um... er... I gather that Gunnar Larsen had an appointment with you today, and I need to get hold of him rather urgently. I wondered –'

'He hasn't shown. I've wasted all afternoon waiting for him,' said McInnes with barely controlled anger. 'Where is he? Have you asked his wife? As you've probably heard, my fish cages were vandalised last night, and it looks very much as if he had a hand in it.'

'Good God! You can't think he had anything to do with that, surely?' Luke sounded genuinely shocked.

'I can and I do,' said McInnes grimly, 'and until I find out what he was doing last night and where he is now I shall go on thinking it. His boat's gone –'

'That's what I wanted to tell him. A couple of my men found her aground in one of those small inlets opposite Cruach Cormac – I don't know what it's called because it's not marked on the map – but we know it as Crab Cove.'

McInnes' attention sharpened and the knuckles of his hand showed white. An inlet off Cruach Cormac? Just where he least wanted Balfour and his louts messing about. 'How did that happen?' he asked curtly.

'We – um, well, they – think she must have dragged her anchor when it came on to blow last night, and ran aground.'

He paused for a moment, then added uncertainly, 'She's a bit scraped though she was still more or less afloat, but there's equipment missing: Larsen's dry-suit and BCD, and one of the cylinders from the locker.' Another silence developed before he said in a lower tone, 'I'm afraid he may have had an accident.'

'Who found the boat?'

'Danna Murison. You know him, of course?'

'Of course.' That superannuated old meddler, always telling tales out of school and poking his nose in where it wasn't wanted, thought McInnes furiously. Yes, it would be him.

'He was bringing his catch home just after dawn, and says he caught a glimpse of green as he passed the mouth of Crab Cove – there's a dog-leg and a bit of a sandbar, but it opens out beyond it into a kind of lagoon with cliffs and caves at the far end.'

Dog-leg, sandbar, bit of a lagoon…yes, he knew them very well.

The hesitant voice went on, 'Danna didn't pay much attention at the time, but later when he'd offloaded his fish, he mentioned it to young Logan, who ghillies for me, and they went past the dog-leg right into the cove, and there was *Shield Maiden* aground on the shingle, close up against the cliff.'

'Go on,' said McInnes when he stopped. 'What did they do then?'

'They couldn't refloat her immediately because the tide was out, but they went aboard and that's when they saw the scuba gear was missing. I've been trying to get hold of Larsen ever since, but his mobile's not answering and it's beginning to look pretty bad.'

Silence again as the implications sank in, then Luke said heavily, 'I think – I'm very much afraid – I ought to call in the police.'

'Now hold your horses, Balfour!' said McInnes sharply. The last thing he wanted was police divers swarming over the area, examining the vandalised cages, questioning Yanis and the boys. Who knows what they would find? What they would uncover? He must at all costs keep control of events before they spun out of his hands. 'I know the place you're describing – it's that odd little kink in the coastline just beyond the belt of pines. I'll send a team down to recover the boat –'

'Oh, we've done that already. Once the tide was up she refloated with no trouble, and we brought her back round here to see if we could work out what happened.'

Hell!

'But I really do think I ought to –'

'Look, Balfour. Before you start panicking and ringing 999, ask yourself just what you're going to say to the police? What grounds do you have for calling them in? Just because Larsen's boat ran aground last night and you can't contact him isn't evidence that there's been any sort of accident. Why not wait until you've spoken to his wife – where is she, by the way? There may be some simple explanation, and you'll feel every kind of fool for going over the top before you've heard it.'

'We-ell...' Luke hesitated.

McInnes sensed he was winning. 'Give it a few hours, make basic enquiries, and I'm sure you'll find out why Larsen's gone AWOL,' he said forcefully. 'Meanwhile, I'll ask around and see what I can do from this end. Wasn't there some suggestion of a Viking festival he wanted to see? He could have decided to go there by road if the engine of his boat was playing up, and that would have meant starting early.'

'You could be right,' said Luke, ever polite though he didn't believe a word McInnes said. What was perfectly plain was that he had no intention of helping search for Gunnar, nor did he want the police to investigate his disappearance. 'OK, then. Sorry to have bothered you. I'll keep in touch.'

He rang off and sat for a few moments at his desk, staring at a pod of dolphins larking round a solitary lobster boat that was chugging slowly towards the Inverclinie jetty. Then he sighed deeply and went in search of Robb.

He found him on the big lawn in front of the house, cursing steadily as he tried with clumsy fingers to disentangle a cat's cradle of overrun line in the reel of a spinning-rod, while Danna stood a few yards away, obviously longing to take over. Beyond them Marina was practising Spey casting, sending graceful loops of line through the air in low figures-of-eight.

'Do buck up, Dad,' she said impatiently. 'Let Danna sort it out or we'll never get there.'

Luke halted beside her. 'Where are you off to now?'

Words spilled out of her: as usual he had to concentrate hard to catch and make sense of the rippling stream. 'We had no luck on the Clinie this morning because the water's still too low, just as you said, but now I'm longing to go up the Dunseran and try that little stream that runs out of Michie's Run, below the rocks – you know where I mean? It looks just the place for a fish to rest and wait for a spate before tackling the waterfall, but it's overhung with branches, so I thought if Dad tried spinning from this bank, and I crossed the bridge and followed him down on the other side, casting under the trees...'

'Sounds a good plan to me,' said Luke. 'Why don't you and Danna go on ahead and I'll bring your father up to join you in, say, half an hour? There's something I want to discuss with him first.'

Marina smiled broadly. 'Cool. See you in a bit, then. Come on, Danna, we're off,' she called. 'Can I sit in front?'

As the little crawler bumped away, Luke turned to Robb, the familiar anxiety clouding his face. 'Sorry to butt in like that, but I wonder if you'd mind giving me some advice?'

Though his voice was carefully calm, Robb saw that his hands were shaking. 'Professional advice, you mean?'

'Well, yes. I'm afraid so.'

Bang goes my lovely, mindless freedom, thought Robb, but his face remained impassive. 'Of course I will. Tell me about it – come on, we can talk as we walk.'

As they set off in pursuit of the Argocat, Luke said awkwardly, 'I – I didn't want to mention it in front of your daughter, but something's come up – or may have come up – that's worrying the hell out of me, and I just don't know what to do.'

'Something to do with Gunnar?' Robb guessed as his heart sank. Gone off on his own, worrying his unfortunate host sick: par for the course.

Luke nodded. 'I can't get hold of him. No one seems to know where he is.'

'Surely his wife does?'

'Apparently not. She's not bothered because she says he often disappears like this. She used to get frantic when he went walkabout without telling her, but now she's schooled herself just to wait until he comes back. Says this is typical. He switches off his mobile and goes missing. Something about his wild Norse blood and needing his freedom. Bollocks. I think he likes stirring things up, getting everyone in a stew so that he can breeze in a couple of days later asking what all the fuss is about. That's really what's stopping me from calling the police.'

'Have you yourself ever known him do such a thing?'

'Well, yes,' said Luke unhappily. 'I've known him a long time and we've had a lot of – well – adventures, I suppose you'd call them. Or misadventures, depending on your point of view. Tight spots, anyway, and they've nearly all come about because he's such a chancer.'

'Meaning what, exactly?'

'I mean,' said Luke, and now there was a touch of anger in his voice, 'that if there are two ways of doing something, one safe and the other dangerous, he'll always choose the second. He teases me because I'm naturally cautious. I don't see the point of deliberately putting yourself in danger.'

'But he likes the buzz?'

'That's it exactly. I think it's hard-wired into him, and that's why I'm uneasy about this particular disappearing act. When I rang McInnes just now, he made it pretty clear that he thinks Gunnar was responsible for last night's breakout at the fishcages, and Big Dougie's not the man to take something like that lying down. He's got his reputation to consider. He's got fingers in every pie locally, owns half the businesses in Stairbrigg, and I reckon a lot of fishermen are in his pay, knowing he'll persuade the cops to turn a blind eye to minor infringements of rules on quotas and so on. I don't want to sound over-dramatic, but if McInnes were to set his hounds on dear old Gunnar, I wouldn't give much for his chances.'

For a time they walked in silence as Robb considered this. It didn't sound likely, but on the other hand he didn't think Luke was the type to panic for no reason. Over-conscientious – yes. A worrier – yes, but not an hysteric by any stretch of the imagination. And on this wild, lonely coast, beside the enormous, relentless sea, aware that an aggrieved Mr Big would be burning for revenge... perhaps he had reason to worry.

Hints of Dougal McInnes' ruthless acquisition of Stairbrigg businesses and manipulation of local authority members by well-tested carrot-and-stick methods – golf club dinner invitations on the one hand or threats to vote against pet projects on the other – had reached him from odd quarters over the past week, though principally from Jess and tattle-tale Danna, but how much of this was factually true and how much exaggerated by their visceral dislike of anyone engaged in fish-farming was hard to assess.

Was Luke making a mountain out of a molehill? By his own admission Gunnar was an eccentric, rich and wayward, and had a long history of getting into – and out of – tight spots just for the hell of it. Was this a tight spot he couldn't get out of? Or needed his godson's help to get out of?

It sounded to him as if Ravenna had wised up to her husband's quirks and was determined to ignore them as one would overlook the bad behaviour of a child.

Luke was watching him anxiously. Robb said, 'It seems to me as if you've got three options. One, call in the police and risk looking an ass for making a fuss about nothing if he turns up in a couple of days right as rain. Two, do nothing and hope for the best. Three, let me see what I can sort out. Correction: let me give my sergeant a call and see what we can sort out together.'

Relief broke over Luke's tired face. He was by nature a conciliator, not a leader, who hated being put on the spot and preferred decisions to be taken by someone else. 'Would you do that? Option Three, I mean?'

'Of course. though I can't promise any better outcome than if you chose One or Two.'

'Better than doing nothing, though. I'm haunted by the thought that Gunnar may be in trouble, and I'm in a state of suspended animation because I don't know where the hell to start looking for him.' He shook himself. 'Sorry! Let's be practical. We've got a new party coming in next week, but I'm sure we can find room for your sergeant. Is he a fisherman?'

Robb grinned. 'Not as you and I understand it. Jim's a city boy, but he's mad about cetaceans – whales, dolphins, you name it. Even goes looking for sharks, which would scare the living daylights out of me. He showed me a pic of an enormous fellow only a couple of yards away, said it was completely harmless. I said I'd take his word for it.'

'So he's done some diving?'

'Loves it. Actually, he got Marina hooked on it. Nothing he enjoys more than togging up in scuba gear and exploring wrecks: South Africa, Thailand, he's been all over the world. That's why I think he'd be useful to us here. If Gunnar had an accident with his equipment – heaven forbid – Jim would probably be able to spot what went wrong and how it happened... and then that would be the time to call in the police.'

While Luke was silent, thinking this over, Robb added, 'As to where to put him, I should suggest the pub – the Old Anchor, isn't it? – or one of the local B&Bs, where he can pick up gossip and get a feel for the place. Better not to have him too closely associated with you here. Or me, for that matter. He can be just a regular tourist, keen on underwater exploration.'

Luke said slowly, 'He'll find diving here rather different from Thailand, but I daresay The Dive Shop would be able to kit him out with a drysuit. That's one of McInnes' little sidelines. It was on the verge of going bust when he swooped in and rescued it, and now I'm told it's flourishing. Midas touch, lucky beggar.'

Or a mountain of debt? Robb filed away that thought and returned to the subject of Gunnar. Who saw him last? When was that? Who knew of his plan to visit the Viking festival? On each of these questions Luke was maddeningly vague, but they had to be asked. He must make a list of everyone who had had occasion to talk to Gunnar since Thursday afternoon, already nearly 48 hours ago, when Robb himself had been watching from above Loch Herrich and seen Gunnar's brief visit to Mhairi's croft.

He thought back. Something about that tiny incident had agitated Logan, who could hardly wait to finish his work and get home himself. It would be interesting to find out why. Marina might know. She had been cross to have her loch-fishing cut short, and could well have demanded an explanation.

So... He must interview Mhairi and her son, and Jess – whom he suspected kept a much closer eye on people's relationships than Luke did.

Then there was Danna, the inveterate gossip who must have the longest memory of bygone days and, of course, Ravenna, who was so curiously incurious about her husband's movements. Plenty of questions to ask, and now he, too, felt a prickle of urgency.

'Look,' he said, stopping so abruptly that Luke, following on the narrow path, nearly bumped into him, 'I think I'll skip fishing this afternoon. If you'll make my excuses to Marina and Danna, I'll go back to the Lodge now and get on to Jim Winter right away.'

'Your sergeant?'

'That's right. If as you tell me Gunnar is missing and so is his diving kit, I don't think we've got much time to waste.'

# CHAPTER EIGHT

# Jessamine

THE DELICIOUS SMELL of fresh-baked loaves filled the kitchen and the subtle aroma from a large glass bowl of strawberries on the central table tempted Robb to filch a couple as he passed, but of Jess there was no sign. Where would she be on this beautiful sunny afternoon? A moment's thought directed his steps along a herb-lined path to the walled kitchen garden, where he found his hostess struggling to resurrect a wigwam of sweetpeas up-ended by last night's gale.

'Hang on, let me give you a hand,' he said to the flushed freckled face peering through a tangle of flowers and greenery; and when the wigwam was once more firmly planted he helped her unwind and tie up the trailing blossoms.

'Thanks. I should have known better than to put it in that corner,' she said at last, pushing damp tendrils of dark hair back from her forehead. 'The wind comes fairly whistling in over the wall, but I thought the foliage would act as a filter to protect my seedbed. Gardening so close to the sea is a continual battle against the elements, although we're lucky to have the Gulf Stream to take the edge off the cold.'

'Do you have any help with this?' To Robb's eyes, keeping the dense rows of vegetables and fruit bushes in such good order looked a mammoth task, and Jess laughed.

'Lord, yes! Half Inverclinie works here off and on, and I've made overtures to people in Stairbrigg, offering them homegrown vegetables if they'll give us a hand, but they're inclined to keep their distance. A bit Us and Them, you know – ridiculous, but there it is.'

'People are very conservative,' Robb suggested, but she shook her head.

'Not exactly. It's because Dougal McInnes discourages them from becoming too friendly with us. Likes to keep tabs on people – a real control freak. Of course, he can't control everyone. Take Mhairi, for instance. She's a free spirit who never follows the crowd and she's got green fingers. She can make anything grow, and Danna does most of the heavy stuff, digging and so on. He used to look after Major Philpott's glasshouses, back in the day. He's incredibly strong and fit for his age.'

Robb nodded, remembering the steely hand that had pulled him out of the Dunseran. 'And Logan? Does he help?'

'Oh, mowing, you know. And he's a whizz with machinery. You could call it a co-operative because we all share what we grow. Then another that bucks the trend is Olympia, who runs the Fish Bar. When she comes over to cut my hair she usually brings a few of her nephews and nieces to pick stuff for her freezers.'

'She's got a big family?'

'More like a tribe! I never know their names, but they all seem to end in 'a' and most of them work locally, in the Smokery or the Fish Bar. It's mainly thanks to Olympia that Stairbrigg isn't your typical West Coast youth desert.' She smiled ruefully. 'Actually she's pretty acquisitive and when soft fruit's in season I have to watch out that she doesn't strip the bushes bare. She likes a good old gossip, too. I think half the reason she comes is to find out what we're doing, who's staying and what they've caught; and no doubt all of that goes straight back to Big Dougie.'

'Would you say the locals are friendly, on the whole?'

It took her a moment to answer, and he sensed her struggling between the pretence that everything was rosy and reluctance to admit hostility. Finally she sighed, exhaled, and said defensively, 'Don't think we haven't tried to get on well with everyone, because we really have. Obviously people here look on us as outsiders – well, fair enough. That's what we are. And on the surface everyone is polite, if a bit guarded, but...'

She left the word hanging and stared at her muddy shoes.

'But?' he prompted.

'It sounds ridiculous, but sometimes I think there's a secret here that everyone's in on but us.' She looked up at him and smiled. 'Of course it would help if one of us had the Gaelic!' Or Arabic, she might have added, since it had long been clear to her where much of Big Dougie's workforce originated, but after all, Robb was a policeman, and some cans of worms were best left unopened.

'You think your neighbours talk about you behind your back?'

'I'm sure they do. And they watch us pretty closely, too. I don't say that any of it is actually damaging. I mean, gossip is one of life's pleasures, but I do admit I find it slightly unnerving to be under constant surveillance.'

'Does it worry Luke?'

'Quite honestly, I think he hardly notices. Or rather,' she corrected herself, 'let's say we have different areas of worry. For instance, take this week. It bothers him that Ravenna spends so much time in Stairbrigg, while for me it's obvious that she'd be bored out of her mind if she had to kick her heels here all day while Gunnar is on the river. And she's helping the museum with their catalogue for next year's exhibition. That's a proper reason to pop over there whenever she can.'

She paused fractionally, choosing her words with care, 'But Luke – who I may say in passing is the least suspicious person in the world – thinks she sometimes spends the night there as well.'

'Why's that?'

'Because he saw someone who looked awfully like her creep into the Lodge through the gunroom before dawn a couple of days ago. We don't lock, because of guests fishing at night, and at this time of year it's never really dark, but he's pretty sure it was Ravenna. Of course, the museum wasn't open then, nor was the ferry running.'

There was a silence until Robb asked, 'How could she get back here, then?'

'He saw headlights on the single-track across the bay, but there are too many trees and zigzags to be sure that was the same car that turned into our drive, and anyway it switched off its lights once it was off the road.'

'Why was Luke up at that hour?'

'When he's worried and can't sleep, he gets up and watches the sunrise on the bay. He says it calms him down.'

Poor Luke – thought Robb, who knew exactly how day-to-day anxieties were magnified at night.

Jess asked hesitantly, 'I know you're on holiday, but did Luke say anything to you about looking for Gunnar ourselves? He's probably perfectly all right, but leaving his boat like that...' Her voice trailed away.

'You think that's out of character?'

'Partly that, and partly because of something odd I saw.' She bit her lip and fell silent as if wondering whether to trust him.

'Tell me.'

'OK. Well, you know Mhairi makes jewellery, mostly silver, which I sell on her behalf to our fishing tenants. She's very talented but a bit – well, reclusive, I suppose is the word. Too modest. She says they're rubbish and can't bring herself to put a proper price on them, but I've no such inhibitions. Anyway, it's a nice little business for both of us.'

'Where did she learn? Art school?'

Jess said uncomfortably, 'Actually that's all rather sad but I might as well tell you so you can avoid elephant traps. Her father was a silversmith in Edinburgh, and a pretty good one by all accounts, and she learnt from him. But unfortunately he strayed from the straight and narrow, got in with a bad crowd, became addicted to drugs and, to cut a long story short, was convicted of handling stolen goods and uttering forged documents relating to their provenance. He did quite a stretch in gaol. When he came out, he moved up here to run the family croft and put all that behind him.'

'So he taught Mhairi? Is that why she keeps a low profile?'

'I guess so. It's a shame because she's really good, but she's very dismissive. Says it's her little hobby for the winter evenings.'

'She's Logan's mother, right? Any other children?'

'No. As far as I can gather, her husband Seamus Brydon was a nice easygoing chap, a bit slow, good with his hands, though apparently he used to hit the bottle pretty hard.'

'He's dead?'

She nodded. 'He was drowned – oh, years ago. Got a rope round his ankle while fishing and was dragged overboard. Drunk, I should guess. Quite a common accident hereabouts, worse luck.'

She paused, and when Robb was silent, went on, 'So Mhairi's big worry is that Logan will take off for the bright lights and get into drugs like his grandfather did.'

'Yet she's doing everything she can to get him into uni, or so Marina tells me. If she wants him to stay with her, isn't that counter-productive?'

'I know. Bit of a catch-22. Because she lost out on further education, she's determined her son should get a degree.'

'Whether he wants it or not?'

'That's about it.'

Robb said, 'You were going to tell me about something odd you saw. Something to do with Mhairi's jewellery.'

'Oh, yes. It really puzzled me.' She paused a moment, remembering. 'I went over to her croft a couple of days ago to say I had run out of stock – the French guests we had here took a fancy to her charm bracelets and cleaned me out – and while I was in the back of her studio seeing what she'd made recently Gunnar came bumbling up the path to her croft, and she went out to talk to him.'

'And?'

'She spat at him!' The shock was still clear in her voice. 'I – I couldn't believe it. That really was out of character – at least out of the character I thought I knew. It's silly to make a lot of it, but it's so surprising when someone as controlled as Mhairi suddenly explodes.'

Over-controlled, he thought. Bottled-up emotion getting the better of her. He said, 'Did he know you were there?'

'No. He just went away. And when Mhairi came back in she behaved as if nothing had happened. She said he'd wanted her to copy a brooch for Ravenna, but she told him she didn't make copies, all her work is original, so she sent him away. Not a hint of why she'd spat at him, but it was so odd.'

She glanced at Robb to see his reaction. 'And later on when I asked Ravenna if she knew anything about getting a brooch copied, she looked very surprised and told me in confidence that curiously enough quite an important brooch from the museum's Viking hoard had gone AWOL – very worrying for her since she had taken it home to examine without telling the curator.'

'How did the museum react?'

'It didn't have to. I mean, she never had to 'fess up because after searching high and low, turning the whole place upside down, even going through the non-recyclable bin in case Morag had thrown it away in the rubbish –'

'Don't tell me, I can guess. She found it?'

'In her make-up bag. Which she had hunted through again and again, turned inside out, looked inside the lining, and was absolutely certain contained no brooch or buckle of any kind. Yet next morning, there it was.'

'Was that where she had left it?'

'She's not sure. She had wanted to examine it in a strong light, and remembers sitting at her dressing table, wondering where to put it overnight, and thinks she decided to slip it inside a spectacle case where it would be hidden but ready to hand, but when she came to look at it with her magnifying glass, it wasn't there.' The lines between her eyebrows creased into a frown. 'She even asked your Marina if she had moved it for some reason.'

'Why should she?' said Robb more sharply than he meant to. 'What would my daughter be doing in her bedroom?'

'Oh, you haven't heard about Ravenna's latest conquest? You haven't noticed poor Logan sighing like a furnace whenever their paths cross?' Jess laughed. 'He fancies himself as a bit of a poet, and gets Marina to slip his deathless verses under Ravenna's pillow. All very romantic – and very silly – but that's teens for you.'

Robb tried not to let his disapproval show, but he didn't like the sound of this at all. 'Go on,' he said. 'What did she do when the brooch turned up?'

'Returned it to the museum asap, and thanked her lucky stars she didn't have to tell them she'd lost it.'

They stared at one another, then Robb said carefully, 'You think Gunnar pinched it and that was what he wanted copied? That he was after a replica to put in his own collection?'

'Well, that did occur to me. He would have had the best opportunity. Pure speculation, of course.'

'Of course.'

'Was it silver?'

'I'd have to ask her. Or Mhairi.'

Robb said briskly, 'The first thing is to find out where Gunnar's gone. Apparently he's pulled this stunt before –'

'Several times, according to Ravenna. She says he's a buccaneer at heart, always has been, and you can't teach an old dog new tricks. I'm not surprised. I'm sorry if it sounds disloyal, but I must admit I've always found him perfectly maddening – though of course he means well.'

And the road to hell is paved with good intentions, thought Robb. So Jess also found Gunnar's ingrained quirks irritating and sympathised with his new wife, which explained in some part the veiled animosity between Ravenna and Luke, for whom Gunnar would always be both benefactor and hero.

Or would he? Was cynicism creeping in to replace unquestioning admiration?

'But she is worried, I'm sure,' Jess went on. 'I heard her asking your daughter what he said to her about some cave he wanted to show her. Where was it? What was in it? The trouble is disentangling fact from fantasy. A lot of the stuff they talked about is utter nonsense – fairy tales. Marina would suggest something and Gunnar would embroider it…well, you heard her at breakfast.'

'Myths, monsters, kingdom of the sea? Yes, she does live in a dream world at times, but at others she can be extremely practical. Typical teenager.' Robb agreed. 'I'll see what I can find out.'

And I will contact my editor asap, thought Jess.

By unspoken agreement, no one had mentioned their mounting worry over Gunnar's whereabouts to Marina, and Robb dreaded her reaction to the news that he was missing.

He found her in sunny mood, perched on the very ledge above Michie's Run where he had foul-hooked his first fish of the holiday; she waved and mouthed, 'Hang on a bit,' and after waiting with mounting impatience for her to fish out the tail of the pool, he watched her edge back cautiously along the spray-slippery rock and eventually plump down in the heather beside him.

'Nothing doing. I suppose it's too hot or too bright – that's Danna's explanation, anyway. Where have you been? I thought you were never coming.'

'Listen, darling. Come and sit down for a moment. There's something I've got to tell you. Something serious.'

'Tell away then. I'm listening.' But even as she spoke he knew that most of her attention was elsewhere, focused on a patch of slack water just below the neck of the pool where a lazy swirl close to the surface looked worth investigation.

He waited while the silence stretched out.

'Go on, Dad,' said Marina at last. 'Is it bad news?' Her shoulders went rigid, her mouth closed tightly in the expression he remembered too well from her first visit to him in hospital after Meriel's death. Then she had been with both sisters for support as they listened to the orthopaedic surgeon listing his injuries and preparing them for the possibility that he would be crippled for life. Was she up to facing bad news on her own?

'I'm afraid it may be. We're not sure yet, but I'll put you in the picture as far as I can. Last night there was a major break-out of salmon from the fish farm cages.'

'Yeah yeah, I know,' she interrupted. 'When I swam round the point this morning everyone was talking about it down on the hard. Some people said seals must have bitten through the netting because they've often made holes in it, but I heard one fisherman say it was sabotage. How could it have been? No one's allowed to go near the cages. They've got all that wire, and a nightwatchman with a torch...' Her voice trailed away. She said in a lower tone, 'I wish Gunnar would come back. It's not so much fun, swimming on my own.'

Robb said reluctantly, 'That's what I want to talk about. We don't know where Gunnar is. No one has seen him since he went off to fish the Lower Rock Pools, saying he was going to get *Shield Maiden* checked at the Templeport shipyard before seeing over the Smokery in the afternoon. After that he planned to go straight on up the Sound to the Viking Festival we were talking about at breakfast – remember?'

She nodded. 'But, surely Ravenna –'

'She doesn't know either. His mobile is switched off, and when Luke rang the shipyard he said that *Shield Maiden* had been booked in for a check but hadn't shown. So then Luke rang the harbourmaster in Corriemill to ask if she'd turned up there, but he said not a sign of her. And then –' for a moment he hesitated, wondering whether to tell her what was for him the clincher – 'this morning when Danna was on his way home from night-fishing, he spotted *Shield Maiden* in a little inlet not far from Stairbrigg.'

'D'you mean Crab Cove?' she asked quickly, and Robb nodded.

'I think that's what he called it.'

'But that's where Gunnar was – ' She stopped abruptly, and colour rose in her face right up to the hairline.

'Was what?'

When she shook her head and didn't answer he went on, 'You know how rough it was last night? Well, apparently the boat – yacht – whatever you call it – had dragged her anchor and run aground on the shingle at the far end.'

'Not possible, Dad.' Marina's flush had faded and she shook her head decidedly. 'I've been there. It's got a very narrow entrance and some awful sharp rocks like a row of teeth. In that wind she'd have been smashed to bits.'

'Well, there she was and that's why we're worried,' said Robb. 'It's beginning to look very much as if Gunnar went swimming last night and – and had an accident.'

'Oh, Dad! Why would he dive at night? It's dangerous, and anyway, he would hardly see a thing.' Marina fiddled with her hair, pulling the end of her ponytail round and nibbling at it.

'Don't do that,' he said automatically, and she wrinkled her nose.

'You sound just like Mum.'

It was progress of a kind that mentioning her mother didn't bring tears to her eyes. She said slowly, 'Are you saying that Gunnar let those fish out? Is that what you think?'

'I'm afraid that's the way it looks.'

He expected her to reject the idea out of hand, but instead she nodded. 'Danna says the same. "Ane rule for Mr Larsen and anither for the rest,"' she said in a passable imitation of the ghillie's hoarse mutter. 'Did you know that his brother is the fish farm's nightwatchman? He's been fined twice for shooting seals, but each time Mr McInnes bailed him out.'

'Where is Danna, by the way? I thought he was ghillying for you.'

She turned and pointed to a clump of heather fifty yards downstream, but so perfectly did ancient tweed and vegetation blend that Robb had to look twice before he could make out the little man's outline as he lay sprawled face-down on the riverbank, one arm plunged up to the shoulder in the water. 'Tickling trout, only he calls it guddling. He's promised to show me how.' She paused a moment, then said quietly, 'Apparently he had a busy night.'

He wasn't the only one, thought Robb. He said briskly, 'Luke and Jess want to call in the police, but McInnes is dead against it. He says they're being alarmist and there's nothing the police could do since there's no evidence a crime has been committed.'

'Doesn't letting fish out count as a crime?'

'Not if it was done by seals, darling.'

'But, Dad –'

Robb said quickly, 'The fishermen may think it was human sabotage, but until we have evidence of that, McInnes is right in saying we haven't much to go on. Yet. So I've asked Jim Winter to join us here and take a look around. You know how he loves scuba-diving.'

Marina's face lit up. She said eagerly, 'I could help him, Dad. He'll need a diving buddy because he doesn't know the bay, but I've been all over it with Gunnar.' She waited, expecting her father to turn the idea down flat, but instead he nodded.

'That's roughly what I had in mind. We won't make a big thing of it, or tell anyone he's my sergeant, but if you and he make a preliminary recce you may spot something that would justify calling the police.'

Am I mad? he wondered. Why should he prefer the evidence of a teenager to that of a police diver? Power and influence, he thought. As his old Super used to say, "Beware the big fish in a small pond". He hadn't liked the way the local cops had so readily enforced an exclusion zone round McInnes's cages. That was illegal. McInnes might no longer be an MSP who had only to whisper his wishes in wee Nicky's ear to have them granted, but the web of patronage he had woven during his years in political power was alive and flourishing, witness the deference with which he was treated around here. From the Fish Bar to the Dive Shop, the Museum to the Council Chamber everyone jumped to do his bidding, and – yes – that was likely to include the police.

If McInnes told them to find nothing, they would find nothing that could have any possible connection with Stairbrigg's favourite son, their very own Big Dougie, the man who put the town on the map.

Marina was watching him with the keen attention of a terrier at a rat-hole, head on one side, forehead puckered. She said hesitantly, 'Dad?'

'Yes, poppet?'

'Do you think – are you telling me – that you think Gunnar might have drowned?'

'It's no good ignoring the possibility.'

'I don't believe it. I just one hundred per cent don't believe it,' she said fiercely. 'He wouldn't have gone without telling me. We had a deal: I was going to help him find his lovely fur coat again.' Her voice rose to a wail... 'Oh, why didn't he wait for me?'

Robb started to say, 'Fairy tales...' but then he saw she was crying, so he pulled her head against his shoulder and held her in silence while she sobbed.

'Sorry, Dad,' she said at last, sniffing and wiping her nose with the back of her hand. 'I've just been getting this feeling that everything here was too perfect and something awful would happen; and now it has.'

'We can't be sure,' he insisted again, 'but I wanted to warn you...'

No good. The first stage of grief had gripped her. Denial. Rejection of bad news.

'I just can't believe it. It's not possible. Not real.'

A shadow fell across them and both looked up. Danna was standing between them and the sun, holding out a net in which were two fish, their spotted sides gleaming iridescent in the sunlight.

'If ye've a mind to guddle a troot for your supper, lassie, I'll show you the way of it now,' he wheezed confidentially; and Robb watched as she drew a deep, quavering breath, wiped her nose on her sleeve again, then rose and followed the little man as he limped back to the riverbank.

He wondered how much of their conversation Danna had heard.

CHAPTER NINE

# Jim

SERGEANT WINTER travelled north by overnight train, local bus, and hired motorbike, and arrived in Stairbrigg at ten on a brilliantly clear morning, to find the sun sparkling on rippling waves in the harbour and the enticing smell of fried fish wafting from Olympia's Bar.

Food first, he decided, choosing an outside table near the water with an uninterrupted view of the swarm of brightly coloured dinghies with numbered sails sweeping down the coast from the north, threading between marker buoys before turning for rougher open water.

'Is it a race?' he asked after placing his order for fish and double chips; but the thin little waitress, who looked barely old enough to have left school, shrugged incomprehension and spoke to a couple at a nearby table.

'She say you.'

A tall, handsome woman with coppery highlights in the single plait that hung over her left shoulder breezed across in a warm waft of expensive scent, smiling as Winter rose politely. 'I'm afraid Leila didn't understand you. Her English isn't too good. Can I help?'

'Oh, it was nothing important.' He kicked himself for instigating this encounter. 'All those dinghies out there. I wondered if this is a race? I don't know much about sailing.'

'Not exactly a race, but it's quite competitive, as you see.' Her voice was a deep velvety purr. 'They're running off the Dragon Class heats in the local regatta, trying to qualify for the Edinburgh Cup. What brings you here? Do you know this coast? It's very beautiful.'

So was she, he thought, and from the boss's description it was not hard to guess her identity. What infernal luck to walk slap into her in his first hour in town! Her elongated greenish eyes were alive with curiosity, inviting further revelations.

'Just passing through on my way to visit an old cousin. She's in a Home, and probably won't even remember me,' he said flatly, boringly, and made to resume his seat. 'Ah, here comes my order. Thanks for putting me right about the race.'

'No problem.'

Accepting dismissal, she returned to her own table, where McInnes was impatiently tapping his nails against his teeth. 'Come on, for God's sake. Can't you see I'm busy? I've got a whole load of work to do, sorting out this mess. Fucking hell, I can't wait here all day while you stand there yammering to every Tom, Dick and Harry in the bar.'

She raised a quizzical eyebrow, enjoying his agitation. So often the boot was on the other foot. 'Hot,' she said complacently. 'Just as I thought.'

'What is?'

'He is.'

'That scrawny biker. Who is he?'

'His name is Jim – Jim Winter, I believe. Sergeant Winter. Does that ring any bells with you?'

Now she had his full attention. He was alert, wary, sensing trouble. 'No. Why should it?'

'Not even if I tell you he's DCI Robb's sergeant?'

There was a long pause. 'How do you know?'

'Because little Marina showed me a pic on her iPhone. Family party – a christening, I think she said – with Robb himself, her two sisters, brother-in-law, baby, and there was your "scrawny biker" – I recognised him at once.'

'Bloody hell!' he exploded. 'That two-faced bastard Balfour must have asked him to come here. I told him to back off because there was nothing to warrant calling in the police, getting divers crawling over the seabed and asking stupid questions, and he said yes, yes, of course you're right…

and now he tries to mount a private investigation without telling me.'

'But what have you to hide, my angel?'

Her sugar-sweet, deliberately provocative purr brought only a black look. It gave Ravenna pleasure to needle him, seeing his self-possession dissolve as he fought to control his anger. He was so accustomed to getting his own way that any opposition, any setback, provoked a furious response quite out of proportion to the trigger. Brooding silence followed by an eruption of fury was one of his strategies for keeping people in line, and at one time it would frighten her too, but armoured by marriage to a millionaire she felt immune to his manufactured rages.

'More coffee?' Leila was standing by the table, and with an effort McInnes mastered himself and stood up.

'I'm off,' he growled.

'Will I see you later?'

'No. Yes.' A moment's thought. 'I'll let you know. Keep in touch, and keep an eye on that bastard.' He nodded towards Winter, now shovelling down fish and chips as if he hadn't eaten for a week. 'If he goes across to Kildrumna, I want to know about it asap.'

Two hefty helpings to the good, and a reasonably priced bed booked in Eileen McKinnon's neat B&B overlooking the harbour, Winter fixed an afternoon rendezvous with Robb, then lost no time in making his number at The Dive Shop, where the proprietor was eager to display his goods to this friendly, knowledgeable newcomer.

'Ye'll have done a fair bit of diving, nae doot, sir?' he suggested, heaping the long counter with drysuits in descending order of price.

'Plenty in the Far East, principally Thailand, but never this far north. So many of my favourite places are over-dived nowadays. Take the Red Sea,' Winter shook his head sadly, 'fifteen years ago it was perfection, fantastic fish, wonderful coral, and then the Russians came in. Animals. Worse than animals. Kicking the coral about, a dozen or more diving together, all filming like crazy. Hardly room to move, let alone enjoy a dive. It's a disaster.'

Davie laughed. 'Ye'll find a big difference here, sir. Wi' us, ower-diving has never been a problem. Oh, we get the odd party come here frae Templeport, but there's plenty room for all and to spare.'

'Glad to hear it.' Winter fingered the Seac Sub Warmdry at £648, and regretfully pushed it aside. 'You've some good stuff,' he said appreciatively. 'Top of the range. Who does your buying?'

'That's Mr McInnes, sir. He won't stock any cheap lines – says quality counts more underwater than it does on the surface.'

'Amen to that,' said Winter heartily. 'I wish everyone thought the same. Well, now. I'd better make up my mind. Tell me, Mr McTavish, what would you yourself recommend?'

'Och, weel, for masel'...' Davie launched into a comprehensive analysis of the pros and cons of neoprene, trilaminate, and vulcanised rubber drysuits, and ended by saying confidentially, 'We'd be willing to hire out any one to ye to see if ye liked it before deciding.'

'That's very good of you.' They negotiated a deposit and Davie packed the neoprene suit together with thermals and a map. As Winter picked them up, he said casually, 'Where's the local dive club? I'll need a buddy to show me around- reefs, rocks, wrecks – you know the kind of thing.'

Davie's smile faded; he shook his head. 'Naething nearer than Templeport, sir. I'd show you around masel' and welcome, if I'd someone tae leave in charge here. Wait, now, while I think.' After a moment he said diffidently, 'There's a young leddy staying at Kildrumna Lodge who might help you. Just a wee bit lassie, but she's a braw diver and she's PADI qualified – got her Open Water certification to 30 metres last year, they tell me.'

'She sounds just the job.' Winter was careful not to sound too enthusiastic. 'What's her name, and where can I find her?'

One of the few animal instincts that modern humans have retained is an awareness of being watched. Whether the stare is friendly, hostile, or merely curious, the sensation of eyes following you is impossible to mistake, and Robb was in no doubt that someone was monitoring his progress up the narrow serpentine path that led from Kildrumna Lodge to the village of Inverclinie. 'We're under constant surveillance,' Jess had said, and now he saw what she meant. In this wild and largely unpeopled landscape, every movement was interesting, and it was human nature to want an explanation of who was heading where, and why.

From high above on the banks of Loch Herrich a couple of days ago, he had watched Jess Balfour run up the same path and marvelled at her stamina; now as his reconstructed jigsaw of a leg carried him steadily to the crest and down the other side without much complaint, he felt a surge of satisfaction.

I couldn't have done that a month ago, he thought. Even a week ago I doubt if I'd have made it without stopping. The surgeon said it would take eighteen months, and I didn't believe him but by God, he was spot on.

Like Jess before him, he avoided the harbour, and instead threaded through the narrow lanes linking the stacked cottages behind the main drag. As the gaps between inhabited buildings and backyards grew wider, he recognised Mhairi's croft at the end, where the track petered out into a thread of path linking a small patch of unripe oats and two unthrifty tussocky fields fenced with sagging wire, in which a handful of resigned and shaggy stirks were lying out of the wind. At the beach, the path ended abruptly.

Talk about living at the back of beyond! he thought. No wonder a boy of seventeen was pining for the bright lights and wider world. Reclusive, Jess had called Mhairi, and certainly she seemed to be taking good care to isolate herself from her neighbours.

Yet she still sang at The Clachan on occasion, and indeed as Robb made his way up the front path outlined with whitewashed stones, he recognised the plaintive Eriskay Love Lilt sung in a sweet, pure soprano that seemed to embody all the wild loneliness of sky and sea and surf around him.

He knocked, and the song ended in mid-phrase but Mhairi's smile as she opened the door was warm, with more than a hint of mischief.

'Come in, Mr Robb, come in and welcome. Let me guess your errand. Could it have to do with a certain bonny lassie? A birthday gift, maybe?'

'Jess told you?'

'Aye, so she did. Fifteen years old tomorrow and her dad had forgotten. You don't deserve her.'

'Don't rub it in,' he said with a grimace. 'I've never been much good at anniversaries. My wife used to do all that stuff, but Jess thought you might be able to suggest something in the way of jewellery that would appeal to Marina.'

'What sort of thing had you in mind – earrings? A necklace? Brooches?'

'Oh, lord! I don't really know. Just something unusual, that would remind her of Inverclinie.'

Mhairi nodded. 'Let's see now if anything in here takes your eye.'

She pulled open the rough wooden door of a long shed set at a right angle to the cottage, hooked it back against the wall, and rapidly keyed in digits on a sophisticated-looking alarm before stooping to lift the handle of a roll-up metal security door. Now the croft's isolated location began to make sense to him, for as she unbarred and threw back the heavy shutters and switched on the overhead light,

Robb saw that the dark space within had been divided into two sections: at the back were showcases and wall cabinets with interior lights, which contained small silver objects, sparkling and glinting enticingly, while a long workbench under the window held Mhairi's tools and materials: baskets of coloured stones, chisels, hammers, tweezers, files, fine-grade sandpaper, bars of silver, small saucepans, a spirit lamp, and machines at whose function he could only guess.

'Aladdin's Cave!' he exclaimed, and she smiled.

'Just my wee workshop, Mr Robb,' she said deprecatingly, but he sensed she was pleased. 'Take your time, now, and have a look round. If you can't find what you want, I'll show you some more designs I've a mind to try out.'

What would Marina like? What would suit her? For a while he wandered from one showcase to the next, trying to imagine her wearing the delicate necklaces and earrings, but it was no good. The more he gazed at them, the more helpless he felt. Jewellery would look ridiculous with her unvarying uniform of jeans, sweatshirt and trainers: now he came to think of it, he had rarely seen Marina wearing a dress.

Mhairi had settled at the angled easel on her workbench, back towards him, and was sketching quietly, and though he was tempted to ask for help he was reluctant to disturb her concentration, but when with a grunt of satisfaction he spotted what he wanted, she swung round so quickly on her revolving stool that he realised she had been watching his reflection in the window.

'You've found something?'

'This little bowl. It's perfect.'

'That's my take on the traditional quaich – the cup of friendship, Mr Robb,' she said, nodding. 'I'm glad you like it. That's a new design I'm trying out. Wait now…'

She unlocked the case and handed him the small wooden bowl, rimmed and lined with brilliantly polished silver. On either side a tiny silver mermaid was perched, her long tail forming a handle as she leaned over to peer into the depths at the small antique coin set in the bottom.

Robb examined it carefully, running his fingers over the surface, admiring the detail. 'Where did you find this wood? It's so smooth – almost like vellum.'

'Och, it's nought but driftwood from the shoreline. Logan brings me odd pieces he finds after a high tide. It may have come from a wreck – certainly it has been in salt water a long while, maybe years.'

'And the mermaids!' He turned it to and fro, catching the light. 'Marina will love them. I've photographs of her in exactly that attitude, leaning over a rock pool. So that's a quaich, is it? Tell me, how much do you want for it?'

But Mhairi was reluctant to name a price, telling him to settle it with Mrs Balfour, who dealt with the business side and would know what to charge. She was curiously uninterested in his praise for her work, but when he asked casually if she'd heard that Gunnar was missing, her reaction startled him.

'I have, and I say good riddance to that buaireadair bampot!' she exclaimed. 'Wherever he goes, trouble soon follows, but I doubt we've seen the last of him yet. What did he want to go stirring up the hornets' nest that way? What good did he think he'd do?'

'You think he let the fish out?'

'Who else? Now Big Dougie's mad as fire and he'll take it out on poor Mr Balfour, mark my words. Those misbegotten salmon will run up our rivers and destroy the few native fish we have left to us, and clear the way for more cages in the bay.'

She stopped, biting her lips, a red flush of anger staining her cheeks. He saw that her hands were shaking as they wrapped his parcel in layers of tissue paper.

'You don't think he's had an accident, then?'

'If he has, it'd be no more than he deserves,' she said more moderately. 'Coming here with his big credentials as a conservationist and then pulling a trick like this. Not for the first time either, as Mr Balfour knows full well.'

'Where is he, then? He can't have vanished into thin air.'

She shrugged. 'That's for you to find out, Mr Robb, but I can tell you this: if he's down with the fishes in Kildrumna Bay, he won't be taking my lad away to the Viking festival next week when he should be studying, nor offering him a job on his cruise liners this winter, and I for one am glad of it.'

'Has he done that?'

'Aye, and if my sister hadn't warned me what was in the wind, Logan would have left his books and been away up the Sound without a word to me. He may say he's a man and has a right to decide his own future, but I won't have him throw away his chances on a rich man's whim.'

Robb said tentatively, 'You don't think Mr Larsen simply wanted to give him a helping hand?'

'No, I do not. He's a rich man, Mr Robb – too rich for his own good in my opinion – and with that money comes a sense of entitlement which is not to my taste. If Gunnar Larsen thinks he can stroll in and out of our lives as he pleases, he has a lot to learn.'

'He used to come here as Major Philpott's guest, didn't he? Mr Balfour showed us the photograph of Danna's big fish. Gunnar Larsen was there, along with his parents.'

'Aye, so he did. I mind it well.'

'That would have been – what? Nineteen years ago? Twenty? How often have you seen him since?'

She was silent, clutching the quaich in both hands, eyes suddenly wary. Time to risk it, thought Robb. He said deliberately, 'How many times has he asked you to let him help his son?'

Her face flamed and she swung round to hide it, dropping the half-wrapped quaich. Robb bent to retrieve it, giving her a moment to recover her self control.

'Was it Danna told you that?' she asked angrily. 'It's a lie, a black lie, and I'll have the hide off him for his blabbering tongue.'

'Nothing to do with Danna,' said Robb. 'I daresay Mr

Larsen made you promises he couldn't keep all those years ago, and you've every right to resent him and everything he represents. But if he wants to make amends to you and the boy – to right the wrong, if you like – it strikes me that by refusing his help you're in danger of cutting off your nose to spite your face.'

She wasn't listening. 'There's some wrongs that can't be righted,' she shakily. 'I know the kind of man he is, and I'm not putting myself in his power again, or shaming Seamus Brydon's memory. He brought up Logan as his son, and his son he will remain while I have breath in my body.'

She said little more as she tied string round the parcel, and her manner was stiff and formal as she accompanied him to the door.

He climbed back up the serpentine footpath reflecting on the female of the species: no embattled mother – be she bear, buffalo or human – ever gave up her offspring easily. Not when she had borne him, protected him, taught him how to survive in an uncertain world. Like every mother, Mhairi would fight tooth and nail to stop her son being lured into a world she despised, even by a man she had once loved.

Words drifted into his mind, a ballad Meriel used to sing:

> *It will come to pass on a summer's day*
> *When the sun shines bright on every stane,*
> *I will come and fetch my little young son,*
> *And teach him how to swim the faem…*

When McInnes reached the cages in the early afternoon, most of the night's debris had been cleared; the damaged cables attaching the netting to the big circular frames were already being replaced by his chastened workforce, and both McTavish boys and Yanis worked in near silence, dreading the lash of the boss's tongue.

Seals, grown bold from their nocturnal bonanza, popped up round the launch, their bulbous eyes and bristling whiskers an infuriating reminder of his humiliation. After the briefest of inspections, he told the team curtly to carry on, and turned the launch towards the series of small inlets that intersected the cliffs opposite Stairbrigg like gaps between the teeth of an ill-used comb. Few of these merited a name on the map, but McInnes had known them like the back of his hand since childhood, when he would scramble about their narrow ledges in search of gulls' eggs to sell at the fishmarket.

Though occasional rockfalls made them dangerous, his particular favoured eyrie commanded a great sweep of coast from the deep-water harbour off Templeport where cruise ships, tankers, and container ships moored overnight, past the Skerries and Inverclinie to the south, and away to the far blue loom of the mountain ranges beyond the broad expanse of sea shaped like an inverted comma that separated the mainland from the long Caillich Peninsula. From here he could survey the comings and goings of local fishermen and yachtsmen alike, while at the path's entrance official warning signs deterred others from accessing this private lookout.

Seating himself on a narrow shelf with his back against the sun-warmed rock, Big Dougie focused his telescope on the cruise ship moored on the outside berth at Templeport, which was scheduled to leave before the gloaming.

Either they were late, or he was too early. He could see ant-like figures still crowding the gangway as passengers slowly re-embarked after their tour of the town with its gift-shops and cafés offering cream teas with fresh-baked scones and gingersnaps. They would have been allowed two hours ashore before the ever-smiling multi-national crew rounded them up and hustled the straggling queue back on board to shower and dress before yet another meal. When they were all bedded down in their cabins, the ship would slip silently away north-west, ready for the following day's cruise.

He shifted his attention nearer, minutiously scanning the coastline from Templeport to Stairbrigg, examining every craft that moved. He liked to know what was going on in his patch. Surfers were out in force on this hot afternoon, making the most of the white-tipped rollers swelling up to break in regular succession on Magill Beach's steeply shelving shingle; and close to the knife-edged rocks of Fulmar Cove, the lifeboat crew was putting its latest recruits through their paces, their grossly inflated day-glo bodies bobbing round its sides like orange sausages.

Then a small, broad-beamed, workaday fishing boat painted an unobtrusive brown nosed out of Kildrumna Bay. He knew it well, and swung the telescope to focus on its occupants. That old meddler Danna at the tiller, of course... The square-built DCI, Martin Robb, seated uneasily in the very middle of the central thwart and gripping the gunwale on both sides, and perched casually in the bows, already dressed head to foot in thermals, the slight figure of Robb's teenage daughter.

McInnes frowned. What were they doing here, and where was Ravenna's scrawny biker? He watched Danna steer carefully through the rocks that guarded the entrance to Crab Cove, and round the dog-leg to the half-moon of shingle at the far end. On the rough wooden landing stage another black-clad figure was kneeling, unpacking equipment. When Marina waved to him, he uncoiled himself and raised a hand in acknowledgment.

Pre-arranged rendezvous, thought McInnes, and smiled sardonically. Whatever they were looking for, they were unlikely to find it. Relaxing, he lit a roll-up and waited to see what would happen next.

Am I mad? thought Robb, but he had gone too far to turn back now. He and Danna, one ashore and one in the boat, would monitor the divers closely, ready to order them out of the water at the first sign of trouble – but what trouble could there be in perfect conditions on a balmy summer's afternoon? Jim Winter was an experienced diver, and Marina knew the cove well. He pushed away the unwelcome suspicion that her mother would have disapproved of involving his youngest daughter in this underwater recce, but Meriel had been a pragmatist and would have recognised the logic of letting Marina take part. After all, she had encouraged her love of the oceans. Teenagers were notoriously impulsive, if not reckless. He could not watch her every minute, so it was surely better than she should do it under supervision than evolve some madcap scheme of her own. Surely?

'She'll be fine, sorr,' wheezed Danna, as if reading his thoughts as they waited on the landing stage for Marina and Jim to complete their pre-dive checks. 'She'll never rest until she's seen for hersel' that Mr Larsen's not doun wi' the fishes in Davy Jones's locker.'

'You don't believe that?'

'What I believe, sorr, is neither here nor there,' muttered the little man. 'All I know is the lads frae the islands have upsticked and are awa' hame. Lady Jean didna care for Moontide's notion of security, I'm told, and Big Dougie's fit tae be tied. He'll have eyes and ears frae Stairbrigg tae Templeport on the watch for whoever cut those cages, and if he finds him, I'm thinking there'll be murder done.'

If there hasn't been already, thought Robb. He paced restlessly along the firm sand at the water's edge, willing Jim and Marina to hurry. How could they enjoy a sport which required so much gear? At Marina's age rugby had been his own passion: as a rock-solid front-row forward he loved the camaraderie and barely contained violence, but to dress like a spaceman and lower yourself into the sea's chilly depths with nothing but a narrow hose to connect your lungs with air took a type of courage he found incomprehensible.

He had briefed Winter with all the known facts about

Gunnar's disappearance, and received in return news of his encounter with Ravenna in the café. Robb frowned: the woman puzzled him. Could she really be as unconcerned as she appeared? She had seemed almost eerily calm and unruffled when they met in the hall after breakfast, him heading for the river while she waited for Jess to finish her shopping list.

'My motto's keep calm and carry on,' she had responded quietly when he asked if she was worried. 'Nine times out of ten my husband returns from one of his solo jaunts ravenously hungry and bursting to tell me all about an exciting new project he wants to invest in. It's his way of escaping the shackles of boredom.' She smiled. 'He can't tolerate boredom.'

With life? Or with his marriage? Robb said carefully, 'And the tenth time?'

'He tells me to come and pick him up from some Godforsaken dump miles from civilisation where an unknown good Samaritan has deposited him after a bender.' Her raised eyebrows challenged him to disbelieve her... 'All right? Any more questions? Now you know why I absolutely refuse to get in a flap because my husband's switched off his mobile.'

Yet she had been quick enough to board the scraped and battered *Shield Maiden* as soon as Danna and Logan brought her back to her usual mooring in front of the Lodge, and when she had confirmed that nothing but a cylinder and Gunnar's diving gear were missing she had removed his laptop and tablet to her bedroom.

'No sense in leaving temptation about,' she said, raising a hand in farewell. 'Sorry, must fly. Jess is waiting,' and off she strode across the gravel sweep, a big, bold, bonny woman in well-fitting jeans and snowy trainers today instead of the voluminous mid-calf skirts favoured by Gunnar, which hid her curves and hampered her movements. Watching her swing easily into the Range Rover's high seat, Robb thought again how differently she behaved when her husband was not around. Was the submissive Nordic wife simply an act? Which was the real Ravenna?

Marina and Winter were ready at last, boarding Danna's boat with all their encumbering gear.

'Come on, Dad,' she called, waving for him to join them, but he shook his head. The small craft was crowded enough already and despite Marina's enthusiasm he had a growing feeling that this dive was mere window-dressing to satisfy her; it would shed no light on Gunnar's disappearance. The cove might be narrow, but even so it was too big for a team of two to search effectively, and Winter had already warned him police divers would be needed to make a proper job of it. Should he go ahead and contact them?

Restless and worried, he followed the water's edge round the dog-leg shore until faced with the choice of wading round the rocky point or scrambling over its shoulder to reach the next small inlet. Warm as it was, he had no appetite for getting wet in water that might be deeper than it appeared, so opted for the scramble on hands and knees up heather-covered rocks and loose scree that had an alarming tendency to give way under his feet.

Steeper and steeper it became, with tough heather roots giving way to bracken which made it harder to see where he was heading, and he soon began to wish he had chosen to wade. Flies buzzed round his sweating face but he dared not raise a hand to swat them away. At last he reached a small ridge, below which the ground fell away in a narrow defile, and sliding down to the bottom of this he was surprised to find himself on a well-trampled sandy path, over which the sides hung so closely that it was almost a tunnel.

Who used this hidden path? Deer, certainly, for their slots stood out plainly, but there were also boot-prints and the faint blurred traces of trainers so worn that even on damp sand their soles left hardly a mark.

Prints led in both directions, but the most recent – which still had dry sand trickling into their track – impelled him to choose the upper branch, which sloped steeply and obliquely along the cliff. He soon had reason to regret this choice as well, for it became ever narrower, the shaley rocks ever more crumbly and the steep drop below ever more daunting.

Instinct plus a trace of tobacco on the air warned him that someone else had passed that way just a few minutes earlier, and since the path seemed to end in a rocky platform overlooking Crab Cove, he might encounter that person coming back.

As the path emerged from the shadow of the cliff, Robb's eye was caught by the glint of sun on glass. Sitting on the very edge of the rock platform with telescope propped between stick and bent knee was a thickset figure in jeans and a faded rust-red guernsey that even from behind he had no difficulty in recognising as Dougal McInnes.

High above the cove, the platform commanded an impressive sweep of sea and shore, with the little whitewashed houses of Inverclinie in the distance separated by the whin-covered low tongue of hill from Kildrumna Bay. Just round the point the fish cages looked like shining coins on the dark-blue water. Small figures in hi-vis clothing hurried to and fro on the surrounding walkway, and several motorboats were tied to the landing stage; but from the steep angle of his telescope McInnes's attention was focused on Crab Cove itself, where Marina and Winter had just hauled themselves aboard Danna's lobster boat, and now seemed to be leaning over the gunwale to heave something heavy out of the water.

'A fine view,' he remarked and McInnes, taken by surprise, started violently. He swung round, glaring, closed the telescope and sprang to his feet.

'What the hell –? Can't you read, man? This path is dangerous.'

But not for you, apparently, thought Robb. Nor for all those other footprint-makers.

'I'm sorry,' he said pacifically. 'Is there a notice? I must have missed it.'

'Then how did you find this path?'

'Climbed up from the shore. It was rougher than I expected, but I didn't fancy wading round the point. I thought I'd be able to see what my daughter was up to from this height.'

'Your daughter?' The darkling frown vanished, replaced by a smile and outstretched hand. 'Then you must be Mr Robb. Glad to meet you. My name's Dougal McInnes. I'm sorry I barked at you, but these cliffs are unstable and we've had several dangerous rockfalls. That's why the Council's put this path off limits.'

'Can you see what they've found?' Robb asked. 'Some kind of tank, is it?'

'Rubbish from a cruise ship, I expect.' McInnes was dismissive. 'It's amazing what the crews chuck out when they come into Templeport to restock. Idle sods. The tide brings the stuff into the cove and after a big blow you find it littering the seabed. It snags the fishermen's nets so it's quite a problem.'

For a moment they watched in silence as the small figures in the boat settled themselves and prepared to leave.

'Looks like they're through with the dive,' said McInnes. 'Ah, well, must be getting on. I'll see you safe back to the lane, and if you take the left-hand fork, you'll find the path goes straight down to Crab Cove, you can't miss it. Nice to meet you, Mr Robb, but take my advice: don't go clambering about these cliffs on your own. It's not safe, and Stairbrigg can't afford to lose a visitor.'

Was there a hint of menace in that last phrase? Robb zigzagged down the permitted path by which Winter had come and found the divers sitting on the shingle, stripped of their scuba gear. Their despondent attitude told him at once the marine exploration had been a disappointment.

'Nothing there,' said Marina. 'We brought up an air tank that Jim spotted, but there's nothing special about it.'

'Hasn't been there long, though,' said Winter. 'I'll take it ashore and test the mixture. It's got the remains of a sticker from The Dive Shop – that's the chap who hires out scuba-gear. He may remember who got it filled. Worth a try, anyway.'

Nobody spoke much as they motored back round the point, and into Kildrumna Bay. Marina was cast down by their failure to find anything, and Robb was preoccupied. He now had a fair idea what the locals were keeping quiet about, and thought that Jess probably guessed too, but had he any right – or inclination – to blow the gaff? This wasn't his patch. As a visitor here he owed his hosts a measure of consideration, but if he began crashing about making accusations and disrupting the local economy the backlash would certainly imperil the Balfours' relations with their neighbours, which as Jess had hinted, were already delicately balanced. On the whole he thought it better to keep his mouth shut and let well alone. Jim wouldn't see it that way, but where the law was concerned his sergeant was a black-and-white man, with zero tolerance for grey areas.

'Dad,' said Marina, breaking in on his thoughts, 'is it OK if I go out to help Logie with his creels tomorrow morning?'

It was the kind of question he dreaded: Meriel would have known exactly what to say and how to say it. God, how he missed her quiet calm authority! As a father his instinct was to refuse permission. Protecting his teenage daughter from the wicked world meant fending off males – boys of seventeen or men of seventy and every one in between. Boys were predators: he knew because he had been one himself. But why should it be more dangerous to check lobster traps at dawn with a boy than to spend all day on the river with him?

'How early?' he asked to buy time.

'Low tide.'

'When's that?'

'Five-fifteen.'

Even for an early riser, this seemed an ungodly hour, but if Marina wanted to cut short her night's sleep for the dubious pleasure of hauling cages out of chilly water at sunrise, who was he to object?

'Surely you need some kind of permit?'

'Oh, Dad! Do stop making difficulties. Logan's got a licence, and Mr Balfour has a special permit for hobby fishermen – I checked it all out with him, OK?'

'OK,' he said reluctantly.

'Cool. It can be my birthday treat. Thanks, Dad.'

'Mind you're back for breakfast.' And don't think I'm a soft touch because you got your own way again, he added silently. It was happening too often for his liking but he didn't see how to stop it.

A drifting veil of mist, dense in patches and gossamer-thin where stirred by the southerly wind, lay over the bay next morning as Logan set a course for the far line of jagged rocks on the edge of the Reekie Sound. Huddled in the bows, wishing she had put on her puffa, Marina stared into the grey, shifting gloom and wondered how to cheer him up. Since wishing her a happy birthday as she hopped aboard, he'd hardly said another word: not surprising when his hopes of landing his dream job had vanished, though Marina herself doubted that Mhairi would ever have let him go – and quite right, too, she thought. Working on a cruise ship was not a fate she would have wished on anyone.

She had often seen and shuddered at vast, slabby, multi-decked hulks looming over ancient Mediterranean cities or tiny Scandinavian ports, ugly and out of scale, obliged to moor in deep water because unable to enter their harbours. She imagined hundreds if not thousands of passengers queuing on gangways to disembark and spend a few hours ashore – what a nightmare! Each of these leviathans required dozens of crew members, cleaners, waiters, kitchen staff plus an invisible army of storemen, maintenance workers and engineers to keep it functioning: where was the satisfaction of being a tiny cog in such a vast machine? Even with a good word from the Chairman's wife, how could a teenager like Logie ever hope to battle his way to prominence?

Whereas with a workmanlike, well-found little craft like this, freshly varnished, brasswork shining even in the mist, he was his own master and the world was his oyster.

'Was this your father's boat?'

'Aye.' He smiled at last and ran a caressing hand over the gunwale, scratching off a dried fish scale. 'He and Danna built Jenny B the winter before I was born: she's named for my Gran, and she's ideal for this job. They put in a lifting keel so she can run in anywhere. When he died, the boat, the gear, and the Swarovski were what he left to me, and I had to fight to stop my mother selling them before I could use them.' Plainly Mhairi was still in his bad books. 'Uncle Danna was the one said she should keep them. "He'll grow soon enough," he told her, and he was right. He showed me where to put my traps and how to handle the boat, and by the time I was twelve I could make a living at it for her and me.'

'Plus her jewellery. Don't forget that.'

'Not likely to, am I? It's little enough she gets for it, forbye. Mrs Balfour drives a hard bargain.'

Marina said wistfully, 'You're so lucky. I wish I had my own boat.'

'She's all I have. You've got lots of other things I'd like.'

'Snippy-chippy,' she teased, and he laughed unwillingly.

'It's true enough. But she's a good boat, you're right there. She may be built of whatever Dad could scratch up, but she's reliable. She was always under-powered with the old Daihatsu, but last season Uncle Wully snapped up this big Mariner Long Shaft when Mr McInnes wanted to upgrade, so he got it for a song. Makes a big difference.'

Conversation died. Cocooned in the fog, they were alone in an unreal world, with only the haunting screams of seabirds and an occasional splash to vary the slap of waves and muted putter-putter of the outboard. Logan daydreamed, while Marina strained her eyes into the murk, hoping they wouldn't hit a rock.

'Where are we going?' she said at last. 'I didn't realise your traps were so far out.'

'I checked the inshore cages last night,' he admitted, 'so

with the mist and all I thought we'd try somewhere better today –' he paused, then added hastily – 'but you're not to tell Mr Balfour because I might get in trouble.'

'Why?'

He resisted the temptation to tell her not to ask so many questions, and said patiently, 'Because no one's allowed to land on Skerry Mhor, so I don't – not really – I just moor at one end and scramble through the rocks.'

'But, surely –'

'It's OK, don't worry. It's only because SNH don't want the seals disturbed when they're breeding, but there won't be any pups for a few months yet, and anyway, they're well used to me. It takes me just a few minutes to check my cages and bait them. All right? You're not scared, are you?'

'No.'

It wasn't true, but all week Marina had wanted a closer look at Skerry Mhor in its ring of rocks, because Gunnar had insisted on giving them a wide berth. He said too many ships had run aground on them in storms, keels sliced off and bottoms ripped. She was silent, remembering this, as they crossed the rough water at the tail of the Reekie, and as they hit the open sea the mist lifted as if an enormous hand had drawn a cloth across it, leaving Kildrumna Bay shrouded in gloom behind them. A brisk breeze made Jenny B buck and bob, with white water breaking over outlying rocks, but Logan steered confidently for the gap between two tall pillars which stood as if guarding the entrance to a sheltered inlet.

He cut the engine, and let the boat ground gently against the shingle. Seals were everywhere – in the water and heaped together on tiered shelves – and though a few slid into the bay, most of them quickly overcame their uneasiness and settled down again, honking and grunting, their eyes fixed on the intruders.

'Quiet, now! Follow me, and don't go falling in.' He scooped up a hanging curtain of kelp and draped it from bows to stern, making an effective camouflage, then splashed ashore.

Slipping and stumbling on the weed-slick boulders at the water's edge, she had difficulty keeping up as he zigzagged over small rivulets and jumped from one stepping stone to another with practised ease, an empty bucket crooked on one elbow and the tin of bait bulging from a pocket. So intent was she on placing her feet in his tracks that when he stopped suddenly she cannoned into him.

'Down!' he hissed, gesturing fiercely and dropping to his knees. After a moment's stillness, he cautiously raised his head and began to crawl forward to peer round the group of rocks just ahead.

What had he seen? Should she follow? Before she could decide, he was wriggling backwards to join her, then crawling quickly the way they had come with the bucket dragging at his arm. Under the overhanging cliffs he stopped.

'Big Dougie's here,' he whispered in her ear.

'Did he see you?'

He shook his head. 'All I saw was his launch, but he's close, no question.'

'What shall we do?' She thought of her father, worrying if she was late for breakfast.

'Hide until he goes. I doubt he'll stay long with the wind getting up.'

'Why's he here? What's he doing?'

The ghost of a grin. 'Same as us, I reckon. Mam says he was aye a great forager, and he's a nasty way with those who hinder him.'

He's scared of that man, she thought. Everyone's scared of him – except Ravenna. She wished she hadn't told Logan she wanted to see the seals on the Skerries and he hadn't taken it as a challenge, a chance to show off. Now they would have to sit it out until Big Dougie finished whatever he had come to do, and who knew when that would be?

Logan had raised himself to a kneeling position between two rocks, telescope propped on a handy ledge, and was carefully examining every inch of the inlet where the white launch was moored. Presently he grunted, and touched her arm.

'Down there,' he said, pointing. 'See that patch of sand at ten o'clock to the boat? Follow it up to the clump of whitish grass above... that's where he's sitting, looking out to Templeport. Here, try this.' He handed over the glass, but she could not focus it. With the naked eye she could see what might be a seated figure, but it was too far away to be sure.

Far more interesting to watch were the whirling birds – gulls, guillemots, gannets, shearwaters – swooping and diving over the water, and the seals, slumped like bulky sag-bags, shoving one another about on their ledges, or smoothly plunging into the depths. Farther out she saw a school of dolphins head-and-tailing in a concentrated patch, mackerel hunting, no doubt, but so quickly did they move that her own small binoculars could not pick them up before they submerged.

'He's watching for something,' Logan murmured.

'See that boat? Perhaps that's it.'

'Where?'

She pointed. Low in the trough of waves, still indistinct in the veils of mist, was a flash of orange. Staring until her eyes watered, she made out life-jacketed figures packed into a rigid-hulled inflatable that was heading fast towards the Skerry, planing over the surface with bows well out of the water and a foaming wake astern.

From the tail of her eye she caught movement by the shore and nudged Logan. 'Don't move!' she breathed.

They both froze as a kammo-smocked figure came into sight, picking a careful way over the broken slabs, slick with guano and seaweed, storm-collar up and fore-and-aft deerstalker pulled well down. It seemed impossible he would pass without seeing them, but with eyes on boots he went by and vanished down the slope.

'We'd best be off and forget the lobsters today,' whispered Logan, backing away from the rock.

'Hang on. I want to see who's in that boat.'

For a moment she thought he would object, then he crouched down again and raised the telescope. 'From a cruise ship, by the look of it. Five of them. Four kids and a crewman, see his logo – what the hell...? It's the wrong day...'

His voice died away. In silence they watched McInnes wade out to grab a painter and pull the inflatable into shelter, then help its occupants to scramble ashore. They moved stiffly as if chilled to the bone, and huddled together in a tight group while the boatman tossed bundles and boxes after them. For a moment he conferred with McInnes, then raised an arm in salute and skimmed away in the direction he had come.

'Migrants,' said Marina quietly. It was a scene she had watched many times on news-clips, but never expected to witness for real.

Slickly conducted, well-practised, the whole manoeuvre had taken no more than five minutes. In silence they saw the refugees hustled aboard the launch and the cover pulled over their heads as McInnes unmoored and started the engine. His companion swung a leg over the gunwale and they were off with a flurry of foam stretched out behind them like a long fluffy tail.

'Bloody hell!' Logan muttered. 'He might as well put up a notice. Keep off. Landing reserved for migrants.'

'Smugglers. People smugglers,' she said slowly. 'You knew?'

'Yes. No. Forget it.'

'That's not an answer.'

She stared at him until he shrugged. 'OK. I did and I didn't – if that makes sense to you. These foreign kids in Stairbrigg couldn't all be Olympia's family, could they?' he said angrily, 'but I'm sorry for them. Who wouldn't be? I can't shop them; get them banged up in some immigration centre for months on end. Think what they've been through! Those camps in Greece are hellholes; good luck to anyone who can escape from them, but their families have to pay through the nose to get their kids over here, and who pockets the money?'

'Big Dougie.'

'Sticks in my craw. Ask no questions and you won't be told a lie, so no one talks about it.' He shook his head, frowning. 'Shop him, and what happens to those kids? Back to square one, no job, no money, no family.'

Marina said hesitantly, 'But it's illegal…'

'Think I don't know? Oh, what's the use? Listen, Marina,' he swung round to stare at her directly, 'don't you go blabbing to your dad about what you just saw. Remember, these migrants are the lucky ones. They come from rich families and they get five-star treatment. When security got so tight that sneaking onto cross-channel lorries and hiding under the freight was nigh on impossible, and crossing the shipping lanes landed them in the arms of Border Force, Big Dougie and his mates in Greece worked out this way of getting youngsters to the promised land and giving them a start. Never more than five at a time. Small numbers paying big prices. So remember, you didn't see them, or I'll be in trouble. OK?'

'OK.'

'Come on then, back to the boat. Good job he was too busy to notice us,' he went on, setting such a pace over the weed-slippery slabs that Marina found it difficult to keep up.

'What about the other one? The lookout?'

He stopped abruptly. 'Walked right past us, didn't he?'

'He came round behind us. He could have seen us land and –'

'You worry too much.'

And seen where you left your boat, thought Marina, hurrying after him, but when Logan pulled aside the curtain of kelp the little brown craft was still tucked neatly against her rock. For an awful moment she imagined the lookout's eyes had flickered towards their refuge and then away, but that was all it was, she told herself: imagination.

Logan picked up the funnel and fuel can. 'Best top up before we start. You hop in, and put this on. Over your life jacket.' He lobbed a bundle of oilskin towards her. 'Wind's getting up – look over there... Likely we're in for a wetting.'

A swirling black cloud was racing towards them, and the moment they left the shelter of the inlet, the wind redoubled its force. The last shreds of mist had blown away and the deep water looked more black than blue, with a following wave menacing them over the stern as Jenny B's sturdy clinker-built bows butted into choppy, white-tipped seas. When a heavy packet of spray dashed aboard she draped the oversize oilskin over herself, legs and all, finding a creased sou'wester in the pocket and tying the strings with a double knot.

Logan was right: big drops of rain from the black cloud to the north swept over them, blotting out the Skerry and flattening the waves, and the wind rose to a roar. Rain? More like hail, she thought, stinging needle-sharp against her face. Just in time to avoid a sousing she ducked her head below the gunwale, and was alarmed to find water swilling round her feet.

Quick! Where's the baling can? She spotted it under the forrad thwart and began scooping as fast as she could, but despite her efforts the water kept rising. Was it the rain, the spray, or was it – might it be – coming through the bottom? Moments later there could be no doubt. The floor was awash and she needed a bigger bucket to keep pace.

'She's leaking!' she shouted above the howl of wind, but Logan didn't answer. He was turned away from her, fiddling with the engine, twisting the accelerator to and fro. A cracking double backfire, and the engine died, then revived in an erratic flutter instead of a steady beat. Logan knelt up, peering down at the screw, and again there was a volley of backfiring, a few choking coughs, then silence.

Old but reliable, she thought. Oh, God! Frantically she plied the baling can, but in the few instants she had stopped to listen to the engine the sloshing water had gained on her and was halfway up to the central thwart.

Logan's face was scarlet as he pulled the starter-cord again and again, the only response a muted stutter that died at once. 'It won't catch!' he shouted. 'We'll have to row.'

But how could they, with water coming in so fast? Didn't every boat have a hole for drainage? The bung must have come out. Elbow-deep in fishy slurry, she began to scrabble at the boards under the thwart, trying to remember what Logan had said about a lifting keel, but it was hopeless. Her fingers were too cold to detect the leak, and now he was scrambling towards her, yelling through the gale.

'Leave that! Keep baling! Oars under...'

Under what? Through a haze of spray she saw him fit rowlocks and pull one oar from beneath the thwarts, but there was no sign of its pair, and her vague suspicion that had been hardening ever since the boat began leaking abruptly turned to certainty. This was no accident but deliberate sabotage. Whoever had done it intended them to sink. To drown.

The Skerry was dangerous and they must still be close. Much too close. How far had the engine carried them before it conked? Gunnar had warned of the wicked rip-tide setting towards the face that had drawn numerous fishing boats to their doom.

We need help, she thought frantically – but how? Ring ICE? Dad? She scrabbled under the oilskin for her phone, standing up to unzip the waterproof pocket, her fingers clumsy and shaking, blinking away water as she pressed the button.

'Hang on! Sit down!' Logan's yell reached her faintly just before the boat struck with shattering force, rearing up so steeply that he was flung into the scuppers, while Marina catapulted over the stern and the tide-race whipped her away.

The telephone shrilled through the kitchen just as Jess opened the door to the garden, and for an instant she was tempted to let the answerphone pick up. If it was important the caller would ring again, but if she was late getting down to the harbour, the fish market would be over and her party would go hungry.

Then she remembered how worried Robb had looked when his daughter did not turn up for breakfast and how despite all their assurances that she had her mobile with her and would be safe in Logan's boat, he had spent most of the meal staring out of the window, hoping to see it crossing the bay. Reluctantly she turned back.

'Kildrumna Lodge. Hello?'

'Mrs Balfour? This is Jean Allen from Eilean Breck,' said the clipped, decisive voice, and Jess frowned. What could the queen of the island fish farmers say that she, Jess, wanted to hear?

'How can I help you, Lady Jean?' It sounded stiff, she knew, grinning manically at the kitchen door, trying to inject a little warmth.

'I'm sorry to ring you out of the blue like this, but I wondered if you could help me get in touch with Gunnar Larsen. It's – it's rather urgent. His office tells me he's on holiday this week, and that he may be staying with you.'

'That's right,' said Jess coolly, then corrected herself. 'At least he was here until a couple of days ago, when he left to visit the Viking festival out at Kinvarnoch.'

'Damn, so I've missed him!' Lady Jean didn't bother to hide her annoyance. 'I had the devil's own job to get those box-tickers in his office to give me his mobile number, and then when I rang it didn't answer. Eventually I persuaded them to tell me where he was staying, but now you say he's already left. I must speak to him before he puts in his reports to SNH and the SEPA, and that will be any day now.'

'I'm sorry –' Jess began, but Lady Jean cut her short.

'When are you expecting him back?'

Brusque, barely civil; Jess controlled her irritation as she explained Gunnar's movements were seldom cut and dried, but since both his wife and his boat were at Kildrumna she assumed that he intended to return at some point.

'Huh! No picnic entertaining him, I imagine.' Lady Jean sounded more human. 'I remember thinking when he came to inspect us up at Eilean Breck for his last report that he was a bit of a force of nature. Unpredictable, you know.'

'I certainly do.'

'I mean, he turned up two days before we were expecting him, and I had the feeling – oh, it's difficult to pin down – that he wanted to catch us out in some way.'

'And did he?'

A cackle of laughter. 'No. In fact his report gave us a very fair crack of the whip, I'm glad to say, which was good for business – but I thought then that if he hadn't liked the way we do things, he wouldn't have minced his words. That's why it's so important for me to speak to him now, before he completes his update. There are things going on in your area that he ought to know about.'

Jess said cautiously, 'I heard you and your colleagues were taken round the Smokery in Stairbrigg, and went out to the Moontide cages.'

'A shambles. A complete and utter disgrace! Yes, you're right: that's why I'm trying to contact Larsen and warn him. If he doesn't grasp the nettle and get him booted out of the industry asap, that smooth-talking scoundrel McInnes will ruin it and all the jobs that depend on it. Hundreds of them. Thousands.' She paused, then asked sharply, 'So you knew I'd been to Stairbrigg? More fool me! I shouldn't have touched it with a barge pole. What else did you hear?'

'That you'd agreed to join his consortium and invest in the Smokery.'

'I've done nothing of the kind! The man's a liar and he'll drag us all through the dirt if he gets the chance. Once the public loses confidence in farmed salmon, it'll be the devil's own job to get it back, and so I'll tell Gunnar Larsen. Well, I'm sorry to have bothered you, Mrs Balfour –'

'Jess.'

'Thank you for putting me in the picture.'

'Sorry I couldn't be more help, but if –'

Jess's impatience to end the conversation must have

shown in her voice, because Jeannie said hurriedly, 'Look, if I give you my mobile number, would you ring me the moment Larsen surfaces?'

'It's a promise,' said Jess, her heart singing. For so long everything and everyone had seemed to be pro-McInnes and against them, but here at last was an ally who had seen through his bonhomie and meant to do something about it. With the island queen on their side, things looked very different, and she could hardly wait to share the news with Luke.

Then the big snag kicked in: without Gunnar, they could do nothing. How typical of him to go walkabout just when they really needed him! And come to that, where was Ravenna? Not for the first time Jess wished she had more control over their visitors. They were on holiday; they were adults; they could come and go as they pleased, and she had no right to ask them to account for their movements.

As her head broke water, Marina twisted and turned like an eel, struggling to free herself from the stiff folds of oilskin. While it enveloped her arms the life jacket was useless, and that damned sou'wester with its strings knotted beneath her chin flapped over her eyes, blinding her. She spared a hand to wrench it off and immediately realised how far the current had carried her. Briefly she glimpsed the boat, with Logan clutching his arm as he knelt in the bows staring back at her – white-faced, appalled, and very distant: no help could come from him.

'Don't fight the water,' dive instructor Pablo said in her mind. 'Make it your friend and it will keep you safe.'

True enough in the balmy Mediterranean, but here the cold was numbing, creeping relentlessly from hands and feet to arms and legs, and in its grip her strength was ebbing fast. Water bubbled against her lips and she blew out hard, fighting down panic; then turned on her back, arms wide, desperate to keep her head clear of the waves.

Above her loomed a sheer black cliff – no possibility of getting ashore on iron-bound rocks while she was dragged along by this powerful undertow. She had only minutes – seconds – before it and the cold would overwhelm her. The oilskin had gone, stripped away by the rush of water, and though her life jacket buoyed her up the deadly chill was rapidly paralysing her limbs so that her body rocked and tossed, unable to steer away from those lethal cliffs. One big wave, and she would go under.

She was struggling to breathe, blacking out, choking, helpless as a beetle swept down a drain. This is it, she thought. I am drowning. This is the end, but strangely she felt no fear, just resignation. She had tried to beat it, tried to survive, but the sea was too strong and she was too cold to fight any more.

Darkness swept over her as consciousness retreated, but subliminally she was aware that another force had taken over the struggle she had abandoned. Powerful hands clamped her chest, holding her steady against the swirl of current, dragging her into slack water.

'Lie still, kittunge, don't fight,' rumbled a voice behind her.

'I knew you'd come,' she tried to whisper, but water roared in her ears and blackness swept over her.

# On the Skerry

JOGGING DOWN THE winding path to the harbour, her mind churning with possible ways to turn Jeannie's call to their advantage, Jess nearly collided with Mhairi, hurrying uphill in such a flurry of string bags, shawls and flying hair that she barely recognised her.

'Oh, Mrs Balfour! Thank God you're here.' She reached out and clutched at Jess with both hands. 'I was coming to find you... to tell you...' She stopped, gasping for breath, her face contorted.

'Tell me what? Calm down, Mhairi – what's happened?'

Mhairi made an effort to control herself and said more steadily, 'Terrible news. Terrible. I don't know how to tell you. There's a boat wrecked on the Skerry rocks, just this morning – a wee brown boat. Yanis saw it. He's sent to tell them to launch the Templeport lifeboat.'

'He saw it? But that's so far away. Surely he couldn't...?'

'He was watching seals through his glass.' She gulped and said painfully, 'He says – he thinks – it's my son's boat, and the two in it were Logan and little Marina Robb.'

'Oh, no!' Cold clutched at Jess's heart; she felt stunned as the full horror began to sink in. What could those crazy teenagers have been doing, so far out in the Sound? Logan knew that no one was allowed near the Skerries, and why would he risk it on a rough morning like this, choppy waves, wretched visibility... and that awful sucking undertow that dragged ships towards the rocks like corks down a bath-plug. Why? Why? This was no time to ask the questions that bombarded her: she must act at once.

Word was spreading like wildfire through the remains of the fish market and the harbour resembled an overturned anthill as fishermen unmoored their boats and engines roared into action.

Luke arrived at a run, skidding to a stop on loose pebbles, with Robb, ashen-faced, close on his heels.

He looked round for Winter, who had passed him on the hill. 'Where's Jim? Tell him to get on to –'

'He's already gone. I saw him jump in Davie McTavish's boat – the green launch out in front. He'll get there first and find out what happened.' Luke handed Robb his binoculars. 'Here, take these. There's nothing we can do now but wait.' He drew a deep, shuddering breath and said heavily, 'That's always the hardest part.'

An hour later, the drama was over. As the rescue fleet dispersed, and grumbling, honking seals hauled out once more on their rock shelves, Danna limped purposefully to where Jenny B wallowed in the swell.

Winter soon joined him. The boat was a sorry sight, planking ripped into sharp splinters; creels, bait, boathook and cans floating in an oily pool under the thwarts, and a heap of slimy bladderwrack draped over the starboard side where the waves had deposited it. Water gushed in and out of a gaping hole amidships. Only the outboard, which had sprung up and now rested on its supporting hook at a 45-degree angle, appeared unscathed.

'I suppose she's a write-off,' said Winter, inspecting the damage.

Danna frowned his disapproval, wrinkles creasing round his narrowed eyes as he assessed the damage. 'Hae ye no notion o' make do and mend, man? I'll fettle up the planking in ten days, without shipyard fees, forbye. Nay...' He bent over the outboard, removing the fuel cap and sniffing, looking closely at the starter cord, then standing back with a defeated air. 'The problem's here but I canna put ma finger on it. Wully wad see it in two ticks – he's the great man with engines.'

'You don't know what's wrong with it?'

The little gnome shook his head. 'I'll get Wully tae strip her down. The engine started fine, so what stoppit her a hundred yards frae the rocks?'

'How do you know she got that far?'

'Man, I was watching.'

'Watching. You saw the accident?'

'How else wad I get here soon enough? If ma boat had been a wee bit farther off the lassie would be drownded, for sure.'

Winter stared at him, taking this in, then nodded. 'You'd better tell me how it happened.'

They sat side by side on the edge of the flat rock above Jenny B's resting place while Danna described in his hoarse whisper how he had been returning with his night's catch when he spotted Logan's boat heading for the Skerry – 'Where he had nae business, the scallag, as well he knows –' and had changed course to intercept him and, 'gie him the rough o' ma tongue.'

When he reached the outer ring of rocks, Jenny B had vanished – 'There's a wheen hideyholes she could slip frae view' – so he had waited nearby with his engine idling until her brown bows nosed out of a narrow cleft a few hundred yards away. That was when he saw that Logan was not alone, and as he recognised Marina his anxiety rose because Jennie B was pitching steeply. It had begun to blow hard and black clouds heralded a sudden squall.

As she cleared the outer rocks and headed for the tail of the Reekie, Danna saw puffs of smoke erupt from Jenny B's stern. He saw Logan bending over the outboard, pulling the cord again and again, and moments later she was drifting back towards the rocks.

Even at full throttle, it took him several minutes to close the gap between the two boats, and he was half-blinded by the driving rain.

'I never saw her strike, but young Logan was still aboard when she canted ower, and I could see the lassie in the tide-race, all wrappit up and trying tae free herself. She'd a lasted but a wee while in that sea…'

He fell silent, faded blue eyes in his mahogany face gazing back in memory at those frantic seconds.

'You caught her with your boathook?'

'Aye.'

Though Winter was not an imaginative man, he shuddered to think how easily the hook could have missed its mark, but Danna was still preoccupied with Jenny B's engine failure.

He rose and examined the splintered hull again, then detached the outboard and transferred it to his own boat. Winter helped him gather up the remnants of Logan's gear, and when the wreck was empty they heaved her over clear of the tidemark, to drain.

'We'll be awa' the noo,' said Danna, untying his mooring rope. 'Will ye come aboard?'

'What about Jenny B?'

A grim twitch of a smile. 'She'll no' move in that condition. She can bide here until I fetch her hame.'

Neither of them spoke much as they crossed the lacy foam of the Reekie and headed for Kildrumna Bay. Hunched over the tiller, Danna seemed to be wrestling with a problem which he was on the point of revealing, only to shy away like a horse refusing a jump. Winter knew better than to question him. Every small community had secrets, and word of his own connection with the police would now be widespread: hardly surprising that Danna preferred to keep his mouth shut.

As they slid into calmer water, the big orange lifeboat passed them at high speed, heading for Templeport.

'Someone's in a hurry,' Winter remarked.

Danna followed it with his eyes. 'Young Lachlan wants his dinner, I ween.'

But when they reached the Kildrumna jetty, both Luke and Robb were waiting for them.

'Bad news,' said Luke, his voice shaking despite his efforts to speak steadily. 'The coastguard just rang to say that Gunnar's body has been found a few miles along the coast, washed up in Rowan Bay, in that little inlet called Cladh nan Ron. They're taking him in to Templeport, but they think he's been dead some time.'

# CHAPTER ELEVEN

# Chakrabatti

'A NASTY KNOCK. She was lucky – very lucky,' said Dr Chakrabatti, stepping away from the bed. His deft brown fingers tucked away his stethoscope as he surveyed his patient. 'She'll have a sore throat for a few days and that big bruise by her eye will take some time to go down, but her lungs are clear enough and otherwise I'd say there's no damage done. Full marks to whoever gave her CPR.'

'Teamwork,' said Robb. 'Danna was first on the scene and pulled her out, but he admits he thought she was a goner.' He drew a deep, shaky breath. 'Then my sergeant took over, and she started to cough.'

'Danna Murison? Splendid old boy. Knee-high to a grasshopper, but strong as an ox.' Chakrabatti smiled. 'Must be seventy plus, but no sign of slowing up.'

'I know.' Robb remembered the iron grip that had hauled him out of the Dunseran. 'But when I think what might… in just a few more minutes…'

'Don't think about it. Children are tough, and as I say, she was lucky. Now, about the boy – Mhairi Brydon's son – what's his name?'

'Logan.'

'Of course. Stupid of me to forget. That shoulder of his is more serious. Bit of a mess. I sent him in to Glasgow for a specialist team to deal with.'

'Did his mother go with him?'

Chakrabatti nodded and grinned. 'Her croft's not exactly set up for a hospital ward – Spartan's an understatement! Her uncle will see to the livestock, she says – that's Danna again, I imagine.'

'And my daughter?'

'P &Q's the best prescription I can give. Let her sleep as much as she can. The sedative may make her a bit woozy, but that's all to the good. Don't worry, Mr Robb.' He clapped him briskly on the shoulder. 'As I say, there should be no lasting damage, and in a couple of days she'll be right as rain. How long are you staying, by the way?'

Robb considered. 'We were due to leave on Wednesday, but I suppose it really depends on how Marina gets on. I'll have to discuss it with Luke and Jess.'

'Ah, the joys of an infinitely expandable house!' sighed Chakrabatti, who lived alone in a two-up, two-down cottage. 'I'll pop in and see her again tomorrow and meanwhile just keep an eye on her and let her sleep.'

Through the hazy lethargy that overwhelmed her, Marina listened to their footsteps on the stairs, in the hall, on the gravel, and finally the diminishing purr of the doctor's little sports car. The house was very quiet. Jess must be out in the kitchen garden, Luke on the river or down at the boat-house; her father perhaps making himself a cup of tea before coming up to sit with her.

Questions assailed her. Was she ill? What had happened? Her head ached and snippets of conversation floated through her mind, different voices, light and shade; impressions of people crowding round her and others telling them to stand back, give her a chance.

Wet clothes rasping and constricting movement and the horrible gushing of water from her mouth and nose. Relentless hands pumping her chest so she couldn't even scream at them to stop, to let her breathe…

An accident – yes, that was it. That must be why she was lying here on a sunny June day when she should be fishing.

Besides the headache she had a raw, sore, barbed-wire throat that made it painful to swallow. Listening to the doctor's staccato, lilting speech she had tried to piece together what had happened since she and Logan set out into the mist, but all her memories blurred and she fell asleep again.

When she next woke she could see from the shadows that it was evening, and her father was in the room, chatting quietly to someone at the door.

'Still out for the count,' she heard him say, and tried to tell him she was awake, but nothing came out but a croak.

'Poor pet. How much does she remember?' That was Ravenna's voice, soothing and low.

'Can't tell. She hasn't said anything yet, but the doctor told me not to try to hurry it. Sometimes a bang on the head blots out memory completely for years, or it may come back overnight. You just have to wait and see.'

'What a terrible, terrible thing to happen! Thank God Danna was there to save her. And all on top of -' A pause, a gulp; then she said softly, 'Look, would you like me to sit with her for a bit while you have supper?'

'It's very kind, but no... You don't want anything else to worry about. Not at the moment.'

'Go on, Martin. I've already eaten what I could force down and, frankly, I'd like something to focus on. To – to distract me – you know, take my mind off...' There was a curious little break in her voice, as if she was trying not to cry. Why would Ravenna cry?

'Besides,' she said more firmly, 'it would save Jess having to carry up a tray. She's run off her feet as it is.'

Silence, then Robb said, 'OK, then. Thanks.'

Marina heard the door shut behind him, and sensed Ravenna bending over her, watching her at close quarters.

'Marina? Can you hear me?' she said softly. When Marina did not reply, she went on, 'The hospital rang. They're going to operate on Logan's shoulder in the morning. They say he's going to be all right. I thought you'd want to know.'

Logan's shoulder. A piece of jigsaw slid into place as the image of his contorted face flashed behind her closed eyelids. She had fallen out of the boat and he had been clutching his shoulder, unable to help her. The engine had stopped and he couldn't start it, and the rip-tide had dragged them back against the rocks...

Marina swallowed painfully and forced her voice to croak, 'Is it broken? His shoulder? I was afraid –'

'Mhairi spoke to Jess and told her they're going to wire it together. It should be good as new. Can you remember what happened?'

'It's all blurred.'

'Tell me anyway.'

Slowly, with many pauses, Marina fished from her memory the random scenes haunting her dreams. Like a badly-wound film, shrouded in mist, she saw herself crouching against rocks, hiding her face, praying that someone would not see her. A rigid inflatable planing over the waves, bows clear of the water. A sleek white launch at anchor. Migrants in life jackets. Big Dougie... The splintering crash and sudden shock of cold.

Something she mustn't tell her father. Mustn't blab about... or Logan would be in trouble.

Ravenna's smooth, cool hand was stroking her forehead, 'Poor poppet, you've had a horrid shock but you're safe now. Here –' she offered a glass of water – 'have a sip and swallow this to help you sleep. You'll find everything much clearer when you wake up.'

'OK. Thanks.'

True to her mother's advice, Marina accepted the small yellow pill and tucked it in her cheek. She turned over, spat it into her hand, and plunged back into sleep.

Next time she woke the bedside light was on, and the rich smell of onion soup wafted across the room as Robb carefully balanced a bowl on a plate and sat down by her bed. She realised she was hungry.

'Dad, what happened?' she said huskily.

'I hoped you could tell me that.' He put down the bowl and hugged her. 'How's your head?'

'Sore.' Her fingers explored the bump on her forehead.

'D'you think you can eat some of this? Jess made it specially when I said it was your favourite. Come on, I'll help you sit up.'

He watched as she dipped bread and drank a few spoonfuls.

'Can you tell me what you were doing so near the skerries?'

Marina screwed up her eyes in an effort of memory, then shrugged helplessly. 'Sorry, Dad. I don't seem able to sort out what's real and what's a dream. The engine stopped and Logan couldn't get it going, and water came into the boat. I was baling, and the current was dragging us towards the cliffs. Then we hit a rock. That's real. I remember it clearly. But after that…it seems to blur. I was struggling, and it was so cold…' She gulped, and took a long breath. 'I had to give up. I couldn't fight it any more and thought I must have drowned, but then – then Gunnar caught hold of me.'

Robb took her hand in his. Sooner or later he would have to tell her the truth and it might as well be now, before she embroidered any more fantasies. 'You dreamed that part, I'm afraid.'

'I can't have.' Colour surged in her cheeks and she said in an agitated tone, 'He told me – he promised me he would come.'

'No, darling. It was Danna. He caught your life jacket with his boat-hook and pulled you into his boat.'

'But he called me 'kittunge.' Only Gunnar calls me that.'

'Listen, darling. It's very sad news for all of us, especially Ravenna, but the fact is that poor Gunnar has been drowned.'

'You mean he saved me and drowned himself?'

'No.'

Her mouth opened soundlessly and he remembered her earlier reaction of disbelief when he told her Gunnar was missing. Drowning had been a possibility then, but now it was certain.

'How do you know?' she said after a moment.

'The coastguard patrol found his body quite a long way down the coast in Rowan Bay, where dead seals and dolphins sometimes wash up. Something to do with underwater rock formations in the Reekie Sound. He was still wearing his BCD and oxygen cylinder... Hey, darling! Steady on!'

He made a grab for the soup plate which had tilted dangerously as Marina bounced up in bed, her eyes shining. 'So that's why he's gone!' she exclaimed.' Of course!'

'Why of course?'

'Oh, Dad! Don't you see? He left everything behind because he didn't need it any more. It means he's found it – the fur coat a mermaid stole from him long ago and he's been looking for ever since. Now he can go back to live in the sea again. No more BCDs and steamers. No more masks and fins, just a lovely thick fur coat.'

Could she possibly believe that? He stared down at her, baffled. 'But, darling –' he began, then stopped. What was the use of arguing? She was probably concussed.

'He told me that's what he's always wanted,' she said drowsily, and cuddled down under the bedclothes. 'I think I'll go to sleep now. Good night, Dad.'

'Sleep tight, sweetheart.'

He left the room reflecting on the human capacity for self-deception. Marina might be satisfied with her private fantasy, but it did nothing to address the little matter of the 9mm bullet holes that pocked the back of Larsen's BCD, nor the rip in his regulator hose.

'How much does she remember?' asked McInnes when Ravenna at last responded to his texts.

'She got quite a crack on the head. She's still confused.'

'Good. Let's hope it stays that way.'

'She said she had to hide from a man on the rocks and saw migrants in orange life jackets landing on the Skerry. Then she said it might have been a dream.'

'She called them migrants?'

Her silence confirmed it. 'Christ! And her father's a cop.'

'Exactly.'

'What about the boy? Has he said anything?'

'According to Jess, who spoke to the registrar, they've got him sedated, but even when he wakes up, I think he'll keep his mouth shut. Think about it,' she said before he could contradict her. 'He lives here. He's got nowhere to hide. What would happen if he blabbed? His creels would be stolen. He'd be outcast, his mother ostracised. No one would buy his fish.'

'And if the Smokery was affected the boys would run him out of town. Yes! You're right, Venny. The girl is the one we've got to worry about. I'd better warn Olympia asap.'

'Relax,' she advised. 'Don't panic, you've plenty of time to cover your tracks. I gave her one of Hoffnung's Specials, and she'll be in no shape to remember anything tomorrow. Leave her to me – I'll talk to her as soon as she wakes.'

Sitting at the kitchen table, Danna blew on the mug of scalding coffee handed him by Jess, and took a cautious sip. 'I blame masel,' he said wearily, and rubbed his eyes. 'If I hadna told him o' the Island fish farmers' plans, he'd never have risked it that night, though I warned him over and over.'

'Would he have listened to you?' asked Luke. 'He certainly wouldn't to me. The more I told him to leave it alone, the more determined he was to give McInnes a bloody nose. I think the antagonism went back a long, long way.'

'Right enough. They were like twa thrawn tups that canna leave one another be.'

'Men!' said Jess disgustedly. 'Idiots would be a better word.'

'Whatever the one had, the other wanted it. The first year it was Mhairi – but she chose to wed puir Seamus Brydon, a steady man for all that he was near kin and ower fond o' the bottle – then, the next summer, Dougie McInnes stole away Isla, the Major's niece, under Mr Larsen's very nose.' Danna wiped his mouth with the back of his hand. 'Twenty years later when he brings his bonny new bride here, what happens?'

'Ravenna?' said Luke. 'Same pattern?'

'Ye'd be blind not to see it.' Danna drained his cup and rose.

'Sit down,' said Jess. 'Tell us the whole story. Did Gunnar know about his wife and Dougie McInnes? When did you last speak to him? Did you know what he was planning?'

But Danna was already limping to the door, muttering that if he didn't check on the stirks they'd be in the oats again, leaving Luke and Jess staring at one another over their coffee mugs.

'D'you think he's right?' said Luke quietly.

'About Ravenna?' She gathered up the mugs and shook her head decisively. 'No way. She looked absolutely shattered when she heard: I thought she was about to keel over. I asked if she was all right and she said it was what she had always dreaded. Actually, it was a mercy Martin Robb was there to say the right things and calm her down. I suppose he's used to breaking that sort of news; all in the day's work for him. And good of him to go with her to identify the body.'

Luke blinked rapidly, trying to clear his head, feeling he was in a dream: a nightmare. The whole day had been a blur of horror piled on horror – strangers coming and going, telephone ringing non-stop, meals forgotten, vehicles thronging the drive – all wanting him to make decisions though one thing alone filled his mind. Gunnar was dead and he – Luke – must pick up the pieces. Never again would he feel that warm glow of relief when he managed to extricate his godfather from a perilous situation. They had been in so many tight spots together, but this time he had been excluded from the adventure. Gunnar had gone it alone, without consultation or back-up, and perished as a result.

Throughout the police questioning, the taking of statements for the Procurator Fiscal, the ever-increasing difficulty of fending off media interest, he had felt inadequate and helpless, almost as if part of him had been destroyed.

'I should have gone with her,' he said in a faraway voice.

'Much better left to a pro.' Jess put a hand on his shoulder. 'Darling, don't beat yourself up about it. Gunnar was a law to himself. You couldn't have stopped him – no one knows better than you how impulsive he was. How reckless. Keeping tabs on him must have been a nightmare for Ravenna.'

But Luke was recalling the cloaked figure slipping into the house before sunrise. The sleek look of a satisfied cat at breakfast, and the intensity with which she had studied the photograph of Danna's record catch. How much did she remember of the Major's household during her visit here as a teenager?

While Robb was in Templeport, Jim Winter pursued his own enquiries. When he went back to the Dive Shop just before it closed that afternoon, to return the hired scuba gear, he thanked Davie McTavish warmly for his speedy reaction that morning. 'That boat of yours is a real flyer. I honestly thought she was going to take off over those waves,' he said admiringly. 'Good job she's so fast. I don't think the girl would have lasted much longer.'

'Aye, I take her out whale-watching, and she's a grand boat for water-skiing, too. There's only one faster in Stairbrigg, and that's the white Gran Turismo that McInnes has on appro,' agreed Davie.

'Was that there this morning?'

215

Davie shook his head. 'Not down at the harbour, that's for sure.' He glanced at his watch and said diffidently, 'I'm by way of closing the shop now, sir, but if you'd fancy a cup of tea I know my wife would like to meet you and hear all about it first-hand. It's only a couple of steps away.'

Winter was always in the market for a cuppa. He glanced at his watch: time enough before he was due to meet Robb, and after only the briefest hesitation he said, 'That's very kind. Sure it won't be a nuisance for her?'

'Not at all, sir. Not at all. I'll give her a call now.'

He flipped out his phone and spoke briefly.' You'll be doing her a favour,' he assured Winter. 'She's troubled with the arthritis and doesn't get about much, and she'll be full of questions I can't answer.'

Doing me a favour, too, thought Davie, as he led the way through the shop and locked the back door. Elspeth had been in a strange mood ever since news of the lifeboat's grim discovery had filtered into Stairbrigg. She seemed at once excited and scared, was short with the boys and snapped at him: one moment cautioning silence about her own visit to *Shield Maiden*, and the next dredging up snippets of scandal dating back to her days working at the Lodge. She talked of friction between Gunnar Larsen and his parents when they visited Kildrumna: wrangling over business, women, and even how to tie salmon flies; the arguments went on for days. Gunnar was a risk-taker; his father a cold and cautious man. Once she had overheard Olaf declare he would leave everything he owned to his younger son Bjorn if Gunnar continued to defy him.

She remembered vividly how he and Dougie McInnes had quarrelled at the summer ceilidh in Templeport, causing Isla to burst into tears and storm out of the dance hall with Mhairi in tow; and how Gunnar used to swim round the point to Inverclinie on nights when Seamus was away with his nets, and haul out on the shingle, 'furry as the Great Selkie himself and naked as the day he was born.'

Does she need to dredge up all this? Davie had wondered. Surely to God now the man's dead such tittle-tattle is best forgotten?

But when he suggested she should let sleeping dogs lie, Elspeth turned on him fiercely. 'He ruined my sister's life and she's washed her hands of him, but it's the injustice that riles me. I can't shut my eyes to it. All these years he's got off scot-free, and never faced a reckoning. How many times have I told her that?'

'She won't listen?'

She shook her head. 'Once her mind's made up there's no shifting her. For the boy's sake I had to try one more roll of the dice, but I'm greatly afeared I left it too late.'

Housebound as she was, Elspeth's reputation for a warm welcome and fresh-baked cakes tended to draw members of her family to the bungalow at teatime. Not only were her sons already at the scrubbed table demolishing a large stack of dropscones, but both Wully and Danna, white foreheads contrasting strangely with leather-tanned faces, sat side by side at the far end, carefully boning kippers. Despite the difference in physique – Wully thin and rangy, Danna short and square – the family look was unmistakable, but while Danna exuded his usual mischievous brand of self-confidence, Wully seemed subdued, even cowed, and his knobbly hands shook as he extracted fishbones. Loss of status? Missing his dog? Had he been sacked after the mass escape?

All the men rose as Davie introduced him, and Elspeth limped forward to greet him. 'Sit you down, Mr Winter, and try a scone,' she said, handing him a cup of tea. 'I'm told you're the hero of the hour, bringing that poor bairn back from the brink.'

'Far from it,' said Winter, embarrassed. 'It was Danna who saved her and your husband who got me there in time to help.'

'Wheesht, that's not what I heard, but never mind.' She lowered her voice to a respectful whisper. 'Is it true that the coastguard found Mr Larsen's body washed up in Rowan Bay? That's a bad business.' She clicked her tongue. 'I hear his wife's gone to the hospital morgue, along with Mr Robb.'

How news got about! On that front there was little Winter could tell her that she didn't already know, but he confirmed enough to satisfy her, while straining to hear the two old brothers' low-voiced wrangling about Jenny B's engine failure. Apparently Wully had rescued it from the crusher.

'Naething but a heap of scrap metal. Why else wad Big Dougie ha' chucked it?' asked Danna and Wully bridled.

'I tell ye I paid for it. The lads at the shipyard said it was a bargain at twenty pound.'

'Twenty pound for a thousand-pound engine that could ha' cost the boy his life? That's the kind of bargain ye'd do weel tae avoid.'

'Much ye know about engines!' grunted Wully. 'If ye told young Logan tae use a filter on his fuel maybe he wouldn't end up in Glasgie General wi' a busted shoulder, and ye putting blame on me.'

'Filter, is it now?'

'Choked wi' grit, small wonder she stalled. Time he learned how tae maintain his machinery. Look at how he treats yon Argocat – overloads her wi' turf and pulls the guts half out of her then hands Mr Balfour the bills.'

On his other side the hulking teenage Alick, spotty and unshaven, quick dark eyes barely visible under a tangled fringe, was trying to get his attention.

'Have you finished repairing the fishcages?' Winter asked, but his brother cut in before Alick could answer.

'Waiting on the boss for further orders,' said Hamish smoothly. With his fair hair sleeked down and beard carefully trimmed to outline his jaw, he was a heftier version of his father. He added, 'There's a new type of reinforced netting he wants to use.'

'With a built-in alarm to wake the dead,' put in his brother, with a glance at Wully, who rose to the bait at once.

'There was never an alarm to match old Nipper, and don't you give me that look, boy, nor tell me I shoulda roused up the boss when the fush escaped. If he didna pick up ma call, whose fault is that? Did he want me to quit ma post and go haling into Stairbrigg in search of him with the seals all round the cages and the bay thick with fush?' he demanded hotly.

Winter leaned forward. 'So what did you do?'

'What about that old gun you'd shoot off to scare them. Where's that gone? Who gave you another?' insisted Alick, ignoring his brother's frown.

'I wanted to tell Jim –'

'Mr Winter to you, boy,' reproved his father and Wully, pale beneath his tan, advised him gruffly to save his breath to cool his porridge.

'I don't know anything about seals,' said Winter. 'I never saw one close to until this morning and was surprised how big it was. Are you allowed to shoot them?'

The question sparked a chorus of conflicting views.

'I'd say that's a grey area.' At the head of the table, Davie McTavish nodded judiciously. 'There's laws and there's regulations, but there's no' a lot of clarity. They're a protected species, but in certain conditions shooting them is permitted – with a licence, if you've evidence to show they're harming your business, which can be hard to prove.'

'Uncle Wully didna have a licence,' chirped Alick, who seemed bent on earning himself a clip round the ear. Wully grunted and glowered but said nothing intelligible and Winter, wary of provoking a family bust-up, hastily turned the conversation to cetaceans, in which he was more interested.

'I see you've got a poster on the door about whale-spotting,' he said to Davie. 'What do you expect to see here? Minke, I suppose?'

'Oh, aye. Minke, fin, orca, bottle-nose dolphins, porpoises – we get all sorts.'

'Humpback?'

'Aye, and blue whales, too. There was a pod round the

Shanty headland close inshore last week. They like the strong current when they're hunting krill and saithe. Sometimes they'll come right into the bay here, though there's always a risk they'll strand in the shallows. I blame those damned acoustic deterrents which play merry hell with their sonar.'

'Are those to keep them away from fish farms?'

A frown creased Davie's weathered face. 'So they say. It's the pity of the world that we canna leave those great beasts alone to hunt as they please without traps and nets and alarms. Tell me, Mr Winter, did you ever dive in South African waters? I spent four years on the beach there and it was the happiest time I ever had.'

'Until you ran out of money,' said his younger son, but Davie affected not to hear.

When eventually Winter took his leave, he was not surprised to find Danna limping after him down the cobbled street and halted at the corner to let him catch up.

'If ye're thinking now it was ma brother Wully who shot Mr Larsen, ye're on the wrong tack altogether,' he said aggressively.

Clearly the coastguards had been talking out of turn, but for form's sake Winter frowned. 'Who said anything about shooting? I thought he had drowned?'

Danna snorted contemptuously. 'Don't play games wi' me, man. It's all over town that his BCD was holed and the regulator hose punctured; but I'm telling you now that my brother had naething to do wi' that. What could a twelve-bore do against a tank tested to withstand pressure at depth? Zero! The pellets would rattle off like dried peas on a drum. And so ye can tell Mr Robb.'

With his ruffled hair standing up in a crest and wrinkled indignant face, he resembled nothing so much as a furious lizard. Without waiting for Winter to trot out soothing platitudes or ask for further revelations, he turned on his heel and limped rapidly back to Elspeth's bungalow.

'Always nice when a concerned citizen decides to do our job for us while we're still waiting for Forensics to report. I'm surprised he didn't give you the gun's make and serial number while he was at it,' said Robb sourly. He had had a trying afternoon and had not been impressed with his colleagues in Templeport, whose pasty-faced Chief Inspector Selwyn Gray, bursting out of his uniform, seemed determined to pin the shooting on Wully Murison, no ifs, no buts.

'Hauled him in for questioning within a couple of hours of seeing Larsen's body,' said Robb with disgust. 'No wonder the old boy was in a funk when you turned up at teatime. I gather he's been done for shooting seals before, so Gray thinks he's back at his tricks again and all he has to do is frighten him into a confession. Talk about a one-track mind! My suggestion of interviewing McInnes didn't go down well at all.'

'A nettle that might sting?' Winter suggested.

'Certainly one he wasn't keen to grasp. Much muttering about local sensitivities and the media. Trouble is, he's the big benefactor here – you should have heard the CI go on about what Big Dougie's done for the area. The Smokery, the golf course, the new wing at the museum. On and on. He even got Gray's missus invited to Holyrood to hear the debate on the Education Bill – five star treatment, and a word with wee Nicky herself. Big deal.'

'Which makes him untouchable,' said Winter thoughtfully.

'Makes him think he's untouchable. Strikes me they're all dead scared of antagonising Big Dougie for fear of political repercussions, and those go right to the top. No skin off our noses, of course; but it doesn't look good when the police prefer to pick on the little guy and leave the big fish alone.'

'I'd forgotten they used to call you Red Robbo.'

'None of your lip, my lad.'

Winter said tentatively, 'That boy – Alick – he works

at the fish farm. Cocky little blighter. Attention seeker. Each time he tried to tell me something the brother headed him off. Maybe if I talked to him outside the family circle he could shed more light on Wully's armoury...'

'You work on that,' said Robb with sudden energy. 'I'm going to find out what Danna was doing hanging about the Skerry rocks at dawn today, and see if I can jog his memory of Friday evening as well. I hear Mhairi's due home from Glasgow, too. Let's meet here at nine and exchange notes.'

For most of the return journey from Templeport Hospital, Ravenna had been silent and withdrawn. From the driver's seat Robb could see that the hand on her lap was clenched into a fist, while the other fiddled with the heavy gold links of her necklace.

He left her to her thoughts and concentrated on the twists and turns of the narrow coastal road with its humps and dips, and sudden swerves towards the cliffs where only a flimsy barrier separated it from the foaming waves breaking on rocks below.

Explosions of golden gorse punctuated the dull green of bracken along the verge, and against the skirts of the blue hills were occasional clusters of white-washed cottages clinging together for company in the huge empty expanse of moorland. No gardens or flowers that might attract the attention of deer, and every henhouse was a miniature fortress protected with electrified wire against foxes and polecats, and roofed with netting to deter crows. Even in high summer this tree-less landscape was bleak the moment the sun went in; he found it difficult to imagine how stark and unforgiving it must look in winter.

'I should never have married him,' said Ravenna at last, as if continuing aloud the conversation she had been holding in her head. 'All my friends told me not to. They warned me something like this would happen and they were right:

he would never settle down, though God knows I tried to persuade him to. For nearly two years now I've had my heart in my mouth whenever he went missing, dreading every telephone call…and now it has happened.'

'I'm so sorry.'

Silence fell again. After a while, Robb said, 'He was certainly unusual. A one-off.' and this time she seized the lead eagerly, words spilling out almost too fast for him to follow.

'That's it. I'd never known anyone like him – larger than life, you might say. Everything about him was supersized. When I first met him, I was overwhelmed. You hear about women being swept off their feet – well, that's what happened. It was like riding the crest of a great wave. He was so strong, so generous, so full of enthusiasms –'

So rich, thought Robb.

'– and when I saw him just now…' She drew a long, quavering breath, 'All that was gone. Vanished. An empty husk. I couldn't help thinking of the time I'd wasted. How could I have done more to make him settle down? Stop his crazy longing for danger. For adventures. But I couldn't – he wouldn't listen. It was like a drug.' Her voice trailed away.

Robb said quietly, 'Don't blame yourself.'

'But I do! I can't help it. If I had given him a child, things might have been different. He loved children. Well, you saw how he and your Marina understood one another. All those fantasies and silly practical jokes. At heart he was a great boy who had never really grown up, a teenage adrenalin junkie. All he ever wanted was the buzz he got from adventures that might be dangerous, and because he could afford it, that's what he went looking for. The conservation work was an excuse for going to the kind of places where he might find it.'

'Some of the situations he got into were pretty hair-raising, according to Luke,' said Robb. 'Close encounters with narco barons. Somali pirates boarding his boat off the Horn of Africa, isn't that right? Challenging Japanese whalers? Luke said he was often scared stiff.'

'Poor Luke. He was roped in, Sancho Panza-style, though I don't think he really enjoyed that kind of thing. I didn't either, but Gunnar believed adventures always had happy endings.'

Not this one, thought Robb, and wondered why she was suddenly so keen to spell out her feelings. Sorrow? A degree of guilt? Probably both. Sheer relief at getting this disagreeable formality over and done with? No matter how sympathetically it was handled, identifying a body was an ordeal, and Ravenna's stoicism up to this point had been exemplary. Probably too exemplary. Bottling up emotion brought its own problems, and a sideways glance showed her on the verge of tears.

She said in a choked voice, 'Can you stop for a moment? I – I feel a bit sick.'

'Sure.' He parked on the sheep-cropped verge and she got out with her hand pressed to her mouth. 'Take your time,' he said. 'I'm in no hurry.'

She walked off towards the cliffs and leaned on the crash barrier, breathing deeply, staring out to sea. He wondered if he should join her or if she preferred to be alone, but before he had resolved the question she turned and came back to the car, looking more composed.

'Better?'

'Much better,' she said and managed a watery smile. 'You're a dear to come with me today. I couldn't sleep last night, thinking about it. Dreading answering questions. Seeing him dead.' She touched him lightly on the arm. 'How is Marina doing?' she asked in a different tone. 'Has she remembered any more of what happened? Why they were there?'

Robb shook his head. 'She says it's all a blur, and the doc told me not to press her about it. Either her memory will come back in a rush or it won't – no way of telling. The great thing is that she has bounced back physically: I had quite a job to get her to stay in bed this morning, and she's getting up for supper.'

'And no more panic attacks?'

'Not a sign of one for days.'

'Wonderful,' said Ravenna. 'So will you be leaving on Wednesday as planned?'

'Touch wood. Luke and Jess have been endlessly kind, but they've got another lot of visitors due in three days' time, and we really can't inflict ourselves on them any longer.'

She sighed. 'Same goes for me, though I'll have to stay on until I've got all the official stuff sorted. I'll probably move to a hotel, where I can wrap up my work for the museum as well. Gunnar's solicitors have been in touch already, saying they want to talk to me asap, and they've had the sense to detail a PR firm to deal with the Press. Keep them off my back.' She grimaced then said quietly, 'I'll be sorry to see you go. You've been a wonderful support.'

'Me? Nonsense! I've done nothing.' Robb ducked his head, embarrassed.

'Au contraire. Having you here – knowing you were on my side – has made all this bearable for me.'

Where did sides come into this, he wondered. Suddenly acutely conscious of her closeness in the confined space, the warmth and fragrance of her body as she leaned towards him, and unwilling to prolong a conversation that threatened to become too personal, he started the car.

'If you're OK now, we'd better be getting back,' he said. 'Just tell me to stop if you feel sick again.'

Mindful of her promise, Jess had rung Lady Jean's mobile to warn her of Gunnar's death, but voicemail didn't seem a suitable way to convey such a message, so she merely asked her to call back as soon as possible.

Asap turned out to be half past eleven at night, when the yawning Balfours were about to go to bed. It had been a long day.

'Jean Allan returning your call,' said the clipped voice,

barely audible against a background of static and clinking glasses. 'Has Larsen surfaced? Where can I get hold of him?'

'It's bad news, I'm afraid.' Jess switched the handset to her other shoulder and gestured to Luke to turn off the bath-taps.

'On a cruise? Where to?'

'News. Bad news!' Jess shouted. 'Gunnar Larsen has been drowned.'

'Sorry, didn't catch that. Bloody awful reception up here. Hang on a tick – I'll put you on speakerphone.' A pause, accompanied by muttering: 'Which button? No, that's not it. Try the next one along – bottom left, and shut that flaming door, I can't hear myself think. Aah...that's more like it.' Suddenly her voice came through loud and crackly. 'What were you saying? Larsen's gone on a cruise?'

Slowly Jess repeated her message, which was greeted with a shocked silence. Then – 'How the hell did that happen?'

'We don't know for sure. You remember the night the salmon cages were sabotaged?'

'Saw the result with my own eyes, didn't I? You mean that was Larsen's work? Sorry, but can you speak up a bit? I can hardly hear you. Did you say it was Larsen who sabotaged those cages? I – I find that hard to believe.'

'So do we,' shouted Jess, 'but that's what it looks like. The police think Gunnar swam out to the cages and cut holes in the wire, and old Wully, the nightwatchman, thought it was a seal attack and shot him.' She paused, then added, 'The major snag with that theory is that Wully's old twelve-bore was confiscated a few months ago because he hasn't got a licence. Someone – not hard to guess who – had lent him another, but a shotgun is pretty useless against seals and twelve-bore pellets wouldn't penetrate a BCD.'

Jeannie said sharply, 'Only had a 12-bore? Eyewash! Typical police – they haven't got a clue. Listen: when I saw Wully next morning, the old ruffian was stoned to the eyeballs and couldn't have shot a barn door at twenty paces, but he certainly had an automatic.'

'You saw it?'

'I did indeed. There was a seal with half its jaw missing, all tangled in the netting, and I told McInnes to look sharp and put it out of its agony, so he nipped into the cabin, brought out a machine pistol and emptied the magazine into the poor creature.'

'It wasn't a shotgun?'

'Nothing of the kind. I only got a glimpse – it all happened very quickly – but I'd say it was a Glock or Beretta or H&K. Something of that order. Nine mill. Ratatattat! Ratatatat! Semi-automatic. Definitely.'

Jess said slowly, 'That alters things a bit.'

Silence but for the fizzling and crackling until Lady Jean said, 'Look, this is no bloody good. I can't hear you. Tell you what: I'm coming over to the mainland sometime in the next couple of days, so I'll drop in on you so we can discuss this properly. OK?'

'Fine!' shouted Jess as the line went dead.

'Now what was all that about?' asked Luke. 'What alters what?'

Jess took a deep breath and put down the handset with fingers that shook. 'The Lady of Eilean Breck, who sounds as if she knows her way around guns, says she saw McInnes kill an injured seal – not with a shotgun, but a semi-automatic pistol from the feed barge. This could mean old Wully is in the clear.'

'Or that both he and McInnes were lying,' Luke pointed out.

She shook her head emphatically. 'Don't be like that, darling. Wully's been fined twice already for shooting seals. I remember him saying, "The pollis warned me, Three strikes and ye're oot,"' so I'm sure he wouldn't risk it. He'd be scared of going to prison… And don't forget he lost poor little Nips, who was the only person he ever really cared for.'

Luke recognised gut instinct kicking in and knew it was useless to point out the lack of logic in this argument. Her liking for lame dogs had led Jess to pay the vet for Nipper's wormers and painkillers because Wully couldn't afford his fees, and he thought it likely that the practice had the stroppy little terrier registered as hers. Now that same gut feeling was insisting Wully was innocent of shooting Gunnar, so who did that leave pulling the trigger?

She said angrily, 'How absolutely typical of our very own Teflon Man to throw Wully to the wolves and slide out of it himself. Can't you just imagine him saying, "If you so much as open your mouth to the cops I'll make sure you never get another job in this town." Come on, Lukey, can't you?'

He felt sleepy and depressed and wished that she would leave the whole mess to sort itself out without her involvement. Or his. The trouble was that he could all too easily imagine Big Dougie saying exactly that.

He made an indeterminate sound which she took for agreement, and Jess went on, 'All the same, I think with a bit of input from the Lady of Eilean Breck we may still manage to pin it on him. Come to bed, darling, and in the morning we'll make a plan.'

'Must we? Can't you leave the police to do their job in their own way? After all, it is their job, not ours.'

'And have them throw the book at an innocent man? Send him to prison for something he didn't do? I can't believe you said that. You know what they're like where Big Dougie is concerned: Yes, sir; no, sir; three bags full. We've seen it again and again.'

She pummelled her pillow into shape as if she wished it was McInnes's head, and said with quiet intensity, 'Of course he must have shot Gunnar, and yes, it's up to us to make sure he takes the rap for it. We owe it to Ravenna. Big Dougie's got away with too much for too long. He can't be allowed to get away with murder.'

# CHAPTER TWELVE

# Alick

A ROUNDABOUT CONFIRMATION of Lady Jean's assessment came when Winter tracked Alick to the dimly lit, sparsely-patronised bar at the Clachan, all smokedoak and brass horse plates, where he was moodily throwing darts Around the Clock.

Winter bought himself a Coke and settled at a nearby table to watch. No doubt about it, Alick was good. When he finished his game with a triumphant bullseye, Winter sauntered over.

'Neat!' he said sincerely, and the hulking boy's scowl of concentration was replaced by a tentative smile.

'You play?'

'Now and then.'

'Give it a go? 301 or Around the Clock?'

Winter had hesitated, glanced at his watch and shook his head.

'Come on,' urged Alick, producing another set of darts. '301 doesn't take long. House rules, OK?'

Winter nodded. 'Suits me.'

He stepped up to the oche and threw a double and two low trebles. Alick looked unimpressed. He licked his lips, pushed his heavy fringe out of his eyes, and used his turn to score double 12, treble 14, and 9.

He's right, thought Winter: this won't take long. It'll be a massacre.

At 164, with his opponent still trailing by a hundred points, Alick grinned, glanced at the barman, and winked.

'Right! Here we go…' and in a swift flurry he threw double 18, treble 20 and a bullseye. '18,' he said with satisfaction.

Winter countered with a feeble double 8, 17, and treble 4, and stepped back. 'Over to you.'

One, four, double six. Winter wondered what Alick was playing at. Left on one a player was bust. Was he deliberately throwing the game?

Alick's smile widened. 'House rules, OK? That means I have to split the 11, right?'

Casually, apparently without aiming, he threw his first dart into the tiny space between the upright digits, watched it stick there, quivering, then swung round to bow theatrically left and right.

'Brawly fecht!' called the barman.

'Well done!' clapped Winter.

'Party trick,' said Alick with a modest smirk. 'Rematch?'

Winter shook his head. 'You're a sight too good for me. What are you drinking?'

'Same as you, ta.'

They settled at a table against the wall, and hefty balding Fergus, his scalp freckled like a Maran's egg, bustled over with two Cokes and bags of crisps. Buoyed by his easy victory, Alick was more at ease than at his mother's tea party, though plainly disillusioned with his work and scared of his boss.

'He'd give our jobs to those bloody foreign kids if he could, but then he'd wave goodbye to his grants for employing local labour,' he said moodily.

'You could always leave.'

'And pull the plug on Dad's business? No way. He's up to his neck in debt and If Mr McInnes didna support him he'd go under in six months.' He sank half his Coke in one swallow, and Winter signalled for another. Alick muttered, 'You tourists come up from the south don't know how hard it is to find jobs here, or how easy to lose them.'

'You've got a good eye. Have you thought of taking up darts professionally?'

A contemptuous shrug. 'That's nobbut a game.'

'What else do you play? Footie? Snooker?'

'Total rubbish.'

Chippy Youth: my speciality, thought Winter, mentally preparing his fail-safe blend of praise, sympathy, and careful flattery. All these unhappy teenagers had something eating them. The trick was to find out what it was. Munching crisps and sipping Coke, he listened to the familiar depressing litany of complaint from the overworked and underpaid at the bottom of the employment heap, who asked nothing from life but instant stardom, fame and fortune – money, money, money – all with the minimum of effort.

In Alick's view, Yanis was a slave driver, McInnes a tyrant, and his own talents neither recognised nor rewarded as they should be. His dream was to own a fleet of speedboats and jet skis and start a water-skiing business here on the coast between Stairbrigg and Templeport.

'Great idea,' said Winter. 'What's stopping you?'

Money, of course.

'Wouldn't your boss lend you enough to get started?'

A derisive laugh.

'You could start small,' Winter persisted. 'Get your dad to lease you that launch that took me out to the Skerries. It's a flyer.'

'It's not his. The boss charges him to use it.'

Impasse. Winter picked up the tab and felt for his wallet. 'I'd better be off.'

'Wait,' Alick said, suddenly galvanised. 'Something you should know.' He leaned forward and began to speak rapidly. 'You're a cop, right? Knew it the moment I saw you at my mam's. Well, the pollis say my Uncle Wully shot Mr Larsen, but I'm telling you now he never did.'

'But –'

'Listen. You've seen that Gran Turismo launch the boss has got on appro? Lovely job – proper flyer, she is. Uncle Wully's mustard on engines, and he keeps it in good nick in case it has to go back to the shipyard, but he says Big Dougie's always fussing, saying it's running rough or noisy. Needs adjustment, tuning, anything'll give him an excuse to keep it longer.'

'Doesn't the seller object?'

'Poor sod needs the money, see?' Alick's mouth turned down. 'He knows, and Wully knows there's bugger-all wrong with it, but the boss has got him over a barrel. Just like he has my dad. "Let me help you out, Mr McTavish",' he mimicked grotesquely, 'and before you know it the business is his, all but the name over the door, and Dad taking orders and wondering how he lost control.'

'Is that what happened?'

'Look. Take this Gran Turismo. Last weekend, Friday, the seller gets fed up, asks the boss to decide one way or the other, he's got someone else interested, OK?'

'OK.'

'Well, the boss doesn't want to pay the asking price, and he doesn't like being pushed around, but all the same he wants to hang on to it for a few more days. Why? He's got a load of bigwigs down from the Islands and he wants to impress them. So after they've gone to bed that night he takes the Gran Turismo out to the cages, tells Wully he thinks there's something wrong with the engine, doesn't sound right to him, and he'll have to get it sorted before handing it back. Can't risk the seller claiming it was returned damaged, can he? Well, a nod is as good as a wink to Wully, so off he goes for a spin round the Skerry and back, puts the boat through her paces while the boss keeps watch over the cages because there's been talk – only a rumour, mind – that a certain friend of Mr Balfour's is taking rather too much interest in how the fish are managed and treated –'

'Mr Larsen?'

A blank look. Behind Alick, at the bar, Winter was aware of Fergus's bulk bent forward, listening.

'Course there's nothing wrong with the launch at all –

but to play the boss's game Wully says he'd like to strip down the engine and give it the once-over before it goes back to the shipyard. And with that the boss gets back in the launch and that's the last Wully sees of him that night.'

'Go on,' said Winter as Alick stopped abruptly.

'You know the rest.'

'Not in detail.'

'OK, then. So the boss has everything nicely arranged for his bigwigs. Rubbish gone, rat droppings swept out, every sick fish dumped in the nearest bog hole, so he loads up his visitors in the Gran Turismo,' said the boy rapidly, 'and when they reach the cages, what do they find? Wully stoned, Nipper drownded, and the biggest bull seal you ever saw with its jaw shot away. Don't tell me Wully did that.'

'Because he hadn't got a gun?'

Fergus was moving around the bar uneasily, clinking bottles, clattering glasses and clearing his throat.

In warning?

Alick muttered, 'Boss doesna like us speaking to tourists, and if Fergus here wasna a mate of mine I'd worry about word getting back to him.'

'Then it's lucky I haven't understood a word you've said.' Winter levered himself off the sticky vinyl bench. 'Thanks for the game, and good luck.'

He sketched a wave and left without looking back.

'Hearsay,' said Robb moodily. 'Circumstantial. Nothing we can get hold of there. I think Luke's right and we should leave it alone. We're not on our own patch. We've no dog in this fight.'

'Boss!'

'No good looking at me like that. Think it out: what can we do? We're visitors here. We've no official standing. Everything suggests to me that Larsen was up to no good and got himself killed by accident. You never met him, but to my mind he was a bit of a bully who liked to lay down the law though he reckoned the rules didn't apply to him – you know the sort. Classic mischiefmaker. And despite all the bombast, he was quite childish about practical jokes and fairy tales. Mythology. He and Marina were on the same wavelength there, so of course they got on like a house on fire...'

He paused, remembering the old photograph of Danna's great catch. 'He used to come here with his parents years ago, when McInnes was working as the gardener's sidekick, and apparently the pair of them clashed even then. Women were the problem, I gather.'

Winter said disbelievingly, 'You mean McInnes cast aside his humble beginnings and rose to the dizzy heights of Holyrood in twenty-odd years?'

'Marrying the Major's niece probably helped careerwise.'

'Ah. Yes. So how do you suppose Larsen felt when he came back here to find his old bugbear the local big cheese? Had the passage of time mellowed their relationship?'

'I think,' said Robb deliberately, 'that the iron entered into his soul, and he decided to damage Larsen's business by releasing those salmon himself, and then publishing a damning report on how the fish farm was managed.'

'But you can't prove it.'

'Correct. Pure surmise based on observation. And I also think – surmise again – that while he was dressed in his scuba gear and busy cutting those cages open, someone – either old Wully or McInnes himself – got lucky with a burst from a semi-automatic they shouldn't have had on the barge. You can't call that murder. Accident, at most. An unfortunate accident.'

Winter shook his head. 'Pity. What about the machine pistol? Mrs B said the old trout who rang last night was sure she'd seen one.'

'Lady Jean Allan is a well-known eccentric,' said Robb with regret. 'Not the most reliable of witnesses, and she admits she only got a quick look at it. Somehow I don't think anything she says will cut much ice with the local police. It's no good, Jim. I don't like it any more than you do, but McInnes has them in his pocket and the last thing we want is for them to make things difficult for our friends here. The Balfours know they're not popular locally because of their opposition to fish-farming, and this might be the final straw.'

'What d'you reckon to the foreign kids that would take Alick's job if they got a chance?' persisted Winter. 'Youngsters waiting in the bars and restaurants. Packers at the Smokery. How did they get here? Why did they get here? All above board, d'you think?'

'Mrs Balfour says they're related to the Greek woman who runs the fish restaurant. Olympia.'

'All of them?'

'Apparently she has a big family,' said Robb blandly. 'Lots of nephews and nieces. They help her and she helps them. Temporary visas. Visitors.'

'And how many of those visas are still in date?' Winter demanded sceptically. 'How many of those nieces and nephews work until their visas expire and then vanish into Glasgow's black economy?'

'Look, Jim, it's no good trying to get answers from me because I don't know and as a visitor here myself I've no right to ask.' Especially not that tight-assed box-ticker of a Chief Inspector in Templeport, he added silently. 'There's nothing I've heard to link them to friend McInnes, though Mrs Balfour thinks it's a bit of an in-joke locally.'

'Joke?'

'You know what I mean,' said Robb impatiently. 'A secret — that's more like it — which everyone except them knows about and keeps mum. The Gaeltacht taking the mick from the Sassenach. It's a well-known Scottish amusement.'

'You won't do anything about it?'

Robb thought it over and shook his head. 'I don't see that I can without getting egg all over my face. I can just hear Police Scotland telling me politely to back off. They'll do what's necessary in their own way without instruction from visiting Englishmen.'

He paused, feeling he owed him an apology. 'I'm sorry, Jim. I'm afraid I dragged you up here under false pretences. When there seemed to be a sporting chance of finding Gunnar Larsen alive, I thought we could tackle it together, me on land and you in the water, but now we know for certain he's dead, well –'

'You find I'm surplus to requirement.' Winter forced a grin.

'Don't take it to heart, Jim. Pity it turned out to be a wild goose chase.'

'No worries.' Winter shrugged. 'I've hired the bike for a week, so I might as well get some mileage out of her and see a bit of the country. You staying long?'

'We'll leave on Wednesday morning, crack of dawn, so should be able to make it home in one hop. Then Marina's due to stay with Helen for a week over at Marlow to get some riding as well as helping her with young Timmy, while I think about getting back into harness.'

'Sure you're up to it?'

'Rarin' to go.'

Winter said cautiously, 'She seems a lot better.'

'We both are. This place has done her a world of good, and you should see me go uphill now. Everest next stop.'

'Mind you don't overdo it, or your girls will have something to say. I texted Sal last night to put her in the picture, and she sent you a message: tell Dad to watch out for wealthy widows.'

'Cheeky monkey!' Rob laughed and shook his head. 'Poor Ravenna, actually I feel sorry for her. By her account she had a hell of a time trying to keep Gunnar out of trouble with his crazy adventures, and now he's given her the slip and got himself killed just as she always feared he would.'

'Inheriting a few million should soften the blow,' said Winter dryly as he took his leave.

# CHAPTER THIRTEEN

# The Challenge

'LAST DAY,' SAID Marina sadly as she pushed open the kitchen door. 'It's gone so quickly. I can't believe we've been here nearly three weeks, and now we've got to go home.'

'You must come again next summer,' said Jess; if we're still here and solvent, she added to herself. For the past three nights the terms of Gunnar's will had been coming between her and her sleep.

'Oh, yes!' Marina's face lightened as she noticed the be-ribboned parcels by her place. 'But what can these be?'

'You didn't get much of a birthday, poppet, what with one thing and another,' said Jess, leaving the stove to give her a hug, 'so we thought we'd have a re-run and celebrate today. This is from your father, the oblong one from Ravenna, and this is from me and Luke. Let's wait for them to surface before you start opening.'

'Cool! I know Dad's awake, and Luke's just coming up the path. I'll put stuff on the table.' Marina darted to the larder and gathered an armful of cereal canisters, jams, honey, Marmite, butter and sugar which she plonked on the sideboard. 'Anything else? Shall I make toast?'

'I'm going to miss your help,' said Jess.

'Just at breakfast?'

'All the time! Some people stay for weeks and haven't a clue where things are kept. Even our sons are pretty vague. I always wished I had a daughter.'

'Dad's got three. He might do a swap.'

'What might I swap?' Robb stomped in, fresh from the shower, just as Luke joined them through the garden door.

'Happy Birthday!' he exclaimed. 'How does it feel to be fifteen?'

'Plus three days,' corrected Marina. 'OK so far, thanks.'

'Come on, see what's inside,' Robb urged, nudging his parcel forward. Marina felt it carefully through the paper. 'Round. Quite hard... Hmm. Can't guess.'

'Open it.'

She untied the ribbon and began hunting for the end of the sticky tape.

'You'll need these.' Jess passed across the kitchen scissors to snip the many layers with which Robb had armoured his parcel.

'Honestly, Dad! It's like getting into Fort Knox.'

Everyone watched as she unwound the final sheet of tissue and drew out the silver-lined quaich.

'Oh!' Scarlet-faced and momentarily bereft of speech, she turned it this way and that, minutely examining the little mermaids on the rim, the incised scales on their long tails, the smooth driftwood with its silky finish.

'Do you like it?'

'Like it? I love it! Oh, Dad. It's the most beautiful thing I ever saw in my life!'

'Well, not quite, perhaps...' He broke off as she flung her arms round him, gabbling thanks with an enthusiasm he never expected from the most reserved of his daughters.

'It's perfect, and look – two handles! It's a loving-cup. Where did you find it?'

'Mhairi made it. Jess suggested I should have a look around her workshop, and I spotted it in one of the display cases.'

'It's called a quaich,' put in Jess. 'The Cup of Friendship. May I look?'

They passed it round the table, admiring, commenting on the workmanship, while Marina tore open the other parcels.

Ravenna had given her a tartan cashmere scarf – 'Not quite the weather for it, but you may find it useful this winter,' she said deprecatingly – but when Jess's colourful paper was stripped away to reveal a large curiously-shaped shell, with spiral ends and the iridescent sheen of mother-of-pearl, Marina's eyes widened, and she put a hand to her mouth.

'Wh – what…? Wh-where…?' she stammered.

'It's a conch – a queen conch,' Jess told her. 'My aunt picked it up on a beach in the Caribbean and brought it home so that she could listen to the sea, no matter where she was. Have a try.'

Silently Marina put the shell to her ear. A slow smile spread over her face and her eyes dreamed into space.

'What do you hear?'

'Waves,' she whispered as if afraid to break the spell. 'Waves crashing on shingle, surf on pebbles…and voices. Voices calling me.' Her forehead creased. She said haltingly. 'It's – it's the Selkies… calling me to join them… under the waves… Listen!'

Ravenna's face froze: she sat very still.

'Nonsense!' said Robb sharply. 'Put that down.'

As he leaned forward to take it from her, she dropped the conch, which rolled off the table and smashed on the tiled floor. Marina picked up the two biggest shards and tried to fit them together, her eyes filling with tears. 'I'm sorry. So sorry,' she murmured. 'Oh, Jess! I didn't mean to drop it.'

'Don't give it a thought,' said Jess, while Luke hurriedly found dustpan and brush. 'Doesn't matter a bit – not your fault at all. Shells are so fragile, and of course it was old and brittle. Something like this was sure to happen to it one day.'

'Can't we stick it together?' Marina was still clutching her handful of shards.

'Not a hope, poppet,' said Jess gently, 'put those in the bin with the rest.' She drew a deep breath. 'Now, let's sort out what we're going to do today. Lukey?'

As usual, he was ready with a plan. 'Both rivers are

unfishable today, I'm afraid. Too low: I looked at the marker just now and it's barely up to 3. Hopeless. Needs a couple of days' steady rain, and we're not going to get that this week.'

'So?' prompted Jess.

'So I think this looks like a good day for the Shanty Fish Challenge, if anyone's up for it.'

'What's that?' asked Marina quickly. She liked challenges, particularly if they involved fish or water.

'It's our home-made version of the classic Macnab. Have you heard of that?'

'Shoot a stag, catch a salmon, bag a grouse, all in the same day,' Robb said promptly.

'Spot on. The difference is that in our version you have to catch six brown trout, land one seatrout, and collect a jarful of shrimps between eleven o'clock and five pm, and the place we do it is the Shanty estuary, about three miles up the coast from here. Would you like to have a go?'

'Sounds fun,' said Robb. 'Count me in.'

'And me,' said Marina at once.

'Ravenna?'

She glanced at Robb, hesitated, then shook her head. 'Sorry, I'd love to, but I'll have to opt out. Gunnar's lawyers want to speak to me – they say it won't wait. Something to do with his will. They've set up a Zoom meeting at half past ten at the internet café in Stairbrigg because your connection here is so dodgy.'

'Did they say what's wrong?' asked Robb.

Again she shook her head, saying with a kind of angry impatience, 'He always liked to be different. There was no need to put in stuff about loyalty and fealty and who owed what to whom as if he was a Viking chief. Apparently he got some jobsworth to look up Old Norse law to get the language right.'

'Don't worry,' said Robb calmly. 'It probably won't be valid here.'

'It just makes everything more hassle, which frankly I

could do without,' she said edgily. And you can bet your boots that Gunnar would have made it watertight, she thought. Legal wrangles meant probate would be delayed, and that was the last thing she wanted.

'Are you sure you can cope? I spend much of my time dealing with lawyers.'

She flashed him a look of gratitude but said firmly, 'I'll manage, but thanks, anyway.'

'Right, so it'll be a straight contest between the two of you,' said Luke. 'We'll get Danna to run us round in his boat, and I'll show you the path up to the two little lochs. They're stuffed with trout and catching half a dozen should be a doddle. It's a bit of a hike to get there, and no one from the Lodge has been lately because the French ladies weren't great walkers. Danna says the only person fishing there is the otter.'

'Oh, I hope we see him!'

'Her. Or rather them. She had kits last year, so there's quite a family of otters thereabouts. The bigger loch' – his finger moved to the crescent nearest the hill – 'has fair-sized fish, but not so many of them, and the small triangular one, Loch Donuil, is absolutely stuffed with tiny dark trout with goggle eyes because they don't get much light under the cliff. The more you can take out, the more food there'll be for the rest.'

'Do you fish them from the bank?' asked Robb, whose back-cast all too often snagged on whatever lay behind him, especially if there was a wind.

Luke nodded. 'You can spin from the sides, though it's difficult to cover much water; but we've also got a small boat on each.'

'Great,' said Robb.

'I've told Danna we'll meet him at the jetty at half ten. He'll take the three of us as far as Shanty Beach and leave us there; then around four thirty he'll bring out Jess with firewood, and we'll cook our shrimps on the beach. OK? Can you put everything together by then, my love?'

'Shrimps! Brown bread and butter. Of course. Nothing more delicious.'

'What's the prize?' demanded Marina, looking up from admiring her quaich.

'Wait and see,' said her father automatically, and she gave a sigh of exasperation.

'But I want to know!'

Ravenna rose, glancing at her watch. 'I suppose I'd better get going.'

Robb followed her out of the room. 'I'm sorry you can't come to the lochs. I'm sure you'd have given us a run for our money.' He looked searchingly at her and asked, 'By the way, what did you make of that business with the shell? Did Marina really hear something, or was she having us on?'

'Goodness knows.' She was silent a moment, then said reflectively, 'It was so strange, the bond she had with Gunnar. I found the way they seemed to speak the same language quite eerie. Perhaps it's just as well you're leaving here tomorrow – giving her something else to think about.'

'I know. Time to return to ordinary life with ordinary worries. And talking of worries, her memory is coming back, though she says it's still patchy. I've told her to stop fretting and put the whole episode behind her.'

Ravenna smiled. 'You're very understanding – she's a lucky girl.' She squeezed his hand briefly, and hurried away.

The Shanty beach was a neat pair of semi-circles separated by a heap of jagged boulders, where fine yellow sands shading to white dunes were tucked under looming black cliffs topped with heather. Beyond them, the hinterland stretched away in a great expanse of marshy peatbog, with blocks of stacked turfs standing out like straight dark streaks against the prevailing yellowy-green vegetation. Between the stacks were trenches like random ditches showing where countless generations of crofters had dug out their fuel supplies.

'Very little digging allowed nowadays,' said Luke, map spread on knees, as Danna's boat chugged towards the shore.

Beside him on the middle thwart, Marina looked keenly from map to land and back again. 'I suppose it's a good thing, conservationwise, but I do miss the whiff of turf smoke hanging over the bay on winter evenings.'

'Mhairi still burns peat,' said Marina. 'Logan told me he has to fetch loads for the stove, and only the Argocat can get across the bog.'

'Ah, yes. Her croft has an historic right to dig a certain number of turfs per year. It dates back to God knows when and she won't be giving that up in a hurry – not while she's a strong son to lug them home for her. Mhairi likes to do things the traditional way, but it's heavy work!' said Luke, laughing, 'I tried it once and it nearly killed me.'

He called to Danna at the stern, telling him to head for the smaller of the two beaches. 'We never take the boat beyond the headland,' he explained, 'because the tail of the Reekie sweeps right up the coast from Inverclinie and there's a terrifying whirlpool close under the cliff face. It's done for any number of fishing boats when they tried to take a quick way home.'

Marina's finger moved over the map. 'What's it called?'

'The whirlpool? There's some unpronounceable Gaelic name on the map, but locals call it Red Donald's Skillet.'

'Oh, that's the one you told us about. I didn't realise it was so close.'

He laughed. 'The whole coast is riddled with caves and strange rock formations, and most have gruesome stories attached – probably to warn people to keep clear of them. Whoops!' He clutched at the map. 'Hang on until we're through the surf. There's a hell of a current running at high tide, but once we're in the estuary it calms down.'

Moments later the boat grounded gently on shingle and Marina splashed ashore to pull it up the beach.

'Out you hop,' said Luke as Robb fumbled around for his rod and net.' Don't bother with a gaff, you won't need it here, there's nothing much more than twelve ounces in the

243

Shanty lochs. Right, then. Easy does it' – as the boat lurched – 'got your piece?'

Robb and Marina looked at one another and nodded. 'Fine. Let's have those rules again: first we catch our trout, then come back and try for seatrout off this beach?'

'Off the rocks over there –' he pointed – 'that's your best bet. And after that you have to look for shrimps in the rock pools. I'll leave the nets and jars here by the mooring post.'

'And how do we get to the trout lochs?'

'Straight up the path to the big boulder where I've painted arrows to each of them. The boats are on the bank with oars underneath. Any more questions? Right, then, off you go. I want a word with Danna, then I'll probably catch you up. Tight lines!'

'Race you to the top, Dad?'

Robb grimaced. 'Tortoise and hare? Thanks, darling, but I'll go at my own speed.'

As Luke turned back to the boat, Robb and Marina who had drawn Mhor and Donuil respectively, waved to Jess and set their faces to the heather-covered hill.

Davie McTavish swung his muddy 4x4 into the lay-by overlooking Kildrumna Bay, and Winter's laden motorbike pulled in behind him. Both men got out and leaned on the crash barrier to gaze at the view.

'There's three good vantage points for spotting whales,' said Davie, fingers busy with a roll-up. 'This is where you'll likely see minke most mornings, cruising along the headland after sand eels, or chasing herring to the surface. If there's a big gathering of seabirds squabbling near the estuary, you can bet there'll be a pod of minke close by. Then we get humpback in the summer, and I've seen blue whales close to the Shanty Rocks. Oh, it's a grand place for all kinds of cetaceans.'

'You're lucky. My parents lived not far from Falmouth

when I was born, and as a kid I saw a lot of dolphins and orcas between there and Land's End, so when my dad died and Mum moved to Reading I really missed sea life, messing around the harbour and going out with fishermen.'

'That'll be why you took up scuba diving, no doubt.' Davie drew deeply on his roll-up. 'Well, now you've seen my best lookouts, and between them all you should get some sightings today. Weather's perfect and I see you've good binoculars.' He sighed. 'I must get back to the shop. I wish I could take you out this evening, but waterskiers have booked the speedboat and the boss has sent his launch in for a check on the engine.'

'No matter,' said Winter. 'Thanks for showing me the lookouts.'

'And I'm sorry we didn't get our dive together.' He held Winter's gaze just a fraction too long, and the thin brown hand planted on the crash barrier was just a little too close.

'Don't worry, I'll be back, and I'll spread the word among my mates at the club. They're always looking for new places to explore,' said Winter heartily. 'Now I'd best be on my way.'

He turned back to his hired motorbike on the pretext of checking the luggage grid, and Davie sighed again, wished him luck and drove away. Lonely, poor sod, thought Winter, and was thankful that he hadn't been compelled to listen to a litany of financial woes he could do nothing to assuage.

When the beat of the Toyota had died away, he stood for a while staring out to sea, then swept the whole horizon very thoroughly with his binoculars. A fretted, broken coastline punctuated with inlets, bays, small islands and peninsulas, the sort of places he had as a boy associated with pirates, smugglers, hidden caves. Golden sands were in short supply here, though now and then he saw a glimpse of pebbly shingle sloping steeply from beneath the stark black cliffs.

He strained his eyes, hoping to see a black triangle break the surface, feeling the age-old frustration of the sea-watcher that no matter how powerful your binoculars they always left you wanting more magnification, more distance, greater clarity.

Nothing. After ten minutes of careful scrutiny he gave up and returned to the bike. If he was going to spend the night in Callinan Braes twelve miles down the coast, he had better get moving before all rooms in the hotel were booked.

As Luke had suggested, catching trout in Loch Donuil was a doddle. The perfect little loch surrounded by gentle hills was a fisherman's dream: fed by two burns with wide reedy deltas, it fairly pulsated with insect life and at this hour hungry trout were keenly on the rise, plopping circles in the still water on the edge of the weedy shore.

After running most of the way uphill, Marina sat on a handy slab of rock partly to recover her breath and partly to decide a strategy while putting up her rod. Should she fish from the boat or cast from the shore? Each had advantages and drawbacks. From the shore she was likely to catch as much weed as fish, and the bigger trout usually lurked in deeper water. On the other hand the wooden boat looked heavy and launching it would take up precious time, which she would prefer to have in hand for her attempt on the seatrout in the estuary. That, she recognised, would be far and away the most difficult part of the Challenge: catching little brownies in the loch was just an appetiser designed to encourage contestants like her father with little or no fishing experience.

From her boulder, she could see him in the distance, and when she put her glass on him it was clear that he had chosen to launch his boat. She waved, but could not catch his attention as he slid it down the bank and awkwardly scrambled aboard. She hoped he would not tread on his rod and break it.

On balance she thought casting from the shore was the better option, if she could find a suitable spot – clear of weed, and with the light breeze behind her to carry out her line. Leaving the boulder, she began to prowl round the loch's edge, flicking her fly into the water now and then before moving on, following the faintest of trails that dipped right down to the water and back again. Probably made by deer, she thought, coming down from the high tops where they spent the summer months avoiding flies to enjoy an evening drink.

Under the shadow of a cliff, she found the ideal spot, where the water was deep and clear with only a gentle ripple to disturb the shining surface. One – two – three casts of a tiny teal-and-silver fly brought the desired response: a dark-sided six-ounce trout with goggle eyes, who came to the net with barely a struggle, and was rapidly followed by three more, identical in size and colour.

Moving on round the loch, she completed her quota of six within the hour, and walked back to the upturned boat to see how Robb was getting on. He was sculling gently across his loch, with the rod apparently held between his feet and line trolling behind. As she watched, he shipped the oars abruptly and rose to stand with the rod bent into a half-hoop. No trout, however heavy, could have achieved that drag: hooked in weed, she diagnosed, and wondered if she should hurry over and offer help like a dutiful daughter or steer well clear of the language such a setback would provoke.

Better leave him to sort it in his own way. She had lowered the binoculars and was gazing dreamily at the smooth water when she noticed a V-shaped ripple moving gently towards her. Close behind it came three more, and her heart gave a leap of recognition. An otter. No, a family of otters, and they were heading for this very bank.

She drew herself farther into the boat's shadow and sat very still, not daring to raise the glasses again in case they caught the movement. Steadily, undeviating, they swam on until they reached a little kink in the turf, where first the bitch otter hauled out, a fish clamped in her jaws, and then her four kits, sleek and handsome but half her size, followed her out of the water and began to romp in and out of the tussocks, wriggling and squirming, wrestling and twining in a tangle of bodies as they slithered up and down a muddy slide, in and out of the shallows.

Fascinated, she watched. Sinuous and supple as snakes, they bent their bodies in knots, ambushing one another with sudden charges or pushing the topmost over like children playing King of the Castle. Their neat whiskery faces probed at pebbles, turning them with their noses and clasping them as a squirrel holds a nut before moving on to the next, while on the bank the bitch crunched and tore at her catch. Presently she signalled to the kits who left their game and joined her in the feast, pulling the floppy remains apart and retreating to gulp it down in private before it could be snaffled by a sibling.

Stealthily Marina reached for her camera.

'Oh, there you are! I've been looking everywhere.'

The otters looked up and froze. With barely a splash, all four vanished under the bank, and Marina saw Ravenna leaning over the boat's upturned keel. Damn the woman! Why did she have to turn up just when she wasn't wanted?

'What on earth are you doing down there?'

'I was watching otters, but you've scared them away.' It was hard to keep resentment out of her voice. 'I thought you'd gone into Stairbrigg to talk to lawyers.'

Ravenna's face was pink with exertion after the climb and she looked hepped up, excited, as she threw the heavy single plait back over her shoulder and said, 'That didn't take long. Boring legal stuff. I wanted to see how you were getting on, so I followed as soon as I was free.'

'How?'

'By boat, of course!' Ravenna laughed. '*Shield Maiden*'s dory, to be precise. She's perfect in these waters. I thought you might like to try for your seatrout from her rather than casting from the beach.'

'Is that allowed?'

'I don't see why not. Luke didn't say whether you had

to be onshore or offshore. And on the way I saw something absolutely thrilling – I could hardly believe it.'

'What was that?' asked Marina without much interest, still regretting her otters.

'A whale! A most enormous whale! I still feel all shaky when I think how big it was. It could easily have swamped the dory.'

Forgetting the otters, Marina snapped to attention, firing questions. 'How big? What kind? What shape? Did it just breach or come right out of the water?'

'Heavens! I've no idea what kind. You'd probably have known. All I can tell you is that it was so huge it took my breath away. And its skin looked kind of rough. Crusty.'

'Barnacles. Do you think it's still around? I wish I'd seen it. Shall we take your boat and have a look?'

Ravenna smiled and nodded. 'That's exactly what I thought, so I hurried up here to find you.'

'Come on, then!' Marina scrambled up and grabbed her fishing bag. 'I've got my six brownies already. I'll just go over and tell Dad what we're doing...'

'Where is he?'

Marina pointed to the other loch.

'That'll take too long,' said Ravenna quickly. 'Peat hags and tussocks – you can't hurry over that without a path...'

For a moment Marina hesitated, then nodded. 'OK. Let's go. He'll understand.'

'You carry the fish, and I'll take your rod,' said Ravenna, and led the way back to the arrowed marker.

With the sun at its height, they were both dripping sweat when they reached the estuary shingle, where *Shield Maiden*'s dory rode at anchor some two yards out from the beach. The tide had turned but the powerful outboard sent the little boat's sharp bows cleaving cleanly through the rough water of the

Reekie's tail and when they turned south-west to skirt Shanty Point the waves flattened into oily swirls of darker blue, with only the occasional slap of froth over submerged rocks.

To Marina's surprise, Ravenna seemed very much at home with both boat and engine as she steered towards a narrow bay a good mile from the end of the Shanty headland. Water rippled along the dory's sleek sides and sunlight glittered on the crest of the following wave, but she could not help feeling uneasy as they left the estuary behind and the looming jagged cliffs closed in on them.

'Luke told me they never brought the boats past the headland because it's dangerous,' she said tentatively, but Ravenna laughed, fine white teeth flashing.

'Luke's an old woman! Doesn't want to lose a paying customer – well, you can see why, the state his finances are in. This coast's safe enough for any decent boat. This is the type the fishermen use in Newfoundland – amazing in rough seas. Not scared, are you?'

'Oh, no.' Just terrified, added Marina to herself. She lowered her binoculars and half turned to stare at Ravenna. Was it imagination, or did she look disappointed? There was something reckless about her slapdash steering, holding the tiller loosely and constantly looking over her shoulder. Marina wondered if she had popped one of the pills she dispensed so freely. She had pulled her thick coppery plait forward and tucked it into her bush-shirt's collar, and her eyes were half-shut against the glare, but the little that showed had a curiously glazed look, as if her thoughts were turned inward, calculating risks, taking chances.

When had she seen that expression before? Her mind dredged up the memory of a kammo-clad figure prowling along the shingle, picking a path through rocks by the water's edge, and the last fragment of missing memory clicked into place. Not a red-bearded man but Ravenna herself, keeping watch, plait tucked under her chin, hat-brim down, collar turned up…and she was alone with her.

Marina's unease increased: she wished she had not come.

'Keep scanning the bay,' said Ravenna. 'We're close to where I saw him. You may spot him any moment.'

But scan as she might, nothing like a whale broke the blue-green surface before the dory grounded on a steeply shelving sandy beach, where random boulders were scattered like pebbles flung from a giant's hand.

'Just the place for seatrout,' said Ravenna. 'Have a go while I tie up.'

'OK.'

Marina slung her fishing-bag over her shoulder, picked up the little rod-case and splashed ashore. There was a promising channel between the rocks, and she was kneeling down to look into it when Ravenna called again. She was sitting with her back against a sun-warmed boulder, and patted the sand invitingly.

'Come and relax for a moment,' she said. 'It's so lovely here. Actually, I've been wanting a private word with you for days, and now's the chance.'

'What about?' said Marina warily. All too often a private word turned out to mean a scolding.

Ravenna propped herself on her elbows and smiled up at her. 'You told your father your memory had come back, hmm? I'm curious to know if you told him what you saw on the Skerries the day you capsized?'

We didn't bloody capsize. You – yes, you – knackered our engine, thought Marina angrily, maintaining her smile through gritted teeth.

'Did you?' persisted Ravenna.

'Well... Some of it.'

'Did you mention migrants?'

'Logan asked me not to.'

'Never mind what Logan said. Did you tell him?'

'No.'

'Why not?'

'Because I felt sorry for them,' said Marina uncomfortably,

resenting the interrogation but aware she was in no position to quarrel. More than ever she wanted to leave this beach and rejoin her father, but Ravenna showed no inclination to move.

'Why was that?'

Why do you think? 'Because they looked so cold and scared. And seasick, poor things. Dad would have had to report it and they would have been put in a detention centre for months, even years. I've seen clips of them on TV and they're horrible, dirty, crowded places. Logan said these were the lucky ones, even if they didn't look it.'

'He got that right, at least.' Ravenna sat up abruptly. 'And so did you. Well done, poppet. If your father had reported them, it would have been you who'd have robbed them of any chance of a decent life, and how would you have felt about that? It's what we aim to give them when we bring them in, just a few at a time —'

You make it sound like charity work, thought Marina, but what does this five-star travel service cost their families? Who gets the money? Logan had said the thought of Big Dougie raking it in stuck in his craw and Marina realised it stuck equally hard in hers.

'That's why anyone who guesses what we're doing has the sense — the simple human kindness — to look the other way.'

'Dad says you don't see what you don't look for,' Marina snapped but when Ravenna frowned she added placatingly, 'Don't worry, he's cool with that. Who are they, anyway, and how do you bring them in? I won't tell anyone, don't worry.'

'You'd like me to spill the beans?' Ravenna chuckled. 'No, no, sweetie. Not even to you. Not even when I know it won't go any further. You'll just have to take it on trust that each of these — let's call them young travellers — belongs to an important family in a country where the rules are — well — different from ours. For one reason or another the parents wouldn't be allowed to settle here, but that's not their children's fault, is it? And they all want their children to come to the UK. They want it so, so much that they're willing to pay over the odds to make it happen. To give their children safe, happy lives – isn't that wonderful? So rather than let these youngsters risk their lives trying to cross the Channel in the back of lorries or those flimsy little inflatables, we offer them a helping hand on our cruise boats. Simple, you see? Win-win. Small towns like Stairbrigg can't survive on fishing nowadays, so we keep everyone happy by ploughing most of the passage fees into local business.'

And the rest goes into your pocket, thought Marina. Aloud she said, 'Did Gunnar know about this – um – business?' and Ravenna gave her a contemptuous, almost pitying look.

'My dear girl! Of course he didn't. Conservation was always his thing: he never took much interest in the cruise boats, not the way I do. I used to work on them, remember, so I know exactly how they operate' – her smile widened – 'and I know every nook and cranny where people can slip aboard while taking on stores, and stay aboard when the boat leaves port. Oh, yes – this special side hustle is strictly my own.'

And Big Dougie your sidekick? Or your little bit on the side? By now Marina was familiar with local gossip and had grasped the extent of his hold over Stairbrigg economy and social life: fancied by most of the fishermen's wives and feared by all the men who owed him money.

She murmured, 'Oh, I see,' as Ravenna lay back on the warm sand, eyes slitted but watchful under her hat's floppy brim.

'Aren't you going to fish? Or swim?' she said languidly.

'Quite honestly, I'd rather go back to the estuary. Dad may be worrying where I've gone.'

'Don't be silly, I'm sure he won't.' She sat up. 'Now we're here, we must at least enjoy a swim in Cladh nan Ron.'

The name rang a faint bell.

'Gunnar loved swimming here,' said Ravenna casually as she glanced at her watch and rose, tall, strong and formidable in her pale green bush-shirt and wide-legged capris. 'Come on, just a quick dip and then we'll go back. See that cone-shaped rock? I'll race you there, OK? Ready? Go!'

How could she refuse? Better get it over with. Marina stripped off T-shirt and jeans, and kicked off her trainers. Ravenna was still tussling with the zip at her waist as she plunged into the clear blue water, immediately out of her depth on the bay's steeply shelving floor, and struck out for the weed-covered rock a hundred yards away. The usual feeling of intense pleasure suffused her being as the initial shock of cold subsided into cool, energising perfection, soothing sunburnt skin and erasing worries. Luxuriously she stretched her cramped muscles and exulted in the way every kick, every stroke of her arms propelled her forward. She forgot Ravenna's troubling interrogation, forgot the nagging memory of where she had heard of Cladh nan Ron, forgot everything but the simple joy of swimming faster than her rival.

She touched the rock and somersaulted to face the beach, searching for Ravenna's coppery head among the waves. Had she meant 'there and back,' or just 'there'? What did it matter? She was confident that over a short distance she could outstrip even a Channel swimmer like Ravenna. In a more leisurely fashion she began to doggy-paddle back towards the cliffs.

The choppy waves were increasingly turbulent and it seemed a longer swim on the return journey.

The tide, of course! Had she left her clothes far enough from the water? Perhaps Ravenna had moved them to safety. Suddenly worried, Marina scrambled ashore and ran to where they had been sitting, but her clothes were gone and water had nearly reached the sun-warmed boulder.

Where had she put her rod? It was a relief to find it still by the narrow channel in the rocks. She snatched it up and slung the bag on her shoulder, then ran along the hard damp sand at the water's edge to where they had left the dory.

It was gone.

'Ravenna!' she shouted, and 'venna...enna...' echoed faintly from the cliff. 'Come back! um ack... ack...'

An icy chill seemed to grip her stomach as she remembered when she had heard the name of Cladh nan Ron, and the horror of the situation hit her. This was where Gunnar's lifeless body had washed up along with disorientated whales and seals with bullets in their skulls, and she was marooned. No boat. No clothes. No way to summon help. How could she have been so naïve as to trust Ravenna? No wonder she had wanted to know how much Marina had told her father before talking so freely. She'd known that information wasn't going anywhere, not while the person she'd told was trapped in a blind inlet with the tide coming in.

She felt helpless and vulnerable as a hermit crab without a shell; even the idea of climbing those sheer cliffs made her shiver, and the lack of a tide mark made it horribly clear that at high water there was no beach, no refuge at all. Even the big standing rocks would be submerged.

She contemplated swimming into the rising tide rather than wait for it to reach her and dash her against the cliffs. How long could she resist the chill, the relentless tug of the current? Her mind darted to and fro seeking a way out as she ran to the very top of the beach, and then worked right round the cove, carefully examining the rocks for hand and toe-holds, ledges or cracks by which she could climb high enough to escape the waves. The only split in the cliff was so narrow that it could hardly be called a chimney, and it ended a mere twelve feet above the beach. Above and to its right, a single rowan clung to the cliff, leaning perilously forward in search of light, but between it and the chimney yawned a smooth expanse she could see no way of crossing without crampons.

I'm done for, thought Marina, as tears of frustration and fury at herself for falling into this trap rose to choke her. She brushed them away and went back to examining the rocks. Somewhere, somehow, there must be a way of escape.

# CHAPTER FOURTEEN

# Whale watching

SO FAR SO good, thought Ravenna, glancing yet again at her watch as the dory sped back to the estuary, exulting in the slap of water on its sides as the sharply pointed bows parted the waves. So far so good, but there was a long way to go yet and time was tight.

It was now 3:15; high tide was 3:40. She had scooped up Marina's watch along with her clothes, and must place these where Danna and Jess were bound to spot them as they arrived at the picnic rendezvous at 4:30. Long before that the dory would have slipped away, hugging the coast to avoid meeting Danna's boat, and be moored in Stairbrigg harbour near the museum before anyone realised the girl was missing.

She smiled to think how she had separated her from the rest of the party as neatly as a collie pens a single lamb, weaving back and forth to frustrate its attempts to break back to the flock. Apart from one nervous moment when Marina looked like insisting on telling her father where she was going, the girl had accepted every suggestion that drew her into the trap. Now she could rely on the high tide to complete the job, and she would be ready with comfort and consolation for the bereaved parent.

That shouldn't be too difficult. She sensed that Robb was already attracted to her: if she put her mind to it she wouldn't take long to convert Work in Progress into Mission Accomplished, and Dougie could like it or lump it.

Still smiling, she swung the tiller across and was heading towards the estuary's shingle shore when she noticed

Marina's rod case and bag were not under the thwart. Damn! In her hurry to scoop up all the girl's possessions she had forgotten them.

No matter, she thought. They would be washed away together along with their owner as soon as the tide reached its height, and her chances with Robb would be much improved without that little minx looking on. She jumped out quickly as the dory grounded and, without bothering to use the kedge, she placed the neat pile of folded garments just above the tide-line, hopped aboard again and departed at full throttle.

She had done it! She was free. Rich and free at last. Lovers would be queuing for a piece of the action. Euphoria swept over her, or was it the pills kicking in? No matter: as Dougie predicted, she had fallen on her feet, not with any element of luck, either. Careful, patient planning had done the trick, freeing her from Gunnar's control and breaking the last link that connected her to people-smuggling.

A golden future stretched before her: wealth, liberty and luxury beckoned from a sky of clear, cerulean blue. Just one small cloud no bigger than a man's hand marred that serene azure arc, a cloud in the shape of a question mark. What had Gunnar meant when he warned Marina to beware of the lights of cruise ships, which lured mermaids into lifelong slavery? Had it been his usual fantastical nonsense, or had the remark been aimed at her – his wife? How much had he known or guessed about her private side hustle?

The small cloud spread, blotting out some of the sun. Why had Gunnar so recently changed all his passwords, denying her access to his laptop? Why had his lawyers been so uptight on this morning's Zoom call?

No matter. She pushed the niggling worry aside. She was safe enough now. Marina would tell no tales and in future Big Dougie could make his own arrangements.

Now she must concentrate on dodging Danna. Like old Safety-First Luke, he always made a long, time-consuming and – to her mind – quite unnecessary detour to the north of the Skerry before turning east along the coast and heading for the estuary. This, she assumed, was in obedience to the notices warning boats to give the rocks a wide berth, since landing there to photograph or harass the seal colony in any way was strictly forbidden.

Danna and Luke were rule-takers. She was not, particularly since she knew that Big Dougie used the warning signs as a blind to cover his own activities. It would be just like him to have lobbied the tourist board and council to get them erected. In any case, she saw no reason not to use the obvious shortcut home, hugging the coastline and slipping through the channel between the towering cliffs of Craig Baillie and the Skerries' outlying rock stacks.

A mile away, flecks of bright colour showed racing dinghies setting off from Templeport harbour in a straggling line. The finals would be held tomorrow, when McInnes would present cups and trophies, and congratulate the regatta committee on drawing so many tourists to the area.

As she neared the Skerries, the outlying rocks stark, jagged and black against the blue-green sea, with a froth of white foam like a frilly petticoat round their ankles, the dory began pitching skittishly in the swell, and for a moment her confidence faltered. The channel between the highest cliffs was narrow, with a powerful current sucking the dory's bows towards the rocks as if magnetically attracted.

Adrenalin surged as she fought to keep control, and before the walls of cliff hid her view of the bay, she glimpsed Danna's boat, with Jess in the bows, taking the long way round as she had predicted. So her instinct had been right. It would take them half an hour to reach the estuary and find Marina's clothes. By the time they realised what had happened and raised the alarm, she would be innocently working in the Stairbrigg museum, with *Shield Maiden*'s dory moored to a bollard as if she had never moved all day.

She was halfway through the channel before a violent lurch to starboard caused the tiller to jerk in her hand. As she corrected, the dory lurched again, and peering down through the glassy water, she saw a line of rocks dead ahead, only inches beneath the surface.

'Shit!'

Before she could reverse or kill the engine, the boat struck with a tearing crash, turned broadside on, and water poured over the gunwale. Ravenna leapt up and clutched at the nearest rock as the dory began to sink, but her fingers slipped on weed and she fell backwards, head down; in a moment her body had been sucked into the narrow, fast-flowing handle of Red Donald's Skillet and spun helplessly into its ever-whirling current.

'Seen anything?' After closing the Dive Shop, Davie McTavish joined Winter at the layby barrier rail again and leaned on it, raising his own binoculars.

'I'll say!' Winter's normally pale face was flushed and his habitually impassive manner transformed. 'Fin whale. Orca – twice. Lots of dolphins, porpoises. Something that could have been minke, but they didn't hang about long enough for me to be sure. Wonderful place for spotting; and I've enjoyed watching the birds, too, though I can't identify most of them.'

'Verra guid.' Davie's sun-wrinkled features cracked in a grin. 'It's a grand prospect you get up here, though I say it masel'. Did you find a bed for the night?'

'Every hotel room for miles booked out –'

Davy nodded. 'On account o' the regatta.'

'– and no luck with the B&Bs, either; but I found a room with a nice old biddy down in the harbour, Queen Street, name of Emilia Menzies. Maybe you know her?'

'Indeed I do. Bakes the best shortbread on the West Coast, but don't tell my wife I said that! You'll be right enough wi' Milly Menzies.' He lowered the binoculars and stepped back, rubbing his eyes.

Winter said, 'I've had a great afternoon. Non-stop action – never a dull moment up here. Even when cetaceans don't show, there's always boats to look at. After a bit you begin to recognise them. There's a little green boat with pointed ends that's been up and down the coast twice since I've been watching. Regular commuter, you might say. Tucks right in to the coast – d'you see the one I mean?'

'Oh, aye.' Davie put up his binoculars again and frowned. 'Taking a bit of a strange course, but he'll know what he's doing, nae doot.'

'Why strange?'

'See those rocks?' Davy pointed. 'They're outliers of Red Donald's Skillet. Many a ship's foundered on them in days gone by. There's a channel between them and the cliffs…' His voice changed and he nudged Winter sharply. 'Look over there, man! Quick! Yon's your minkes, two of them, right there in the bay itself. Clear of the water, forbye –'

'Where?'

'Eleven o'clock frae the fish farm. You canna miss them. Tae your left, man. Left!'

Winter whipped up his binoculars just in time to see the sleek, fluidly elegant bodies breach in a smooth parabola and their flukes smack the undulating water in unison before they slid from sight.

Both men sighed with pleasure.

'How's that for luck?' said Davy, and Winter turned a glowing face to him.

'Wonderful!' he exclaimed. 'Thanks, mate. I wouldn't have missed that for worlds.'

He swept his binoculars across the bay, hoping for another glimpse, but both minke had vanished…

'I don't like the look of that,' said Jess, spotting the pile of clothes on the empty beach.

'Take her in right there, Danna. I don't like it at all.'

The old man grunted and changed course. Without waiting for him to moor, Jess swung her legs over the gunwale and splashed ashore. Marina's dark-blue T-shirt, jeans, and a quilted jacket that had seen better days were instantly recognisable, and so was a baling can marked Loch Donuil, half full of very small dark trout, now dull and curling.

Danna looked worried, but said hoarsely, 'Dinna fash, missus. Yon lassie'd more sense tae swim oot wi' the tide making. We'll find her fishing frae the rocks...'

They turned as one and scanned the empty sea, hoping for the bob of a head ten or twenty yards out, but there was nothing.

Jess's heart began to race at the memory of Marina holding the conch to her ear at breakfast. What had she said? Something nonsensical about the waves calling her... seals calling her... but no! A thousand times no! She wouldn't – she couldn't take such rubbish seriously! Not while her father was fishing only a few hundred yards away, and they were due to leave tomorrow.

She drew a deep breath and tried to swallow her fear. 'Take a recce up and down the shoreline, Danna. What's the time? Four-ten? Any minute the tide will turn and if she's swimming it could sweep her right out to sea. I'll run up to the lochs and tell the men to come quickly.'

'No need, missus. There they are on the bend in the path,' Danna began to say, but she was gone, brushing through the scratchy marram grass topping the dunes and pelting up the rocky trail towards the two distant figures. They saw her coming and hurried to meet her.

'What's up?' asked Luke sharply.

She grasped his arm, her nails digging in. 'Something awful. Marina's vanished. Looks as if she's gone swimming and there's no sign of her. Just her clothes on the beach.'

'The tide!' exclaimed Luke, looking at his watch. 'Come on, quick!'

Both men started to run, Luke's long stork-like legs easily outpacing Robb while Jess doubled up, gasping, clutching the stitch in her side. Minutes later when she caught up with them they were standing by the forlorn heap of clothes, with Robb scanning the sea through binoculars and Luke on speed-dial to his friend and frequent fishing guest Johnny Somerville, currently SAR commander at Prestwick.

'Thanks, Johnno. Quick as you can. We'll meet you there.'

He rang off and nodded to Robb. 'All in hand. They're scrambling Johnny's newest toy, the big Leonardo. I've given him details and of course he knows this coast like the back of his hand. They'll be here asap. At least the weather's in our favour, but –'

He stopped abruptly. No good pointing out the obvious. One bobbing head in the strong outgoing tidal current would be all-but-invisible. Instead he waved to Danna to bring the boat in, and said. 'We'll get back to the Lodge to co-ordinate the search. I'll get on to the coastguard now and put out a general alert.'

Silently Robb nodded, picked up the discarded clothes and heaved himself aboard. Jess put an arm round his shoulders as he stared fixedly at Marina's jacket.

'I don't believe this. It's all phoney. Staged,' he said at last, his voice cold with anger as well as fear.

'How d'you mean?'

'Look at those clothes! Marina never folded anything in her life. She just drops them on the floor. It's a classic set-up – missing person, clothes at the water's edge. Think Reggie Perrin, think John Stonehouse. Someone left those here for us to find, to make us think Marina had swum out to sea...'

He hesitated, looking back at the beach as the boat roared out into the estuary, packets of water flung over the bows. 'Where's her rod? Her fishing bag? Someone took her away.'

'But why? Where? Who?'

Ravenna, thought Robb, his mouth set grimly. It had to be her.

'Don't worry. The chopper's on its way. We'll find her,' said Jess steadily, and wished she had more confidence in her own words.

The recovery of her rod and bag spurred Marina into action. A glimmer of a plan; a tiny spark of hope. Once again she stared at the narrow rock chimney: even skinny as she was, it would be a tight fit to squeeze her body into it, let alone wriggle upward. She turned her attention to the rowan. How high up was it? Well clear of any tidal surge, for sure, and it must be firmly rooted. If she could only reach the branch that hung out from the cliff, some twenty feet above the beach, she might be able to able to cling on long enough for the water to subside.

Her father had teased her for carrying too much kit. 'Why pack that bag so full when you've got to lug it about all day? You don't need three fly boxes,' he'd said, 'nor four different kinds of cast,' but in the tradition of women who can't leave the house without loading all life's necessities, real or imagined, into their handbags, Marina liked to cram in anything that could be useful. Now she rootled through the bag, pulling out and discarding most of the contents. Tin boxes for trout flies, salmon flies, Mepps, minnows…all useless. Another see-through box for swivels and lead weights – keep those. Packets of made-up casts, half tubes of Polos, smudged and folded maps of the Clinie and Dunseran pools, a tidal chart, a priest made of lead-filled horn, a green midge-veil wrapped round a folding multi-tool knife with scissors, blades, screwdriver heads, and a marlinspike – now, that could be useful.

Again she plunged her hand right down into the bottom of the bag, praying that she hadn't taken out the one thing that could really help in this emergency, and felt a surge of relief as her fingers touched cold metal, the telescopic gaff which she had concealed there for fear of Luke's disapproval. Tucked in beside it was a reel of white floating line, which she attached to her rod with shaking fingers.

How strong was it? Would her idea work? Only one way to find out, she thought, as a long tongue of water slid up the remaining beach before retreating.

Hurriedly she clipped the heaviest of her lead weights to a swivel and tied it to the white line with a double knot, stepped back for another look at the overhanging branch and then, standing parallel to the cliff face, she gave her rod a couple of brisk swishes to pull out a big loop of line and cast directly upward.

It nearly succeeded first shot. Carrying the white line with it and pulling out yards more, the lump of lead soared past the end of the branch, rattling the leaves, and fell back onto the beach.

Close, she thought, reeling it in for another try.

Twice more she missed; then at the fourth attempt the line looped over the branch, checked for an instant among the leaves, and plummeted onto the sand close to her feet. Marina seized it and tugged, gently at first, then with her whole weight. It held firm.

With another anxious look at the waves curling gently up the beach, she repeated the operation with another lead weight, and would have done it yet again if she had not reached the backing. Now her lifeline was four-stranded, but it still looked alarmingly frail, and the position wasn't perfect. Of the three branches visible to her, this was the thinnest. It sloped downward, scaly-looking grey bark ending in tufts of leaves, with the doubled white line looped less than a foot from the fork with the main trunk.

She slung the near-empty bag over her shoulder and tied the line round her waist to free her hands, Keeping tension on it, she stepped sideways and forced her body into the narrow chimney. It was slimy and dripped water, but at the cost of some painful scrapes she managed to wriggle upward a few feet into a wider space where she could brace her back against one wall and toes against the other. Rock-climbing in a bikini was not to be recommended, but bare feet were an advantage. By alternating right and left hands and bringing each foot up in the same rhythm, she inched higher like a leech until her head emerged from the top of the cleft and she could go no further.

Behind her water had started to surge into the little chimney, and she had no idea how high it would rise. Evidently she needed to gain a few more feet to be safe, but the rowan tree was still out of reach, and her hands were beginning to shake with the strain.

She heaved herself up to sit astride the spur of rock at the top of the cleft and encircled it with two turns of the line that had been round her waist, securing it with a fisherman's knot. For a moment or two she rested, regaining her breath, dreading what she must do next. No more than six feet above her and to the right, the rowan seemed as distant as the moon and the doubled white line now stretched between her rock and its nearest branch looked as fragile as cobweb. Dared she trust her weight to it, thin and slippery as it was, breaking-strain unknown? Clear and unwelcome came the childhood memory of her sister Sally launching herself confidently from a rope swing, and shrieking as the rotting manilla parted, depositing her in the stream. She pushed it firmly away, and looked down at the water still rising in the chimney. There was no choice. She would have to risk it, and the more she thought about it the more difficult it was to start.

Though the rock had looked smooth from the beach, closer inspection showed little excrescences in the basalt, and small cracks into which she could thrust her marlinspike as a kind of primitive piton. Narrow horizontal ribs too small to be called ledges would nonetheless provide toeholds. Taking a firm grip of the four strands of line with her left hand, she reached out with her right to thrust the spike into the nearest crack, then shuffled sideways along the face of the cliff, bare toes clenching on every small protrusion.

'Oh, Mum!' she murmured.

Now there was no going back. A wrench, and the spike was ready to be moved to the next crack, her feet to grasp the next striated rock. With three moves she found herself halfway along her lifeline, but now the support was slacker, her tendency to lean outward more pronounced. With a sharp squawk a big grey seabird erupted from the rocks almost beside her and she lurched sickeningly, head spinning as she caught a glimpse of the waves dashing against the cliffs below. Paralysed with fear, she froze, unable to move hands or feet.

Never look down.

Time passed. Spreadeagled against the rock-face, it was pain from the line cutting into her palm that brought back her power of movement, and with it a grim determination. Very cautiously she shuffled forward, then eased the telescopic gaff from the shoulder bag and extended it to its full length. That plus her arm should reach the rowan branch.

It did, but to use it she had to unclench her hand from the white line which felt like abandoning her last support. Jab it in hard, her mother had said as she gaffed her first salmon. Don't think about it – just do it.

Reaching up through the nearest clump of leaves, Marina struck the sharp hook into its midst as hard as she could, feeling it penetrate solid wood. Cautiously she dragged the branch towards her perch. Seconds later she had grasped it with both hands like the bar of a trapeze, and pulled her body up monkey-fashion until she was lying across a thick but alarmingly flexible branch, which dipped under her seven stone and threatened to tip her into the sea far below. Hastily she swung a leg over to straddle it, then wriggled backwards to where it forked from the main trunk. There she crouched, panting and bleeding from a dozen scratches, hardly able to believe that against all the odds she had made it. She drew deep breaths as her thundering heart gradually quietened, and took stock of her situation. For the moment at least she was safe, but how the hell was she going to get down?

Ravenna, thought Robb. His brain churned sluggishly like stirred porridge, torn between anger and fear. Neither he nor Meriel had believed in wrapping children in cotton wool and all three of their daughters had crashed through childhood with plenty of scares and scrapes, learning the hard way how to extricate themselves from danger without calling in grown-ups.

'You've got a job and so have I. We won't always be around to yank them out of trouble,' Meriel pointed out. 'Much better they learn to deal with it themselves.'

She had been tougher on them than he was; but Stranger Danger was a lesson she had taken care to impress on them all. He did not believe that Marina would ever have left the beach with someone she did not know, let alone remove her clothes first. She would have been wearing a swimsuit as usual, a bright red bikini or a black one-piece, but without shoes, jeans and sweatshirt she was uniquely vulnerable not only to cold water but also to biting insects. Midges brought her out in a rash; the long-bodied silent cleggs raised painful lumps with a single bite. It was inconceivable that she would have spent any time out of the water without the protection of clothes, so how had they turned up on the beach?

As the youngest of three daughters, fighting for attention, Marina had always been a bit of a drama queen, creating fantasies which her sisters studiously ignored. A typical example was that nonsense at breakfast about seals calling her – yet someone had decided to make use of it. And who had been so keen to know just how much she remembered of falling overboard last week? Who had insisted on sitting by her bed while he snatched some supper? The more he thought about, it the more inescapable the conclusion: at some point during that ill-starred quest for lobsters Marina had seen more than she should have...

And what was that? The answer was blindingly obvious. He cursed himself for not spotting what was right under his nose. Marina's unconvincing pretence of amnesia. Ravenna's solicitude. Her repeated enquiries about her loss of memory... The local secret the Gaeltacht were careful not to share with nosy Sassenachs.

Those subdued, treacly-eyed girls with netted hair and delicate hands, the sallow, skinny lads with wispy beards and imperfect English, wiping down bars in Stairbrigg, serving restaurant tables, loading dishwashers and packing smoked fish. Too old to pass as unaccompanied children; too young to claim the minimum wage. Far from being part of Olympia's extended family, these were McInnes's private work force, cheap, biddable, vulnerable; they were also illicit migrants transported to Scotland on Gunnar Larsen's cruise boats, whose families must have paid through the nose for their passage. No wonder McInnes could splash the cash as he did. A new wing for the museum, a club house for the golf course, an upgraded lifeboat? Roll up, take your pick from Big Dougie's Magic Money Tree!

Someone – probably young Logan – had allowed Marina to see how all these foreign youngsters came to Stairbrigg, and she in turn had admitted this to Ravenna.

Robb's anger grew as he unravelled the connections. Could Larsen himself have condoned such an enterprise? Unlikely. According to Luke, the cruise line had soon bored Larsen and he had abdicated from its day-to-day management as soon as the new board was appointed. Though he remained in nominal ownership, rubber-stamping the board's decisions was all he did nowadays, he had claimed, with his booming laugh. This Robb had doubted initially: now he was convinced it was the simple truth. Gunnar's interest lay more in conservation than commerce.

No: it was Ravenna who had duped him. Duped them all. Far from being the submissive wife of a hectoring old bully she was an active participant in – possibly even the organiser of – this scam. He, Robb, had felt sorry for her, tried to cheer her up and soften the blow of her sudden bereavement. More fool him! How she must have been laughing as she led him on, accepting his sympathy with a grateful smile, gently laying her hand on his arm.

Something had changed all that. Was it fear that Marina might tell her father about it that made Ravenna decide she must be silenced before they embarked on the long drive south? Sitting side by side for hours on the motorway, it was tempting to exchange confidences, and Marina might think all need for secrecy ended once they left Kildrumna.

Ravenna was strong, determined, and would be ruthless in protecting her own interests. Where had she taken Marina? Robb felt cold with fear. Useless to remind himself that when his girls had lessons in self-defence, teak-tough ex-SAS instructor Sergeant Donovan had praised Marina's fighting spirit.

'But she's so small,' Robb had said, concealing his pride.

'Size don't count for much when it comes to hand-to-hand, sir. It's will to win makes the difference, and your little wildcat's got that in spades. Talk about tooth and nail! Anyone who messed with her would soon wish he'd picked an easier target.'

Yet Robb knew all too well that in any struggle Marina wouldn't stand a chance against Ravenna's size and strength.

Pale beneath his tan, Luke's thoughts had followed the same track. 'Ravenna,' he said. 'I always suspected she might be a wrong 'un. A bit too good to be true. Alarm bells started ringing when I saw her sneaking into the lodge at dawn like a cat after a night on the tiles, but I knew Gunnar would never listen, so I kept schtum..'

Robb nodded, and both men looked skyward as the heavy whumping beat of rotors reached them from the south.

'Quick work,' he said.

'Johnno doesn't hang about.' Luke was determinedly cheerful. 'Like as not he'll have spotted them before we're back at the jetty.'

Leaning side by side on the lookout's guardrail, admiring the view of distant hills and basking in the still-warm sun as it began to cast lengthening shadows over the coast's fretted inlets and bays, Winter and Davie McTavish had enjoyed swapping whale stories for nearly half an hour and had made a date for next afternoon before Davie reluctantly decided it was time for his tea.

'Four o'clock at the jetty then, OK? There'll be no trade at the Dive Shop because everyone will be out at Templeport watching the prize-giving at the regatta, and we'll have the bay to ourselves.'

'Sounds good. Shall I bring my –? Oh, hang on a tick...' Winter, turned away as his phone chirped.

Davie waited, listening with keen attention to Winter's terse replies. Something was up, he gathered. Someone was missing.

'Wilco. I'm on my way.' He cut the connection.

'Trouble?' asked Davie diffidently.

'Possibly.' Winter hesitated, but the story would be out soon enough. 'The boss asked if I'd seen his daughter – you know, little Marina. They'd gone with Mr Balfour to fish at the Estuary, and when Mrs Balfour came to join them and brought a picnic, they couldn't find her. He wonders if she could be with Mrs Larsen. Trouble is, she didn't tell him she was going and –' again he paused – 'she left her clothes on the beach.'

'She's a braw swimmer, but surely to God she'd not go into the Estuary on her own?' Davy frowned, chewing well-nibbled fingernails. 'But Mrs Larsen, now. Didn't you say you'd been watching her from here? Wondering why she was going up and down the coast?'

'I was?'

'Yon green dory, man. *Shield Maiden*'s jollyboat. Who else would be in her but Mrs Larsen? Whereabouts was it you saw her?'

Winter stared at him blankly, opened his mouth, shut it again, and said rapidly, 'It's hard to explain because I don't know what all these bays are called, but it was about halfway along from those big rocks –'

'The Skerries.'

'– a narrow inlet, sort of L-shaped, with trees on top of the cliff. I saw the boat go in and come out –'

Davy was nodding. 'Oh, aye. That'll be Cladh nan Ron at the tail of the Reekie. Where the seals' bodies wash up. It's where they found Gunnar Larsen.'

Winter was not an imaginative man, but he swallowed hard. 'Hang on, you'd better speak to the boss yourself,' he said and pressed Recall.

'That's her. It's got to be!'

Hardly able to trust his eyes, 'Stormy' Withers directed the searchlight's powerful beam into the dark recesses of the cliff to pick out what looked like a small striped ape clinging to a branch and waving frenziedly. Just one solitary tree growing out of the black rock face and the girl was wedged against its trunk. 'How the hell did she get up there?'

'Worry about that later,' snapped the 2-i-c, leaning closer to the windscreen. 'Hell of a place to get her out of. Winch job, and we'll have to go in close.'

Switching his gum to the other side of his mouth, the pilot nodded imperturbably, and the helicopter rose vertically to hover above the very edge of the overhanging cliff while the crew swung smoothly into action. Winch, harness, first aid kit: 'Tell her we've seen her and we're on our way.'

'We're coming to get you! Don't move!'

As if! Cramped and chilled as she was, aching in every muscle and itching from innumerable bites, Marina was seized with a mad desire to laugh as the great disembodied voice boomed and bounced off the rocks. Leaves thrashed in the downdraught, the engine roar was deafening. Hands and feet, arms and legs were numb, her white-knuckled fingers clamped immovably round slim twigs: she dared not stir so much as an inch for fear the sloping branch she sat on would break away from the trunk and tip her into the foam licking hungrily at the cliff's base.

She had been crouching here for what seemed an eternity, trapped like a kitten on an aerial, unable to go up or down. Hope made her heart leap when she first heard the low thunder of rotor blades, quartering the Sound methodically as a gundog searches for game, only for it to sink despairingly when it passed and repassed the entrance to Rowan Bay without deviating from its course. How could she attract attention?

'I'm here!' she screamed hopelessly.

Only on its third run up and down from Stairbrigg to the Estuary did she realise that it had begun to focus on the cliffs themselves. In and out of the fretted inlets it chuntered, the bulbous red and white body with its canopy sparkling in the sun, the heavy beat drawing nearer while its brilliant light probed every cleft, every cave... and then came the voice.

They had seen her.

Relief made her sway, suddenly dizzy, and stare up through the rowan's meagre branches as the monstrous insect rose high above clifftop level, an orange line spooling out of its belly.

Cling on, she told herself. Don't go and fall off now.

Down came the snaking line and with it a bulky figure in hi-vis orange. His hand touched her shoulder. 'Hi, I'm Sam,' he shouted above the engine roar. 'Are you hurt, hinny?'

'J-just c-c-cold.' So violently were her teeth chattering that she could hardly pronounce the words.

'Two ticks and we'll have you snug as a bug in a rug.' His warm Northumbrian voice cut through the din, as his big deft hands snapped and clicked straps and buckles. 'That should do the trick –' He picked her up as if she weighed nothing – 'Up we go, now. Up, up and away!'

As the winch took up the slack, he pushed them both clear of the rowan branch that had supported her so long, and together they rose smoothly into the sky.

RODS HAD BEEN taken down, the car packed: farewells loomed.

'I wish you could stay on a day or two,' said Jess, and Robb grinned.

'I thought you'd be longing to see the back of us!'

'No way.' She hugged Marina warmly. 'How will I manage without you? We're missing you already, but you'll come for a week next summer – promise?' Now she knew their future at Kildrumna was secure, the zigzag crease between her eyes had smoothed out. She looked years younger.

'I told you Gunnar would never let us down,' Luke had said, passing her the solicitors' letter, adding sadly, 'But I'd much rather have him than his money.'

No more crackly calls from the far ends of the earth. No more summons to share in crazy adventures or death-defying stunts. No more teasing challenges to his law-abiding, risk-averse little godson to lighten up and live dangerously. His world without Gunnar would be a duller place.

He couldn't expect Jess to share this sense of loss. She had always regarded his godfather as an alarmingly loose cannon and found his bluff, noisy ways overbearing, even rude. Jess was a pragmatist: without exactly welcoming his death, she would not regret it in the way he did.

Now even as he listened to her wishing the Robbs a safe journey, he knew that at some level she was already planning menus and the allocation of bedrooms for the incoming fishing party, and working out how to be ready for them.

Robb said quietly to Luke, 'Still no news of Ravenna?'

'Nothing. My guess is that she's hiding out in the cruise boat. She could have gone straight on to Templeport after leaving Marina marooned. Should we try to get it searched?'

The searing blaze of anger that engulfed Robb when he heard Marina's story had settled overnight into a steady glow: nevertheless he shook his head. He doubted if CI Selwyn Gray and his team would either agree or make a good job of it.

Luke went on thinking aloud. 'She'll have to come back here for her clothes – and we can't keep *Shield Maiden* moored here for ever. I'll let you know the moment she surfaces. I suppose you'll put in a report?'

'Certainly. We'll get her, one way or another.' Robb was silent a moment, then sighed and said, 'For me this is unfinished business, and you may say it's unprofessional, but I can't remember when I've felt more angry. That woman tried to kill my daughter. Not once but twice, so this isn't a professional matter: it's personal. She took us all for fools and I want to see her go down.'

Jess was trying to catch his eye. 'I've been telling Marina we'd love you to come back next summer. No more dramas, just fishing.'

'And swimming. And sailing. Oh, we will, we will!' said Marina, who had begun to fidget. 'Come on, Dad. It's not that I want to go, but I hate saying goodbye.'

Jess laughed. 'Then we'll say Arrivederci –'

'Hasta la vista –' called Luke.

'Do svidanya!' added Robb.

'Good journey! Safe home!' said Luke, and waved them on their way.

❖ ❖ ❖

Mhairi had a visitor. A small blue Datsun automatic was parked by the gate, and the front door was shut, but women's voices, passionate and indignant, could be heard before they were halfway up the path.

'Cat fight,' said Marina, instantly recognising the timbre. She halted, clutching her quaich, and Robb remembered the fiery temper that lurked beneath Mhairi's habitual calm. They hovered uncertainly, listening.

'I can't believe you went sneaking to him behind my back – you, my own sister,' she declared bitterly. 'Didn't you promise me? Didn't you say hell would freeze over before you'd shame me? I swore I'd never accept a brass farthing in payment and now you've betrayed me. Haven't I been punished enough?'

'Nothing ever punished you but your own wicked pride and I've no patience with it. I helped when you needed me, but now I've had enough,' said Elspeth tartly.

'Traitor! You dare say that to me?'

'What shame is there in telling the simple truth? Call me all the names you like, but I did it for your bairn's sake. You've no right to make him suffer for your stupid, stiff-necked, stubborn, wrong-headed pride.'

'You call it pride. I call it honour, but you wouldn't know what that is.'

'Take that back or I'll –'

A crash. A shriek.

Oh lord, thought Robb, a Domestic. When they start throwing crockery it's time to beat a retreat. He jerked his head at Marina, and they had turned to go back to the car when Logan burst from the woodshed and ran lopsidedly after them. His right arm was strapped across his chest and a broad grin split his unshaven face.

'Stop! Wait! Mam said you were leaving today.'

'What's going on?' said Marina.

He laughed, clear blue eyes narrowing to slits of amusement. Norseman eyes. Viking eyes, thought Robb. The resemblance was unmistakable. 'Call it a family discussion. A wee difference of opinion between sisters. Why else would Danna have missed his breakfast while I hide in the byre until the dust settles?'

'What's the problem?' she persisted.

His face wore a curious expression of mingled pride and disbelief. 'You could say it's me.'

'Your exams? Uni?'

'Nothing of the kind!' He was longing to tell, bubbling with suppressed excitement. 'You really want to know?'

Without waiting for her answer, he drew a deep breath and addressed himself to Robb. 'You mind the day we were up at Loch Herrick, sir, and saw Mr Larsen moor his boat and walk up here to the croft?'

'I remember.'

'And d'you mind how Mam shut the door on him?'

'That's what it looked like.'

Puzzled, Marina glanced from one to the other. Logan's look of ill-contained excitement had gone and he spoke seriously. 'Well, sir, he had come to tell Mam he'd set up a trust for me but I couldna touch it until my twenty-fifth birthday.'

'Who -ay!' gasped Marina. 'What did your mum say?'

'She wouldn't listen.'

'You mean she sent him away?'

'She did. And it wasna the first time. Whenever he came for a visit he'd try to give her money, but she wouldn't take it. She thought he was trying to lay claim to me – trying to buy her off. She's stubborn as a mule and wouldn't accept a penny from him.'

'But why?' burst out Marina and both men looked surprised, as if they had forgotten her existence.

'Because he was my father,' said Logan simply. 'I've thought for a while that must be why Mam gets so angry if I mention him, but Uncle Danna tells me not to rile her, she's spent her life here living down my Grandpa's disgrace and bringing me up on her own after Dad died.'

She could have been an artist herself, reflected Robb, remembering Aladdin's cave within the calf-shed. All that talent left unfulfilled, turned to bitterness at the man who betrayed her. Yes, a proud, frustrated woman might well have reacted as she did, determined not to admit she was an adulteress and her son a bastard.

'So what made her change her mind?'

'He found a way round it. See for yourself, sir.' With reverence akin to one handling Holy Writ, Logan drew from his pocket a stiff envelope and pulled out the enclosure.

Robb skimmed it rapidly. Yes, there it was in black and white, written in stern legalese, the sum of half a million dollars to be held in trust for 'my natural son Logan Brydon until he shall attain the age of twenty-five years or marry whichever shall be sooner…'

No wonder the boy looked like a dog with two tails. Each page was initialled and finally signed by the appointed trustees: Daniel Murison's careful script contrasting with the flowing cursive signature of Jessamine Balfour.

Reading over his shoulder, Marina reached the end and looked at Logan with awe. 'Half a million dollars. That's nearly five hundred thousand pounds! What will you do with it?'

He grinned. 'I'll have time enough to think about that before I'm twenty-five.'

'Isn't your Mum pleased?'

'She's mad as a box of frogs, but this way she canna stop it. Aunty Elspeth says it's only because he's dead that the truth has come out now. He wanted it kept secret another seven years, but when his will was read, everything changed. My aunty spoke to him the very evening he broke open the cages —'

Logan stopped speaking, swallowed hard and looked away. After a few moments' silence he said, 'I'd have wished to know him better, though he'd always bite my head off if my work wasn't just to his taste. I thought he didn't like me. Whiles he'd shout at me…'

'Nobody's perfect,' said Robb, and certainly not that selfish old bully, he added privately.

'You're always dreaming. He wanted to give you a kick-start,' said Marina, brutally honest. 'Why didn't you shout back if you didn't like it? I would have.'

'We're not all like you, God be thanked,' snapped Logan, but before a slanging match could develop they all became aware that croft was silent: the sisters' argument had ended...

'Kiss and make up time?' suggested Marina.

The door opened, and Elspeth limped awkwardly down the path, balanced between her sticks. Her face was flushed with lips compressed, but her eyes had the light of victory.

'Good day to you, Mr Robb, and you, mo chridhe,' she said, halting beside them. 'You're leaving today, I hear? Forgive me if I don't stop now, but I wish you Godspeed and a pleasant journey.'

'Aunty –'

She turned to Logan, hovering anxiously, and murmured so only he could hear. 'All settled, laddie. Done and dusted. I've had my say and she'll get over it, but it'll take her a wee while and now she's greeting sair. She loved him, ye ken, for all she wouldna admit it. My advice is to take your boat and your creels and stay away until suppertime if you know what's good for you.'

His face cleared.

'And don't go boasting to anyone of your great inheritance,' she added. 'The less said about that the better. Put that letter away now and try to forget all about it.'

'Yes, aunty.' Reluctantly he stowed the long envelope.

'Good lad. Now give me a hand into my car.' She patted his shoulder briefly, reorganised her sticks, and accepted his arm for support.

'Come on, darling. Time we got going,' said Robb. 'It's a long drive.'

'Wait a sec, I've got something special to say.' Marina was gone, running up the path before he could stop her.

Mhairi was sitting at the kitchen table, back to the door, head bowed, but when she looked round and smoothed escaping wisps of hair, only her red-rimmed eyes gave a clue to recent emotion.

'I wanted to thank you for this.' Marina held out the quaich, and Mhairi's face lightened. She took the little cup and stroked its smooth surface.

'I hoped your dad would choose it, for it was seeing you sit on the harbour wall gave me the notion. It will help you remember Kildrumna.'

'As if I could forget it! Anyway, Jess has asked us to come back next summer, so I'll see you then.' She held out her hand but with a quick, graceful movement Mhairi rose and pulled her into a hug.

'Godspeed, little mermaid,' she said in a muffled voice.

Gently Marina disengaged herself and Robb, watching through the open door, heard her say, 'Don't cry any more, Mhairi. I know he's gone, but he'll always be here under the waves, keeping an eye on you – and his son. Remember that.' She stepped back, cradling her quaich, and added carefully, 'Mar sin leibh, Mhairi.'

The beautiful ravaged face broke into a watery smile. 'Very good, little mermaid! I wish you the same: Mar sin leibh – an-drasta. Goodbye – and come back soon!'

## THE END

FURTHER READING FROM MERLIN UNWIN BOOKS
full details: **www.merlinunwin.co.uk**

**The Stalking Party** D.P. Hart-Davis £14.99
**Death of a High Flyer** D.P. Hart-Davis £14.99

**My Animals and Other Family** Phyllida Barstow £16.99
**A Job for all Seasons** Phyllida Barstow £12.99
**Ascension**: *the story of a South Atlantic island*
        Duff Hart-Davis £16.99
**The Countryman's Bedside Book** BB £20
**The Naturalist's Bedside Book** BB £20
**The Best of BB** £20
**The Shootingman's Bedside Book** BB £20
**Sport in the Fields and Woods** Richard Jefferies £15.99
**The Way of a Countryman** Ian Niall £16.99
**The Sporting Gun's Bedside Companion**
        Douglas Butler £15.99
**The Complete Illustrated Directory of Salmon Flies**
        Chris Mann £20
**The Poacher's Handbook** Ian Niall £14.95
**That Strange Alchemy**: *Pheasants, trout and a middle-aged man*
        Laurence Catlow £17.99
**The Black Grouse** Patrick Laurie £20
**Geese!** *Memoirs of a Wildfowler* Edward Miller £20
**The Airgun Hunter's Year** Ian Barnett £20
**Advice from a Gamekeeper** John Cowan £20
**The Gamekeeper's Dog** John Cowan £20
**Vintage Guns for the Modern Shot** Diggory Hadoke £30
**The British Boxlock Gun & Rifle** Diggory Hadoke £30
**Hammer Guns** Diggory Hadoke £30
**Feathers**: the game larder José Souto & Steve Lee £25
**Venison**: the game larder José Souto & Steve Lee £25
**Much Ado About Mutton** Bob Kennard £20
**The Yellow Earl**: *almost an emperor, not quite a gentleman*
        Douglas Sutherland £20